Sue Gee is an author and creative writing teacher. She ran the Creative Writing MA programme at Middlesex University and currently teaches at the Faber Academy. Her novel *The Mysteries of Glass* was long-listed for the 2005 Orange Prize, and she has published many short stories, some of which have been broadcast on Radio 4. She lives in London and Herefordshire.

COMING HOME

Will and Flo have found themselves, and each other, in colonial India — but as the war and the age of empire draw to a close, so they must make their way back to England. There, they and their young family attempt to fashion a new life for themselves in rural Devon. But managing a farm proves harder than Will anticipated, while Flo struggles to marry the pressures of domestic life with her desire to write. The 1950s and 60s — the decades in which their children will come of age — will challenge some of the Sutherlands' deepest certainties. But through all the misunderstandings and heartache, this less-than-perfect family remain committed to each other above all things.

SUE GEE

COMING HOME

Complete and Unabridged

CHARNWOOD
Leicester

First published in Great Britain in 2013 by
Headline Review
an imprint of
Headline Publishing Group
London

First Charnwood Edition
published 2015
by arrangement with
Headline Publishing Group
An Hachette UK Company
London

A catalogue record for this book is available
from the British Library.

ISBN 978–1–4448–2524–4

Published by
F. A. Thorpe (Publishing)
Anstey, Leicestershire

Set by Words & Graphics Ltd.
Anstey, Leicestershire
Printed and bound in Great Britain by
T. J. International Ltd., Padstow, Cornwall

This book is printed on acid-free paper

To the memory of my parents
And for my brother David

The child is the eternal being. The grown-up is the ghost.

Hélène Cixous

Contents

Prelude

1947

She was writing her last letter home in the café of the Grand Hotel. Though an awning shaded the window from the morning sun, the room was splashed here and there with points of light: on the china, on the snowy tablecloths, and the waiters' crisp starched shirts; against teak panelling blackened with years of cigarette and pipe smoke. And as people lit up now, in uniforms and mufti, tapping out a Player's, tamping down a wad of tobacco, smoke drifted through the crowded room, to and fro between the little tables, over the tarnished gilt mirror on the wall, up through the slow-moving paddles of the ceiling fan.

Darling Parent-Birds...

Through the glass-panelled door she could see all the comings and goings in the marble foyer, and hear, as it opened and closed, the shouts for a luggage wallah, for a taxi to the harbour, where troop ships were moving out of the dazzling Bombay waters, sounding the siren, taking home the last British officers of the Indian Army. In less than an hour, she'd be on one of them.

Darling Parent-Birds, We've got here! What a journey...

All the way down from Tulsipore, a place on the Nepal border as far from civilisation as you could get.

3

When they'd first arrived last autumn, setting up house as newlyweds in the old wooden bungalow, Will drove her out to the jungle by moonlight, holding her hand as they walked along the paths. Enormous vines hung from the trees. She and Will made out the shapes of roosting birds, the dark silhouette of a sleeping monkey.

'I saw a tiger drinking here once,' he told her, as they came to the glinting bed of a stream. 'Stayed up all night in a tree to wait for him. The most beautiful creature I'd ever seen.' He drew her closer. 'Until I met you, of course.'

'You didn't shoot him,' she said, when they'd finished kissing.

'Shoot him? Of course not.'

But he'd shot a panther once, he told her, as they walked back to the car. 'That was different — he was taking the villagers' goats, prowling around the compound at night. They asked me to get rid of him, and the headman took some jolly good photos afterwards, with my Brownie. I've got the head and skin in store: he'll come back to England with us one day.'

When he went off to work, riding out to the sugar cane fields at daybreak, leaving her with cook, bearer and his old black Labrador, she lay in a green cane chair in the shade, slept inside in the afternoons, listening to the creak of the punkah, dreaming of his return. *We're so in love*, she wrote in her diary. *Can it really have happened to me? At last?*

Each evening they had their drinks on the veranda, watching the sun go down behind the distant peaks of the Himalaya, the fall of night so swift, so sudden — and then those stars, a vast shower of silver in the inky sky. Will knew them all, had watched stars and birds and animals all his life. Their bearer brought out supper, stood waiting quietly. As soon as they'd finished, they went to bed — *We just can't keep our hands off one another!* she told her diary. In a couple of months she was pregnant.

And then all this began, she wrote to her parents now, in her corner of the café. Ex-Indian Army officers were entitled to a free passage home, but wives must be paid for — and no woman more than four months pregnant was allowed on board. *By the time we heard that, I was already three! So we had to get weaving — one of Will's favourite expressions! — in order to buy my ticket.*

It had taken a week of train journeys: to Cawnpore, then Delhi, then Bombay. In Cawnpore, headquarters of the Sutherland plantation, they said goodbye to everyone at the Club. *One or two are staying on after Independence — they can't imagine living in England now. But Will's been here so long, he can't wait to come home. And I can't wait for you to meet him!*

She broke off, looked out across the smoky room. Where was he?

'You stay there, my darling,' he'd said, when he'd tipped the luggage wallah. The room off the foyer was heaped with cases. Their trunks were already on board in the hold — *stuffed to the brim, and including the panther!* Then he was off, striding away to the little white house on the pier again, where he'd been told at Army HQ in Delhi he should buy her ticket. *But yesterday it was shut up tight — I only hope it's open now, or we're stranded!*

A huge urn hissed on the counter.

'More tea, memsahib?' said the old waiter suddenly at her side. Perhaps someone wanted her table, but she wasn't going to move.

'No, thank you.' She still had only a phrase or two of Hindi. Will had been fluent for years.

'*Tik hai?*' he called, every time he came home.

'*Tik hai.*' She held out her arms. 'All's well.'

The waiter moved to the next table, the door to the foyer swung open and shut, officers came and went. But still no Will. Of course, he was saving taxi money until they left together — *one special last night in the Grand has almost broken the bank!* — and it was quite a walk to the harbour. And she thought of her first sight of it, eighteen months ago, leaning out on the ship's rail beneath the awning as they came steaming in: the bright cotton saris of the women selling *chai* and knick-knacks along the wall, the dusty palms swaying in the hot sea breeze.

You were so right to tell me to come here, she wrote to her parents, and as she turned the thin blue page of airmail paper, she saw herself, with the other RWVS girls, Judy and Ann and poor darling Rhoda, laughing all through the voyage: over their G & Ts, over the games of deck quoits, and flirtations with handsome young officers returning from leave — men looked so gorgeous in khaki! Out for an adventure at the end of the war, getting over her broken heart at last.

6

India! India had saved her.

It had saved Will, too, from a deadly London insurance office. When his father died in '34 — a heart attack at the Rectory breakfast table, what an awful thing — he'd left his mother and sister in Norfolk, upped sticks, and come out on his own adventure. Wealthy Uncle Arthur had given him a chance.

'And you know, I took to it at once,' he'd said, telling her all about himself on their first date, as men did. They were having drinks in the Club in Delhi, she with her curls springing out from under her RWVS cap, he meltingly handsome in uniform.

'I found the Europeans a dreadfully stuffy lot,' he went on — oh, how he went on! — over his ice-cold beer. 'But the young Hindi chaps — we got on like a house on fire.'

He'd picked up Hindustani in no time, and quickly been promoted, spending ten years with Sutherlands: riding out to district plantations, supervising the growers, buying their cane. 'Must have ridden about ten thousand miles overall,' he said, lighting his pipe. 'Had a super horse.' Then the war came, and he'd joined the Rajputana Rifles, one of the best regiments in the Indian Army. 'One of the best in the world!' He became a weapons trainer, rose to major, fought in North Africa, was wounded at El Alamein, almost lost a leg . . .

'Now what about you?' he said at last, as men always did, though you could usually tell, as they leaned forward, and asked if you wanted another drink, that they weren't all that interested in

7

what you actually *did*.

Which was just as well, because one way and another she hadn't done much with her life, so far. Before the war — well, lots of boyfriends, of course, and in between she'd tried all sorts of things: doctor's receptionist, kennel maid, nursing home assistant . . . Then: then she'd thought she should do something serious, get a proper nursing training, and that had ended in —

Oh, she couldn't bear to think about that time.

As for the war — she'd done her bit, pushed a lot of planes about in the Ops Room with the WAAF, but frankly it was fun with the officers in the evenings, which was what the war had really been about. Until one of them broke her heart.

'Well,' she said, with a little laugh, perched on the edge of her chair. Waiters hurried to and fro between the potted palms, glasses chinked on brass trays, people up at the bar were roaring with laughter. The atmosphere in here was terrific, everyone letting go now the war was over at last.

'Well?' he asked, giving her what was suddenly the sweetest, truest smile, and suddenly she couldn't look back at him, couldn't give one of her flirtatious little looks, could only sit gazing at the bubbles of tonic, fizzing away in her glass.

★　★　★

Gosh, she'd been miles away.

I'd better finish, she scribbled. *Will's bound to be back in a minute!* And she thought of them all

8

in an English spring, Father at one end of the breakfast table, pushing his specs up his nose as Mother, at the other end, listened to her news.

Soon the British flag will run down all over the country — Will says it's bound to happen, and he thinks it's right. I'm sure Father has been following it all in the paper.

Vivie would be making toast, and Hugo swinging his legs, stroking the cat beneath the table and longing to get back to his train set.

There's just a little matter of a job, of course, but he's so competent, he's bound to find something.

'All I want to do is look after you for the rest of my life,' he'd said, as they kissed one another to death in the back of a Delhi taxi. 'Marry me, marry me.'

Such an outdoor chap, of course — he's talking about farming. I do love farms! Anyway — I'll post this on the way out, and I'll see you soon!

And she signed it with all her love, as always, but not as Felicity, but with her new nickname. *I know you find it hard to get used to, but once Will said, 'Flo, Flo, I love you so,' I'm afraid that that was it!*

She licked the envelope. She wasn't Felicity Davies any more, either. *Mrs William Sutherland*, she wrote on the back. And just *The Grand Hotel, Bombay*, because they didn't have an address now.

She put down the letter, and looked across the room. In the huge gilt-framed mirror she saw herself amidst the hurrying waiters, amidst all

9

the officers and wives: a woman in her thirties, newly married, expecting her first child. Happiness and pregnancy lit her up, she knew it, though she'd been told she was pretty all her life. 'You're very bad for a man, Junior,' gorgeous wicked Guy had told her, trying to get her into bed, as they all did. Then he went back to his wife. She hadn't even known he was married. But now — now all that was in the past, and she was a different person.

Was it true? She looked at herself through the drifts of smoke, and saw an officer at a nearby table look back at her, in the mirror. She'd been so used to men's glances: now she turned quickly away.

Had flirtatious, impetuous, scatter-brained, oh-so-emotional Felicity really gone for ever?

Felicity Davies.

Mrs William Sutherland.

Flo.

Could a new name make you a new person? There were so many things she wanted to leave behind. No more weeping. No more feeling an utter fool. She was going to make something of herself at last.

And as she thought of the fun she'd had, writing her letters home, and of all her Indian diaries — notebook after notebook from the bazaars, packed away in her trunk — it came to her. One day she would write about her time here, and how it had changed her life.

She tucked the letter into her bag, and pushed back her chair. The baby kicked. And then the glass-panelled door swung open, and there was

Will, striding in at last, making his way through the tables towards her.

'My darling. Still no ticket wallah — I waited for ages. But we can get it on board, apparently, from the purser's office. A chap's just told me.' He helped her to her feet. 'So sorry I've made you wait all this time.'

'Doesn't matter,' she said, and her heart went flippity-flop as he kissed her. 'I've been writing away. And the baby's just kicked again.'

And he said that was splendid, he was so glad, and then he paid the astonishing bill, and went to get their cases, pointing out to the luggage wallah the green leather one he'd given her as a wedding present, and his old brown army kitbag. Both were stencilled with their initials: he'd organised that, as he had everything else.

A born organiser! she'd written to Vivie, telling her all their wedding plans. *Getting married in Delhi within three weeks of meeting — I can hardly believe it! And yes, I know it's the right thing. Promise.*

She followed him out across the cool marble floor.

'On you go,' he told her, as a boy in white jacket bid sahib and memsahib goodbye, and opened the great wooden door to the street. 'That's it.' And she walked through, and he swung the bags after her, and out into the sun.

Part One

Rain, Hens, Mud

1

It lay at the back end of nowhere: a square brick farmhouse a mile up a deep Devon lane from a hamlet. An old wooden platform for milk churns stood in long grass at the gate, overhung by trees. Beyond stretched twenty-five yards of mud.

'Well, here we are!' said Will, as the taxi, a roomy old Austin, pulled up in the pouring rain. He shoved the passenger door open and through the streaming windows Flo watched him race out into the wet towards the gate, where an ancient wooden letter box was nailed on the post. The gate looked heavy and old, and she saw him struggle with the iron catch, but then he heaved it over stones and swung it wide. 'Done it!' he shouted. 'On you go!'

And he stood there, saluting, as the taxi went bumping through. The driver, entering into the spirit of things, gave two hoarse toots on the horn, as Flo and the children waved wildly from the back. 'I'll follow you up!' he called.

He swung the gate to, just in case Baba went running out — you had to watch her like a hawk, you never knew — and for a moment, in the driving wind and rain, he looked up towards the house.

The snapshots Fitz had sent had been taken in the spring: apple blossom, scudding clouds, a lilac by the door in bloom: that sort of thing.

Cousin Fitz had money, the only one in the family who had, left a fortune by old Uncle Arthur. Like a saint, she had come to the rescue.

'I'll buy it, Willie, and you can lease it from me! How about that?'

She said it was empty, the old chap gone and his son selling up; she said there were seventy acres, and a lot of potential for a good mixed farm. Home from India with a new wife and baby, up in Norfolk with Mother and Agnes, finishing off at agricultural college, it had all sounded pretty good. Marvellous, in fact. Looking at it now, all grey and shut up — well, you had to start somewhere. And he pulled down his cap and made a dash for it, as the taxi drew up before the porch and Flo leaned out of the window, calling, 'You've got the key!'

So he had. He ran up, squelching in the mud. 'Here we are!' He felt in his pocket and pulled it out, a big old iron thing, the kind of key Flo would call romantic. 'Here we go,' he said, as she and the children got out and ran into the porch, Freddie in Flo's arms. Behind them the driver was opening the boot.

'Stand back, you kids,' Will commanded, hardly room for all of them in the freezing entrance, and Baba pressed back against the wall while Flo held Freddie close. Will shoved the key into the lock, turned it, and pushed the door open. 'In we go!'

In they went. At first it was so dark they could hardly make out a thing, just bare wooden stairs up ahead, and a bit of light from a window at the top. All the downstairs doors were closed, and everything smelled shut up, mildewy, dusty and damp. It was perishingly cold. The children were silenced, their eyes enormous in the gloom. Behind them the driver was dropping their baskets and bags and cases in the porch, where the rain was splashing in.

'I think that's it, zur.'

'Jolly good. Thanks so much.' Will felt for his wallet. 'Mind if I stay here with the family? I'm afraid you've got to do the gate again.'

'That's all right, zur, you carry on.'

And he was gone, bumping away with a last toot on the horn.

Will heaved the stuff into the hall. Two of the cases had come home with them in '47, each with their stencilled initials. In January 1950, it felt amazing to see them here.

A new adventure, he had written to Fitz in his Christmas card from the Rectory, *and all thanks to you!*

Flo, Freddie still in her arms, opened the door to the kitchen. Will followed. They gazed at the chipped white sink, the unlit range, an airer hanging wonkily above it; at a table thick with dust and a couple of chairs, likewise. Their own stuff was coming down with Pickfords tomorrow: their beds, the high chair, the pram, the Windsor chair. Everything. Should've been today, of course, but there'd been a balls-up.

Baba was running about. Will put his arm round Flo.

'We'll soon make it a home.'

'I know.' She gave him a wan little smile.

'Come on, let's have a look at the rest.'

17

Off they all went through the house, Baba racing ahead through every door: into the sitting room across the hall — bare boards, a fireplace and an old red sofa; up the echoing wooden stairs to the bedrooms, one big, one small, one tiny.

'Like the three bears,' said Flo brightly.

'This is my room!' said Baba, running across the floorboards to the window. Water was seeping in through the frame, and the sash was broken. They looked out through the rain, saw an ancient caravan parked by a gate, then empty fields and the misty hills beyond. Will made out a track, leading between tall hedges towards more fields. He supposed all this was his now, thanks to Fitz.

For a moment he had a flash of the last land he'd managed: saw the endless rows of Cawnpore sugar cane, tall and feathery, stretched out beneath the sun, and the dazzling white dhotis and turbans of the workers walking in bare feet along the earthen paths. He heard the sound of the billhooks, slashing away at harvest time.

'Tik hai?'

'Tik hai, sahib!'

'Will?'

He followed her voice. 'How are we getting on?'

The bathroom was floored with cracked green lino. An unclean basin, a WC with an ancient cistern. He pulled the chain, and nothing happened. Pulled again.

'Try the taps,' he told Flo, and she turned on one on the bath. Not a drop, not a dicky bird. A spider the size of an egg cup crouched over the drain.

18

Freddie was starting to grizzle.

'I'm hungry,' said Baba. 'I'm starving!'

'They've turned off the stopcock,' said Will. 'That's all it is. I'll go and have a look for it.'

'I'm hungry!'

'Now, then,' said Flo, taking her hand. 'This is the moment for Grandmother's picnic, don't you think?'

'I should say so,' said Baba.

Wherever did she pick it all up? Eyes like a hawk, ears like a — well, he couldn't think what it was now. But they laughed, and trooped down the stairs again, and while Flo was digging about for the basket he went to look for the stopcock, finding it where it should be, under the sink. Devil of a job to turn the thing on, but at last —

'Done it!' he shouted, and banged his head on the sink as he got up again. Flo hated him swearing in front of the kids, so he just took a few deep breaths and turned a tap on. Water came gushing out. Thank God for that. Of course, they would have to boil it.

★   ★   ★

What a fool I was, thought Flo that night, as they all lay shivering on the bedroom floorboards. What a fool. What had she seen, when Will suggested farming? A white-painted gate leading into a meadow. Will leaning over it, smoking his pipe. There were cows, with someone to milk them. A dear old cart horse. There were hens, with eggs to collect, such a happy thing. The children would be country children, brown and

19

fit, and she would watch over them while she sewed beneath the trees. There was a beehive, and it was always sunny.

She must have been mad.

'Will?' she whispered, over the heads of the children.

'My darling.' He reached over and squeezed her hand. They were lying on his old army greatcoat, spread as far as it would go, so the children could be out of the draughts coming up from the gaps in the boards: draughts were a killer, her mother had told her that. 'You don't feel the cold, but the cold feels you, my darling.' What would they do out here, if one of them got ill? They were all still in their clothes, her own winter coat and his jacket snuggled round the children in the middle, and she and Will left to pull on every jumper they had. And their gloves. She wound her woolly scarf round her mass of curls, and he kept his cap on.

'What a hoot!' said Baba.

They lay there now, listening to the wind roaring all around the house, and the rain beating against the windows.

'Would you say it was funny?' whispered Will.

'Just about.'

★   ★   ★

Next morning, the rain had eased off but there were puddles everywhere and the sky still grey. The cold of the house was terrible: they were still in their coats, but Will found the last of the coal in a bunker, enough for a good few days, with a rusty old scuttle and paraffin can. A cardboard box half full of damp kindling and a heap of newspapers were in the pantry. He spread out the kindling to dry on top of pictures from the 1949 Devon County Show, and lit his pipe. Then, while Flo and the children had a breakfast of milk and jam sandwiches, he went out to look round the yard.

A barn, a cowshed, dairy, calf pen and tractor shed. Everything was in a hell of a state: rusting iron, missing tiles, rotting timber, cracked concrete flooring. In the cowshed, twenty neck chains, icy to the touch, hung above twenty feed bowls. Rain dripped from the gutters, moisture shone on the brick walls. He'd be out here twice a day. He strode through to the back yard, where the cattle would stand when they came in from the field.

Old wet straw lay here and there on the concrete; as in the parlour, a channel led out to the slurry pit, which he could smell from here. It was fenced in, with a rusting padlock on the gate; even so, he'd tell the children it was out of bounds. Not to go near, understand? Nowhere near!

And he went out to the front again, looking into the barn, still with a few old bales heaped up, and into the tractor shed, where a 1938 Massey-Harris, bought with the lease, stood waiting. A pretty good buy: they lasted for ever if you looked after them.

Through the rain he heard the back door opening, and Flo bringing the children out. Baba came splashing through the puddles in her wellies.

'Want a ride?' he asked her, seeing her eyes grow wide at the sight of the towering tractor, the enormous wheels still caked with mud, the headlamps hung with cobwebs, the cab so high. And he swung them up one by one, behind the muddy wind flap and into the seat.

'Go!' shouted Baba, Freddie on her lap. She grasped the wheel. 'Go go go!'

The iron seat was lined with old sacking; they slid about.

'How are things?' he asked Flo. 'How're we getting on?'

'We're getting on,' she said, shivering.

'Chin up.'

She nodded dumbly. And then there was a hooting from the lane.

'Pickfords!'

'Thank God.' He ran down to the gate.

★   ★   ★

They spent the rest of the morning getting everything into the house, keeping the children out of the way as the big iron bed was taken up the stairs in pieces and banged together again. Then came Baba's bed, and Freddie's cot, and Will's old army camp bed, which could come in useful for visitors. If they ever had any.

In came the chests of drawers, the wardrobe and cupboards, the tea chests of linen and clothes; all the kitchen things. Everything, except for the wall clock that had hung in the Rectory study, was post-war utility, cheap and varnished. The Windsor chair they'd bought at an auction

22

in Norfolk. 'We have to have one nice thing,' Flo had said, when Father had sent her a birthday cheque. Now it sat by the stone-cold range, and now Will must get the thing going. He pulled out the matches from his jacket pocket, thought of the pleasure of sitting in that good old chair in the evenings, smoking his pipe in the warmth.

It took three goes and the last of the paraffin before it all caught. 'We're off!' he shouted. 'Come and look at this!' Flo scooped up Freddie again and they all huddled round it, their faces lit up by the flames. Then he closed the door.

'Think that's about it, sir,' said the Pickfords foreman, bringing in a long mirror, wrapped in a blanket. 'Where'd you like this?'

'Flo? Where do you want the mirror?'

'In the bedroom,' called Flo, looking at the boxes of china and crockery waiting to be un-packed, wondering how soon she could get the children down for a nap.

'I'm hungry,' said Baba. 'I'm starving!'

Hawkchurch was all that way down the lane; she'd have to go down there tomorrow. But now —

'Hold on a minute.'

'I'm starving!'

She put Freddie down and rummaged in the box for rusks. That would hold them off for a while; then they could have another couple of jars of Cow & Gate.

Tonight they could even have them warm. Even as she thought it, she could feel the fire begin to die.

The windows shook in their frames and let the rain in. She went round stuffing towels in the gaps. There was no electricity, of course: they lit oil lamps every evening. The range was a nightmare, needing constant attention. There was no time for constant attention: that was what the children needed, inside and out.

We are surviving! she wrote to the parent-birds. *That's all I can say!!* She posted the letter, a scrawled half-page, in the letter box outside the Hawkchurch shop, which was also the post office. The mile-long walk was one she got to know all too well, bundling the children up in coats, leggings, hats, boots, mittens, getting the pram out, with its little seat for Baba to ride on when she had a mind to, Freddie asleep or propped up at the back. They bumped over rough ground down to the gate; she hauled it open, pushed the pram through, hauled it shut again, set forth down the sloping lane. Pushing it back up again was a hell of a thing.

'We're singin' in the rain, just singin' in the rain' she sang to the children when she had the strength.

Everything was non-stop. They were up with the children at six, Will outside straight after breakfast, banging about with repairs, getting the tractor going, taking it out over the land to see what needed doing. Indoors, she was learning to cope. The Ostermilk book had given her a good routine when Baba was born and she hadn't had a clue, not really, living in the Rectory while Will went to college, Mother-in-law watching her like a hawk. Get baby into a routine, said Ostermilk. First feed, bath, swaddle, sleep in the pram, change napkin. Second feed, walk in the pram in the fresh air, kicking, change . . .

Then Freddie arrived. Ostermilk didn't talk about having two children. Baba pulled the ribbons out of the white matinée jackets, while he yelled for his breakfast. She hid the little bootees. She sat in her high chair and turned the bowl of semolina upside down on her head. The book hadn't talked about living on a primitive farm, no electricity, having to boil all the drinking water, mud.

One day, when Flo had five minutes to herself, she'd write about it all. And as the Devon rain poured on and on, she saw herself three years ago, waiting for Will in the Grand Hotel in Bombay. One day, she'd thought then, she would write about India, the great experience of her life.

She must! She must dig out her diaries, and get it all down . . .

Rain gurgled in the ditches, huge shaggy hedges towered above them. You only saw the fields when you passed a gate, and then there was nothing to see, the cattle all indoors for the winter: only soaking grass or ploughland, bordered by bare trees, the kind of view to make your heart sink, if you let it.

'Happy again,' sang Baba, perched on her little seat. The children were certainly having a good time, and that was the main thing. If they had nothing else, they had space, inside and out, and no beaky old Mother-in-law to have to worry about, as Baba raced from room to room, Freddie crawling after her. She built towers of bricks and sent them crashing on to the floorboards, clambered over old hay bales and jumped down shouting, with no one to tut-tut-tut.

Never had Flo said goodbye to anyone with such relief: waving from the window at Mother-in-law and Agnes standing side by side in their dreary hats on the Norwich platform and sinking back into her seat as the train puffed away — 'Thank heaven for that!'

Will had looked a bit hurt — they were his mother and sister, after all, and of course they'd been terribly good and kind — but they were difficult, no two ways about it: M-in-law such a starchy old thing, typical clergyman's widow, and Agnes so — so what? Awkward. Shy. But snappish, waspish: you never quite knew what would come out.

'You don't know anything about farming, Willie,' she'd said, when he'd told her his brain-wave. Willie! No man should be called Willie, ever. And pouring cold water over his great idea: it was horrid.

Of course, Flo should be eternally grateful to her.

'My brother is coming for the weekend,' she'd said, as they got settled into their billet with the RWVS. The sun of a Delhi afternoon filtered through slatted wooden blinds on to their beds and suitcases. From outside in the teeming street came the cries of the bazaar, a frantic ringing of

26

bicycle bells. 'I'll introduce you,' said Agnes, hanging up her jacket.

In Will came to the dining room in his khaki shirt, brown and fit, with that lovely moustache and dark hair, that laugh. As soon as she saw him, she knew. They both did: that first drink only confirmed it. *All I want to do is look after you for the rest of my life...* But poor old Agnes — going out and coming home alone. Of course, she was jealous: she must be.

Anyway, she'd been wrong! Here they all were on the farm, and going to make a go of it, come what may. But you couldn't take your eyes off the children for a minute. Yesterday they'd got stuck in the mud, unable to move an inch until she ran out and rescued them. Meanwhile the range went out, heaps of washing piled up — *and so on and so on,* she'd written to her parents, *can't stop now!*

She'd have to get help: perhaps she could put up a notice in the post office window. No good putting an ad in the *Lady* — no one with any sense would come down and put up with somewhere so primitive, it would have to be somebody local, some good strong Devon girl who was used to it all. *Mother's help needed for busy farmer's wife.* Never, in all her born days, had she thought she'd be that.

2

'The cows are here, the cows are here!' shrieked Baba, as two huge trucks drew up at the gate. They'd been talking about it for days. Will ran down, shouting.

'Well done! Good show!'

Through the gate came the cattle trucks, and Flo and the children all went outside, watching them go bumping up and along the track to the fields. Every now and then a great bellow sounded. Through the wooden slats they caught glimpses of wild dark eyes, muddy flanks, horns.

'They've got horns!'

Freddie was thrashing about in her arms.

'Promise me,' said Flo, as Baba jumped up and down, 'promise you will never, never go near them by yourself. Not in the yard — keep still, Freddie — not in the field, never, never, never.' She felt suddenly sick. What did she know about cattle? What, frankly, did Will? Of course they had taught him milking, calving — what else did cows do? But getting up close to a great horned animal, managing a herd?

'Promise?'

'Promise.'

'Off we go, then.' For alarmed as she was, she was also excited, wanted as much as the children to see what came next. They hurried down to the second field — goodness, how heavy Freddie was — panting as they reached the open gate and saw the trucks bump through.

'Wait for us!'

'You stay there!' called Will, slamming the gate to, and she perched Freddie on the top rung while Baba scrambled up, and clung on. Wind whipped over the field. Then the men jumped down, one with a clipboard, and stood talking to Will. Snatches of 'Friesian — Dairy Shorthorn — dockets,' blew towards them, with verdicts on the weather.

'Come on!' called Flo. 'We're freezing here!'

The men glanced towards them and smiled.

'Big day, isn't it?'

And in a minute or two they started to lift the iron bars across the back doors and swung them wide. Even from the gate they could sense the great shifting inside. Down came the ramps.

'Steady! Stand back!'

Little bits of straw fell on to the grass, and then the first cow came down.

Baba clapped her hands to her mouth.

Huge with calf, the black-and-white horned beast stumbled slowly into light and fresh air, over the slatted ramp towards the ground, where she stood, and looked about her.

'Poor old thing,' murmured Flo, and held on tight to the children as the men all stood round with their sticks and a great smile spread over Will's face. On the cows came: ten, eleven, twelve, black and white, dull brown, tan and white. 'I like that one,' said Baba. 'Do you like that one, Mummy?'

'I think that's a Guernsey,' said Flo, remembering the books opened out on the dining-room table in Norfolk, when everything about farming was a happy excited dream.

'Go on with you!' the men were shouting, getting them out across the ground. 'Garn!'

Thirteen, fourteen, the last a muddy white. And then it was over, the cows moving slowly away from the trucks, the men climbing back in the cabs and Will striding over to the gate.

'Get down now, kids!'

They stood back with Flo as the driver came through, waving and sounding the horn, and Will swung the gate shut once more. Off went the empty trucks, rattling away, and more bits of straw came flying out on to the mud.

'Done it!' said Will, and put his arm round Flo and kissed her. 'Not bad, eh?'

'Not bad at all,' she said. And then, 'Will you really be able to manage?'

'It'll be all right, you'll find.'

And they all turned back to the gate and beheld the herd — their herd — getting the measure of the place, looking round them, beginning to graze, as the sun came out a bit, and shadows and cattle moved over the bright spring grass.

★　★　★

It was dark when he got up, the alarm clock on the chest of drawers ringing its head off at five. Dark and cold as charity. He pulled on his clothes and felt his way out along the landing as quietly as he could: Flo, still fast asleep, wouldn't thank him if the children woke. Downstairs, he stoked up the range and filled the kettle, lit and turned up the wick on the lantern. Then he pulled on his jacket and boots and went out, the lantern swinging before him.

In dry weather the rutted ground and hedgerows, the huge shapes of the barn and outbuildings, were outlined by starlight and the fading moon. Often, however, it had been raining, or was raining still, and the lantern was his companion in the dark and wet, as he walked along the track to the cow field.

Once, the land he knew had been cleared from jungle, and he on horseback overseeing five hundred square miles of it, riding old Kolynos all day in the heat. He put up his tent in a village, setting up next morning to issue the workers' chits, count out rupees, hear the endless stories of why, *This particular week, sahib, I am in special need. The jackals are eating my crop, the crop is drying out, the nilgai are lying in it, somebody has been stealing...*

But now: now he was home. England, green and rain-soaked. And already each morning the birds were up, whatever the weather, and the songs of thrush and blackbird, finch and warbler, never failed to please him, no matter how tired he was.

He'd loved birds all his life: the songbirds of his Norfolk childhood; the starling and pigeons he watched rising and falling over the fountains of Trafalgar Square, from his deadly insurance office. Fitz's father had saved him from all that: out on the P&O liner in 1934, twenty-two years old and suddenly fatherless.

'*Of course you must go, Willie darling.*' Poor Mother.

And as the dawn birds sang on, and he opened the field gate, he saw again the croaking crows of India, and the wicked old vultures, like specks in a hazy sky.

The cattle were moving slowly towards him.

'Come on, then, come on, come on.'

He always left his stick by the hedge; took it up now and waited as they came filing through: Hatpeg and Daisy, Bluebell and Guernsey Noo. Flo and Baba had named them, had favourites, Guernsey Noo the best beloved, as Kipling might have said.

'Go on! Go on!'

He gave a nudge to Bluebell, followed her out, huge haunches swaying ahead of him, the rain slanting down, everything muddy and wet and lantern-lit. As they came into the yard he glanced up at the house, still dark and silent. All you could hear was the slow steady footsteps over the concrete, as the cows filed into the shed, the stream of piss with a lifted tail, the splatter of shit, running down the gulley to the slurry pit. He got them all settled with their feeding bowls, he went for the pails. Half-past five, and this lot to milk before breakfast.

Once, he'd shot jungle fowl and a panther. Once he'd had garlands hung around his neck. Here, all that felt like a dream. There were snapshots somewhere, everything still in a muddle from the move. Perhaps Mother had them. He settled himself on the stool against Hatpeg's dun-coloured flank, felt for the teats on

32

her swollen creamy udder.

'Right then. Off we go.'

★ ★ ★

Fitz drove over from Dorset in her marvellous car. When she hooted at the gate, on a windy April morning, even from the porch they could see its sleekness and splendid comfort: the gleaming chassis, the running boards.

'That she drives herself is a miracle,' Will had said, when she wrote to say she was coming. *How you are getting on?! Longing to see it all.*

'She should have a chauffeur, you mean?'

'I mean it's extraordinary that she learned how to. Got herself behind a wheel.'

Fitz — Francesca, but she couldn't say her name when she was small, and Fitz it stayed — was the only child of elderly parents. She had always been delicate. The excitement of a birthday party made her sick. School made her anxious. A cold would inevitably go to her chest. She came home early from dances. So it went on.

Will knew all this from his mother, first cousin to Fitz's father. He'd shown Flo a photograph in her album: the family, circa 1910, the parents arm-in-arm on a terrace, she small and white-haired, Sir Arthur Sutherland tall and white-moustachioed. Sitting at their feet, Fitz in a frock, smiling bravely.

What saved her was music: she played, she even taught. Having young pupils come to the house was not too taxing; she could even go to

33

their homes without too much anxiety. Incredibly, she learned to drive. And Mozart, Chopin, Schubert — the sound of the piano filled the drawing rooms of Dorset. Then, in her thirties, she found the love of a good woman.

This was something Will had spoken of to Flo only once, treating it with both a light touch and a deep distaste. *A couple of funny old lesbians.* No one else ever mentioned it, and Flo had to suppress a giggle, when told, at the thought of Mother-in-law's reaction. Fitz lived with her best friend, that was what everyone said.

The best friend was Eleanor, a pale-haired aristocrat who had, it seemed, left her husband for Fitz. He was never spoken of, but she kept her married name: Lady Eleanor Forster. For years, the two had lived contentedly, and very comfortably, in a whitewashed house near Lyme Regis. Fitz (still a martyr to ailments) played, taught, summoned the doctor and watched her investments; Eleanor read, gardened, painted watercolours: the Dorset lanes, the coast.

Staying with the family in Bournemouth soon after Baba was born, Flo had gone down there with Will to be presented, and been welcomed with open arms.

'Flo! We meet at last! Willie, give me a kiss!'

Now, as he swung wide the farm gate, and this magnificent car came slowly up the track, she thought of the Turkey rugs and comfortable sofas, the grand piano, the cabinets of silver and porcelain treasures, honeycomb for breakfast. What on earth would Fitz make of the way they lived here? Then she reminded herself that if it

34

were not for her they would not be here at all. While Agnes had poured cold water, Fitz had consulted an estate agent, seen its potential, bought it. Just like that.

'My dears!'

Will, running up behind, pulled open the door and she emerged: tall, slender, in the best of all possible tweed, with a plum-coloured felt hat stuck with pheasant feathers.

'Catch!' And as she strode round the gleaming bonnet she pulled off the hat and sent it spinning towards the children. Flo leaped and grabbed it before it landed in the mud, Baba squealed and Freddie was dumbstruck. He could stagger about these days, and stood gaping at the car with his dark brown eyes like saucers.

'Flo! My dear!'

Then it was all hugs and kisses and exclamations.

'I want to see *everything*! Who's going to show me round?'

'Me! Me!'

The wind blew through the lilac, sun and cloud played over the mud, the bright spring grass, the rattling windows. Fitz produced Wellingtons from the awesomely capacious boot and she and the children, each with a streaming cold, each with a hand, marched through to the yard. She was shown the milking parlour, cowshed and tractor shed, the water trough, the barn and calf pens.

'But where are the calves?'

'Next month,' said Will. 'We've got six due.'

'But where are they now?' demanded Baba.

35

'Under the gooseberry bush.'

'Where's the gooseberry bush?'

'I can't remember now. Come on, you introduce Fitz to Hatpeg and Molly.'

And while Flo got the lunch on, they all went out to the fields, walking down the track, past what would be the hen field, past the old empty caravan. The cows looked as if they had been here always: grazing beneath the windswept sky, ambling over to the water trough. Birds flitted in and out of the hawthorn hedge and sang in the ash and elm.

'Well done, Willie,' said Fitz, as they leaned on the gate. 'Jolly well done.'

'All thanks to you, Fitz,' he said, pulling his pipe out. 'I've got the first of the arable fields ploughed up, you'll be glad to hear. I can show you after lunch, perhaps; they're further down the track.'

'And what are we sowing?'

'Come and see the henhouse!' said Baba, tugging at a slim gloved hand, as he began to tell her.

'You're quite wearing me out.'

They walked back to the empty field opposite the house, where a battered old henhouse rested on wheels in the grass.

'Where did you find that?'

'Local paper advert — they drove it up here from Axminster last week. Going to do it up — I've got three dozen point-of-lay pullets on order.'

'I'm going to have my own hen,' said Baba, wiping her nose with the back of her sleeve.

"May I have my own hen," said Fitz, as they all walked back to the house. 'Manners maketh man. Where's your hankie? Freddie, hold my hand.'

Lunch round the kitchen table was a happy affair and, in Flo's eyes, a miracle. She had cooked a roast! She had cooked it on the blasted range! A miracle, a triumph. And fantastically expensive, of course, using up all the meat coupons for a month, but no matter for once: Fitz, accustomed all her life to the best of everything, should have the best they could do here — God knows they owed it to her.

What a happy visit! Thank you both so much! said the letter which came two days later. *Alas, I caught the children's colds, and am writing this in bed.*

3

The three dozen pullets came up to the farm a
fortnight later. 'Rhode Island Red,' Will told Flo,
as the crates were opened up and the birds
released. They had a field to themselves, they
had the huge old henhouse, newly creosoted and
cleaned out, with perches, fresh straw in the
nesting boxes and white china eggs to give them
the right idea. They had a ramp at their own little
door. Everyone was enchanted.

And did the hens stay in their field? Did they
lay in the nesting boxes?

'Get off!' shouted Flo, coming out one
morning to find one perched on the hood of the
pram. And then, two days later, finding her
snugly arranged inside it. '*Get* out! Get out at
once!'

She scooped her out and flung her away. Baba
burst into tears.

'Don't throw her!'

'They're tough,' said Flo, as the bird ran
squawking into the lilac, and had found that this
was true. Tough and implacable. That hen — yes,
that one — came back to the pram the moment
her back was turned, and soon she grew used to
inspecting it for eggs before putting anyone in.
There were hens all round the porch, rushing up
for scraps. Will had a bucket in which every
potato peeling, uneaten crust, eggshell and
cabbage stalk piled up; the birds grew plump,

grew glossy, and more persistent.

'This one doesn't look very well,' said Baba one morning, clutching a bird to her chest.

It was true. She was thinner than the others, she had a drooping air. They put her in a box in front of the range, with her own tin lids of grain and water, and her own cardigan.

'Darling, are you sure — '

'She's cold,' said Baba happily, tucking her in.

Needless to say, the hen enjoyed all the fuss, and recovered nicely. And would she go back with the flock?

'She's my hen,' said Baba. She christened her Brownie and carried her everywhere. Everywhere. Flo found her in Freddie's cot, in Baba's bed, tucked up next to Squeaker the bear.

'She cannot come upstairs! Cannot!'

Baba burst into tears. 'Poor Brownie! Don't be cross with her!'

Down in the playpen, Freddie began to roar.

'Now what?' Flo raced down to find his finger trapped between the double wheels of a small brown cattle truck, a present sent by Fitz. Oh, for crying out loud.

'It's all right, darling, Mummy's here.' She hauled him out, yelling, sat him on her lap and gently prised out the swollen little finger. 'Poor Freddie, it's all right now.' She put the finger to her lips and kissed it. 'There we are.' He snuggled up against her, and the roaring stopped at last.

'Brownie's staying downstairs now,' Baba announced, bringing her in to settle on the beaten-up old sofa beside them.

'I'm glad to hear it. Give me a kiss.'

'Kiss Brownie.'

Flo put her lips to the cold red comb. I've got to get someone to help me, she thought again. Will nobody answer that ad?

★ ★ ★

Josephine was sixteen, and tied her hair up in a turban. Its little wings stuck out at the front and became a delight to Freddie, when she carried him about.

'You keep those hands to yerself,' she said peaceably, as he tweaked and tugged. The turban was made of whatever came to hand — an old scarf, an old tea towel it sometimes looked like, but no matter: it spoke of her workmanlike attitude to the day ahead. She arrived in gumboots, always, kicking them off at the door to do inside chores in a pair of carpet slippers, which she carried up the lane in a tool bag. This was also of interest to Freddie, who rummaged, or from time to time stored things in it.

'Lawd sakes,' said Josephine, at the end of the afternoon. 'What you go putting this here for?' She pulled out bricks, spoons, bits of rusk.

Beneath her coat she wore a pinny, bright and flowery and edged with bias binding. No one ever saw her without it, though she sometimes rang the changes in the flower department.

'That's pretty,' said Flo, who did everything she could to encourage, praise and generally hold on to her for the three days a week they could just afford. Within hours of her answering

40

the advert, she couldn't think how she had ever managed without her.

'That's pretty, Jofaween,' said Baba.

'And that's a nice ribbon in your hair this morning,' said Josephine, hanging her coat up. 'Terrible windy,' she added, pulling on her slippers, and then, 'Lawd sakes!' She hopped about, tugged off a slipper and shook it. Out fell the cattle truck. 'You'll do me an injury, you will,' she told Freddie.

'Leave Josephine's things alone,' Flo told the children, time and time again.

'Now, then, Josephine, if you could just hang up the washing while I make the beds . . . '

Out she went with the basket and peg bag, out went the children after her. Peace, perfect peace. Upstairs, Flo made and straightened the beds, picked up the vests and dungarees and jumpers that Baba had scattered wildly over Freddie's room while she was getting him dressed. Sun fell on to the dusty floorboards, the eiderdowns, the bears, and she stood at the window in Baba's room and looked out on to the land.

Will had done the milking and was now out in the fields, and though she couldn't see him she knew he'd be happy on a day like this, just as she was, seeing the sheep from other farms sprinkled over the distant hills, the fields greening up, the cattle grazing, the hens let out and foraging everywhere — everywhere! And by the back door the lilac was in full flower at last. The clothes line was round the side of the house; she could hear, just, the children's voices, carried by the wind.

'Here's a peg! Here's a peg!'

41

Now, then. What next? Lunch for five.

Downstairs the front door banged. Josephine was calling up from the hall.

'What next, Mrs Sutherland?'

Up came the children, bang bang bang on the bare wooden stairs.

'We're hungry! We're starving!'

Could two children be stronger and fitter and happier?

'Just going to muck out the cowshed,' Baba announced after lunch, and set off with an enormous broom. 'I'll be back tomorrow night.' Flo grabbed the camera and followed.

'Just going to drive the tractor,' Baba said next morning, and sat beaming on Will's lap as they chugged out of the yard. 'This is the gear lever,' she told him.

'Daddy's little Baba.' He held her tight as they drove along the track. He'd taken the hood down now spring was here and he yawned in the petrol fumes.

'Are you sure it's not too much for you?' Flo had asked at breakfast. Sometimes he looked so weary.

'Of course not.' He tucked into rationed bacon and their own eggs — jolly good ones. Freddie was banging his dish in the high chair, Baba fed little bits of toast to Brownie under the table. The kettle hissed on the range; the sun came pouring in. He had a family he loved, he'd manage. But, God, he could do with a hand.

★　★　★

42

Then a letter arrived. Letters were Flo's lifeline, the sight of the post van at the gate the most cheering thing in the world: she pulled on her boots and ran down to the box, lifting the old wooden lid — and often lifting up one of the children, too, if they came with her. 'Take!' said Freddie, pulling out letters from Norfolk (dull) from Bournemouth (joy! With a cheque from Father, perhaps?), and from Fitz in Dorset: *How are the hens?!* There were also feed bills, quite a lot, and copies of the *Farmer and Stockbreeder*. But today the envelope that Freddie waved at her was addressed to Will in a hand she didn't know, with a postmark from Suffolk. Who on earth was that?

'Good Lord,' said Will, coming in for elevenses and ripping the envelope open. 'It's from old Mike Geering. Chap I knew in the war. What's he got to say for himself?'

What Mike Geering had to say was that since he came home he'd been selling Ewbank carpet sweepers door to door. *Not a lot of fun. Got your address from the regimental secretary. Just wondering if you could do with a bit of help.*

'What do we think?' asked Will, putting the letter down. 'Could be damn useful.'

'But where would he sleep?'

'In the caravan?'

'It's filthy! It's freezing.'

'He's tough,' said Will, getting to his feet. 'Let's give it a go.'

And so, as her father would say, it was settled. They scrubbed out the caravan and put in a paraffin stove. Flo found a couple of chairs in an

43

ad in the post office window. She made up the bunk bed. Three weeks later, on a sunny afternoon, Mike arrived, getting the bus from Axminster to Hawkchurch and walking up the lane with his army kitbag, a wiry dark chap in his forties with a thin moustache and a strong handshake.

'I'm very glad to be here,' he said. 'What needs doing?'

* * *

Now things were easier: two men to do the milking, that was the main thing, as well as the work in the fields and the endless odd jobs on a farm. And now, on Josephine days, Flo was cooking for six. Each Sunday evening she went through the ration book, counting out the coupons before the week ahead. Two ounces of butter, lard or margarine per person: five years after the war, it was still bread and scrapings. Bread: she was learning to make it. What a performance. Her arms ached with kneading.

'Mummy, look!' They came in one afternoon to find a hen sitting snugly on the bowl of dough, left in front of the range, covered with an old tea towel. 'Get off! *Get* off!' Out ran the wretched bird, scattering little bits of dough from her yellow toes.

Tea was still on ration and they drank gallons: sometimes she used the same tea leaves twice. 'Ugh! Flo! What's this?' Coffee was coffee and chicory. Pretty patriotic tins in red, white and blue, but a revolting drink. Still, they only had it for

44

elevenses and everyone got used to it. No more dried egg, thank God: now they had more eggs than they could ever need. She and the children boxed them up — 'Careful! *Careful!*' — and took them down to the butcher in Hawkchurch, or Will took them into Axminster on market day. Quite an income.

They also had milk, of course, and the children lived on milk puddings: good strong teeth and bones. And then there was the veg: Will had sown barley, kale, sugar beet, swedes and potatoes and mangelwurzels, a name that made the children shriek with laughter. Soon they'd be pretty self-sufficient, thought Flo, as she scraped and chopped. For someone whose life before the war had centred on men, clothes and shopping, she wasn't doing too badly.

'I did try to be serious,' she told Will, when they were getting to know one another, and it was true, though it had been a disaster. There was a year in her life she could still hardly bear to remember. 'I love you just as you are,' he told her, kissing her again. Oh, whatever would have become of her if they hadn't met? One day she'd get it all down.

Finally, she bought an exercise book in the village shop. It was dusty pink, a school book with multiplication tables on the back, and cost four pence ha'penny, which she took from the egg money. All the way back up the lane, pushing the pram with Freddie propped up against the cushions and Baba perched in front — 'This is fun!' — she thought about what she would write.

That evening, when the children were asleep,

she found a pencil and began, sitting at the kitchen table, while Will, in from milking, sat with his pipe by the range. Mike, as quite often, had gone down to the pub. And she began their story, as only she could tell it: how she'd gone out to India with a broken heart, sailing out on a troop ship, right at the end of the war.

I joined the RWVS, and we were sent out to cheer up the troops! I thought it would be an adventure, help me get over my misery. I made a lot of friends on board, but we lost touch in different postings. Then, in my billet in Delhi, was a girl called Agnes, terribly awkward and shy, though she could have been pretty. One day she said: 'My brother is coming over this weekend.' And as soon as I saw him I knew! It was love at first sight!!

'What are you writing?' asked Will, tapping his pipe out, looking over.

'Our story,' said Flo, turning and pressing down the page. 'How we met and fell in love.'

'Good Lord.'

He stretched, yawning, and heaved himself out of the chair. The range was getting low again: he lifted the scuttle and shook in the last of the coal.

'What a sweet thing to do,' he said, going out to the bunker.

Flo turned back the page and read what she had written. She sounded like a schoolgirl. Not that she'd been any great shakes at school, nor done anything terribly clever afterwards, until —

Before the war I was training at one of the big London hospitals, she wrote. *I wanted to be a good nurse more than anything in the world, but unfortunately —*

Unfortunately she hadn't been able to stop crying. She wanted to do it so well, and she found it so hard.

I suppose I'd had rather a sheltered life until then —

She stopped, put down her pencil, sat there at the kitchen table. The wall clock ticked steadily, the coal settled down in the range. Here, all around her, was her new, unimagined life. A draughty old farmhouse, chilly even on a summer evening. Her children asleep upstairs, her husband working his socks off. And she at the centre of it all, finally finding her place.

I suppose I had a kind of breakdown.

There had been nothing she could get right, nothing she could take in, or do on time. All that anatomy: she took endless lecture notes, sat up for hours learning it all, then went into a panic in the tests. She knew it, she knew it, how could she have failed? All that disease, all that disinfection: on the ward she dropped things, and Sister shouted. She rolled up yards of bandages, then got the folds all wrong when dressing a real live wound.

She made eyes at one or two real live young male patients, she couldn't help herself, it was how she was made, but oh, the ticking-off in Matron's office. She went into theatre on observation and fainted at the first incision. They were all supposed to be tip-top London nurses and she was useless. She couldn't sleep. She cried and cried.

When she started to cry on the ward, they sent her home.

Even now, thinking about it, even though it was years and years ago, Flo felt darkness stealing in. She picked up her pencil again.

I can feel darkness stealing into me — it frightens me, even now.

Will came in again with the scuttle.

'How are we getting on?'

'Oh — ' she shook her head quickly — 'I've done enough for today.'

Had he really understood how frail she'd been, how utterly inadequate?

'Flo? You're looking a bit off.'

'Just being silly,' she said, and she closed the book. The cover, printed in black on that dusty pink, showed Britannia in a plumed helmet, one hand resting on a shield embossed with the Union Jack, the other grasping a trident. She was gazing out over a landscape lit by a setting sun. Or was it rising? The Supreme Exercise Book, it read, with places for Name and School. British Made.

'I'd better write something supreme,' she said, as Will shook coal into the range. The bright fuel seen through the open door always cheered her up. All the clothes on the airer stirred a little in the sudden wave of warmth.

'What's that?'

'Nothing. Just thinking.'

That landscape was a funny thing, though: not rolling English hills but jagged mountains. She

48

supposed it was Scotland or somewhere, but it took her straight back to the distant glittering peaks of the Himalaya, her happiness in love. Oh, let me remember that, she thought. Let me be a proper person now.

4

The morning was bright and fresh. As he drove down the track between the fields Will watched sparrows and tomtits flit in and out of the hawthorn hedge, everything greening up. The thin blue line of smoke puffed out of the stove-pipe chimney on the bonnet; when he pulled up, and turned off the engine, all he could hear was a deafening silence, and then the thin bleating of the goats, two white kids he'd bought on a bit of an impulse and then regretted: one more thing to think about.

He climbed down, pulled out the sack of feed from the cab.

'Back a bit!' he told them as he pushed open the half-door. 'Move!' He filled the trough, turned over the bedding. Then he began the walk-about, field by field, striding along the paths, inspecting. Row upon row of young corn and kale and sugar beet were pushing up nicely, with turnip and swede: good food for hungry people still on rations, good animal fodder, and all with a guaranteed price from the Min of Ag and Fish. Farmers were highly thought of these days: after the war they were going to get the country fit and strong again.

Hard to believe what it had looked like when they arrived, lying fallow or forgotten, everything choked with sorrel and dock. He'd seized the place by the balls.

Not that it wasn't taking it out of him: no use pretending — even with Mike to help out, he was feeling his age. Still: look at that. Look at those acres of green. Something to be proud of. Not to mention strong calves, and the Milk Marketing Board setting a good price for milk. Not to mention two growing children and a loving wife. They'd done it: against all the odds they were making a go of it.

The wind was whipping up a bit as he turned and walked back up the track, hearing once more the plaintive cries of the goats, sticking their heads out through the door. It got to you, the wind — it could go right through you, no matter how many layers you pulled on — and as he came up to the tractor he felt again something that kept coming and going, a tightening in the chest, then a sick swimmy feeling. Probably just the end of a cold, but — he stopped, put his hand on the bonnet, breathed and breathed. There: it was gone.

★　★　★

What I've decided, wrote Flo at the kitchen table, *is just to write about now. So much going on! So silly to think about the past! And things are getting easier all round now Mike is here — though there's even more washing! As for the goats...*

When they put out the washing the goats were waiting: they'd have tea towels and dusters off the line before you could say jack rabbit.

'Jack rabbit!' said Baba, shrieking with

51

laughter as they bounded away.

Freddie is teething, so we've had a few broken nights, poor little chap. But other than that —

Behind her the windows were rattling. She looked up. A shower was blowing across the yard, Will pulling up in the tractor. Across the hall the children were in the playpen, put in a corner of the sitting room, still uncarpeted, dusty and full of rainy light. They were banging about with bricks. Time for elevenses, and a mountain of wet washing to hang above the range.

★　★　★

Summer unfurled, and the farm felt settled, with Mike smoking his pipe on the caravan step at the end of the day, Josephine heaving the gate open three mornings a week, calling out to the children as she reached the porch. 'Hello, my ducklings! What are we up to now?'

She took them out to collect eggs in the hen field: Freddie hauled an enormous basket, and Baba held Brownie close. 'You're my very own,' she told her, stroking her face. At evening milking, Mike heaved Baba up on to Guernsey Noo's bony back, and held her hand as they swayed along. Will kept an eye on Freddie, stumbling along with his stick.

Everyone's happy these days, but other than Josephine we hardly see a soul! Flo wrote home. *Only the milk lorry and the vet.*

Then came a letter from Wimbledon. That dreary flat! Flo knew what it would be like, without ever setting eyes on it. Mother-in-law and Agnes, moved from that lovely old Norfolk rectory, setting up home together, getting on each other's nerves, putting up horrible curtains.

'Auntie Agnes is coming to stay,' she told the children. Of course, they couldn't remember her.

It was June, everything full and sweet-scented: the summer grass, the hay in the nesting boxes. Even the smell of the muck heap in the yard was good — this was the country, after all. Flo made up the camp bed in Freddie's room, pushed his cot across the landing into Baba's, ironed a guest towel, if you could call it that; nothing new bought in this house since she didn't know when.

She went outside and stood amongst the hens round the door, watching the sun play over everything, the mud all dried away, the children running about. It all looked picture-book; if she and Agnes couldn't get on now they never would — this was as good as it would ever be, with plenty to do, plenty to show her — 'Don't know anything about farming' my foot.

And Agnes, it seemed, was coming down for a reason — 'Something to tell you,' she said in the letter to Will. As always, it ended, 'Give my love to Flo,' and as always it felt a bit chilly and tacked-on.

Stop it, she told herself, calling the children in for elevenses. Look how much you have to be thankful for, and poor old Agnes living with that stick of a mother.

Will went down to Axminster on the tractor to meet the train and Agnes, squeezed laughing into the cab beside him, arrived in a pretty summer frock and a very good mood for once.

53

'I had to cling on for dear life!'

The children ran up as she clambered down on to the footplate.

'Let me look at you! How you've grown! Flo — let me give you a kiss.'

It all got off to a splendid start.

But then: 'I've brought you a little present, Flo.' Agnes gave her a book in a brown paper bag. 'I hope it will be helpful.'

Flo pulled it out. '*How to Run Your Home without Help*,' she read aloud. 'Gosh. Well — thank you, Agnes. Of course, I do have Josephine now — but still. How kind.'

She gazed at the contents: What Running a Home Entails. Have a Plan. Planning the Kitchen — oh, ha, ha, ha. The Weekly Cleaning. More Weekly Cleaning.

'I'll look at it later,' she said.

'Only I know you're not very domesticated,' said Agnes.

Flo bit her lip.

'Watch it, Sis,' said Will after lunch, as he showed her round the farmyard. 'Flo's doing pretty well, you know.'

'I'm sure she is.' Agnes peered in at the dairy. 'It's just — well, she's been a bit spoiled till now, hasn't she?'

'I wouldn't say that. Come and look at the hens.'

She looked at them, spread out over the sunny field. 'I mean, she's always had money behind her. What did you say her father did again?'

'I think he's in biscuits,' said Will, lighting his pipe.

'Biscuits?'

He led her down the track, introduced her to the goats.

'You mean he's in trade.'

'Honestly, Sis, does it matter a damn?'

At last she stopped.

And that evening, when the milking was done and the children were asleep, he poured everyone a whisky and they took it outside with the kitchen chairs and sat by the lilac watching the sun go down.

'Cheers!' he said, and then, 'Well now, Sis. What's up?'

'Well,' said Agnes, quite sweet again now, and she blushed all down her neck. 'Something's happened.' She looked into her glass, which Flo saw could do with a wash. 'I've met an awfully nice man.'

'I knew it!' said Flo, for what else could it be? What else could she have to tell them, from life in Wimbledon?

Agnes gave a little giggle. A giggle!

'Well, that's absolutely marvellous,' said Will, getting up and kissing her. 'Splendid! Jolly good show!'

Watching them, Flo thought: she's pretty. Deep down, she's really attractive — that wavy dark hair, those shining eyes. She's even got a pretty bosom — how did I never notice that? How did no man? Something's been unlocked, she realised, as Will sat down on the rickety chair again.

'Now then, tell us all about him.'

They had met in church — where else,

thought Flo, and gave herself a mental smack. He was called Neville, he was retired, a tax inspector. Well, you couldn't get much duller than that, could you? (Another smack.) But if he was retired —

'He's much older than me,' Agnes confessed.

'How much?'

'Ssh, darling. Let her tell us in her own good time.'

Neville, it seemed, was sixty. Agnes was thirty-eight. As they took in this gaping fact, Will said kindly, 'Well, just as long as he makes you happy, old thing.'

Agnes looked down again into her smeary tumbler. 'The thing is,' she said slowly, 'he has a bit of a dicky heart.' Pause. 'We wouldn't be able to have children.'

From out across the fields came the sounds of the hens, scratching about as the sun sank low. Pigeon made for the trees and sat crooning softly: *My toe bleeds, Betty, my toe bleeds, Betty* — the country words that Will had taught Baba and Freddie. Now, all at once, Flo, not knowing what to say, heard only, *We can't have children, we can't have children...*

How awful. How absolutely awful.

Agnes looked up. 'What do you think I should do?'

Will cleared his throat. 'Well, I — '

'Do you love him?' Flo asked her. 'I mean, really?'

Agnes blushed again. 'I do,' she said shyly. 'We do both love each other very much.'

'Well, then,' said Will. 'There's your answer.'

He went up to London for the wedding.

Mike was waiting on the tractor; Will climbed up and hung on. He waved all the way to the gate.

'I don't like it here without Daddy,' said Baba, as the strangest silence fell.

'Neither do I,' said Flo.

The two days ahead felt yawningly empty, even with Mike striding about the place, Baba running after him, calling, 'I love you, Mike!' And though in the evenings Flo had time to write, it wasn't the same, somehow, all by herself at the kitchen table.

I'm just not good at being alone, never have been. I should make the most of this, but it just feels ghastly.

It did. The Rectory wall clock ticked away, something she rarely had time to notice, except when Will wound it up each week. Now, when it should sound steady and comforting, it just sounded horribly loud. Reproachful, even, in the silence all around her.

If you were a proper person, you'd be all right on your own. Was that true? Didn't all women just want to get married, deep down?

How on earth do widows manage? I'd be absolutely hopeless! And even thinking about it was like looking into a pit. *Stop it,* she wrote quickly. *Stop thinking about yourself. You know what happens.*

She closed the book. This one was dusty blue: The Scholarship Exercise Book. Ha ha, great scholar she'd been.

Hopeless at nursing, hopeless at school, the clock ticked away at her. She shut her eyes. Things were different now. *I'm a wife, I'm a mother — what's more important than that?* But summer dusk had fallen, and her stomach churned.

★　★　★

Soon after Will came back — 'Tik hai? Everything all right?' 'Oh, thank God you're home!' — the wedding photographs arrived, in a big brown packet. They gazed at Agnes and Neville outside a flinty church, smiling at each other with unmistakable affection. Agnes wore a long cream dress and a hat that was not inelegant — *But black? For a wedding?!* Neville, in morning suit and buttonhole, looked charming, kind, happy. And old.

★　★　★

That evening, herding the cattle back out to the fields, Will had another of what Josephine would call funny turns. The day had been ordinary enough; he didn't feel, as he sometimes did, that he'd overdone it, even though it was Mike's day off and he'd hardly stopped since six. The weather was fine, as it had mostly been for weeks, putting everyone in a good mood. So what was this?

He stopped on the track and everything, once again, went swimmy. Then something roared in his ears and the world went black; for a moment he thought he'd pass out, and he leaned on his stick and couldn't move. The cows were treading away, but he couldn't see them; he just breathed and breathed in the darkness — and then it was over. He straightened up, took a few more deep breaths, wiped the back of his neck. It felt horribly clammy. Ahead, the cows were swaying steadily towards the field. He stood there, just watching them go.

5

Darling Parent-Birds, wrote Flo, on pale blue Basildon Bond. How I wish you could come down for a visit! But farms were beyond them now, even in high summer, and as she wrote she pictured her father slowly opening the post in the Bournemouth breakfast room, saw everyone round the table: her mother, such a frail little thing these days; Vivienne pouring the tea; Hugo, home for the summer holidays, itching to get down and back to his Meccano. She could almost smell the toast. Send Hugo, she wrote. He's old enough to come down in the care of the guard, and Will can meet the train at Axminster and bring him back on the tractor! He'd love that! She took out an envelope from her writing case, Will's first present, saw she was out of stamps, added them to the shopping list.

I miss everyone, she thought, walking down to Hawkchurch that morning. The pram was empty, both children running ahead on the shady verge, stopping to poke about in the ditch. And as she stood there, she wrote up her diary entry in her mind. She was almost at the end of The Scholarship Exercise Book; she'd finish it tonight. Oh, how different it felt, when Will was in the house.

Time for a bit more background! She stood there with the pram beneath the trees, miles and miles away. My sister, Vivienne, had rotten luck in her marriage, so sad. She's always been the *prettiest, kindest thing — someone I've looked up to all my life.*

There was the sweetest snap somewhere: Vivienne and Johann in the garden, he as tall and good-looking as any chap in a romantic novel, she in the most fetching frock you could imagine, both smiling radiantly at the camera.

But he turned out to be an utter cad — left her when Hugo was tiny, supposed to be making his fortune for them all in the Dutch East Indies, and never came back. Utterly broke her heart. So she went back to live with the parents —

Flo broke off, suddenly aware that everything had gone a bit quiet.

'Children?'

The lane stretched away, filled with sun and shade. Where were they?

'Baba! Freddie!'

She looked round. Cattle were grazing behind the hedge, swallows skimmed low before her. A perfect summer day, suddenly shot through with dread.

'Children! Where are you?'

'Here we are!' came a little voice, and her thumping heart almost missed a beat as two small heads bobbed up before her in the ditch, all overgrown with weeds. 'We were hiding,' said Baba, as they scrambled out, covered in mud, feet and sandals soaking. 'You couldn't see us at all!'

'I certainly couldn't,' said Flo, pulling stickleback out of their hair. She drew them close and hugged them. It had been only a minute, and how silly of her to panic — how far could they be, after all?

61

But all the way down the summery lane she felt the old feelings gnawing away.

It was a lesson, she wrote that evening, sitting outside on a kitchen chair, scribbling away on her lap. *I've got to keep my eye on things, no use dreaming away as I did at school. Looking after the children — this is the one thing in my life I've got to get right.*

She looked up to see Will walking up slowly towards her. He's aged, she thought all at once. How have I not noticed that?

★ ★ ★

Hugo arrived two weeks later: tall and dark, with his new school suitcase. He climbed slowly down from the tractor, grasping the suitcase firmly, and stood there, waiting for things to happen.

'Hugo!' cried Flo, running out with the children, giving him a hug. 'Lovely to see you! Did you enjoy the ride?'

'Very much, thanks.' Bits of straw from the cab clung to his shorts.

'And the train journey? How did that go?'

'It was fine, thanks.'

'You look so grown up! You remember Baba and Freddie?'

'Of course.' But he'd seen Freddie only as a tiny baby. He gave a polite little smile as they stood beside her, Freddie's thumb clamped firmly in his mouth. Flo removed it.

'I expect you're hungry. Come and wash your hands and have tea.'

She took him upstairs and showed him the

bathroom with its old green lino, and the camp bed she'd made up in Freddie's room.

'All boys together!' she said brightly, as he gazed at Freddie's cot. How idiotic that must sound to a nine-year-old.

'Thanks very much.' He put his case down neatly.

'Now, then, teatime!'

Cups of fresh milk and heaps of bread and jam loosened him up by a whisker. They heard his best subjects at school were science and maths.

'Gosh. You *must* be clever!'

Hugo blushed. 'Not really.'

'Come and watch the milking,' said Baba, when they'd all had enough. She took his hand and led him out across the yard, Freddie running after.

'Hello there, old chap!' called Will as they appeared in the doorway. 'Come to lend a hand?'

The evening sun, dancing with stray stalks of hay, came slanting in through the door and lofty airbricks. The air was rich with the smells of cow, slurry, cattle feed, milk. They all stood together inside the doorway, watching the two men moving from cow to cow, the pails filling up and taken through to the dairy.

'Is this the milk we had for tea?' Hugo asked suddenly, as Will went past with a bucket.

'It is.'

Hugo coughed. 'Are there germs?'

'Lots,' said Will cheerfully. 'Don't look so worried, old chap, they'll do you a power of good.'

'Come and see the calves,' said Baba, and

added kindly, 'You'll like that.' She led him out and across the yard again, Freddie in tow, and in through the door to the pens. The calves shied away in their straw, banging against one another. Then they came nervously forward on their long legs, thrusting bristly wet muzzles through the wooden bars, their eyes enormous.

'They want their milk,' she said. 'We feed them by hand, you know.'

Hugo didn't know, but found out when Will came over with a couple of buckets and a bag of clean bottles.

'They still need to suck,' he explained, and showed Hugo how to dip his fingers in the milk and give them to a hungry calf. 'Go on, you have a go, they won't hurt you.' Hugo had a go, but he squirmed at the urgent clamping of slobbery toothless gums. 'I know,' said Will. 'It does feel funny at first.' And when Baba and Freddie, squealing, had had their turns, he dipped in a bottle and filled it to the brim. 'Try this,' he said, slipping on the rubber teat. Hugo tried it; the calf had the bottle drained in moments.

'We'll make a farmer of you yet.'

★   ★   ★

As the days went by, Hugo settled in. He fed the calves morning and night, let the hens out after breakfast, was introduced to Brownie when she came to call, and searched for eggs in the afternoons, carrying the basket with enormous care. When it rained, he set out an elaborate city of bricks on the sitting-room floor, with, as he explained to Flo, a palace, a market place, houses and animal enclosures.

'I love you,' Baba told him, as they all went into the kitchen. 'Come and sit next to me.'

Next day it was fine and Flo took them out to the barn. The straw bales were heaped up at one end for bedding and the loose hay heaped up at the other, for feed, so Will and Mike could pull it out on pitchforks. They all scrambled up to the top and slid down, Freddie on Flo's lap and Baba on Hugo's. The hay was warm and soft and slippery, and after a few goes it was like whizzing down a slide — 'Whee!' — landing at the bottom in a laughing heap. Hugo had hay in his hair and all over his jersey. ''Gain!' said Freddie, and they scrambled up together. Flo ran inside for the camera.

After lunch, Will gave them all a ride in the trailer as he went out to the fields. They bumped along, amongst old sacks and straw, past the hayfield and a field of barley, dusty yellow and bright here and there with poppies. The trees were heavy and dark with the fullness of summer. Will pulled up, lifted the children out one by one.

'You're brown as a berry,' he said to Hugo, swinging him down. 'And I do believe you've grown.'

He watched as they all walked down the paths between the crops, the children in their sunhats dwarfed by hay, grass and barley, Hugo in his shorts and navy jersey tall above them. What a good kid he was, poor chap. Couldn't be much fun in a house full of adults. Still — he'd had a

65

good few days; he could come down again. If we last the course, he thought, yawning in the heat.

★　★　★

On Hugo's last evening they all went into the sitting room and played records. Will put on 'Honeymoon Lane' and the children ran about over the floorboards. The room was still almost empty of furniture, just the battered sofa, the playpen in the corner with the toy box, and the table for the gramophone.

There's a little white house,
with a little green door,
At the end of Honeymoon Lane . . .

The song went very fast: they raced up and down. Then it all began to slow.

'Come here,' said Will, and took Flo into his arms. They danced slowly, cheek to cheek, as the sinking sun shone through the dusty window.

Flo closed her eyes. They'd bought this in Norfolk, not long after coming home. *We were so in love. Still are...*

Will drew her close, stroked the wild springy curls, hearing only the song, their footsteps on the boards. Then he saw Hugo, watching them, just standing there, his arms at his sides, looking as stiff and locked away as he had when he arrived.

'All right, old chap?'

'Fine, thanks.'

And he turned and looked out of the window,

66

though there was nothing much to see at the side of the house, only grass and trees.

The record wound slowly down.

'Time for bed,' said Will, giving Flo a kiss and releasing her. 'Long day for you tomorrow, old fellow.'

'I don't want you to go,' said Baba, as they climbed the stairs.

'It's been jolly good fun,' said Hugo.

★ ★ ★

The harvest approached, but it wasn't just crops they'd be selling: a lot of the good fat hens were going down to the butchers in Axminster.

'Do you know how much we've made in eggs?' asked Flo at breakfast, totting up the book. 'Three pounds since Easter! Isn't that good?'

'Marvellous,' said Will, draining his mug of tea. But the laying was poor in the autumn, and in winter would almost stop. Time for a bit of a cull, he'd told her the night before.

Here was Josephine, calling from the porch. 'Morning, all!'

'Let her bring the kids down to watch,' he said to Flo, pushing his chair back.

'Is that a good idea?'

'It's fun. Do you know what happens when you wring a hen's neck?' he asked Baba, who was finishing her toast. 'They don't feel a thing, but they go on running about.' He lifted his elbows. 'Flap flap flap! Come and see.'

He's kindness itself, wrote Flo, as the children set off with Josephine a bit later. *But sometimes*

67

. . . You could call it callous. Or tough, I suppose. How can you farm if you're not tough? Let alone fight in the war. She put away the exercise book — she was on to a red one, now — and began to clear the table.

Down in the hen field, Will was sitting on an upturned bucket, birds all clucking and milling round him, where he had scattered their grain. It didn't take a minute to wring a neck: a squawk as he grabbed them, then over before they knew it. But then —

'Look at that!' he called, as the children and Josephine came through the gate. He gave a twist to the bird on his lap, and chucked her down. 'Dead as a doornail! Now watch!' And the hen, with her neck hanging limply, began to run across the grass like a mad thing.

Josephine burst out laughing as the children watched in astonishment, and then suddenly the bird took flight. 'Well, I never!'

The hen flew on, her dead head swinging from side to side as they clapped their hands to their mouths, and then it was over, and she thumped down and lay there, amongst all the live birds pecking away. Will bent and scooped her up, flung her on to the pile beside him.

'Next!' and he made a grab amongst all the fluttering birds and swung one up on to his lap. By the time they'd drawn near he'd done three more, though only one went running away. He pounced on another.

'Wait!' said Baba suddenly, as his hands went round her neck. 'That's Brownie!' she shouted, above all the clucking, and Josephine shouted too. 'Mr Sutherland!' They all ran over the tussocky ground. 'Lawd sakes, Mr Sutherland! That's Brownie you've got there!'

Too late. She lay limp on his lap.

'Oh, bloody hell,' he said, getting up as Baba ran crying towards him.

He set down the bird on the grass.

'Brownie!' She flung herself down beside her. The hen's head lifted; then it flopped back.

'Make her live! Make her come alive!'

'Darling, I can't, I'm so sorry. What a bloody fool I am.'

'Now don't take on, Baba,' said Josephine, hurrying up with Freddie in her arms. 'Don't get overheated.'

'Brownie!' Baba was sobbing. The grass was spattered with droppings and grain, and a heap of dead bodies lay beside the bucket. She sat there stroking Brownie's head, and half an eye gazed blankly up at her, through a drooping lid. Will kneeled beside her, and feathers came floating down.

'She's gone to heaven,' he said, putting his arms around her. 'Hens have a lovely time there.'

'You bloody fool!'

★　★　★

The day was ruined.

'How could you?' said Flo.

'How the hell am I supposed to know one blasted bird from the next?' He stalked out, banging the kitchen door. Freddie began to howl. Baba ran upstairs. Flo picked up Freddie and followed.

69

Josephine, silenced for once, got on with the washing and left without saying goodbye.

Awful, wrote Flo that evening, coming down after staying with Baba until she had fallen asleep. *Awful*.

'For God's sake stop scribbling in that bloody book.'

She burst into tears. Will didn't move from his chair.

★　★　★

That night, they both lay awake in silence. *As if we were strangers*, Flo wrote bleakly to herself, gazing into the dark. The oil lamp on the landing table gave just the faintest light in here; beyond its pale glow the whole house was as black as pitch, and the endless spread of the fields lay, tonight, beneath a starless sky. Only here, in the depths of the English country, had she known such darkness: in India, except in the monsoon, the velvety skies were pricked with a million stars; even out in the jungle the moon had broken through the dense canopy of the trees, lighting the creeper, the sleeping birds, a stream.

Here, tonight, with things suddenly so horrible, Flo felt the blackness of the land, and the silent farm, more threatening than any jungle. If things ever went really wrong between them —

'Will?'

'I'm tired,' he said stonily, and turned away.

★　★　★

By the time the harvest came they had put it all behind them. Here was a huge excitement, a vast trailer hired and fixed on to the tractor, loaded up with scythes, Freddie racing out there, all the men gathered for the fray: Will and Mike, and the man with the trailer.

'Be a good day for it all.'

They'd been watching the weather for days.

'Me!' shouted Freddie, making a desperate attempt to clamber up on to the trailer wheels. 'Me come!'

Will scooped him off, kicking and yelling. 'You can come down later, old chap. Come and help later, OK?'

Off they went, leaving him howling, and the kettle was on the range all day, Josephine and Flo taking it in turns to walk down the track with fresh flasks of tea and sandwiches — for elevenses (with Freddie, who would have stayed watching for ever), for lunch, for tea (with both children). By the end of the day the air was full of dust and chaff, the stalks lying in swathes along the hedgerows. The children sat in the shade with the men, drinking tea and talking; everyone was sweaty and tired and in a good mood.

'Just as long as the weather holds.'

'There's a rabbit!'

Then it was time for the milking. When it was done, as Will came into the house and up the stairs, Flo, bathing the children, thought she had never heard him sound so slow.

'All right?' she called, amidst the splashing.

He came along the landing, put his head round the door.

'Hello, chaps.'

'Daddy!'

It wasn't often he was up here at bath time.

'Just going to lie down.'

Flo looked at his drawn face, pale, even grey, beneath the sun tan. Yes, he had aged, but it was more than that.

'Whisky?' she said lightly.

'In a bit.'

But when, after shushing the children and tucking them up, she went quietly into their room, she found him deeply asleep, still with that awful greyish look. She drew the curtains, rattling them along the brass rail, but he didn't stir.

6

They were burning the stubble. Flo took the children down to watch the flames ripple all along the rows, the black smoke rising high and dissolving into the October sky. The summer days were gone: wind blew leaves all through the yard and it rained and rained. Will and Mike were out in the soaking wet, turning up swede and turnip and mangelwurzel. Then the ploughing began: more long, long days. They herded the cattle down into the cowshed where they would spend the winter. At least that meant no more tramping over frozen mud into a windswept field in the dark. And then the clocks went back.

Flo, undressing, watched Will turn the hands on the alarm clock, which woke them every morning: now he'd be getting up for the milking an hour earlier, in the pitch-dark. She pulled her nightdress over her head — *Gosh, I could do with a new nightie!* Then, as every night, they kneeled on either side of the bed to say their prayers.

'Dear God, keep my darling safe and well,' she said silently.

'God bless Mummy and Daddy and all the family,' she said aloud with the children every night, naming everyone. She must keep them all in view, something to hold on to in between visits. And then: 'God bless all the animals.' This could take ages, if Baba went through special cows. Not to mention the hens. 'Keep Brownie safe in heaven.' Sometimes her own prayers felt like writing in her diary. *Another happy day!*, or *Give me strength!* when it all got too much.

'Amen,' she said quickly now, feeling the chill in the room, and scrambled into bed.

The china globe of the oil lamp on the chest of drawers shone softly, like a moon. Will got to his feet and went over to turn it out.

'Here we are,' he said, climbing in beside her, and they snuggled up. 'I love you, Flo,' he told her, as they told one another almost every night again now, and she waited, hoping. Almost every night they were asleep in moments — *We hardly make love any more, but it doesn't matter — well, not much!* When she thought of their honeymoon — two people in their thirties, starved of love for so long —

'Will?'

'Sorry, darling. Not feeling too good.'

He mustn't hear her sigh. 'Tell me.'

'Worn out. Going to see the doc.'

I can't remember the last time he set foot inside a surgery, she wrote to herself, as he yawned and turned over. *Please make him be all right.*

★ ★ ★

Next day, after milking, he drove the tractor into Axminster. Flo waited all morning for his return. When he pulled up in the yard, and got slowly down, she was shocked by how drawn he looked.

74

'Doc says my blood pressure's high as a haystack,' he said, coming into the steamy kitchen. 'Gave me a chit for some pills.' He sank into the Windsor chair. 'Got to go back in a fortnight.' And then, 'Chin up, darling. Don't look so worried.'

★ ★ ★

The pills made him feel like death. Or perhaps he would have felt like death anyway, already worn out and now getting up in the dark all over again, walking over frozen puddles in the yard, the cowshed like an ice house. He and Mike barely spoke, just hung up the lanterns and got on with it, their hands raw with chilblains, their breath hanging in the air before them. Sometimes they let one another have a lie-in, but the whole round took for ever on your own, and with the cows indoors there was all the feeding and mucking out on top of the dairy work. Anyway, the kids made a lie-in impossible, no matter how Flo tried to keep them quiet. But he'd manage. He'd always managed.

Then one morning, as he and Mike rolled the milk churns out of the trailer and heaved them on to the platform at the gate, he was gripped by such pain in his chest that he thought: This is it. He stood there panting.

'Will?'

He leaned on an icy churn, streaming with sweat.

'Be all right in a tick,' he said at last.

'You'd better get inside.'

Slowly they walked back over the frosty mud.

'Go to bed,' said Flo, the moment she saw him.

The stairs rose like Everest before him.

'Come on, old boy.' Mike had his arm around him.

'Daddy in *bed*?'

Flo lit a paraffin stove and brought up the stone hot-water bottle. He shouted as it touched the chilblains in his feet. Then he slept for hours.

★ ★ ★

That evening, down in the lamp-lit kitchen, he sat drinking soup in the chair by the range, like a bloody old man. Now what? Now what?

'Whisky?' said Flo, hovering.

You weren't supposed to drink with the pills, but to hell with that. She got him a double and it kicked him back to life.

'Good girl. Where's the *Farmer and Stock-breeder*?'

He lit his pipe, leafed through the ads in the back: Farm Manager Wanted. Dairyman Wanted. Piggery for Sale. Washing steamed above him: his shirts, Mike's shirts, their overalls. Flo, sitting opposite on a kitchen chair, drinking her own whisky, looked tight with fatigue and worry. The range was sinking low. He flung down the magazine, went out to the freezing bunker.

I've never seen him like this. What are we going to do?

★ ★ ★

Baba woke up in the night. The paraffin stove had been turned out, but a chink of light came in from the landing lamp. She lay there listening. Something was going on. She heard the clanking of the chain in the bathroom, and swearing. Then the door was opened and there came a horrible groan. More footsteps. That was Mummy. She clambered out of bed, tugged open the door.

Daddy was standing in his dressing gown up against the wall. His hair was sticking up, he was holding his chest. He looked like a horrible mad thing, and then he saw her.

'Go back to bed!'

'What's happening?'

'It's all right, darling.' Mummy was there, with a white face. 'Daddy's not feeling well, you go back to bed.'

'Mummy come too.'

Then he snarled at her. 'Do as you're bloody well told!'

She burst into tears. A wail came from Freddie's room.

'Oh, Jesus Christ!' He went staggering along the landing and slammed their bedroom door.

'Mummy! Mummy!'

'I'm here,' said Flo. 'Run to bed, I'll be back.'

They were up half the night.

★   ★   ★

Next morning, Will gave them all a hug. 'I'm sorry. Everything's going to be all right.' Mike was doing the milking — *I ran down to the caravan and hammered on the door, still in my dressing gown! God, what a hell of a do.* They were still in their night clothes for breakfast, rain beating against the kitchen windows, the children subdued and pale. 'Come on, Baba, give me a kiss. Daddy says sorry.'

She nodded. 'Poor Daddy.' She let him kiss her, his moustache all tickly.

'Me kiss,' said Freddie, his blanket trailing after him.

They all went up to get dressed.

'I'd better get out there,' said Will.

Flo didn't argue. She stood with the children at Freddie's window, from where they could see the yard. Rain swept over it. The cattle were filing out from the milking parlour, through the back yard in the mud and the wet, into the cowshed.

'There's Hatpeg!'

Mike and Will were following. They had their collars up in the rain, their caps pulled down. Baba banged on the window and they looked up and waved.

'Daddy's better now.'

Downstairs the porch door banged.

'Morning all!' called Josephine. 'Lawd sakes, what a filthy old day.'

★　★　★

He took himself back to the doc.

'Thought I was a goner,' he told him, standing there holding his vest up while the stethoscope moved from place to place. The window on to the garden dripped with rain.

78

'You're going to have to ease up.' Dr Brett put the stethoscope back in its box, sat down behind his desk as Will got dressed. He wrote out another prescription. 'This is on top of the blood pressure pills — it'll thin down your blood a bit. But I've got to tell you, old boy, if you don't slow down you could be in trouble.'

Will took the prescription, slowly pulled on his jacket. 'What the hell am I going to do?'

* * *

I've never seen him in such a black mood, wrote Flo next evening. The rain had set in as if for ever, no Josephine, and the children cooped up and fretful.

'Now what are you writing about?' asked Will, coming in from the milking, streaming wet.

'Oh — nothing.' She closed the book.

'I've never seen so many pages covered with nothing.' He was pulling his boots off, slung them out into the hall. 'What's for supper?'

'Macaroni cheese.' She got up. 'I'll put it in now.'

He grunted, went over to the range and shovelled in coal. 'I was hoping grub would be ready. I'm starving.'

She slid the dish into the oven. 'I'm so sorry, darling, I didn't realise how late it was, I'm so sorry — '

'There's a clock on the wall, for God's sake.' He sunk into his chair. 'But of course, if you're writing — '

'Oh, Will — ' But she didn't go on.

Can't even get a meal on time, she told her diary, as she laid the table. *But my God, it's not often I let him down.*

She turned to see Will leaning back in the chair, his eyes closed.

'Will?'

'Shut up.'

She went out into the freezing hall, stood with her head in her hands.

* * *

Eventually, they made it up.

'I've been a pig. I'm sorry.'

'It's all right, I do understand.'

'You're an angel.'

They were in the sitting room, the fire lit, the children asleep upstairs. So much of their time was spent in the kitchen that it felt almost like a holiday to come in here. They sat on the sunken old sofa, finding a place between the broken springs. The children had bounced it to death.

'We're not going to make it,' said Will, his arm around her.

For a moment she thought he was talking about them, their marriage.

'You mean — '

'Here. I just can't go on. And I don't know what to fucking do. Sorry. Any thoughts?'

She hadn't a clue. Her stomach was like water, all the old feelings flooding through. Even with the firelight, even with Will and her back together again — why couldn't she think? Why couldn't she help?

80

★　★　★

The winter went on and on, and then it snowed. Magical as it was with the first thick fall, the children standing awestruck at the windows, the sun next morning dazzling, nothing would heat the house. As for the caravan — they brought the old camp bed down to the kitchen and Mike slept there.

'Haven't lain on one of these things since '45.' He barked his shins on the iron frame and swore.

Baba went to bed with the snow leopard gloves Will had given Flo in Tulsipore; Freddie wore his woolly hat. The milk froze in the dairy, and anyway the lorry couldn't get up the lane. For days they were snowed in, enormous icicles hanging from every gutter, nothing to be done but huddle round the range.

At least it means Will can rest a bit, scribbled Flo. *Once the milking's over, there's nothing can be done outside.*

She and the children made Christmas cards. When the thaw came she bundled them up in everything they had and took them down to Hawkchurch. Water gurgled in the ditches, melting snow dripped from every tree. They posted their cards and stocked up, after days of mousetrap cheese on toast. Flo used the extra Christmas rations for stocking treats: chocolate and sugar mice.

When they got back, they found Will and Mike had brought in a tree. It stood in a bucket in the sitting room — *Earth everywhere! Men!!* — and the whole house smelled of pine.

Next day she dug out the box of decorations.

81

'There'll be tears before bedtime,' said Mike, hearing the excitement, but came through to hang up an angel.

'Whatever else, we'll have a good Christmas,' Will said, pouring them all a whisky that evening. For once they had a fire in there, though it barely took the chill off. They huddled round it, raising their glasses. 'Then we'll see.'

★   ★   ★

January was foul: as windy and wet as when they'd arrived a year ago. February was worse. Shaving after milking one morning Will nicked himself with the razor. 'Bloody fool.' He reached for a holey flannel, pressed it to the cut, stood there before the steamy mirror and gave it a rub.

He was grey as an elephant. He was drawn and grey and ill. He was on another lot of pills. They made him feel dopey and sick. He was thirty-nine, with a wife and young children. He'd come back from India happy and fit as a fiddle, retrained, done his best, and now —

'Oh, I don't know,' he said aloud.

'What don't you know, my darling?' asked Flo, passing the open door. The beds were done; she put her head round, saw his haggard face.

'Any bloody thing. Never mind. I'll be down in a tick.'

He took away the flannel, saw the cut still bleeding, sat down on the edge of the bath. From downstairs came the sound of wails and quarrelling: the children were fractious, cooped up day after day.

Down in the kitchen, he had a cup of stewed tea, lit his pipe and looked through yesterday's paper, brought up by Flo from the village. No point in looking for jobs in there any more, he'd said when she dropped the new *Farmer and Stockbreeder* on the table, though he always checked prices, read up on the county shows. Now, the children out of the way in the sitting room, Baba putting on records, deft little thing, he picked it up and gave it one more go. Surely, in the new year, there might be something.

'Flo? Come and look at this.'

He showed her an ad. The Rural Landowners Society, looking for regional secretaries to recruit new members, in Leicestershire and the Midlands. They wanted a farming background and sales experience. 'Salary and commission paid. Car useful.'

Old Mike had sales experience, poor bugger. Will had never sold a thing in his life. Sugar cane, of course, but that was different, on a different scale entirely. But farming background: he had that all right, even if he hadn't got a car. Bus and shanks' pony: what was wrong with that? Or a push bike.

'What do you think?'

From across the hall came the crackle of music and the children's racing footsteps.

> There's a little white house,
> with a little green door,
> At the end of Honeymoon Lane . . .

'I think you'd be perfect,' said Flo.

83

The interviews were in London, at the RLS headquarters. On a cold March morning he set out, Mike giving him a lift into Axminster, slow on the wet roads, arriving just as the train came puffing in.

'Good luck, old man.'

'I'll need it.'

They shook hands and then Mike strode back to the tractor, parked in the station yard. 'What would you do if I got this job?' Will had asked him as they drove in.

'I'd find something.'

'Perhaps you should apply for this.'

Mike shook his head. 'My sister's starting a chinchilla farm. Back in Suffolk.'

'Good Lord.'

'Might help her out for a bit. You go after it, Will.'

He'd go after it. He bought his ticket with moments to spare, the platform full of steam, the whistle blowing, and ran through the hall, shouting.

★   ★   ★

Next day, the rain eased off, and a watery sun lit the soaking fields. The children went out in their Wellingtons and splashed about in the puddles. Flo left the door open so she could keep an eye. Wet hens came wandering into the kitchen. '*Get* out! *Get* out!' She wiped up messes and footprints, checked the clock for the thousandth time.

'When's Daddy coming back?' Baba asked at lunchtime, through a mouthful of semolina.

'Tomorrow. He's staying with Auntie Agnes, I've told you. And Uncle Neville.'

'Why?'

'He hasn't seen them since she got married. Darling, please don't eat like that.'

'Why are you looking at the clock again?'

'I'm not.'

They hadn't told the children a thing: why unsettle them when nothing might come of it all? Anyway, Freddie was too young to understand. But she'd had butterflies ever since he'd left — *anyone would think it was me being interviewed!*

'Listen!' She leaped to her feet, banging her knee on the table.

'What? What?'

'Ouch. Nothing. Wait there.'

She ran to the door, looked out. There it came again, the ring of the bicycle bell, and there was the telegraph boy in his cap, wheeling up over the mud. She ran down towards him, Baba following in her socks — when did that child ever do what she was told? — and Freddie calling from the high chair.

'Telegram,' said the boy, and then: 'Your little girl's got no shoes on.'

'I know. Thank you.'

She signed, and ripped it open. Two words.

'GOT IT.'

★ ★ ★

The children were in bed: slowly he climbed the stairs. Baba's room was growing dusky as the pale spring sun went down. It was still very cold.

'Baba, I want to tell you something.' He sat on the bed beside her, and took a breath. 'We're selling up.'

'What's selling up?'

'I've had to sell Hatpeg,' he told her, and felt his eyes fill with tears. 'I've had to sell them all. I'm a tired old Daddy, too old for farming.' He patted his chest. 'Ticker playing up a bit. Can't go on any more.'

She looked at him, sat up, pulled up Squeaker beside her.

'Where's Hatpeg?'

'She's still here, but she's going with Guernsey Noo and the others to another farm.'

'You're crying.'

'No, I'm not.'

Then he was sobbing his heart out.

She put her arms round his neck and he hugged her tight.

'Done my best,' he said at last.

★   ★   ★

There came a terrible day. Three cattle trucks came to take away all the cows and calves. They backed up one by one in the yard and Will and Mike and the drivers rounded up the animals. Flo and the children stood at the kitchen window and watched, as the cows bellowed and sticks were used to drive them: out of the back yard where they had stood since early milking,

86

across to the ramps and up, into the dark inside. They bucked and bounded, rolling their eyes.

'Garn! Garn! Get up there!'

'That's Guernsey Noo!' shouted Baba.

'Poor Guernsey Noo,' said Flo. 'Poor old things.'

The last truck was for the calves, faster than the cows at leaping sideways, darting away on their long thin legs.

'Over there — over there — quick, get him!'

At last it was over, the trucks rumbling away down the lane and the gate swung to. Will and Mike stood looking at the empty yard. There were cowpats everywhere, and bits of straw. Will shook his head. Then he and Mike went into the cowshed, to swill it all out for the last time. When Baba and Freddie went out to play they could hear the fierce sound of the brooms, brushing and brushing the concrete, over and over again.

Part Two

Honeymoon Lane

1

They stood in the lobby on a swirly carpet, their luggage all around them.

'Home!' said Freddie, looking around him. His eyes were enormous. 'Home!'

The hotel was called Saunt's Pump — who was old Saunt, and where had he put his pump, Will wondered, trying to jolly everyone along a bit, but answer came there none.

'Home!' There he stood in his little brown corduroy dungarees, clutching Flo's hand.

'Come on, old chap.'

But when he saw Flo's exhausted face, Will felt his own heart sink. The girl who'd let them in had said the proprietor would be along in a minute; now, across the foyer, they could see the same girl in the dimly lit dining room, serving supper. She plonked down a dish before a wavery old boy trying to tuck a napkin into his collar.

'Mince and mashed potato,' she announced. He looked up hopefully; she was gone in a flash. There were only two other people there, a chap who looked like a commercial traveller and an old girl with a book.

'I'm hungry,' said Baba.

'Ssh,' said Flo. 'Mrs Thing will be here in a minute. Will, do ring.'

'Me ring,' said Freddie.

'Go on, then.' Will scooped him up and

91

Freddie patted the bell in a series of faint little tings. A large woman finally appeared, brushing crumbs off her cardigan.

'I'm ever so sorry. You must be the Sutherlands.' She beamed at Freddie, still in Will's arms. 'Aren't you a big boy, banging away on that bell?' She reached for the keys behind her, heaved an enormous book up on to the counter. 'If you could just sign in, Mr Sutherland. My name's Mrs Burnett, by the way.' She beamed again.

Soon they were tramping up the swirly-carpeted stairs.

'On and on,' sighed Freddie.

They had two front rooms, with an interconnecting door. The children's room was floored with lino and a rag rug. Baba had a little bed up against a wall, and Freddie a battered old cot. Will and Flo had a creaking double bed and the same kind of utility furniture they'd had on the farm. An enormous wireless stood on top of a hideous chest of drawers. There was a carpet of faded cabbage roses. Was there a faint smell of mouse?

They stood at the windows, Freddie in Will's arms, and looked down on a dusky square. At this hour, on the farm, the cows would have been filing out of the yard, the first stars pricking the sky above the fields. Now, on a cold spring evening, they made out a steeple and a market hall, watched people hurrying home beneath the streetlamps. The hotel sign swung in the wind.

'Home,' said Freddie again.

'This is home now, old chap.'

He buried his head in Will's neck.

＊　＊　＊

They were in Market Hampden, an old
Leicestershire town of some substance and
charm: that was how Fitz had described it,
quoting from the Shell book. *'Charles I stayed
there in the Civil War! Where will your office be,
Willie?'*

It was in a narrow street off the Square, just a
few minutes' walk from the hotel. There was an
estate agent on the ground floor, some kind of
dressmaking outfit above. He was in a rented
room at the top. 'Pretty primitive and poky,' he
wrote back to Fitz a few days later, 'but actually
it's rather fun. Atmosphere, character, that sort
of thing.' There was a big old desk, a swivel chair,
and a telephone — joy, as Flo would say. Also
a bloody great typewriter he'd have to get the
hang of — 'though apparently a girl comes in a
couple of days a week. Looking forward to that!'

A vast green army filing cabinet stood in the
corner, with a kettle and cups on a tray. A map
of the Midlands counties was pinned to the wall,
studded with coloured pins.

On his first day he was shown the ropes by the
Area Director, last seen at the interview in
London.

'Sutherland. Charles Denning. Well done
— good to see you again.'

Denning was big and tweedy, and owned, it
seemed, half of Northamptonshire. 'You were in
India, I remember. Sugar, before the war, that
right?' He strode across to push up the casement
window. In came the sun and a distinct whiff of

tomato soup. 'That's from the Symonds factory.'
He pushed the window back down a bit. 'Tinned
soup and veg. You get used to the smell pretty
quickly, I'm told. Now, then.'

They spent the morning going through it all.
Recruiting procedure, and all the benefits of
joining up: advice on renewing derelict buildings, on mechanisation, and saving wages; on
insurance, tax, pension schemes, death duties.

The pins on the map showed RLS members
and potential members: Will took in the names
of farms and villages, saw himself pushing open
other people's gates on to field and farmyard,
walking over graceful parkland and huge estates,
with nothing to do except talk. No milking, no
ploughing, no heaving of churn and hay bale. He
felt better already.

★　★　★

To sit at a table and be brought a meal! The
children gazed round them at the other guests.

'Mummy! That man's got a drip on his nose.'

'Ssh.'

'It's disgusting!'

It was. Poor old boy, all alone in the world,
you could sense it a mile away, no one to tuck in
his napkin or cut up his gristly bacon. But Baba
gave the room a radiant smile as they left after
breakfast.

'Goodbye, everyone!'

'What a little pet.'

Mrs Burnett — she must stop calling her Mrs
Thing — looked up from the desk as they all

94

came down, the children in their reins.

'Going out? Let me open the door for you.'

In came a flood of sun.

'Off we go!'

Extraordinary, after all this time, to be out and about in a town. With Freddie in the pushchair, Baba's reins wound around her wrist, Flo gazed at all the shops.

'What's that smell?'

'Daddy says there's a soup factory. I expect we'll get used to it.'

Tomato? Mulligatawny? They walked along the street. Hoardings bore huge advertisements.

Two children, a little girl in plaits and a toddler boy, were walking away down a country lane, hand in hand. An enormous sunburst awaited them, in their knitted hats and good strong shoes. Start-rite, said the advertisement, and needed to say no more.

'That's you two,' said Flo.

'That's us!'

Inside Boots, she picked up a packet of sanitary towels. In the Hawkchurch village shop STs had been tucked under the counter, but here — shocking, really. And sure enough —

Baba stood on tiptoe at the counter, reaching up. 'What are you buying?' She patted the big soft packets. 'What are they?

'Never mind, we're off now.' She tucked everything into her bag.

'What *are* they?'

A sign pointed to the library on the upper floor.

'Up we go!'

Three or four tables stood on the floorboards, heaped with books. Flo had a look at them. Perhaps, with no cooking, she might at last get an hour or two. Even start writing again, oh ha ha ha. The exercise books were all tied up in a bundle, down at the bottom of her case.

The children were running about, Freddie at the window, Baba on tiptoe again.

'I want a book!'

'Can I help you?' A spinstery librarian in a fawn cardigan. Always one of those. A bit like Agnes used to be.

How long was it since she'd had time for this sort of thing? A happy hour went by. She joined, took out two picture-books for the children, and the new Monica Dickens for herself, and a book by someone called Elizabeth Taylor. *A Game of Hide and Seek*, a love story, just her kind of thing. *One day I'll write our love story if it kills me*, she told her diary, and tugged on Baba's reins as she made for the door. A man went past pushing a pram. Honestly!

★   ★   ★

The best thing was having a wireless in their room. Like the Start-rite advertisement, it had a huge cheerful sunburst over rather grubby fabric.

'Listen to this,' she said after supper, the children bathed and in their nightclothes. They snuggled down in the double bed, just for a treat. Flo twiddled about with the knobs, past a lot of hissing and fizzing and foreign voices. Home Service — 'Here we are!'

96

'We're Much-Binding-in-the-Marsh!' sang dear Dickie Murdoch.

'This looks like fun,' said Will, coming up from his moment in the bar.

'Much-Binding-in-the-Marsh!'

He burst out laughing. 'Jolly good show. I'll look for a cottage there.'

Already, particulars of lovely unaffordable houses were scattered about. Where would they end up?

'Bedtime,' said Flo to the children, as Dickie Murdoch and Kenneth Horne concluded the week's RAF muddle, leaving her and Will in stitches. 'Time to tuck down.'

'I don't want to tuck down!'

They hauled them out of the double bed, and carried them through, shrieking.

'Shush! Shush! There are other people here!'

'Where? I can't see any.'

'That's quite enough from you. Now look, I've got a little nightlight on the chest of drawers.' Mrs Thing had let her have it. 'Get into bed. Come on, Freddie, darling, in we go.' She heaved him into the cot and ran the side up. Will switched off the overhead light and Flo struck a match. In a moment, the nightlight in its saucer of water was shining through the dark. The children fell silent.

'Good night, my darlings. Sleepy tight.'

They crept out into their own room. 'Time we tucked down,' said Will, as they closed the door, leaving a chink, just in case. 'Come here.'

No milking, no exhaustion, no ghastly blood pressure. She moved into his arms; they lay kissing on the lumpy eiderdown.

'Are they asleep?'

'I'm sure they are.'

So far, so hugely better.

★ ★ ★

Then came the telegram.

'She's gone,' said Will, ripping it open at the breakfast table, going white.

'Who's gone? What's happened?'

'Ssh!'

Will pushed it across the linen cloth. 'MOTHER DIED IN HER SLEEP LAST NIGHT. AGNES.' All around them, the room was murmuring — why did a telegram so seldom bring good news?

'Granny's gone to heaven,' Flo told the children, but they looked blank. They'd scarcely seen her, didn't remember her. Her own parents had seen Freddie only once, and Baba as a toddler God, what an isolated life they'd all been living.

'Will?'

He sat with his head in his hands.

'Be all right in a minute.' Then he got up and went quickly out.

'Is Daddy crying?'

'He might be. Poor Daddy.' She wiped egg off Freddie's chin.

'Mummy not cry,' he commanded.

'I'm not going to, darling.'

She knew she wouldn't shed a tear, even if she went to the funeral, which of course she couldn't do. Will would go and she'd stay here with the children.

What an old bat that woman had been — 'You can call me Mother Beatrice.' Ugh, like some ghastly sect or something. Awful to think of Baba being named after her. 'But we've got to do it,' Will had said, just as he'd said they must call Freddie after his father. 'It's the one thing we can do for her, darling.'

Oh, well. Poor Will. It was his mother, after all.

★ ★ ★

But after the funeral, they all settled down. The hotel was comfortable and warm. True, Freddie had watched wide-eyed from his cot as Will threw a mouse from a private mouse trap out of the window one morning. True, the food was dull, but food everywhere was dull these days: lots of things still rationed and the taste of dried egg in every cake. To think of five hundred hens, and all those fresh eggs every day!

But the best thing, apart from no housework, was that they seemed to cheer everyone up. Lovely for the two old permanent residents to have a young family coming down to breakfast every morning: doddery Mr Metcalfe, with his dripping nose; that poor old trout Miss Forest: they'd somehow fetched up here at their separate tables, along with the commercial travellers, and everyone looked up as the children ran in, had something new to talk about at last.

'Hello, you two,' said Miss Forest, peering over the *Telegraph*.

99

'That's a pretty frock,' said Mr Metcalfe, every time Baba appeared in her worn old farm things, quickly getting outgrown.

'Shall I help you cut up your toast?' She sat beside him, hacking away. 'You need a hankie!' He fished one out with a trembling paw.

'I'm off now,' said Will every morning, getting to his feet.

'Bye-bye Daddy!'

'Be good!'

He gave Freddie a kiss in his high chair, nodded to the room. He looked so brisk and purposeful, so cheery, as he and Flo kissed goodbye. 'Have a good day, darling,' she told him.

And with the sadness of the funeral behind him, he mostly did.

Already he'd signed up two new members, catching the bus out of town along country roads, striding in his cap and Wellingtons down splashy lanes in Leicestershire, Rutland and Northamptonshire, getting the OS map out, finding his way about. Blossom in the hedgerows — marvellous. He was visiting old farms getting themselves back on their feet, just as he had done. Lots to talk about: he knew just what they were up against, just what the RLS could offer, and he spoke the farmers' language, talking about milk yields, subsidies, crop rotation. Scratching the head of a huge Ayrshire bull cooped up in a byre, he thought of the bony white bullocks hauling their carts of cane along the dusty paths, turning the wheel of a village well.

'I got a couple of bulls behind the plough once,' he told the farmer, when they got talking about the past. Hens scratched around at their feet.

'Bullocks, you mean.'

'No, bulls,' he said. 'In India.' And he told him how two young bulls were destined for slaughter until he came up with his mad idea. The Ayrshire drooled through the ring in his bristly nose, leaning out over the half-door into the wet, as Will and the farmer shook hands.

'Got another!' he told Flo that evening.

And now — house-hunting!

'We must concentrate our minds.'

They sat with all the particulars in the hotel lounge.

'Oh, please don't call it a lounge!'

'Darling, it's a hotel, what else would they call it?'

'I don't know, it just sounds so awful.'

He passed her a brochure. 'What do you think of this?'

They gazed at the pasted-on photograph of a whitewashed thatched cottage: three beds, small garden front and back, friendly village.

'I do love thatch.'

'I could grow our own veg.'

Flo had a flash of cabbages. Cabbages! In the front garden! Not to mention sprouts. Too awful.

'Always wanted a veg patch.'

Had he really? Had he *really?*

'But can we afford it?' she said, looking at the price.

'The thing is, of course, now Mother's gone

. . . Got a bit more to play with.'

Fitz had been so generous when the farm went on the market. *Of course you must have any profit*, she wrote. *You've been paying me rent all the time and I only ever wanted my money back. Take it! Take it!*

He took it. Enough for a deposit. With Mother's money it all beefed up nicely.

'We can always make an offer.'

'What about this?' Flo fished out a heavenly Georgian house, fine village position, four beds, large gardens, orchard. Orchard! Now that would be a dream. She saw it all: tea under the apple trees, Will up a ladder in autumn —

He pointed at the noughts. 'Sorry, darling, out of the question.'

The apples fell sadly into the long grass.

'Could we just *look* at it?'

'Not much point, is there?'

She bit her lip. And then a thought struck her like a thunderbolt.

'Will! I've got an idea.'

He was lighting his pipe. 'What's that?'

'Father could help us to buy it. I know he would.' Oh, that house, that heavenly, gracious, glorious house! The orchard! They could stay there for ever and ever.

Will threw down his match.

'Now look, Flo . . . '

'Look what?'

'I don't want you getting silly about this.'

'What do you mean?'

'You know what I mean. I don't want to be saddled with more debt than I can manage, and

I certainly don't want to be in debt to your father.'

'He wouldn't mind!'

'That's not the point. And anyway, what the hell do we need a Georgian house for?'

There was simply no answer to that.

★　★　★

'Now, then,' he said, a couple of days later. 'School. How are we getting on?'

Flo was still upset. But no need to dither between thatch and an orchard here: there was only one school in Market Hampden.

A little dame school, she had written to Vivie. *Run by three spinster sisters. Funny little place, but I think Baba will love it — high time she went, little chatterbox!*

They were waiting for a place. Ideally, of course, two places, and five minutes to herself for once, if there were a nursery. There wasn't.

'Still haven't heard,' she said. 'I'll go and see them again.'

Will leaned back beside her. 'Good idea. Reminds me: I must put Freddie down for Mountford as soon as we get settled. I'd love to see him there.'

Mountford Park was Will's old Hertfordshire prep school — a creeper-smothered mansion in glorious parkland — he'd shown her the photographs. It did look gorgeous.

'He's so small,' said Flo.

'You wait — he'll be eight before you know it.'

Flo tried to imagine it. Freddie wasn't like

103

Baba, all loving smiles and off we go. She tried to imagine explaining. Saying goodbye. She didn't want another quarrel, but —

'Darling, I'm really not sure . . . '

Will put his arm round her. 'Leave it to me.'

★ ★ ★

'I'm starting school today!' Baba announced one September morning.

'Are you now?'

'Sorry I can't cut up your toast, Mr Metcalfe! I have to go!'

They waved her off.

There were three Miss Beasleys. There was the Bride Miss Beasley: she was the prettiest — though she, like the other two, could be strict. Then the Middle Miss Beasley: plain, ordinary, nothing more to be said. Often wore a green jumper. And then, in horn-rimmed specs, there was the Fat-Bottomed Miss Beasley.

'Huge!' said Will.

There were two classrooms, both on the upper floor. The one for the little ones had tables and chairs, and overlooked the garden. There was an alphabet frieze all round the wall. A was for Apple and B was for Bear. And Baba, of course. The classroom for the bigger ones was run by the Bride Miss Beasley, and overlooked the street. They had desks in there. Inkwells! A piano! And all the Times Tables were pinned up on the walls.

Baba started off with the little ones. As soon as she could read, said the Middle Miss Beasley, she could go up. Baba prayed for this every night. Some of those children were eight!

'What are you going to do today?' Will asked her, as they walked through the town hand in hand.

'Reading,' she said firmly. 'And writing. I've got a new copybook.'

At the door of the school he kissed her goodbye, and watched her climb the stairs without a backward glance. 'Bye, darling!' Then he was off, raising his cap to all the mothers coming up with their own kids. 'Morning! Good morning!'

Inside, Baba was settling down.

'Good morning, children.'

'Good-mor-ning-Miss-Beas-ley.'

The Fat-Bottomed Miss Beasley gave out all the copybooks. Baba pressed hers open and flat. She took a pencil from the jam jar. Now then.

The pages were lined in rows of three. On the top was something to copy: pot hooks or biscuits. Today it was biscuits. The other two lines were where you wrote: one line for a little letter and two for capitals — that was when you were allowed to do letters. You had to get good at pot hooks and biscuits first.

★ ★ ★

Meanwhile, Freddie and Flo were having a high old time.

'Mummy!'

The moment Baba and Will were gone, he was banging on the table of his high chair, wreathed in smiles. 'Mummy, Mummy, Mummy!'

'Freddie, Freddie, Freddie!' Flo finished her toast and marmalade, helped him finish his egg and soldiers, and then they were off. Every day they walked through the town, looking at this and that. Tuesday was market day: as soon as they woke up they could hear the trucks rattling along, and hear the moos. The children rushed to the window. 'Look! That one's a Guernsey!'

Now they walked through the side streets, and now the smell of animals mingled with the smell of the soup. Inside the market, she and Freddie wandered hand in hand along the rows of pens.

'Pigs!'

Huge pink bristly sows lay on their sides in a heap of hay, little pink piglets clamped to the teats.

'Suck, suck, snuffle, snuffle,' said Flo.

Freddie was weak with giggles. 'Suck, suck, snuffle, snuffle!'

In one of the pens stood an enormous boar, patched with black. Flo gazed at it. From somewhere the words British Saddleback came to mind. Honestly, whoever would have thought she'd spend her married life thinking about breeds of pig. *I ask you!* she wrote to Vivie.

'Going to be a farmer when you grow up?' asked a man in an overall.

'I is a farmer,' said Freddie.

Shafts of sun streamed through the holes in the roof, dancing with hay dust. Little bits of straw spun through the air, and here and there a sparrow flew chirping up to a ledge. Flo leaned her cheek against Freddie's.

'My very own.'

As well as recruiting new members, Will had to keep the old ones happy, of course. Sometimes this meant half an acre and a cow; sometimes, as today, a huge estate.

In came the train to Leicester, clouds of steam lit by the morning sun. He climbed on, feeling the warmth on his back, first time for ages he'd been on a train without the family. And all at once he saw a young man hauling himself up on to a train packed to the gills, the platform crowded with Indian families, steam drifting away in the heat, the *chai* wallah shouting with his tray of chinking glasses, that smoky smell of tea and pungent spices everywhere, the whistle blowing as he made his way down to his compartment. They were off!

As he settled down now, looking out on to a quilt of English fields, bright with English sun, the landscape of the past rushed by.

And on the way home at the end of the afternoon, looking out of the window as the train chuffed once again past farm and village, he saw a little place he liked the look of.

2

'There's a little white house, with a little green door, at the end of Honeymoon Lane!'

★ ★ ★

They all sang away in the back of the taxi, luggage crammed into the boot, everyone wild with excitement. Then they got there.

Red brick, tiled roof, a porch. Two up, two down, with the kitchen at the back.

But a huge garden, leading through a gap in the hedge to an orchard. An orchard! 'Thought we could keep a few geese,' said Will, as the children went racing about. There was a garage alongside the path, large enough for a car at the front, if they had one, and a playroom at the back, if they put a partition in.

At the front, the garden was small and walled, looking on to a lane. To the left was the Crown — 'That looks pretty good.' To the right took you out on to the main road, with a council estate a field or two away, and a footbridge over a canal, thick with duckweed. And in front was a hedged-in bit, which also belonged to them.

'That's where I'll grow the veg.'

The first thing Flo did with the housewarming cheque from Father was to have the cottage whitewashed. And the front door and windows painted black. *A little black and white cottage on a quiet lane,* she wrote to Vivie, on new headed writing paper. Tile Cottage, Melcote Magna, Leicestershire. *Sweet, now we've had it done up.*

Freddie picked up the telephone in Will's office, across the tiny hall from the dining room. He dialled at random: sometimes got nothing at all, sometimes a person. 'Hello! Hello-a-lo!' They'd never had a phone of their own: Will let him get on with it for the first few days, shooing him out for his nap. But essentially, he told Flo, the phone was for work, not social chit-chat. Of course she could use it when she had to. But —

'Will Sutherland here, just phoning to let you know my new number . . . Yes, splendid, thanks. We're just settling in.'

Everything came out of store. Jolly old Pickfords once again, the van squeezed into the narrow lane. In came the long green cane chairs they used to lie on in the garden in Tulsipore. 'Better put those in the garage.' In came the gate-legged dining room table, in came the elephant table he'd bought Flo as a wedding present. Four great elephant heads, with ivory tusks, bearing the carved wooden top. Hadn't seen it for years, what a splendid thing. Did it look a bit odd, in a country cottage?

'Where'd you like this, sir?'

'Flo? Darling? Where d'you think this should go?'

'In that corner. I'll find a lamp for it. I'm going to do something about lunch.'

Cooking again! And endless tea for the men, of course, tramping in and out in their overalls.

Might as well be back on the farm at harvest time!

★ ★ ★

The men had their tea and sandwiches out in the lorry, the family scrunched round the kitchen table for bread and cheese and Symonds tomato soup —

'Tastes better than it smells, don't you think?' said Will.

Nobody thought that it did.

A knock at the door. 'Ready to start again, sir?'

In came tea chests of stuff they hadn't seen for years. The barometer!

'Glass is going up,' said Will, propping it up on a chair.

Then, all packed up separately, came the huge old portraits. Grandfather, in Victorian jacket and cravat, and sideburns black as pitch, his hand resting on the head of a dear old spaniel. Grandmother, in her white bonnet and red paisley shawl. He'd never met either of them, Father and Mother in their forties by the time he came along. Twelve years married before starting a family. Perhaps they couldn't quite get the hang of it.

Not like him and Flo.

He'd seen her honeymoon diary once, for 1946: *23 September! 24 September!! 25 September!!!*

'Where are those going?' she asked now, squeezing from the kitchen into the hall. She gazed at bonneted Grandmother. Another old

110

stick from the Sutherlands.

'Out in the garage for now,' said Will, seeing her face, and as the children came running in he turned to another tea chest.

'Careful! Stand back!'

All the stuff from India. Little things in a box. The ivory elephant and the little ivory owl. 'Let me hold!' 'Let *me*!' Then came the line of elephants, marching across an ivory bridge over an ebony river. He set them on the mantelpiece. Marching through Leicestershire now.

'What is an elephant most afraid of?'

Nobody knew.

'A mouse. And do you know why?'

They shook their heads.

'Because — ' He raised his arm and swung it from left to right in front of them — 'because when an elephant goes tramping through the long dry grass of India, he lowers his great big trunk to see if there's anything interesting to smell. Like this.' He waved his hand, snorting. 'And if there's a little mouse down there, it sees a nice dark hole and runs up it! Right up inside the elephant's head!' He shook his head violently, and gave a sneezy roar. 'And he can't get it out!'

'Ugh! Ugh!'

'What happens?'

'I expect he goes mad.'

Here was a box of books, not many, never been a great reader, never had time, but he dug out the volumes of Arthur Mee's *Children's Encyclopedia* — the kids might like those one day. He ferreted about a bit — there was something slipped down the side, a picture or something. He pulled it out. Good Lord. Not a picture, but his poem, the only thing he'd ever written, and published in the *Times of India*.

'You must get it framed, darling,' Flo had said when he showed it to her, so he had, down in the bazaar, just a simple little wooden thing. He picked it up, blew the dust off.

> Out of Burma, out of Burma,
> By the long and dusty road,
> By the bullock, by the steamer,
> Thousands came and bore their load . . .

1942. The Japanese invasion. There were captioned illustrations: Mule Transport in the Hills. Food Dropped by Aircraft. Finally — Journey's End. And there were his initials, at the bottom.

'Flo? Flo? Guess what I've just found.' But she was banging about in the kitchen.

'Guess who wrote this, kiddos?'

But they were playing with the elephants.

He put it aside. Now what? Something in a box on its own, wrapped in brown paper. Ah!

'Guess what this is.'

He pulled it out. God, it was heavy. He laid it on the table, great bulky thing, and rustled the paper excitingly. The elephants were abandoned.

'What? What is it?'

'It's a big — bad — panther!' He tore off the paper from the head, and the children screamed.

'Mummy!'

'Now what?' Flo came down the hall from the kitchen. Green glassy eyes glared at her across the room, huge sharp teeth bared themselves in a snarl. 'Oh, for pity's sake.'

'Mummy!'

'It's all right, Freddie, he's stuffed, he can't hurt you. Look at his funny old ears.'

His ears were tufty, his coat smooth and — amazingly — still a good colour. What a handsome beast. They stroked him, shivering with fear and courage.

'Daddy shot him,' said Will, and delved into the chest for the skin. 'He was a big bad panther, frightening all the villagers.' There was a photograph somewhere, everyone out in the sun, he garlanded up to the gills, smiling and holding his rifle, surrounded by the village men in white. He laid the skin down on the floor.

Freddie came cautiously over and stroked the soft tail.

'That's the ticket. He can't hurt anyone now.'

Next day, he drilled a hole in the dining-room wall. He put in a couple of Rawlplugs, a couple of screws. Then he hung up old Panther on his wooden mount, glaring across from above the fireplace. Looked pretty good, though he said it himself.

⋆   ⋆   ⋆

In a month or two, it felt as if they'd been there for ever. And there were people in Melcote they could talk to! Make friends with!

There's the owner of Manor Farm, wrote Flo in a letter home. *Donald Gibson — terrifically handsome! His wife's a bit fierce, I thought, but they have three boys and they invited us for drinks almost as soon as we got here. Donald's a member of the RLS already, knew all about Will. Gorgeous house, up a drive. When we got back here I must say it looked — well, not poky, exactly, but still pretty small. But so nice for Baba & Freddie to have other children to play with at last, and the garden here makes up for everything. Will's been to a farm where they breed geese (!!).*

At the drinks do we also met a nice chap who works for Symonds, though we never met him in Market Hampden. Roddy Byatt. He's pretty gorgeous, too. Will said he recognised his wife from the school gate — vivacious, and frightfully pretty. Anyway, they have a little girl who I'm sure will make friends with Baba. Nancy. Funny little thing, bit of a lonely only. And — wait for it — there's also a Literary Agent! He and his wife live a little way out of the village, in another tiny cottage. All a bit Bohemian there...

★ ★ ★

She put down her pen. Mid-morning, Freddie having a nap, worn out with all the excitement, Baba at school — *and the best thing is that there's a school run! I won't have to take her in to Market Hampden on the bus every day, thank the Lord.*

Will was in his office across the hall. She could hear him through two closed doors, talking the hind legs off a donkey on the telephone — 'Will Sutherland here! Good morning!' — or tapping away with two fingers on the Remington, brought with the swivel chair from Market Hampden. The RLS had given an advance for office equipment, and a vast great thing had been delivered.

'What on earth is that?'

'A Gestetner. It's a copying machine. You type your stuff on a stencil and hook it up here . . . and the ink goes in here . . . ' He pulled a black bottle out of a box. Dark, oily stuff.

Flo beat a hasty retreat. Office life: never understood it. Never wanted to. And so strange to have Will at a desk, in the house, after all that outdoor life in Devon. Of course, he'd be out and about recruiting: he loved that.

The sun came pouring through the unwashed windows — something else she'd have to get organised. Dust everywhere, and still bare floorboards.

What I need is domestic help, of course, she continued to Vivie. *Don't know how easy it's going to be to find that.*

Agnes's wretched present from the farm had emerged from a box and was waiting, with *Mrs Beeton*, to go up on a kitchen shelf. *How to Run Your Home without Help.*

Washing-up is a task regarded with particular horror by many, yet really it needn't be so bad. During the war, when soap was too scarce to allow of it being used in the washing-up bowl, it was certainly harder, but with the coming of liquid soap substitute one can luxuriate in nice sudsy water . . .

She'd snapped it shut with a shudder. *Honestly,
Vivie — luxuriate! In the washing-up! I either
want to luxuriate in a bath, or —* Or what? What
did she want? She wanted to get to her book.

*One day I'll get my exercise books out again,
and flutter my eyelashes at that Literary Agent!*

Flo put down her pen. Was it mad, to think of
such a thing? An agent, considering her work?
When she hadn't even begun, not properly, just
scribbled away in snatched moments on the farm.
Perhaps I can't do it, she thought, as the sun
slanted in through the dusty glass, and Will went
on tapping away. And then: I've never done anything proper, not really.

She shook her head. It didn't do any good,
thinking like that.

''Pale hands I loved beside the Shali-ma-ar,''
Will sang in his office, banging a drawer shut.
And then, 'Flo? How's lunch getting on?'

'On its way,' she said quickly, and as she
signed the letter with lots of love, as always, and
as he swung round in his swivel chair, roaring his
way through India's most haunting love song,
she was waiting once again in the crowded café
of the Grand Hotel to board the troop ship
home, and start her new life. Mrs William
Sutherland. She was going to make something of
herself at last.

So do it, she told herself now. Be brave.

3

Chapter One

Mary Marshall was a pretty young woman with a broken heart. She went out to India just after the War, having served in the WAAF. (Before that she'd been a nurse in a London Hospital.) She'd pushed a lot of planes about on boards, tracking Operations, and she went out with lots of good-looking Officers in the evenings. Unfortunately, she fell for one of them in a big way, but though he seemed as keen as she was, at the end of the War he said he must say Goodbye!! She was heart-broken . . .

*   *   *

Flies came buzzing in, and got stuck on the flypaper hanging from the kitchen ceiling. Wasps swarmed at the open window and drowned in the jar of jam and water she'd set on the sill. Freddie was fascinated by this: if she stood him on a chair by the sink he'd watch them for ages.

But now Mary was making a new start! She stood on Deck with other young things, looking out over the sea. Sparkling sea? . . . looking out over the sparkling sea. Much better. *The sparkling blue sea.* Perfect.

'Mum-my!' A cry from the garden, where

Freddie had woken from his nap beneath the apple trees. Every afternoon she snuggled him up with pillow and eiderdown on a long cane chair.

Heavens, where had the time gone? And there was Will, opening the office door once more.

'Flo? Any chance of a cup of tea?'

She put down her pen.

Was it any good? she asked herself, as she put the kettle on and went outside. Jenny Lewis, the literary agent's wife, had asked her to tea again. Chaos in there! Children everywhere, a baby on the way, and Michael in his office — just like Will, but more intellectual, of course. Through the open door she could see piles of Manuscripts.

'Mummy!' There Freddie was, all flushed from sleep, in the dappled shade (that was a nice phrase, she must use that somewhere) beneath the apple trees.

'Hello, my darling, had a good nap?'

$$\star \quad \star \quad \star$$

Sundays, and Will and Baba off to church. They walked down through the village, hand in hand. Over the railway footbridge, along the road.

'Morning! Good morning!' There were the Gibsons, crunching on the gravel as they came out of their drive, Daphne in a pretty fearsome hat, kind of thing Flo would have something to say about. 'Donald, old boy, how're things?'

'Pretty good, thanks.' He gave Daphne his arm.

Time they had them up for a drink. Always so much to do.

Over the footpath across the Green, the bells ringing, the sun out, and Baba hopping and skipping beside him. There was the west door open wide.

'OK, darling, walk nicely now.'

In they went, all the old dears settling down, and he tried to get the same place each week, down on the left near the front. They sat, had a look at the flowers, nodded to new arrivals as the organ sweetly played.

Sometimes, as they sat there, his mind went to the wayside shrines of India: not the great temples and mosques of Bombay or Delhi, but the simple little statues — dolls, really — propped up in the grass, with a wilting bunch of flowers, or a dish of milk. Krishna with his flute. Hanuman, the monkey god. He thought of the women making *puja* under an old banyan tree in the village near his first bungalow, and how he had mocked them once, with one of his men, and had been reproached.

'Where do you think God is, sahib?'

'Well — I think He's everywhere.'

'Then perhaps He is in that tree, sahib.'

He'd felt quite humbled by that.

Now the organ sounded a new note. They were off, getting to their feet as the padre came out from the vestry and stood before them. Jeremy Scott: seemed a good chap. And it was 'All Things Bright and Beautiful' — Baba's favourite.

'All things wise and wonderful,
The Lord God made them all.'

Sweet little voice. The church was full, the sun streamed in through the stained-glass windows.

'The purple-headed mountain,
The river running by . . . '

Behind him a funny fellow was roaring away at the top of his voice: you always got one or two, often an old girl warbling just a bit too loud, a bit too high. Got on your nerves, like this chap. Will found himself making up a little song as the bellowing went on. He'd sing it to Baba later.

Afterwards, as they all came pouring out, she gave in her hymn book to the sidesman. 'Thank you!'

Scott was in the porch, greeting everyone.

'Morning, Padre. Thanks so much. Jolly good sermon, I thought. Right, then, Baba, off we go.'

Hoppity-skip, hoppity-skip.

'What do you think of this?' Will asked her, as they came to the Green, and he cleared his throat. ''I sing very loud, and I make a lot of noise: I'm asking God to give me some toys.' Who's that?'

'That man behind us! Sing it again.'

They sang it together, swinging hands: ''I sing very loud, and I make a lot of NOISE!''

Then they were home, with a marvellous smell of lunch, and Freddie lining up his potato men on the windowsill.

*   *   *

The major excitement of the following year, as Will put it later, was the Coronation: 2 June 1953, the whole village getting geared up for it weeks beforehand, television aerials sprouting everywhere. He couldn't run to that, but he bought a Union Jack and a secondhand wireless in Market Hampden, and had the whole family standing for the National Anthem. Then, as the morning's rain blew away, he marched them out to the party on the Green.

'Come on, kids! Flo, you ready?'

She was doing her lipstick, wondering who they might meet. Was it all old biddies and children?

No: as they walked over the footbridge she could see the Gibsons striding up, their boys ragging about behind them, and Roddy and Rosie Byatt already there, she in a pretty print frock, pouring tea, and quiet little Nancy looking up and waving as Baba raced ahead. Yards of soaking bunting dripped between the telegraph wires; old dears had whipped the covers off trestle tables set out on the wet grass. The village children, in paper hats, were crammed round on schoolroom chairs, waiting for sandwiches and orange squash.

'Sweet frock,' Flo said to Rosie, taking her cup.

'My dear, I ran it up a couple of days ago, it's a pattern I use all the time.' And then: 'Didn't she look *beautiful?*'

'We just heard it all on the wireless,' said Flo,

121

'but I'm sure she did.' She smiled at Roddy, standing a little apart from it all on the grass. Usually she only glimpsed him picking up Baba for school, or dropping her off again, raising a hand from the wheel as little Nancy waved wistfully from the back. Next to bluff Donald Gibson, slapping Will on the back, greeting Rosie with a hearty 'Hello, Mrs Byatt,' he looked — well, more *subtle*, somehow.

'How are you, Roddy?' she asked him, taking an iced cake from an old girl as she went over. 'I gather you watched it all.'

He nodded politely, said it had been super.

'Nice to have a day off, I expect!' said Flo, noticing all at once how tired he looked, as he gave a little smile and said yes, true enough. *Weary round the edges*, she told her diary. *Such a sweet face, but* . . . Dreary old Symonds Soups — how did a chap like him come to be working there? Of course, a lot of people had had to do funny jobs after the war.

'Nancy must come and have tea one day,' she said brightly. 'It's high time. She and Baba get on so well.'

'Baba gets on with everyone,' said Roddy, watching her pull on her paper hat and beam round at the table. 'Nancy's a little bit shy, I'm afraid, but I'm sure she'd love it.' He cleared his throat. 'You're finding plenty to do in the village, I expect.'

She could feel him making conversation, not quite looking at her, but making the right remarks. Well, what was wrong with that? Nothing she could put a finger on, and of course

122

it was a long time since she'd talked to any man on her own. Perhaps she seemed a bit self-conscious, too, as she said that yes, she loved it here, thanks.

'I'm actually writing a book,' she heard herself say suddenly. 'Well, a novel, actually.' She gave a little laugh.

'Are you really? How frightfully clever. What's it about?'

'It's based on our time in India,' said Flo, and then, as he murmured, 'How interesting,' she saw he was looking over her head to where Rosie and the Gibsons were chatting away with Will.

'I'm afraid I don't read as much as I used to,' he said, making his way towards them, and she followed, saying she was sure he didn't have time, and it was like Will, he never opened a book if he could help it, only John Masters, and people like that. She could hear herself going on rather wildly, not quite sure if it was a good or bad thing to be thought clever, or bookish — a writer, even! — not exactly something she was used to.

But it gave her a little lift. Oh, I'll make something of it, she thought, as the bunting danced in the breeze.

★ ★ ★

But of course there was hardly a moment to write after that.

You know I mentioned geese once, she wrote in her letter home. *Well, they're here!*

They came in the back of a van, one Saturday

morning. *Nothing like looking in the small ads! Will says you could find an elephant there if you looked hard enough!*

'This way!' he called now, swinging the side gate wide.

The children were hopping up and down. They stood with Flo on the long path as the driver backed slowly up the lane.

'That's it, that's it, well done!'

Off went the engine, out came the driver, walking round to the back. Slowly the doors were opened, down came a wooden ramp.

'Where do you want 'em, sir?'

'Up in the orchard, I thought.'

A couple of old boxes stood inside.

'I can see their *heads!*'

The driver tipped the boxes up. Out they came, pit pat paddle pat down the ramp, just like the ducks in *Tom Kitten*. Five greylag geese and a great big gander. Honk. Honk honk. They looked about them with their beady eyes.

'They're awfully *big*, Will.'

In moments, they were all shepherding the blessed things along to the end of the garden, and through the gap in the hedge.

'Look at that. Marvellous!'

As with everything else, in a day or two it felt as if they'd always had them. They kept the long grass down, and their droppings turned it emerald green. They were huge, but the children got used to them, only dodging old Gander, who was fierce, no two ways about it. But in the afternoons they slept beneath the apple trees: head under wing, a watchful eye. Adorable. In the spring there would be goslings. That would be fun. Possibly. In the meantime, Baba took one of the geese for her very own, and called her Grey Fluffy Yellow Toes.

Geese?? wrote Vivie. *Honestly, Flo, I don't know how you manage. And how are you ever going to get down here? You've got to come down for Father's birthday, geese or no!*

★ ★ ★

Nancy Byatt came to tea a couple of Saturdays later. 'We're making a worm house,' Baba told her, taking her hand at the door. Rosie gave a pretty little shudder, and said she would leave them to it.

Will put his head round the office door. 'Stay and have a cuppa when you pick her up,' he said, as the afternoon sun slanted through the porch and lit up her soft brown hair. But Rosie said she was off to Leicester, thanks, doing some proper shopping for once, and it would be Roddy who came.

'Bye, Nancy!' she called, and in moments was in the car. 'Bye! Thanks so much!' And she was off, with a bright little toot.

Nancy held tight to her doll, as Baba led her round to the garden.

'Sweet girl,' said Will.

'Which girl is that?' asked Flo, and he laughed, and said Nancy, of course, and he'd be out in the veg garden if needed. Flo went into the kitchen and washed up the lunch things, keeping an eye through the open kitchen window. She could see

125

Baba showing Nancy the cardboard box with its cut-out door and windows, and Freddie digging up fresh worms with a spoon.

'We're making aprons for them,' said Baba, passing scraps of red gingham. Nancy pushed back her pale hair and looked doubtful.

'I don't really like worms.'

As for the geese —

'You mustn't mind them,' said Freddie stoutly, brandishing a stick as one or two came wandering through the gap in the hedge, but Nancy shrank away. 'Back!' shouted Freddie. Out came Gander, stretching his long, long neck and hissing. 'Go on with you!'

Nancy turned and ran.

'One of them's mine,' said Baba, running after her. 'That's Grey Fluffy Yellow Toes, she won't hurt you.' She took her hand. 'You can stroke her if you like.'

Nancy smiled uncertainly, and kept her distance. 'You're safe now!' called Freddie, driving them back through the hedge. The sun warmed the garden, the worm house was abandoned. Now what?

'I know!' said Baba. And while Freddie rode his bike up and down on the path, she and Nancy fetched the dolls' tea set from indoors. Then they brought out Squeaker and sat him down beside Nancy's doll, and by then she was settled, pouring water from the plastic teapot, passing daisy biscuits.

'Had a good time?' Roddy asked, when he came to pick her up, and Nancy nodded, her pale face smeared with jam.

'I like it here.'

He smiled. 'That's good to hear.'

'Stay and have a drink, old boy.'

Roddy hesitated, looking at his watch, saying that Rosie would be home any minute.

'I don't want to go home,' said Nancy. It was the kind of thing children said all the time when they were enjoying themselves at a friend's house, but all at once her anxious little look was there once more, and Flo watched her as Roddy laughed a bit stiffly and told her to come along. Something not quite right. And why couldn't Roddy just unwind and stay for a drink?

'Perhaps another time,' he said, and they all walked round to the front.

'Bring Rosie!' said Will.

'Come again soon,' said Baba, kissing Nancy goodbye.

'Bye, Nancy!' called Freddie, swinging on the gate. The sun was going down and the lane was full of shadows. He watched the two of them walk slowly away towards the village. 'Bye, Nancy!'

★ ★ ★

'My dear, you must come round!' said Rosie Byatt, bumping into Flo and Freddie in the village shop. 'Come after school tomorrow.' She leaned dramatically forward, showing her bosom in another pretty frock, as Freddie eyed the sweet jars. 'We've got kittens!' she whispered. 'Just arrived!'

And so it was that Flo and Freddie walked

down through the village after his nap next day, meeting Baba and Nancy at the Byatts' house, collected from school by Roddy. And where was he now? Was he joining them for tea?

Rosie shook her head, and ushered the children outside. 'Show them the kittens, darling.' They raced through the flowery garden towards a shed. 'Not too much noise!' she called. 'Be kind to Tabitha!' And she took Flo through to the kitchen, where a pretty tea was laid. 'Roddy's gone for a walk,' she said, filling the kettle.

'Will's a great walker,' said Flo. 'Where does he go?'

'Just through the fields, or along the canal. He needs a bit of time to himself after work; he does get terribly tired.'

'He looked a bit weary at the Coronation do.' Flo looked around. Everything neat as a pin, and not a toy in sight. She thought of their own muddly kitchen, and she thought of Roddy, a good-looking man in his forties, tired out working for a soup company.

'I'm afraid he's terribly sensitive.' Rosie warmed the pot. 'He never talks about it, but the truth is, he never quite got over the war. Still has nightmares. Needs lots of time to himself. Don't tell him I told you.'

Flo said she wouldn't dream of it.

'I expect Will's the same,' said Rosie. 'Do sit down.'

Flo sat before the spotless tablecloth, and said that Will didn't, actually, have nightmares, and that since they'd moved here his health was better than it had been for years. No more chest pains, no more sleepless nights. He was settled and happy, they all were.

If anyone was a bit under strain — she didn't tell Rosie this — it was she herself, waking up now and then after some peculiar dream, her heart pounding, especially on snatched writing days, for some reason. But it was only occasionally — once the day got going she forgot about it. In August, she said, they were going down to see her family, the first holiday for years, for her father's eightieth birthday.

'Lucky you,' said Rosie, setting the pot on the table. 'Melcote's a sweet place, of course, but you need to get away. I do get a bit restless, what with one thing and another!' She gave her pretty laugh. 'Can't do the housework for ever, can you? Once Freddie's at school I expect you'll feel the same.'

'Actually,' said Flo, for the second time in a month, 'actually I'm writing a book.' Though actually, of course, she wasn't, not just at the moment.

'A book! My dear! What on earth's it about?'

'It's based on our time in India.' How interesting and strong that sounded. 'Roddy might have mentioned it,' she added, but Rosie shook her head.

'He never said a word. Well, you know men!'

'Come September I'll be able to give it my all,' said Flo, somehow wanting to put a distance between herself and restless Rosie, whose only child seemed such a sad little thing. And as Rosie said again, 'Lucky you,' and went to call the

129

children in from the door, she thought of the quiet dining room, of spreading out her papers, writing away. Making a name for herself, perhaps, introduced at parties. *This is Felicity Sutherland, our resident novelist —*

'Mummy!' said Baba urgently, running inside. 'Mummy, one of them's *white*!'

4

The Gibsons' gardener came to feed the geese.
Mrs Thing from church said she'd love to look
after Snowy.

'We can't *leave* him!'

'He'll be all right, darling.'

'It's only a cat.'

'He's *our* cat. He's only a *kitten!*'

At last they got away.

Such a long journey to Bournemouth!

'One day we'll have a car,' said Will, as they
stood on the platform at Leicester station. He
gave Flo's hand a squeeze. 'Tik hai?'

'Tik hai,' said Flo, returning the squeeze.

''Ladies' Rest Room,'' read Baba. ''Station
Master's Office.''

'Don't wander off,' Will said, eyeing her. 'Hold
my hand now, both of you — here comes the
train!'

They leaped back, shrieking, as it came
roaring up and hissed to a mighty halt. Two
blackened figures leaned out from the firelit cab,
pushing their caps back. Freddie was in a daze of
joy.

Will was checking the carriages.

'This way, this way! Hold Mummy's hand! In
we get!'

At last they were settled.

'What are the wheels saying?' he asked the
children, as the train gathered speed. They

hadn't been on a train for years. 'Listen: you can make them say anything you want.' They listened: chuffity-chuff, chuffity-chuff. 'Bacon-and-eggs,' he told them. 'Bacon-and-eggs.'

'Oh, yes!'

He took Flo's hand again, as they sat there chanting.

'Happy, my darling?'

'Very. Almost as excited as the children.'

Their faces were pressed against the smutty glass. The outskirts of the town, then sunlit fields flashed past.

★ ★ ★

'Hello! Hello, hello, hello!'

There was Vivienne in a pretty cotton frock and a fresh perm, the front door opened wide. There was that darling house again.

'There's Hugo!'

They tumbled out of the taxi. Flo flew up the path.

'Vivie!' Never had they hugged so hard. 'Hugo! Hello, darling.' He stepped forward shyly. 'Give me a kiss. You're so tall now! And so handsome!'

He blushed to the roots of his dark hair. Behind him, the parent-birds were coming slowly down the shadowy hall. Flo burst into tears.

★ ★ ★

Pemberton Road: tree-shaded, broad and quiet. Trolley buses ran on the main road into the centre of town; here, just a few cars went by.

'Why is this house so *big?*'

'It's Edwardian,' said Hugo, who knew everything.

'What's 'Edwardian'?'

'It comes after Victorian. Queen Victoria was our longest-reigning monarch.'

'It's Queen Elizabeth now.'

They were up in his bedroom, right at the top of the house. A train set ran round a table placed against a wall. Hugo pressed a switch and an engine with four cream and maroon carriages went humming round the track. There was a station, with little people on the platforms. There was a signal box, and a tunnel, covered in grass. Cows grazed in the fields. Freddie gazed and gazed, and ran after the engine.

'Me want a train set like this!'

'It's a Hornby,' said Hugo. 'I've been collecting for a long time.'

On another table stood a big cardboard box.

'That's my Meccano set.'

Masses of flat green rods with holes in, and masses of nuts and bolts. Wheels, with rubber tyres. Hugo showed them the things he'd made: the best was a crane, with a pulley, so it went up and down. He manoeuvred the scoop to pick up nuts and bolts.

'And I've made a message carrier.'

He took them out on to the landing. Two long strings on a pulley hung over the banister: he tugged on one of them. Up came a green Meccano tray, bumping and banging. They hadn't noticed that, as they climbed the endless stairs. Inside was a piece of paper. He unfolded it.

133

'What does it say? Can I read it?'

He passed it over.

'"Hope you'll come to the beach with us this afternoon," read Baba. ' "Love from Uncle Will.' That's Daddy!'

'You're a very good reader.'

'I know. Who else sends you messages?'

'Mummy and Grandpa, when they've got time. Sometimes I send them to myself.'

They peered down through the banisters, all the way down to the great dark hall. There were two old leather chairs in the corners, with brown velvet cushions. Between them stood an enormous brass gong, which Freddie and Baba were allowed to strike at lunchtime and supper-time. They could see the top of Auntie Vivienne's head, as she came out of the kitchen.

'Chil-dren!' she called up. 'Lunchtime! Who's going to ring the gong today?'

They hurtled down the stairs.

'My turn!' gasped Freddie, as they reached the bottom.

Beyond the dining room was the conservatory, where Grandpa grew grapes. He snipped off the bunches with long silver scissors.

'Here you are, Freddie.' He passed him a juicy black grape. Freddie didn't know where to put the pips, so he spat them into his hankie.

Grandpa's bedroom was downstairs, along the hall and past the kitchen. He had his own lavatory next door. In his room he kept a big round Coronation sweet tin. Baba and Freddie perched on the bed and unwrapped stripy humbugs.

134

'We're only allowed sweets on Sundays.'

'I won't tell.'

From the window in here you could see out into the garden, where there was a ping pong table, and Grandpa's apple trees, and deck chairs. Mummy and Auntie Vivie were in them now, chatting away. You could hear babies crying from the house next door, a Home for Unmarried Mothers. On and on they cried.

★   ★   ★

'There's Whoopoo!'

There he sat, the biggest cat in the world, next to the box of Sunny Jim cornflakes, up on the kitchen shelf. It was his favourite place. Every time a grown-up went past they rubbed foreheads with him, they just couldn't help it. Hugo lifted up Baba and Freddie so they could do it too.

'He tickles! Do it again!'

'I love you, Whoopoo.'

They all loved him.

Everyone came and went in the kitchen, but mostly it was Mummy and Auntie Vivie, talking and talking as they got the meals ready. There was a Help, who came to clean.

'Mind out, duckies.'

She pulled out broom and mop and bucket from a cupboard and pretended to sweep them away. They bolted into the drawing room, and banged about on the piano. Plink plonk plonk. When Auntie Vivie played in the evenings it sounded like magic.

'That's enough, kids,' said Will. 'You'll drive Granny mad.' He went over to the hi-fi. 'Sit down and listen to this.' He pulled out a record from its brown paper sleeve, set the needle on it. 'Haven't heard this one before.'

> There was an old lady who swallowed a fly
> I don't know why she swallowed a fly,
> Perhaps she'll die . . .

He roared with laughter. 'Flo! Darling! Come and listen to this!'

But she was upstairs, talking to Granny in her bedroom. Hugo came instead. He sat on the sofa and Baba climbed on to his lap. Freddie was bouncing about on the velvet pouffe. By the time the old lady had swallowed a horse, and finally kicked the bucket, as Will put it, they were laughing until it hurt.

In came Grandpa. Will got to his feet at once. 'Father. Come and sit here.'

Grandpa walked slowly across the room and the sun winked off his glasses. Soon it would be his birthday. He was going to be eighty. Eighty! Freddie and Baba tried to count it before they went to sleep. It just went on for ever.

★   ★   ★

In the afternoons they all went down to the beach. All except Granny and Grandpa, who rested, in their different rooms. 'I've been to that beach a million times,' said Auntie Vivienne, as they all set out. 'But not with me for years and

136

years,' said Flo, taking her arm. Baba gave her bucket and spade to Hugo, and put her hand in his. He gave it a little squeeze. At the end of Pemberton Road they caught a trolley bus. Sparks flew from the overhead wires; it rocked along the tram lines.

'Tickets, please!' said Freddie. He tucked his into his pocket.

'Sixpence for the first person to see the sea,' said Will.

They craned their necks.

The bus went all through the town and ended up by the prom. There was the sea, glinting in the sun. They scrambled out.

'Hold my hand! No wandering off, do you understand?'

They all walked down to the beach.

'I've got sand in my sandals.'

'Come on, let's get you undressed.'

There were so many things to take off. Cardigan, frock with buttons down the back, Liberty bodice, knitted pants. Granny knitted those, with lemon-yellow wool and elastic threaded through the waist. Freddie just had shirt and jersey and shorts and no one made him wear knitted pants. He had white cotton ones.

'What kind of pants do you have, Hugo?'

'For heaven's sake!' said Flo, but they were all laughing.

'I'll remember that one,' said Will.

At last they were in their swimming things.

'Aren't you coming in, Mummy?'

'Not today.' She always said that. She and Auntie Vivienne settled down in deck chairs and started talking. They were *still* talking!

'Right, then,' said Will. 'You ready, Hugo, old chap? In we go!'

They raced to the water's edge.

⋆　⋆　⋆

On the last day but one it was Grandpa's birthday. At breakfast he opened his presents.

Granny was there! She sat smiling in her dressing gown at the other end of the table, eating tiny bits of toast. Baba and Freddie had made secret cards, smothered in kisses. Baba's was a house, with smoke coming out of the chimney and flowers at the front; Freddie did an engine, with masses of loopy steam. Grandpa propped them up with the others.

'Splendid. That's a very good engine, Freddie.'

'What about my house?'

'That's very good, too. Thank you.'

Soon the breakfast table was covered with wrapping paper and ribbons. Grandpa had a new shaving brush and bowl, and a new tie, and a bottle of whisky, and a box of chocolates from Hugo.

'Black Magic — my favourite. And what's this?'

'That's from us and Whoopoo!'

They'd bought it secretly, in a shop on the prom. Grandpa unwrapped it, so slowly, trying to guess, that they could hardly breathe.

'A seagull! I've always wanted a seagull. I shall put it in my room.'

After breakfast they all had to brush their

teeth and change. A photographer was coming! Flo pulled a smocked frock over Baba's head, and did up the buttons at the back.

'Mummy? Where's Hugo's daddy?'

There was a pause. 'He lives abroad at the moment.'

'What's 'abroad'?'

'Foreign countries. Places that aren't English. Like India. Where's your hairbrush?'

'When's he coming home?'

'Oh, Baba, that's enough now. Keep still while I do your hair.'

'The smocking's all itchy.'

'Never mind. Now, then, Freddie darling, let's have a look at you.'

At last they were all ready, trooping downstairs admiring each other, and out into the garden. What a palaver, lining everyone up. Hugo held enormous heavy Whoopoo. He was as good as gold.

'That's lovely. If you could look this way, sir. Keep still, children. Very good. Right now — smile!'

Birds sang in the apple trees, the babies in the Home next door went on crying. The photographer popped in and out of his black cloth — 'Just one more, now, lovely,' — and the morning sun shone down. From the end of the road came the hum of a trolley bus, pulling up, then humming off into the distance.

'A big smile now! The last one!'

'Marvellous,' said Will, when it was all over. He and Hugo carried all the chairs back into the house. 'That'll be something to treasure.'

The last plonking about on the piano, the last time watching the engine run round and round the track.

'I love you, Hugo.'

'Thanks.'

'Do you love me?'

'Oh, Baba, leave the poor fellow alone.'

The last sweets from Grandpa's tin, the last rubbing foreheads with Whoopoo.

'I don't want to go!'

The hall was full of luggage. There was the doorbell, there was the taxi. Hugs and kisses and lots of tears. Hugo was going back to school soon. He didn't cry.

'Come on, now, or we'll miss the train.'

Everyone out at the door to wave them off.

'Goodbye, goodbye!'

'Come again soon!'

'Bye Hugo!'

'Sit down!'

Then the taxi pulled out into the broad quiet road and they drove away, beneath the tall trees, in and out of their falling shadows.

5

Crisp September days. 'Glass is going down,' said Will, tapping the barometer in the hall. 'A nip in the air,' said Flo, putting an extra layer on the children, spooning in Haliborange, cod-liver oil, rosehip syrup for last, to take away the fishy taste. 'There! Now then, into your coats.'

Freddie was starting school! For the first week she took them both in every morning, dashing down to the bus stop on the Green, bundling them on to the bus, holding his hand as they rumbled into town.

'I'm in the big class now,' said Baba, adjusting her beret. 'They have Times Tables there.'

Freddie looked out at the fields, his eyes enormous.

'You'll have a lovely time,' said Flo.

'And inkwells.'

Each morning he hung back at the foot of the stairs as the children pounded past.

'Walk nicely now!' called a Miss Beasley from the top. 'Hello, Freddie — up you come!'

'We're the Start-rite children,' Baba told him, as he clung to Flo. There were other new children, but this term they were the only brother and sister. 'Hold my hand.'

'Mummy!'

'Mummy will be here at three,' Flo told him. 'Go on, darling.' At last he let go of her, and went stumping up the stairs.

'Bye!' she called, and fled before he cried, or she cried, banging into Rosie Byatt at the gate.

'Got time for a coffee?'

'I'd love to,' said Flo, 'but I must dash.' Why must she dash? She had a book to write!

From the first moment she stepped on shore, Mary knew she was going to love India.

The sights! The smells! It was all so vivid. The first thing she had to do was take a train up to Delhi, to her Mess in the RWVS. There she would take up her Duties. When she got there, she was introduced to the girl who was going to share her room. She was a rather plain thing, called —

Flo put down her pen. What could she call Agnes? Come to think of it, Mary was an awfully dreary name, though it went nicely with Marshall. What about — got it!

From the first moment she stepped on shore, Miranda knew she was going to love India.

Of course she was! And how could she not have a marvellous, romantic time with a name like that? And the whole point was to make this romantic, to make her and Will's love story as thrilling as possible.

After all her heartbreak in the War with gorgeous Guy — even now, she thought of him sometimes — *Miranda had never thought she could fall in love again. She certainly had no idea that the girl she was sharing a room with —*

Astrid? Astrid was awful, but perhaps it would

142

show up the contrast with pretty Miranda. She'd try it for now.

★ ★ ★

It took a week or so for Freddie to settle, and then he loved it. He loved the bean in the jam jar, the pot hooks, the cutting out. He loved writing an enormous F for Freddie on his pictures.

'We see he's left-handed,' said the Bride Miss Beasley in the second week, when Will picked them up.

'Like my sister,' said Will, as children poured past him. 'I'm afraid she had a tough time in those days. Made to use her right hand, did her no good at all. I hope — '

'Don't worry, Mr Sutherland. We're just keeping an eye.'

'Marvellous. Most grateful. Come along, kids.'

★ ★ ★

Autumn blew through the village. As the evenings drew in, and the clocks went back — *Or is it forwards? I can never remember!* — the children stopped playing in the garden after school. They sat in the lamp-lit kitchen, having their milk and bread and butter, listening to *Children's Hour.*

'Best thing we ever did, getting the wireless,' said Will, coming in for more tea. 'Ah, *Jennings and Darbishire.* Jolly good.' He pulled out a chair and sat down. 'Reminds me of my prep

143

school,' he told the children, as Jennings prepared for a cross-country run. 'You'll go there one day, Freddie old chap. Jolly good place.'

Freddie ran a wooden engine back and forth along the table top.

'He's only just started at Miss Beasleys,' said Flo, scraping carrots at the sink. Another meal, another meal. She put the carrots on to boil. Everyone said a pressure cooker was the thing.

'Better see to the geese,' said Will, as Jennings panted up to the finish to well-bred clapping, and the signature tune told them all it was The End.

'I'm coming too!' Freddie scrambled down from the table.

'Got the torch? Good chap.'

'Wait for me!'

They went out into the dark.

The geese slept at the end of the orchard in an old shed. Another thing Will had found in the local paper. They were already inside when Freddie swung the torch across the grass, honking quietly as they heard their footsteps.

'Safe from Mr Fox.'

They peered inside by torchlight. Up came all the heads. The shed smelled of creosote and straw and droppings. Gander got to his feet.

'Help!'

Will shut and bolted the door. 'Good night, old boy.'

'Good night, Gander! Good night, Grey Fluffy Yellow Toes!'

'Look at those stars.'

They stood in the frosty darkness, gazing up.

'That's Orion,' said Will. 'That's his belt, see that? Those three stars in the middle? And that's the Great Bear.'

'Where? Where's the Bear?'

Light spilled out from the kitchen windows as they left the orchard, back through the gap in the hedge.

'When I was in India,' said Will, swinging the torch, 'there were the most marvellous stars I'd ever seen. I used to sit on the veranda of my bungalow with my whisky and you know night came very suddenly there, whoosh, like a great big blanket. Suddenly it was dark, just like that. And I sat there gazing up and up, into the Milky Way. Sometimes, in the distance, I could hear a jackal.'

He made jackal noises as they raced back into the house.

★　★　★

At weekends everything slowed down. They had breakfast in their dressing gowns, looking out at the frosty garden, and the geese stepping carefully under the bare apple trees. Their water was frozen in the dish; Will went out with a kettle.

'Hello, children everywhere.' Uncle Mac had a Saturday Morning Club; they sent off for badges. Exciting things turned up in the packets of cornflakes: little plastic animals, green and red spectacles that made everything 3-D. Flo found a set of pastry cutters in the village shop: they sat at the kitchen table cutting out rabbits and ducks. They iced them, and had them for tea.

145

'Who made these? You did? Splendid. Can I have another?'

On Sundays, after Will and Baba had been to church, they had lunch in the dining room, under Panther's watchful gaze. Will sharpened the carving knife on a steel. 'Mind out!' They shrank back in their seats as the blade whipped back and forth. 'My father had this carving set.' There was a crest on the yellowing ivory handle: a cat sitting up in profile. 'This is our family crest,' he told them.

'Every blessed thing in this house comes from your family,' said Flo.

'Only because my parents are dead,' he reminded her, sharpening away. A little bit snappy today? Probably needed a rest, like him. 'Now then: who wants what?'

Across the lane in the vegetable garden the Brussels sprouts were yellowing, thick with frost: you could see them through the gate.

'There's Snowy!'

'Can he be our family crest?'

★ ★ ★

Will was in his office. The telephone rang, the typewriter tapped away. The Gestetner pounded out copies of membership forms, advice about insurance. Ghastly dreary stuff. Flo went upstairs, made the beds, dug the washing out of the laundry basket, came down with it, washed up the breakfast things, stood in the kitchen with the mountain of washing on the floor before her. Here we go.

146

In India, a *dhobi* took it all away — 'Very good, memsahib' — brought it back beautifully folded and pressed —

She must get that into her novel.

'If you have an automatic washing machine,' said that blasted book from Agnes, 'you'll work according to the instructions given by the maker.' Oh, ha ha ha. 'Otherwise, whether you use a hand machine or a wash-boiler, or simply the kitchen sink or the bathroom bowl, the job is made easier and more satisfying, too, if you follow a good method. Step one is to collect everything to be washed, and then to sort it. Preferably do this overnight . . . '

Well, she hadn't done it overnight. By the time the children were asleep it was all she could do to get the supper. And here was Snowy, in from his morning prowl, just settling down in the shirts and socks. She scooped him out and kissed him.

And then, for a moment, she suddenly wanted to shake him. Hard. What a terrible thought. Her heart began to pound at the very idea. She carried him to his basket, gave him another kiss. 'Snuggle down, darling.' Now then.

'Put woollies in one pile, silks, rayons and lightly soiled delicate cottons in another. Keep handkerchiefs separate . . . '

A wave of weariness overcame her. She hadn't got an automatic washing machine whose maker would tell her what to do. She had what she supposed was a wash-boiler, awful word, and the kitchen sink, which she saw far too much of, and a mangle. Freddie loved the mangle, posting

147

through dripping wet things, getting soaking wet, turning the handle. Out it all came, flat as a pancake.

At least she didn't have him under her feet all day now.

What a horrid thought. No one should think of their children like that. Especially Freddie.

But as Flo stood there, with that great heap of washing at her feet, she all at once had a vision of shaking *him* — picking him up and shaking until he rattled. She put her hands to her face.

The office door opened.

'Any chance of a spot of coffee?'

She was trembling all over.

'Flo?'

'Coffee,' she said slowly. 'Coffee coming up.'

'That's the ticket.'

$\star$ $\star$ $\star$

Things got a bit better after lunch. They had it together in the dining room, the wet washing hanging on the airer in the kitchen, and on the rail of the range. She'd done it: she'd washed, she'd mangled. She'd got the lunch on time.

'My darling. What have we here?'

'Nothing very exciting, I'm afraid.'

But they chatted companionably over their soup and mousetrap, and then he was off on a Call, and at last there was nothing to do until the children came home, except wash up, go back to the dining room, take out her exercise books from the cupboard and settle down.

At last. Where had she got to?

148

Miranda Marshall stood on Deck, looking out over the sparkling blue water...

She pushed aside that awful moment in the kitchen. Now she could see it all again: the palm trees on the shore, all her darling WAAF friends leaning on the rail beside her, Judy lighting up a gasper, Ann saying Gosh this is going to be fun! If she could only finish the first chapter, she could show it to Michael Lewis. She heard the phone begin to ring. 'Is that Felicity Sutherland?' Of course, she'd put that on the title page. 'Felicity — Flo — I've been reading your chapter. It's really most awfully good — '

Was it? Was it really? She read it all again. Should all those capitals be there? Shouldn't she describe India more, not just say it was vivid? Even though it had been, of course. Vivid as anything.

A sudden squall of rain beat against the window. Already, it was getting dark. She switched the light on, caught a glimpse of herself in the wet black windowpane.

God, what a sight. No make-up, very tired, and very vague. Miles away. A bit mad, even. She swallowed. She mustn't be miles away. She mustn't be mad. She had a family to look after, the best thing that had ever happened to her. She must concentrate on them.

And with that word a dark sick feeling began to spread inside her, something that had been building up all day. Shaking her darling boy — how could she even think of such a thing? Concentrate! All those tickings-off at school, as she gazed out of the classroom window. Thinking of what? Anything except the job in hand, the lesson. All those truly terrifying tickings-off from Matron, as she wept and wept. She'd wanted to do it all so well —

A car was swishing up the lane. Toot toot! They were home! Oh, thank God. She ran to the front door.

* * *

He'd pretty much got the hang of it all now. If anyone rang him with a query — about planning controls, a loan for a new dairy, or the legal rights of a worker in a tied cottage, rent overdue, all that kind of thing — he pretty much had it at his fingertips. Knew where to look for it, anyway. 'I'll ring you back in a couple of minutes, old boy.' 'I'll find that out for you straight away, sir.' From a rundown farm to a great estate: he knew the ropes, knew how to keep them all happy. The Area Director's report from Charles Denning had been first-rate.

The best thing of all, of course, was that he'd got his health back. Hadn't seen the quack since they got here, except to register them all, in the surgery on the other side of the village. *It's going as well as could be*, he wrote to Fitz. *Of course, I shall always be grateful to you for getting me off to a start. Never forget it.* He sat at his father's roll-top desk and banged out his letters and forms. Three counties to look after, each with their County Show — that was something to look forward to — where the RLS always had a pavilion. Leicestershire, Northamptonshire, Rutland.

Rutland, the smallest county in England, was his favourite: the purest England, the prettiest village names — Thistleton, Edith Weston. Brooks and stone bridges everywhere, village greens and duck ponds. As many thatched cottages as Flo could wish for, he noted, getting off the train at Oakham later that week.

He walked through the Market Place, past the butter cross and the stocks, saw the gabled roof of the public school beyond. He could make out the shouts from the playing fields behind. Perhaps this was the place for Freddie one day: he'd love it. In the meantime, he must put him down for Mountford Park, should have done it years ago. Do it when you get home, Sutherland, he told himself, no more shilly-shallying. He looked at his watch. An hour before his first appointment: just time for a sandwich and a pint in what looked like a jolly nice pub.

★   ★   ★

Through the silence of the afternoon, the clock ticked away. She sat at the table, her manuscript before her, and her heart began to pound. Here she was, with all this time at last. There was nothing to stop her writing, and she couldn't lift her pen.

Do it, she told herself. Prove yourself. Her stomach clenched.

Miranda had always had lots of boyfriends. She was looking forward now to cheering up the troops!

Those were the last lines she had written, and how ridiculous they looked. What a silly flighty thing Miranda sounded. She picked up her pen and crossed them out. How messy the page looked now. She picked up another, and its whiteness glared at her. Go on, it said. Go on, you pathetic creature.

An hour or more before the children were home. She put her head in her hands.

★ ★ ★

He had a pretty good afternoon. Netherton Farm was a bus ride out of town, but he got there with a minute to spare, walking like the clappers down the lane, relishing, as always, the mud on his boots, the smell of the country air: earth and manure and livestock. Especially now he didn't have to look after it all. Mind you, it was damn cold. As he came into the farmyard, to the wild barking of a chained dog, he saw a heap of swedes glittering with frost against the wall of the barn. Sheep loved them, perfect winter feed. He'd start the chat off with this, pay the chap a compliment: butter them up and sign them up, that was the thing.

And he gave the madly barking dog a word or two and strode up to the farmhouse door. A light shone in the kitchen: with any luck at all there'd be a spot of cake at some point. Right then: here we go. And he knocked, and cleared his throat.

'Mr Dixon? Will Sutherland, RLS — we spoke on the phone.' He held out his hand to the chap in an old blue jersey, gave his good firm grip. 'How do you do?'

An hour or so later, he had him in the bag.

'My darling!' He kissed her in the tiny hall. 'Kids asleep?' She was in her dressing gown, not looking too good, for some reason. He dropped his briefcase and followed her into the kitchen. 'Had a good day? I bagged two new recruits, you'll be glad to hear.'

She didn't answer.

'Everything OK?'

She nodded, pulling a Pyrex dish out of the oven. 'I'm afraid this is just leftovers.'

'No matter, as long as it's hot. Hello, Snowy, old chap.' He went over to the basket, gave the soft white head a rub, then pulled his chair out. The kitchen looked a bit chaotic, but it was always so good to be home. 'Marvellous,' he said, as Flo set the dish before him, and he patted the chair beside him. 'Come and sit down. Tell me what you've been up to.'

'Oh, Will — ' She just stood there, pale as anything.

'What? What's up?' Little wreaths of steam from yellowing cabbage and pale grey mince rose before him. 'Bad day? Kids playing up?'

'No. Just — you know. My book.'

'Oh.' He reached for the mustard; that might buck it all up a bit. 'That. Thought you had a bit more time for it now.'

'I do, but — '

'Darling, for God's sake sit down. I can't eat while you're hovering.'

She began to cry. 'I'm going up to bed, sorry — '

And she was gone, leaving him alone with the cat and this dismal-looking supper, after what was, quite frankly, a pretty long day.

Women. That bloody book. He'd go up in a minute.

★ ★ ★

Flo woke, and found herself sitting upright. Bolt upright, in the dark. Something terrible was about to happen. What? What was it? She had been dreaming: scraps of the dream whirled round her. Freddie was shouting. And she was ill, she was ill, and no one knew.

'Help — help — ' She could hear someone breathing, very fast and light — it was her, it was her, and the feeling of dread engulfed her. She was on the edge of something terrible — she grabbed the bedclothes, gasping.

'Flo?' Beside her, Will stirred and turned over. Then he sat up. 'What the hell's going on?'

'I'm going to die,' she panted. 'I'm going to die — '

'For Christ's sake.' He fumbled for the bedside lamp, turned back to look at her. She was shaking all over, her ashen face streaming with sweat, hair sticking up like a madwoman's. He pushed back the bedclothes.

'I'll get the doc.'

'Don't leave me!'

What the hell should he do?

'Help me! Help me — ' She began to wail.

'Stop it! You'll wake the kids!'

'Help me — '

He took her in his arms. 'Darling, my darling. It's all right, I'm here, nothing's going to happen — '

She trembled and sobbed against him.

'I can't do it, I can't do it, I can't *do* it!'

'Do what?'

'Anything, anything, anything — I'm going to die — '

He held her and held her. At last she stopped.

'Let me call the doctor,' he said quietly. 'Come on, we'll do it together.'

He helped her into her dressing gown, pulled on his own. Christ, it was cold. They went slowly down the stairs, and into his office. He picked up the phone. She began to cry again.

★   ★   ★

Dawn was breaking. An ambulance came racing along the main road, slowed down, turned carefully into the lane.

6

'Mummy!' Freddie came stumbling down the stairs in his duck pyjamas. 'Where's Mummy?'

Had they heard it all? Will stood with his back to the front door, hearing the ambulance turn on to the main road and gather speed. Had they seen it from their window?

'Where's Mummy gone?' Baba came down behind, her hair all tousled. Like Flo's — that hair awry, that mad lost face, that shriek as they closed the doors. He shut his eyes.

'Mum-my!'

'It's all right, kiddiwinks.' He took a deep breath, went towards them and held out his arms. 'Daddy's here, not to worry.' He kneeled down and hugged them hard. Christ Almighty, what a do. 'Mummy's not very well,' he told them, holding them close. 'She's gone into hospital for a little bit, that's all.' He got to his feet. 'Now then. Let's go and give Snowy his breakfast.'

★ ★ ★

Somehow he got them off to school. Thank God for the run: Roddy Byatt today, pulling up at the gate in the Ford, that long lean body getting out to open the back door. Nice chap. Still didn't know him very well, but —

'Are you collecting?' Will asked him, bundling

156

the children down the path. 'In you go, kiddos, that's it!' They were pale and quiet, still a bit tear-stained, got in without a murmur. He lowered his voice as Roddy closed the door. 'We've had a bit of a crisis, I'm afraid.'

'Oh?' Roddy turned to look at him. In the early morning light the handsome face that Flo was always on about looked drawn. Wasn't there something about shell shock? Could take you years to get over that.

'I'm afraid Flo's in hospital.' He could have lied, said it was appendicitis or something, but no point in beating about the bush at a time like this. Anyway, it was bound to get out, sooner or later. 'Had a bit of a crack-up,' he said quietly. 'Not sure why. But we've had a hell of a night.'

Roddy listened, looked shocked. He offered a cigarette, lighting up. He was sorry to hear it; he understood. He inhaled deeply. These things happened. And yes, he was collecting the kids.

'They can come back to our place,' he said, stubbing out the cigarette underfoot. 'Give you a bit of extra time. I know Rosie would be glad to help.'

'That's awfully good of you. Best not to say anything to the school.'

'Of course not. Best of luck.'

And they shook hands, the smell of tobacco lingering in the air, the pale November sun coming up, and the white-faced children sitting in silence in the car.

★ ★ ★

157

He pulled himself together. The cottage looked like a bomb site: he went from room to empty room, picking up clothes from the floor, stuffing them into the chests of drawers, pulling the bedclothes up. Their own bed was a wreck: sheets all twisted, the smell of sweat everywhere. He flung open the window, let the cold air in, picked up Flo's underwear from the chair, bra, faded pink corset, holey old pants and nylons all in a muddle, and stuffed them into the bathroom basket. Hung up her skirt. When he did that, he almost cried.

She must have been on the verge all day, somehow got the kids to bed, got that ghastly supper, got undressed, dragged on her dressing gown, trying to put on a brave face when he came home. Now that old tweed skirt — 'My working skirt' — hung limply from the hanger. She wore it almost every day, must be years since she'd had proper new clothes, and something he hardly even noticed any more suddenly looked as worn out as she did. Even after the holiday. God, that felt light years away.

He went slowly downstairs. The kitchen, where she always was, looked desolate without her. Hardly touched cornflakes soggy in bowls, Freddie's engine sitting all by itself on the table, ancient tea towels drooping on the rail. His shirts hung on the airer, waiting to be ironed. Who was going to do that?

Who was going to do anything, until she came home?

★   ★   ★

She was in prison: they led her down an endless corridor. One on either side, holding each arm tight. She turned and twisted, trying to shake them off.

'Just keeping you steady, dear. We're almost there.'

The corridor was flooded with light from huge high windows. People shuffled past in dressing gowns. A great fat woman was muttering to the floor, a man had his head flung back and his mouth wide open, stuck there, a gaping dark hole.

'No,' said Flo. 'No, no, no — '

'It's all right, dear.'

She looked out of a window, away from the yawning darkness of that mouth. Wind whipped the boughs of bare trees in grounds that stretched away for ever. Flo felt sick with fear. Those trees — they knew — they knew! She began to howl.

The grip on her arms tightened. She struggled and fought.

'They know! They can see!'

'Now, now. Here we are.'

They led her down a turning. Huge double doors lay ahead. Something was jangling: one of the gaolers was fumbling with a bunch of keys. She unlocked the doors.

'In we go!' She pushed Flo through, and locked them.

★　★　★

They forgot about it all when they got to school. 'Hello, Baba! Hello, Freddie! In you come!' They

159

clambered up the stairs with all the others, hung up their coats on the pegs, the sewn-in mittens poking out, Baba's beret perched on top. They filed into their separate classrooms; the day began.

> 'There is a green hill far away,
> Without a city wall,
> Where the dear Lord was crucified,
> Who died to save us all.'

It was Baba's favourite hymn now. She loved the sad tune, she loved the distant hill, so green and grassy.

The Bride Miss Beasley slowed right down in the last line, pressing on the loud pedal to give it all extra meaning. Then they all bowed their heads, still standing round the piano, while she said a little morning prayer, and said 'Amen.' And then they all went to their desks.

Baba sat between Eddie Gibson and Nancy Byatt, because they came in together on the Run. After school today she and Freddie were going to go to tea with Nancy, and Daddy was going to pick them up from there. For a moment, as she thought of this, Baba felt a queer little twist in her stomach, remembering. Make Mummy be home by then, she told God. Please, she added. Then the Bride Miss Beasley, up at the front, instructed them all to get out their sums books, and thirty lids went up and thirty lids went down again, bang bang bang.

'Quietly, children!' She was chalking up a Times Table on the board. They'd got to six! 'Say it with me,' she said, as she said every morning, pointing with her pointer. 'Then you can copy it down.'

'Once six is six, twice six is twelve . . . '

The sound of their chanting filled the room, soothing as rosehip syrup. There were places where you almost shouted, like the end of a hymn.

'*Five* sixes are *thirty!*'

Next week, they'd have to know it by heart. Baba had so many things on her heart already, she didn't know if there was room for any more.

★　★　★

At lunchtime, down in the noisy dining room, Freddie remembered Mummy. He pushed his mashed potato and swede round the plate.

'Eat up!' said the Fat-Bottomed Miss Beasley, coming round.

'Not hungry.'

'Just try a little bit, there's a good boy. Then you'll grow big and strong, like Daddy.'

'I want Mummy,' he said.

She kneeled down beside him, enormous. E was for Elephant. Behind her thick glasses her little brown eyes were kind.

'You'll see Mummy soon,' she told him. 'She's waiting for you at home, isn't she?'

He nodded uncertainly.

★　★　★

'You two are coming to tea with us today,' Mr Byatt reminded them at the end of the

161

afternoon. 'Thank you,' said Baba, climbing into the car. She pushed up next to Nancy, and took her hand. 'Will Tabitha be there?'

'She's always there,' said Nancy.

They dropped off Eddie Gibson, who had to do homework for his Entrance Exam, and drove through the village. Already it was getting dark.

'You poor little things,' said Mrs Byatt, as they trooped through the front door. 'I've heard all about Mummy, now wash your hands and come and sit down for tea. Nancy, you can put out the biscuits.' She was smiling and nice, but everything was so tidy. Mr Byatt took his tea upstairs. He had a headache. They sat quietly at the table, eating their bread and butter.

'What have you done at school today?'

Nobody could remember.

After tea, Baba and Nancy played with Nancy's doll, whose stiff-lashed eyes opened and closed when you tipped her head. Freddie went and stood by the window, gazing out into the dark.

'There's Daddy!' he said suddenly.

Then it was all hello, kiddiwinks, and thanks most awfully, and coats and mittens on, that's it, off we go, thanks so much again. They walked hand in hand up the cold street.

'Is Mummy home?'

'Not yet.'

'Are we going to visit her?

'Not yet.'

Lights shone out from the Crown, and from their front door, on to the frosty hedge. As soon as they opened the garden gate, the geese started up, as always.

'Now then,' said Will, when they were all in the nice warm kitchen. He lit his pipe and sat down. 'This is the plan.'

★　★　★

Auntie Agnes was coming to look after them! They couldn't even remember her. But when Mrs Gibson brought them home from school next day, there she was, in an apron. Baba sort of remembered her now. She was going to sleep in Mummy and Daddy's bed, and Daddy was going to sleep in the office, on the old camp bed that Mike used to sleep on in the farm kitchen. He brought it in from the garage, banging his shin and swearing.

'Sit down nicely,' said Auntie Agnes, getting their supper. She had dark hair and eyes, like Freddie. 'What a dear little boy you are,' she told him, as he sat there, being good.

'Am I a dear little girl?'

'Of course you are.'

'Have you got children?'

'No.' The wooden spoon went round and round in the mashed potato. 'But we've got a very nice cat. She's called Tinkerbell.'

'What does she look like?'

'Tortoiseshell. Very fluffy. But best of all,' she added, dolloping potato on to their plates, 'I've got you two.' She ladled out spoonsful of stew.

'That smells scrumptious!' And as Baba said it, the word popped up in front of her, just like that. In capitals.

SCRUMPTIOUS.

Auntie Agnes laughed. 'What a long word.'

'Mummy says Scrumptious sometimes.'

'Does she?' She set down their plates before them. 'Where are your table napkins?' They didn't know. 'Never mind. Eat up.'

'Can I make a volcano?'

'What do you mean?'

Freddie showed her, heaping up the sides of the mashed potato, pressing a hole in the middle, scooping in the stew. Little rivers of gravy ran down the side.

'All right, darling, eat it up now.'

'I love this,' said Baba, tucking in. 'Do you like cooking, Auntie Agnes?'

'I love it.'

'Mummy doesn't.'

MUMMY DOESN'T.

★　★　★

'I'm afraid it's a complete breakdown.' Dr Gillespie — a psychiatrist, trick-cyclist, Will supposed — leaned back in his chair and took his glasses off. Flo's file lay between them on the desk. 'I'm very sorry.'

Will cleared his throat. 'Well. Well, I — ' He didn't know what to say. Mental illness — never had anything to do with it, except in the war, of course. People did crack up then. His mind went to Roddy Byatt for a moment, that strained tired look.

'I expect this is all a bit of a shock to you.'

'Yes. Yes, it is. Of course, she's always been

164

highly strung — had to leave nursing before the war. But this — '

He looked out of the window. The place was miles from bloody anywhere, those empty grounds going on for ever: it had taken him twenty minutes to walk up here from the bus. And an hour's journey before that. These huge grey buildings: it felt like some Victorian asylum, probably was, not that he'd ever been near one before. To think of little Flo in here —

'What do you think?' He turned back to the psychiatrist. 'What kind of . . . treatment do you give here?'

'We've given her a sedative. I'm sure you'll find her much calmer. I think we'll just keep her under observation for a bit. If she doesn't improve we sometimes use electroconvulsive therapy — ECT. As you know, that can have dramatic results.'

He didn't know, he'd never heard of it. Sounded like a cattle prod. Jesus. His Flo.

'D'you think she'll be home by Christmas?'

A pause. 'Frankly I doubt it. But we'll see.' He got to his feet, a tall lanky man in a good suit, university sort of chap. Not Will's type, but no doubt he knew his stuff. 'I'm sure you'd like to see her.'

The appointment was over. Some young thing took him down another unending corridor. Docs in white coats hurried past. They came to the tallest double doors Will had ever seen in his life, all dark scratched paint, and she pulled out a bunch of keys.

'Don't tell me you lock them in.' He was horrified.

'It's for the patients' safety.'

And he stood aside as the nurse unfastened a padlock, and swung wide the door. He swallowed. How many women in here? How many?

The ward stretched ahead for ever, bed after bed after bed, the winter afternoon light fading outside and the neon overhead like something out of the army. A few tired nurses were doing their stuff, washing out bedpans in the sluice, ticking off drugs on a trolley. The patients were in dressing gowns mostly, as far as he could tell: a few fast asleep, a few slumped in bedside chairs. Others were wandering, pacing, wringing their hands, waving at nothing, covering their faces, sobbing, shouting out.

'She's over there, Mr Sutherland.'

He looked to where she was pointing, saw a doped-up woman in a bedside chair four or five beds away. Her hair looked lifeless: she looked lifeless, staring at the green linoleum floor.

'Flo?' He walked slowly up to her. 'Darling?'

She looked up, pale and washed-out, her eyes all swollen.

'Will — ' It came out as a whisper.

'My darling. Here I am.' He kneeled down beside her, took her hand. For a second he almost said, 'Daddy's here.' 'How are we?'

'All. Right.' She spoke so quietly, so slowly, he could hardly hear her.

'The kids send their love,' he said, kissing her ashen cheek. She nodded slowly. 'Agnes has come to look after them. Just till you get home.' She frowned, shook her head, as if there were

166

something heavy inside it. 'It's all going fine,' he said. 'Absolutely fine. Just miss you like hell, of course.'

★ ★ ★

It was snowing! It was almost Christmas, and it was snowing! They stood at their bedroom window in their nightclothes, watching it all swirl down. Soon everything was completely covered.

'If you look up,' said Freddie, pressing his face to the glass, 'it feels as if you're going up into it all.'

Baba tried it. It made her feel funny, as if you might never come down again. Auntie Agnes came in to get them dressed for breakfast. No school, no need to hurry, the room full of snowy light.

'Down we go!'

She'd made hot porridge. Daddy was pulling his boots off, after feeding the geese. 'They don't think much of it,' he said, putting the boots by the Rayburn. 'Expect they'll stay inside today.'

But they didn't. They came out of their shed and looked around them. They bent their heads to graze, but they couldn't: the grass was all hidden. They honked, and waddled to another bit. Then they just stood there, as the snow fell on and on.

'Like a Christmas card,' said Auntie Agnes. She had bought them an Advent calendar: they took it in turns to open the tiny doors. A bell, a sprig of holly, a present, wrapped up with a red ribbon bow. For Christmas Eve, the doors were double. It was going to be Freddie's turn to open those, he'd worked it out.

★   ★   ★

'I've got to get home for Christmas, Willie,' Agnes told Will that evening. 'If the trains are running. I can't leave poor Neville much longer.'

'Of course you can't.' He was lighting his pipe, a good peg of whisky beside him. 'You've been marvellous, Sis. An absolute brick.'

They were in the dining room, sitting at the gate-legged table from which, as a girl, Agnes had got up so often, and run upstairs, crying her eyes out. Poor girl, Mother always on at her for some reason.

'The kids have loved having you,' he told her, tamping down the tobacco.

And she'd loved every minute of it, he could tell: getting them dressed and undressed, cooking nice meals — he'd eaten pretty well, too. Got to grips with the wash-boiler thing, given them their baths: he'd heard her laughing away up there. He'd heard her get down on her knees as they said their prayers, starting them off. 'God bless Daddy, and keep him strong. God bless Mummy, and help her to get well soon . . . ' He'd told them Flo had a bad tummy ache: what else could he possibly say?

'I expect all those days as school matron gave you the knack,' he said, drawing on the pipe.

'Assistant matron. But what's going to happen now?'

He didn't know. He just didn't know. How

could he do it all on his own, and work, and visit Flo? How could they all have Christmas without her? Who knew when she'd be home?

'Tell you what,' she said suddenly. 'I've got an idea.'

★ ★ ★

They were going to spend Christmas with Auntie Agnes and Uncle Neville! In Wimbledon — they'd never been there before! Baba started to pack at once. She dug out a cardigan for Squeaker, and told him all about it. They were taking the Advent calendar with them, and Daddy was going to stay here with Snowy and the geese and visit Mummy in hospital.

Outside in the lane she could hear someone clearing the snow. She went to the bedroom window. The paraffin stove was melting the Jack Frost patterns on the pane; tiny flakes of snow still fell past it, on to the whitened hedges of the vegetable garden, on to the lane. Everything was so quiet and still. No one was out, except for the man from the Crown, scraping away with his shovel. It felt like the only sound in the world, so loud in all that silence, and she felt like God, looking down on all He had made. Soon He'd let Mummy come home.

★ ★ ★

'Mr Sutherland? Dr Gillespie here. Sorry to bother you, nothing to worry about, but we'd like to try Mrs Sutherland on a course of ECT.

169

We need your consent, of course — I'm wondering if it's possible for you to come in and sign the papers. Once the roads are clear, of course. We're pretty good over here at the moment.'

Will put down the phone, leaned back in his swivel chair. The room was still full of the marvellous light from the snow, so uplifting you'd think nothing could ever go wrong again. And here was this horrible, hellish thing.

Little white flakes floated softly past the window. He sat there, unable to move.

★ ★ ★

The best thing about where Auntie Agnes lived was the milkman's horse. He came down the street every morning, clippity-clop, and he wore blinkers. As soon as they woke up they listened for him, up in the cold spare room together.

'He's here!' They raced to the window, banged on the pane. Auntie Agnes had ordered Extra, just for them.

'Wait for us!' They hurtled down the stairs. 'Open the door! Quick!'

Auntie Agnes was still in her curlers.

'You can't go out in your nightclothes! Stay here!'

But they were already down the icy path. The milkman turned at the gate.

'You'll catch your death, you will.'

The street was empty, no one about in the early light, only the dear old horse waiting patiently for his sugar lump.

'Please, Auntie Agnes!'

She came down the path in her dressing gown, sugar lumps in her pocket. 'You're spoiled to death.'

'We like being spoiled.'

'Flat on your palm,' said the milkman, and the horse's great big nose came down, all whiskery and wet. He snaffled up the lumps in a second.

'All gone.' They stood there shivering, patting his hairy cheek.

'Now come inside! I've never known anything like it!'

Uncle Neville was coming down the stairs for breakfast. He wasn't as old as Grandpa, but he had an old sort of look. He was thin, and his hair was thin, flattened down with Brylcreem. Daddy used it, too, but he had more hair, so it didn't show so much. He showed them where Tinkerbell's basket was, the afternoon they arrived. She was the next best thing.

And tomorrow the Christmas tree was coming! Auntie Agnes had a box of coloured lights.

'Mummy's got lights like those.'

MUMMY'S GOT LIGHTS LIKE THOSE.

★ ★ ★

They took her out of the ward and along the corridors, slowly slowly slowly, into a great big room. There was the strangest smell.

'That's it, well done, here we are.'

The door closed behind them; she was suddenly with lots of people.

There was a big flat bed in the middle of the room, with things at the head of it. Instruments.

'Now, Mrs Sutherland, Dr Gillespie has explained what we're going to do today.'

She couldn't remember. They told her again. They helped her up on to the bed, they made her lie down.

'What — what — '

'It's all right, you just close your eyes now — '

They were fitting something on to her head. She reached up, tried to push it away.

'Get it off, get it off — '

Somebody flicked a switch. Then the world exploded.

7

Spring came. Spring came at last, and Flo came home. It was still only March, with a blustery wind, but when the sun came out everything danced.

'Mummy — '

Will brought her home by taxi: hang the expense. He paid the driver, helped her out, took her little cream case in one hand and gave her his arm. Such a thin thing she'd become. He clicked open the gate, and the geese started up at once. 'Remember them?' She nodded. Slowly they walked up the path. The children were banging on the dining-room window; they stopped, and ran to the door. Behind them, Agnes hung back.

'Mummy — ' They held hands uncertainly.

'Hello.' She looked around her. What a funny little place.

They came slowly forward; she could not look at them. Then they hugged her legs, and pressed their heads against her.

'All right, now, kids, let Mummy get inside. Come on, Freddie, let go now.'

In the kitchen everything sparkled. Clean sink, clean tea towels, daffs in a jug. Lunch was in the oven. Agnes coughed.

'Hello, Flo.'

'Hello.'

'Say hello to Snowy!'

'Hello, Snowy.'

She sat in a chair; they scooped him out of his basket.

'He wants to sit on your lap.'

He sprang off at once, and made for the back door. Agnes let him out. Off went the geese again.

'Lunch is almost ready.' Agnes gave a little laugh. 'Only cottage pie, I'm afraid.'

'We love cottage pie.'

'Sis has held the fort marvellously,' said Will.

'Oh, well — ' Another little laugh.

Flo put her head in her hands. 'Thank you,' she said to the table. 'It's nice to be home,' she said to the knives and forks.

'Flo? Feeling OK?'

She nodded. 'Just a bit — you know — '

JUST A BIT — YOU KNOW —

'Have lunch on a tray,' said Baba. 'Have lunch upstairs.'

⋆　⋆　⋆

Will took up the tray and settled it on her lap.

'My darling.' Clouds blew past the window, sunlight and shadow flickered through the room. He felt everything come alive again, though she looked so pale and wan still, leaning against the pillows.

'You stay there just as long as you like,' he told her. 'Agnes isn't going back until tomorrow.'

Poor old Agnes — the camp bed tonight, and, God, he'd be glad when all this was over and everything back to normal. He stood there watching Flo do nothing, hearing the clatter of lunch from downstairs. He could do with some himself.

'Eat up, darling, got to get your strength up.'

She lifted her fork, took a mouthful. Nothing tasted of anything much these days, though they said it would get better.

'What about your pills?' he said suddenly. 'Aren't you supposed to have them with meals?' He fumbled amongst her nighties and found them, fetched a glass from the bathroom, watched her knock them back.

'I hate taking pills.'

'I know. Soon be off them.' He put the bottles on the bedside table. God, he was hungry. 'Right, then,' he said. 'You tuck in, that's it. I'll be back shortly.'

And he went downstairs, leaving the door ajar.

Flo took another mouthful. Whatever Agnes had put in it, it tasted of something. That filthy hospital food . . . She had a bit more, put her fork down. That was enough. She pushed the tray away, leaned back against the pillows, watching the clouds change shape in the bright spring sky. Hills and valleys blew past, and something like an alligator. Something with a snout, and forelegs, but nothing to be afraid of. Everything inside her was turned off, now.

★   ★   ★

Next day, Will saw Agnes on to the train. He thanked her for the millionth time. Simply didn't know how he'd have managed . . .

'I just hope Flo won't feel I've intruded.'

175

'Of course she won't.'

He kissed her and waved her off to Market Hampden. Somehow they'd muddled through. And now it was over. Flo was home, and please God it was over.

He walked back over the footbridge. He could see their little lane, he could see the top half of their cottage, so fresh and white and welcoming. Flo had organised that, had painters up ladders before you could say knife. She'd pull through now, he was sure of it.

★ ★ ★

'Where's Mummy?' asked Freddie, the moment he came home from school. He dropped his shoe bag, ran through to the kitchen.

'I'm here,' said Flo, slowly putting tea on the table.

He hugged her round the middle, as Baba ran out into the garden.

'Grey Fluffy! Grey Fluffy! I'm home!'

'Stand still,' Freddie commanded, and then, as Flo disentangled herself, finger by finger, and went to the ice box for milk, 'Look at me. Look at me, Mummy.'

She couldn't. She couldn't look at him, and she couldn't look at Baba, racing back with the drinking can, turning on the outside tap.

'She was thirsty!' she shouted, over the pouring water.

'Mummy,' said Freddie.

'Stop it,' she said flatly. 'That's enough. Baba, it's teatime.'

She had made the sandwiches, poured the milk. What more should she do?

'Shall I take Daddy his tea?' asked Baba.

'If you like.'

Slowly she got up, and filled the kettle. Then she sat down again, and passed them things. 'Tell me about school,' she said, because she was supposed to. She heard herself say, 'Really? That's nice,' and Freddie said, 'But it *wasn't* nice,' and Baba, 'You're not *listening*, Mummy.'

'Aren't I?' she asked the tablecloth, and then Will came in looking for a cuppa, and the children went slowly outside.

'Tik hai?' he asked her, making the tea himself.

'I expect so,' she told the empty sandwich plate, and heard him sigh.

★　★　★

'Look at me,' said Freddie at bath time, as she passed him the sponge. 'Look at me!'

She looked, she saw his anxious face. 'What's the matter?' she asked him, but he didn't know. When she tucked them up for the night, and bent to kiss him, he clung to her neck so hard it really hurt: that she could feel.

'Let me go,' she said, and as she said it a wave of something nameless washed through her, something dreadful she couldn't remember. 'Let me go!' she shouted, and Will came racing up the stairs.

'All right, kids, that's enough.'

He switched out the light, and they lay there

very still, as he led her into their bedroom, shutting the door.

★   ★   ★

And then, quite suddenly, it lifted. It was like stepping over a crack in the pavement: one minute she was dead, the next —

'I'm better,' she said to Will in astonishment, as he brought in the morning tea. Sun was at the curtains, hens calling from somewhere, someone clip-clopping down the lane. She heard all these things and she liked the sound of them.

'My darling.' He drew back the curtains and turned to look at her. 'You're back,' he said, and she looked straight at him and smiled.

★   ★   ★

Perhaps it had to happen, she told herself a day or two later. Perhaps it had all been building up for years, until bang, she finally fell to pieces. Now, slowly, slowly, she was picking them up. ''All the king's horses and all the king's men,'' Freddie sang in the bath, quite restored. ''Couldn't put Humpty together again!'' shouted Baba, splashing madly. But she would have to get back together now, be a proper person again.

She was out in the playroom: the back half of the garage, where Will had hammered up a partition. He'd found an old carpet in the local paper: five pounds for a worn blue thing that covered the concrete perfectly. A little table that the Gibsons didn't want had found a corner. At

178

the far end stood the things they'd never get into the cottage: the bureau, the portraits, the old oak chest, shrouded in blankets. If she looked at them, if she thought 'shroud', she felt funny, but she didn't look at them, she got on with arranging the children's things.

It was starting to rain now, pattering on to the corrugated iron roof, but it was one of those come-and-go April showers, and she turned to look out at the garden, saw the emerald green of the orchard grass, nourished by endless goose droppings, saw Gander step slowly over it and stand beneath the trees. The trees were in blossom, there were eggs in the goose shed: the geese spent most of their time in there now, on nesting boxes thick with hay. *Soon we'll have goslings all over the place!* she told her diary.

And as she did so, she knew she had crossed a divide. Illness and horror lay behind her, life beckoned her back. Perhaps she should buy a new exercise book. *But I won't go back to my novel,* she told the diary, and she ran through the rain to the back door, over the soaking grass. *Not now. I hoped for so much with it, but —*

Even as she reached the kitchen, those terrible feelings of failure began to rise again. And she hadn't even shown it to anyone. She shut her eyes, standing in the kitchen with its smell of coke and matting, and the scents of the wet blowy spring at the door. 'Please, God, make me well,' she murmured. Everyone had been praying for her, apparently, even in church. How awful. 'And I'll keep you in my prayers, Flo,' Agnes had written the other day. She didn't want Agnes praying for her. Couldn't explain it: just didn't.

A sound in the hall: she opened her eyes and there was Will, coming out of the office.

'My darling. How's lunch getting on?'

★   ★   ★

'Never tell the children,' she said to him that afternoon, as they lay in one another's arms in the creaking bed. Neither of them could remember how long it had been since they'd done this: it felt like being in India, on honeymoon even, the sun slanting in through the shutters, the punkah slowly moving above them, their bearer asleep on his cot bed on the veranda, the whole place so quiet in the deep heat of the afternoon. And no children to get up for. Now they had another half an hour before they came home, and perhaps just once more —

'My Flo.'

She sat up, the sheet falling off her, looking down at Will's darling face. 'Promise me,' she said. 'Promise. I never want them to know.'

He took her hand, he lifted it to his lips. He promised.

★   ★   ★

And then they all really did settle down. The rain blew away, blossom fell on the dazzling grass. *The great excitement is the goslings!* Flo wrote to Vivie.

Poor Vivie — how worried she'd been, through all that terrible time. *But I can't come up,*

180

darling, I can't leave the parent-birds. And there was a new development: Paying Guests. *I'm rushed off my feet! And getting Hugo ready for a school trip — skiing in Austria! So please, just keep on getting better...*

She was well, she was well. And now —

'I've seen one hatch! I've seen one hatch!'

The evenings were still pretty cold. Will brought a big wooden box of goslings into the kitchen, and stood it by the Rayburn. He put a thick piece of glass with holes in it on the top. Another little purchase from the small ads, under 'Poultry'. As they had supper, they could hear the tap-tap of thirteen beaks. The kitchen smelled of hay, the last of the sun came dustily in at the window. Tap-tap. Tap-tap-tap.

8

It was Christmas. On the last day of term the children came home clutching glittery cards, smothered inside with kisses. Will was out at some church thing; Flo put the cards up on the dining-room mantelpiece, with those from the family, and people in the village. The Gibsons were giving a drinks party on the twenty-third, and the children were having a babysitter: their first, a nice girl from the village.

Flo looked at the invitation's italic 'At Home' on thick card, next to all the glitter. What on earth was she going to wear? And would people ask her — would they remember? 'How *are* you now, Flo?' everyone in the village had wanted to know, when she first went out and about. She didn't know which was worse: to have them ask, or not to have them ask, as if it were something too awful to talk about. She just told them she was much better, thanks, in such a way that they didn't ask much more.

There came a sudden shriek from the kitchen. Cards and invitation fell to the hearth as she swept round.

'What? What is it?'

Baba was hopping up and down in front of the open larder door. Inside, a goose hung heavy and limp from a hook, her long grey neck slung with string, her eyes half-closed. The yellow beak gaped, yellow feet dangled.

'That's Grey Fluffy Yellow Toes! That's Grey Fluffy — ' She burst into wild weeping.

'Oh, darling, I don't think it is — '

'It is! It *is!*'

Freddie stood silent by the Rayburn rail.

Flo took Baba in her arms. 'Darling, darling.'

'He's killed her! He's killed her!'

'I'm sure he didn't mean to, he just wanted a goose for Christmas, they look so alike — '

'She looked *different!*'

A key sounded in the front door. There came a little whistle. 'Tik hai?'

'No it's not bloody tik hai,' Flo snapped as he came in. 'Honestly, Will — '

Baba buried her face in her shoulder, Freddie dived under the table. Will took in the open larder door, the situation.

'Don't tell me — '

'It was *her*,' sobbed Baba. '*My* goose.'

Nothing he could say could make it better.

★ ★ ★

Which meant that setting out for the Gibsons' drinks do was not quite as happy as it might have been. The prospect of it had been unsettling Flo for days. *At Home.* She stood before the mirror in the bedroom of their own small home, holding ancient things before her. It was one thing to run up a summer frock on the machine — everyone did that — but winter things: you couldn't run up an evening jacket or dress. She couldn't, anyway. She took a worn shirt-waister out of the wardrobe. Where was the belt? She ran her hand

183

along the hangers. God, how dispiriting this was, and oh, how she'd used to love clothes!

Clothes, men, makeup — those were the days. Handsome chaps gazing up at her from their beds in hospital or nursing home, as she shook down the thermometer with a flirtatious little flick. Taking her out for drinks the moment they were better, like the officers whisking her out for dinner after a long day in the Ops Room, in the WAAF, everyone laughing their heads off as they got dressed up to the nines, shrieking as a ladder appeared in rationed nylons. 'Oh, no! Oh, my dear!' Dashing for the soap to stop it running, hearing the horn tooting away outside.

And as for India — all those bolts of pretty cotton rolled out on the dining-room table, the *durzi* ready with his pins and scissors, any number of pretty frocks made up for nothing at all.

Now, as she stood in a cottage bedroom light years later, holding up this old dress, she unzipped her working skirt, pulled her jumper over her head. There she stood, in bra and corset, spare tyre bulging between, too much weight put on, eating to get well again. She was usually in too much of a hurry to contemplate the sight, and now it made her shudder.

She'd danced? She'd sung, getting ready for parties?

Oh, come on, she told herself, stepping into the tired blue dress, running the frayed belt through. You can perk this up with something, surely. And she riffled through a drawer and found a stole she'd quite forgotten about, pale blue and cream check. Had she actually bought it? Was it a present from Vivie? She'd forgotten so much since that dreadful time. But still — it was pretty.

She slipped into her one pair of heels, and wrapped the stole around her.

★   ★   ★

They walked in silence through the darkened village, their footsteps ringing on the frosty ground. A huge Christmas tree stood on the Green, strings of lights swaying in the wind.

'Forgiven me?' Will asked her, as they came to the Gibsons' drive. 'I know it was a dreadful thing. Poor little Baba.'

'Oh, Will.'

Other people were approaching, a torch light swung. She was suddenly sick with nerves. 'Let's forget about it now,' she said, and took his arm.

'My darling.' He squeezed her hand. 'We'll have a super time.'

They crunched up over the gravel towards the house. Beneath the portico, carriage lamps hung on either side of the glossy front door. Light spilled out as the guests were welcomed; even on the doorstep you could smell the logs, the evergreen, the spices.

'Marvellous,' said Will, taking his cap off. 'Simply marvellous.'

A handsome tree stood in the hall, where Daphne Gibson, in a long dull gown, her dog beside her, was briskly directing her boys to take people's coats upstairs. They could see big bluff

Donald serving punch by a vast fire in the drawing room, hailing everyone from behind the bowl.

'That's it, Nick, off you go,' said Daphne to her eldest. 'Will, how nice to see you. And you, Flo. How are you?'

It meant nothing, Flo told herself, slipping off her old coat, saying she was fine, thanks. Nobody cared how she really was, and she didn't have to tell them. But as soon as she stood there, coatless, adjusting her stole, her stomach began to churn. How could she have thought she'd stand up to this? Beside the slinky cinched-waist evening dresses, the wraps and silk stoles all round her, what could she possibly look like?

And here was Michael Lewis, untying what looked like an opera scarf from his elegant neck, handing his good dark coat to another scrubbed Gibson boy. To think she had pinned all her hopes on him, writing excitedly to Vivie — a *Literary Agent!* And look what had happened when at last she'd had time to write.

'Hello, Michael,' she murmured, as he went past, just to see what it felt like, and he turned and looked at her blankly.

'I'm Flo Sutherland,' she said with a little laugh, and he frowned, and then said, 'Oh, yes, of course. Nice to see you. How're things?'

But he didn't care how things were — why should he? — and in a moment, as she said they were fine, thanks, he'd melted away.

Will's hand was on her elbow. 'Ready, my darling?'

'I just need to powder my nose.' She took a deep breath. 'Daphne, could you show me — '

'Of course. Just along the corridor there, and another one upstairs, Nicholas will show you, won't you, Nick?'

'It's all right, thanks, I'll find it.' And she fled past the wagging Labrador, and into the refuge of the lav. In front of the mirror, she pulled out her compact with a shaking hand. Shaking! What had become of her? She'd been doing so well, out and about again — but that was different. Out and about, you could give a wave, have a little chat about nothing very much, go home and shut the door. She looked at herself in the mirror now, seeing herself as Michael Lewis must have seen her, just another housewife wanting to write, with puffy dark circles under her eyes. No pretending that that dreadful time hadn't aged her.

She thought of the children tucked up in bed, the babysitter girl downstairs, just a young thing, with no experience really. Baba had been fine with her, of course, chatting away and showing her things, but Freddie had hung back. What would happen if he woke up and was frightened? He'd been so unsettled, so clingy when she came home — how would he know, if he woke up, that she was coming back?

'Mummy and Daddy are going to a party,' she'd told him yesterday, and his big brown eyes had darkened.

'Mummy not go.'

Someone was trying the door of the lav, coughing politely outside. Flo reached up and pulled the chain and as the water swirled down into the bowl she had a wild image of herself just

187

whirling away within it. Wouldn't that be nice? Gone, gone, and no need to face a soul.

She snapped her compact shut, and opened the door.

'So sorry,' she said brightly, as the vicar's wife, plain old Marjorie Whatnot, stepped back to let her pass.

'How are you, Flo?'

'Oh, I'm frightfully well, thanks,' said Flo with her little laugh. 'See you in a minute!' And she made for the party.

Will was already in full swing, glass in hand, roaring with laughter at something he'd just said, she could tell that straight away, as a group of tweedy chaps laughed with him. Steam rose from the punch bowl, the fire crackled, parchment-shaded wall lights lit the hunting scenes hung everywhere, shone down on the heaps of the *Field* and *Country Life*.

'Flo! My darling!' He reached out an arm. 'My wife,' he told the tweedy chaps, who nodded and smiled, and then, 'Let me get you a drink.'

And once she had some of that punch inside her, she rallied. God knows what Donald had put in it, but after the first glass she thought: I can do this. Just for an hour, I can do it. Soon the crowded room was thick with spices and cigarette smoke: she saw Michael Lewis bend down to light a cigarette for Rosie Byatt, wearing a gorgeous full-skirted dress in emerald-green taffeta, a silky black stole across bare shoulders. Flo watched her inhale deeply, head back, those lovely shoulders raised. And where was Roddy, and where was worn-out Jenny Lewis?

She looked round, sipping her second glass, half listening to talk of shoots, and the Home Guard, which a lot of chaps seemed to belong to. 'We should get you in there, Will, old boy.' Their tweedy wives were in a group of their own, braying away by the fire. Jenny was nowhere to be seen, probably at home with the new baby. Another! Roddy Byatt she saw across the room, nodding and listening to what must be Daphne's sister: another brisk nod, probably going on about hunting. She saw him glance across at his wife, chatting away with Michael.

Then Donald Gibson went up and tapped Rosie on the shoulder, and as she turned and greeted him, and held out her glass with a happy little nod, Flo thought: I can't let that ghastly encounter with Michael in the hall be the last time we speak tonight. I've got to rise above it, show him I'm back in the world. You never know — she had another couple of sips — one day I might write again. One day he might be thrilled to represent me.

And she made her way towards him.

'Michael! Thought I'd just come and have a word.'

Rosie, fresh glass in hand, was laughing in the crowd by the punch bowl. Michael gazed down at Flo.

'How's Jenny?' she asked brightly. 'How is the literary world?'

He drew on his cigarette. 'I think both are in pretty good order, thanks. I'm up in London quite a bit these days.'

'Are you really? How fascinating. With all your

famous authors, I expect!' She flashed him a wicked little look, over the top of her glass.

He gave a half-smile, and she saw his gaze flicker across the room. 'What about you, Flo? I was sorry to hear you'd been ill.'

'Oh, I'm much better now, thanks. I've given my novel a rest, but one day I'll get back to it, I know. It's set in India, did I tell you? Perhaps when I pick it up again, I could show you the first few chapters!' And she drained her glass, and gave him another little look. She had rallied; this was fun!

'Yes, of course,' he said flatly, and then, 'Nice to talk to you — would you just excuse me a minute — '

And he was gone, not even offering to get her another drink, just melted into the throng.

Flo stood there with her empty glass, and felt as if she'd been kicked. Snubbed not once, but twice. Snubbed when she was just picking up again, trying her hardest — and talking to an attractive man for once! And he — and he —

Fool, she told herself. Bloody, bloody fool.

Where was Will? Somewhere she heard his laugh, turned to look for him, felt her head swim horribly, and knew she couldn't move. She tugged at her woollen stole, stranded and helpless.

'Flo, my dear.' Roddy Byatt was all at once before her. 'May I get you another drink?'

She shook her swimming head. 'No, no, I mustn't, thanks.' Her voice sounded distant and strange. She looked up at him, saw such a sweet expression. 'Oh, dear,' she said slowly. 'I'm afraid I — I'm afraid — '

'I know. Parties are difficult sometimes, aren't they?'

'I used to love them,' said Flo. Tears sprang to her eyes; she bit her lip.

'I'm sure you were a huge hit. You've made such a marvellous recovery, I know it must have been hell.'

'Oh, Roddy.' She swallowed hard. 'Please don't be kind, or I'll just make an ass of myself.'

Yet kindness was all she wanted now.

He offered a cigarette; she shook her head. 'Shall we sit down?' he asked her. 'Shall I get Will?'

She looked up at him, and through her misery saw the dark shadows under his own eyes, the lines of strain on such a gentle face.

'I think you've been through a bit of hell yourself,' she said slowly. It felt like the first real thing she'd said all evening, and for a moment they looked at one another with no holds barred, simply an acknowledgement of the truth. Then the shutters came down, and he lit his cigarette, saying quickly, 'Oh, these things come and go,' and then Will was beside them, his arm round Flo, saying, 'My darling,' and, 'Roddy, old boy, good to see you. How's life?'

★ ★ ★

They walked home very slowly, arm in arm beneath the starlit sky. At an icy patch Flo's heel slipped, and she almost went down, but he held her tight.

'Careful, careful.'

Behind them they could still hear car doors slam and voices calling out, Good night! Happy Christmas! Super party!

'Well now, my darling, had a good time?'

All she could think of was Roddy's gentle face. He looked at her. 'You all right?'

'Just a bit squiffy still.'

His arm went round her. 'We'll soon have you tucked up.'

And she leaned her head on his shoulder, seeing Roddy's tall figure, and haunted eyes, as the lights of the cottage came shining out towards them.

9

At a Saturday breakfast in early January, Will pushed back his chair and got up. 'Right,' he announced. 'I'm going out for a bit.' He was always in and out, nobody took much notice, but something made the children look up from their boiled eggs.

'Where are you going?'

'Going to see a man about a dog.'

'Are we going to have a dog? Can we come?'

'It's just an expression,' said Flo. 'Freddie, you've got egg on your jumper.'

He peered down.

At lunchtime there came a toot-toot in the lane. Then a car drew up at the gate. Freddie and Baba, playing upstairs, took no notice. The toot-toot came again; they heard Flo go down the hall. It came again.

'For pity's sake,' said Baba. She went to the window.

'Daddy's in the car,' she said in astonishment. 'Daddy's driving!'

They hurtled down the stairs.

'What do you think of this?' asked Will, opening green doors as they all stood awed and shivering. 'Hop in!'

They scrambled inside, smelling leather and petrol. 'Right,' he said, getting back in to the driving seat. 'Let's go for a spin.'

He hadn't driven a car since the war, but he'd

driven a tractor often enough, and he steered them round the village, toot-tooting at everyone they knew.

'Toot-toot!' called Rosie Byatt, walking up the street in a coat with a sweet fur collar. What a pretty thing she was.

'This is super, Will,' said Flo beside him.

'It's a Ford Popular,' he told them all, braking suddenly as a cat darted out in front. 'Perfect little family car.' He stuck out a bright yellow indicator as they turned right. 'Must join the AA.'

'I feel a bit sick,' said Freddie in the back.

Flo opened a window. Freezing air came in.

'I'm actually going to be sick,' he said, a few minutes later.

'Oh, for God's sake.' Where could he pull up? He found a little turning just in time. 'Out you get! Quick!'

Freddie was sick all over the pavement, Flo comforting him all the way home, holding him on her lap in the front. When they got back she took him straight inside to be cleaned up and have a drink of water. 'Poor darling.' He was ashen.

Baba stayed in the car as Will got out to open the garage doors. He backed, he went forward, he backed again. Gander came waddling down the garden.

'Don't run him over!'

'I'm not going to run him over!'

At last they got inside.

'What do you think?' he asked her, switching off the engine.

'Well done, Daddy.' She gave him a pat.
WELL DONE, DADDY.

★   ★   ★

'I feel sad,' said Nancy, when they were playing at her house. It was a Saturday afternoon, they were up in her bedroom. Outside the sun was shining in a blowy sky, everything ordinary and nice. 'I feel sad.'

Baba fastened the buttons on the back of her doll's dress and stood her up.

'Why?'

'I don't know.' Nancy was sitting on her bed, with its pretty counterpane. 'I just do. I often do.' She began to cry.

Baba told the doll to stay there and went over. She climbed on the bed and put her arm round her. 'What is it? What's the matter?'

Nancy cried and cried. 'I don't know, I don't know.'

'God loves you,' said Baba, tenderly stroking her hair. 'Your mummy and daddy love you.'

'I know, I know.'

'There's nothing to be sad about, really, is there?' She dug in her pocket and pulled out a hankie. 'Here. Blow your nose. Everything's all right really. And I'm your friend.'

Nancy blew her nose. Baba took her to the bathroom, to wash her face in cold water. Nobody seemed to be listening or caring about all this crying: Mr Byatt was out for a walk, and Mrs Byatt was — where was she?

'Mrs Byatt?' Baba stood at the top of the stairs

and called, while Nancy dried her eyes. 'Mrs Byatt?'

She couldn't have gone out, too, and left them all alone. No one would ever do that. Then she heard the ting of the telephone, and pretty Mrs Byatt came into the hall from the sitting room.

'Hello, Baba, were you calling me?'

'Sorry, it's just — ' She stopped. Somehow she couldn't tell her about Nancy being sad about nothing. She didn't think she would understand. 'Just wondering where you were.'

JUST WONDERING WHERE YOU WERE.

'I'm right here,' said Nancy's mother. She looked prettier than ever, somehow, all pink and bright-eyed. 'Tea's almost ready, darling. Tell Nancy, will you?'

★　★　★

Early summer, tiny hard apples on the boughs. Will, with a pay rise, finally agreed to an extension to the cottage. Flo kissed him and kissed him. Fitz was helping, a mortgage would do the rest. 'And this year you really *must* come down,' she wrote, enclosing her marvellous cheque. 'Especially now you've got the car!' Will banked the cheque, wrote to thank her profusely, said he insisted on it being a loan. Though frankly, on top of the mortgage —

Building began, the place all cement mixers and men. Freddie was in heaven. Bang bang slosh slosh hammer hammer all day long, from first thing in the morning until they came home from school, with Will growling away in his office, trying to work, and Snowy hiding under a

196

hedge. By the end of July it was all over bar the shouting: two brand-new rooms, one up, one down, smelling of raw wooden floors and fresh pink plaster. The children went racing about.

'Stop that noise!'

Vivie sent an old carpet up by train, almost the first thing in the house not to come from the Rectory.

And in from the playroom came the bureau, the old oak chest, the portraits, in their heavy gilt plaster frames. Roddy Byatt came to help hang them, one Sunday afternoon.

'He worries me,' Flo said when he'd gone, not staying for tea, thanks. 'Something really not right there. Do you think they're happy?'

At once, she wished she'd said nothing. She thought of that naked gaze, that clearly complicit moment between her and Roddy at the Gibsons' Christmas party. They understood one another. And brief though it had been, talking about him now felt like a betrayal.

Will said how anyone could be less than happy with that lovely Rosie was beyond him, shell shock or no.

'Those are your great-grandparents,' he told the children, pointing at the portraits when they came running in for tea. They gazed up for about half a minute.

And now, finally —

'We've got our own rooms!'

All this new space! *Everyone's wild with excitement*, Flo wrote to Vivie. *And now we've got the car (!!) we're going down to Dorset, to stay with Will's cousin Fitz. She lives with another woman,*

I'm sure I've told you. We tell the children they're best friends, but actually — isn't it awful? Still, they're both terribly sweet.

'Op-pop-pop-pop-poposite the ducks
Is the spot where I unbend,
And among my flow'rs after bus'ness hours,
I am glad to see a friend . . . '

Fitz, singing away at the piano, finished the song with a flourish.

'Again!' said Freddie, banging on the side, and off she went, he and Baba singing along at the tops of their voices. The music floated out through the open French windows on to the terrace, where Eleanor, Will and Flo were sitting amongst the remains of tea. The afternoon sun was warm — hot, even — though with a sea breeze it could be chilly at night. Distantly came the sound of the gulls from Lyme Regis harbour, where the family had spent the day swimming and having lunch in a pub.

'Again!'

'Give poor Fitz a rest,' called Will, polishing off the last of the fruitcake, but she didn't mind.

'How about this one?' And she turned the pages of the music and struck a new tune.

'We men ought to combine,
Ought to combine,
Fall into line!'

she sang brightly, with only the faintest quaver in her less-than-youthful voice.

'All pull together
Like birds of a feather,
And STICK IT through rain and
through shine!'

★ ★ ★

Out on the terrace they were laughing, even
aristocratic Eleanor unbending in a tinkly way.
Eleanor was beautiful: of this there was no
doubt. Her hair had gone white in her twenties,
and now, in her fifties, her pink and white skin
was soft beneath the snowy pile, held up with a
tortoiseshell clip. She was also a bit frightening
— to all of them, not just the children. She was
clever in a way that none of them was: properly
educated, talking of Bach and Chopin and the
Impressionists as if she knew them personally.
And, of course, she had a mind of her own:
decades ago had left her husband, Lord Lacey,
after only two years of marriage, in order to live
with Fitz.

Now she offered more tea from the silver
teapot, and when Will and Flo said no, they'd
done splendidly, thanks, she offered to show
them round the garden. Off they went, over the
springy lawn, gazing at the roses, the raspberry
cage, the herbaceous border, while the sun
slipped down and singing round the piano went
joyfully on. There were quite a few Latin names
to try to get hold of: Flo had a glazed look and
Will sneaked a glance at his watch. Almost time
for a peg.

They had it bang on six, out on the terrace,

the tea things cleared away by Nana, who'd looked after Fitz since she was a baby, and lived now with her sister in a cream-washed bungalow built specially for them across the enormous garden. The house was cream-washed, too, large and light and modern but full of the old rugs and antiques which Flo remembered from her first visit here, when Baba was a baby. Everything smelled of flowers and polish, everything shone. Of course, they had masses of Help.

She took the children upstairs for their bath, noting the two separate bedrooms as they walked along the landing — *so it seems they don't actually sleep together, thank heavens,* she scribbled to Vivie next day, sealing the envelope tight. Or perhaps they did, when no one was here — she couldn't bear to think about it.

'So lovely to have you all here, Willie,' said Fitz, leaning back in her chair, while Eleanor supervised supper. 'And Flo's looking marvellous, after that dreadful time.'

'All behind us now, thank God.'

All week the weather was perfect, the mornings especially, with the sun in the breakfast room winking off cut-glass marmalade jar and glistening honey in a comb.

'We love it here,' said Baba, digging away.

On the last day but one they wrote postcards to Agnes and Neville and searched in the seaside shops for presents. Gulls wheeled over the Cobb, dogs raced up and down. It was windy and bright, clouds scudding by. They found a shell box for Eleanor and a little china duck for Fitz.

200

She put him on top of the piano, and they had a last sing-song together.

'Op-pop-pop-pop-poposite the ducks
 Is the spot where I unbend . . . '

They knew it by heart, they sang it in the bath, they sang it when they drove away, dosed up with Kwells and waving wildly out of the window. Then they burst into tears.

'I don't want to go home.'

'What about Snowy?'

Snowy was in a cattery, but not even the thought of his face as they went to collect him could lift their spirits now.

'Tell you what,' said Will, feeling more relaxed than he had for ages — marvellous little holiday — 'I'll tell you a story.'

'About India,' said Baba and Freddie together.

Sunlit India was always there, always behind their lives.

   ★ ★ ★

A television! It sat in the corner of the big new sitting room, and most of the time there was nothing on at all, only a strange-looking thing like a fir tree, which Will explained was the Mast. Misty circles went round and round it. Later, there was a sort of chessboard, with a little girl with long hair in an Alice band smiling beside it.

'She looks like you, Baba.'

'No, she doesn't.'

By now Baba was at The Rookery and at

nearly nine was apt to stand her ground. It didn't stop her from being as enchanted as Freddie with Rag, Tag and Bobtail, hopping around their garden.

In the evenings were boring grown-up programmes: The News, with talk about somewhere called Suez, Will shouting about That Bloody Man Nasser.

THAT BLOODY MAN NASSER.

With all this, the wireless rather faded into the background, though everyone was still fond of Uncle Mac. Sometimes after lunch on Sundays Will put on *The Brains Trust*, with Julian Huxley, Jacob Bronowski and Isaiah Berlin answering everyone's questions in their brilliant way. Once in a blue moon they had Marghanita Laski, a woman Flo found so terrifying that she took refuge in the washing-up.

She'd finally bought a pressure cooker, supposed to make everything much easier. The idea was that everything cooked together, which it did, but in the meantime there was the frantic escaping of steam, the rush to twiddle the valve, the scalding of your hand.

Feeding the Family, read a chapter title in the dreaded book. There were sections on Nutritional Values, and Choosing Shops Carefully. That had been a laugh and a half, a mile up a lane in the depths of Devon. Even here there was only the village shop and Market Hampden, carrying everything home on the bus unless Will ran her in.

'Are you going to learn to drive, Mummy?'

'No,' said Will.

'Why?'

'I'd never get the hang of it,' said Flo. All those crashing gears, and just the whole idea of it, putting your foot on the wrong pedal and the whole thing running away with you. 'I know I wouldn't.'

Have Oven Days, commanded the book. And Top-of-the-Stove Ones. Have a Repertoire of Tested Recipes.

The Brains Trust was over, Will calling out: 'Anyone for a walk?'

Sunday walks were often along the canal. Green duckweed floated all along the top, and the towpath went on for ever. Once they saw a water snake, poking his head up through the weed, and once a water rat, swimming sleekly through it, like Ratty in *The Wind in the Willows*. 'Come along!' said Will, as they gazed down into the water. 'Off we go!'

OFF WE GO!

⋆   ⋆   ⋆

Flo sat the children down and told them the facts of life. She'd got to do it before Freddie went away to school. God knows what other boys would tell him: lots of parents were useless at this. She got out a little book from the Boots library, and settled them down on the sofa, one Saturday afternoon. She read bits out, she showed them the pictures.

'This should be on the Science Table,' said Freddie after a while. It was all about bees and flowers and Pollination.

Flo tried to tell them about Gander and the geese. 'You know when he flaps his wings and runs after them . . . '

'He's always doing that to *me!*'

Eventually they got round to the real thing, but not with the book, the book was pretty hopeless: 'When your mummy and daddy want to make a baby, they lie down together in a special way . . . '

'What sort of way?'

God, it was difficult. Flo fetched pencil and paper.

'Now,' she said, pressing on *How You Began* on her knee. 'This is the Womb.' She drew a pear, upside down. 'Here are the Ovaries.' They followed her pencil as the Sperm went up and the Egg came down, and met.

'But how does the sperm get *in* there?'

HOW DOES THE SPERM GET *IN* THERE?

There was nothing for it but to spell it out.

'You mean — you mean he actually puts it *inside the mummy?*'

'Yes. And it's a lovely, lovely feeling. For both of them.' If she could do nothing else she could make them understand that. How gorgeous it was, the best thing in the world. She could hear Will opening the office door, after his Saturday Stint. Perhaps they could get the children to bed early tonight.

He put his head round the door. 'What are we up to?'

'Mummy's been telling us how we began.'

'Well, you know where you began,' Will said to Baba, laughing. 'You began in India. Just before

204

Independence.' And he put on his Indian voice. ''At the stroke of midnight, while the world sleeps, Indiah will awake to life and freedom . . . ''

'Where did I begin?' asked Freddie, sliding off the sofa, but Daddy was saying what a marvellous chap old Nehru was, and then he and Mummy were laughing and talking about how happy they'd been then, and nobody heard him.

★ ★ ★

Then something terrible happened. It was autumn, leaves blowing about the garden, the geese needing more feed to fatten up for winter, the evenings drawing in. The children were having supper in the kitchen, Flo keeping an eye on their table manners.

'Half of what you think is right,' she said, as they stuffed in baked potato. 'Baba, you are not a hippopotamus.'

They giggled, as the phone began to ring. It was always ringing; Will was hardly off it when he was at home.

'Elbows off the table, Freddie, sit up straight. When you get to prep school you'll have to behave at the table.'

Oh, how would he manage, so far away?

'Daddy says it's a bun fight.'

The office door opened. Will came slowly in to the kitchen. As soon as Flo saw his white face —

'What? What's happened?'

The children looked up.

'Come here,' said Will, and then, to the

children: 'Stay there.'

She followed him into the office. He shut the door and stood with his back to it.

'Roddy Byatt's shot himself. Out by the canal.'

'No.' She sank into the swivel chair. 'No, that can't be true.'

★ ★ ★

Rosie Byatt had been having an affair with Donald Gibson. It had been going on for ages, apparently. Roddy Byatt suffered from dreadful depression, worse than anyone knew. Long before the affair, apparently: perhaps that was why Rosie —

It all came out, it all went round the village.

★ ★ ★

The vicar had made the phone calls. On the day of the funeral, the church bell slowly tolling the forty-two years of Roddy's life, he stood at the west door to receive the cortège, his face drawn, his cassock blowing about in the autumn wind. Nancy had been sent to stay with her grandparents. Rosie arrived in the deepest black and a veil, something no one had seen for years. She spoke to no one, and nobody spoke to her.

Could Roddy be buried in the churchyard? Wasn't suicide the worst thing you could ever do? Didn't Catholics think you went straight to Hell?

The vicar had said he could be buried by the far wall, and so he was, the rooks cawing in the bare elm trees and the sky a gunmetal grey as the plain wooden coffin sank down.

'And so I should think,' said Will, as he and Flo walked slowly home. 'He's a good man, old Scott.'

Flo couldn't speak. Leaves danced cruelly before her on the path.

By Christmas, Rosie and Nancy had gone.

★ ★ ★

It took a long time for everyone to get over all this. The thought of handsome, kind Roddy Byatt walking along the canal with his gun, walking and walking as dusk began to fall, and the green weed on the water darkened, then ramming the gun to the back of his throat —

They could not get it out of their minds. Prayers were said in church. Snow piled up on the graves, on his grave. It was terrible, terrible.

'What actually *happened*? What did he actually *do*?'

WHAT DID HE ACTUALLY DO?

'I'll tell you when you're much older. That's enough now.'

Will's main concern was that it wouldn't unsettle Flo.

'Are you all right, my darling?'

'I just can't stop thinking — '

Nobody could. But the snow melted, snowdrops lined the lanes, a hazy sun came out. They had to put it behind them.

★ ★ ★

Flo lay awake, gazing into the darkness.

'*Flo, my dear. You've made such a marvellous recovery. I know it must have been hell.*'

'*I think you've been through a bit of hell yourself.*'

The lines played over and over, as they looked at one another. She saw his gentle sweet smile, his eyes dark with pain.

'*These things come and go —* '

'Roddy,' she whispered, as Will slept on beside her, and she saw him, over and over again, walking alone with his gun.

⋆ ⋆ ⋆

At The Rookery, Baba struggled with maths and tennis. She made a new friend called Priscilla and when spring came they went rambling over the countryside at weekends. All by themselves over farmland, no one turning a hair. Priscilla was almost the only thing Baba liked about the new school. She liked the green uniform, and the may trees round the tennis courts, but the maths! The Fractions!

'They're awful,' said Flo. 'I do remember.'

Will tried to help: there were tears. Sometimes amidst these tears, Baba thought about Nancy, who had simply disappeared.

'Can I write to her?'

Nobody knew where she was.

'Try not to think about her,' said Flo, stroking her hair. She was trying, still, not to think about Roddy.

As for the wretched Michael Lewis: he'd been

having an affair with a girl in London. That had all come out, too. And now he'd left Jenny, and the baby, and the nappies and the children and the mess, and set up shop in Soho, living in sin until the divorce came through. There were no prayers for him in church; he'd never gone there anyway.

Isn't it shocking? Flo wrote to Vivie.

She'd told her about Roddy, too, she'd had to. *But I don't want to talk about it ever again.*

★ ★ ★

Baba shut up the horrible maths book. The only thing she was good at was English grammar. Where two-thirds multiplied by one-sixth meant nothing at all, subordinate clauses, conjunctions and relative pronouns sank in and settled down for ever.

And then there was the word thing.

'Mummy? I can see words in front of me.'

'Can you, darling?'

CAN YOU, DARLING?

'Freddie? Do you see words coming up in front of you?'

He wasn't sure.

He was growing fast, now, was strong and fit, into a new stage of being. He was eight, he had shorts with fly buttons. He knew every Times Table backwards, he was in charge of the Science Table. At home, he was a bit short of friends: Flo and Will discouraged him from going down to the Gibsons now. And there was no Nancy, coming up to play with Baba, running away from the geese, or sitting quietly in the car on the school run. He couldn't make it out.

'In the autumn you'll be off to prep school, old chap,' said Will, after church one day. 'You'll have a super time.'

He simply couldn't imagine it.

* * *

And then, out of the blue, came a letter for Will from the RLS Head Office.

'The Deputy Secretary is leaving,' he told Flo. 'They want me to apply.'

'What would that mean?'

'Leaving here, I suppose. Working in London.' He stuffed the thing back in the envelope. 'Well, I'll have a go, shall I? Probably won't get it, probably lots of chaps going for something like that.' He went back into the office.

Flo cleared away the breakfast things in a daze. As she washed up, she saw not the geese grazing out in the orchard, not the long garage-cum-playroom beside the garden, nor Snowy, out for a prowl, but herself, down on the farm, all alone with the children and Mike while Will had his interview in London. She heard the ring of the bicycle bell as the telegraph boy came bumping over the muddy ground, she saw herself run out, and rip the telegram open.

'Got It.'

He'd get it now, she knew.

* * *

Late summer, the swallows gathering on the telegraph wires. They were there every evening, all through the village and along their lane, twittering and preening as the sun went down, getting ready for their long, long journey back to Africa. How could they fly all that way? How could they possibly?

Freddie stood beneath, looking up. The sun was setting, the sky a blaze of gold and crimson, the dark blue-black of the birds in silhouette all along the wire.

Something was aching inside him.

They were moving, too: they were flying away.

He went back through the garden gate, and round to the side of the house. There was a great big iron S there, clamped to the brickwork, holding all the old wall together. He shut his eyes and leaned his head against it.

Part Three

Lights Out

1

Ryehurst was a pretty place, an old Surrey market town lying beneath the springy turf of the North Downs.

'Splendid place for a family,' said Will. 'Good schools, nice shops, and a terrific house.'

Bea — 'Don't call me Baba! Don't!' — counted all the stairs. Seventeen to the turn, five to the first-floor landing. Here was the bathroom, with a separate lav, already piled up with the *Reader's Digest*. Her parents' bedroom overlooked the garden at the back; a big room lay next door, and a little room next to it. That was Freddie's, but he wasn't here.

Then came the stairs to the top floor: fifteen. The wall here was lined with dark old paper, covered in cherry boughs. At the very top was a boxroom — 'Probably the maid's room once,' said Flo — where everything from the move had been thrown in any old how: trunks, cases, boxes of goodness knows what. And there was Snowy, shut away with his dish and his basket, his paws smeared with butter.

'By the time he's licked it all off, he'll have settled down.'

Bea could hear him mewing. Poor Snowy.

'I'll come in a minute!'

To the left was another empty room — 'That can be the playroom.' And here, straight ahead, was her own room: an attic! Right at the top and

215

away from everyone. She stood at the window and looked out.

Garden after garden lay below her: lawns, flowerbeds, sheds, little trees, all fenced along the sides and walled at the far end, where the gardens of the next road began.

'I could keep a pig down there,' Will had told Agnes on the phone.

'Don't be so silly, Willie!'

Everything looked tiny after all that space in Melcote — no orchard, no geese, no vegetables on the Green. No lanes, no fields beyond. But nice in a different way, thought Bea, leaning out in the September sun. She could just make out the tower of the church, and stood listening as the clock struck eleven: Saturday morning, Will home, banging nails into walls.

Her new school uniform hung on a hook on the door; her white-painted bed stood against the wall. There was an alcove, and Fitz had sent up a little desk. It had two drawers, a flap, and pigeonholes. This was where she would do her homework. She'd have quite a lot, apparently.

The playroom next door overlooked the road. On the far side were more houses, set along a path behind a brick wall and trees. Traffic whizzed by. They were on a main road — 'A new experience!' she'd said when they arrived, and Will laughed. 'That's the spirit!' The road led into Ryehurst one way and up towards Croydon the other. It was called Croydon Road, and went on for ever.

'What's wrong with Croydon?' Will had asked Flo, seeing her face.

She couldn't explain.

'It'll be all right, Mummy,' Bea told her, giving her a hug.

'Good girl.' Will was going to have to go up and down to London now, every single day. 'Catch the train at Ryehurst, change at Redstone, change again at East Croydon, arrive at Victoria at 08.30 hours. Do it all again, coming back.'

'A new experience!' Bea said again, but this time he didn't laugh.

'A hell of a thing to get used to. Still — got to be done. I expect I'll have fun when I get there.'

'That's the spirit.'

She turned from the window, hearing Snowy's cries.

'Here I am, my darling.' She sounded just like her mother. Inside the musty little room she stroked and kissed him. 'It'll be all right, you'll find.' She sounded just like her father.

She went out again, closing the door quickly as he made to escape, and went slowly down the stairs. The cherry wallpaper made it so dark up here. It had probably been bright and cheerful once, but — 'Put up before the Flood,' said Will. She could hear him, far below, hanging up Panther in the hall.

'Pass him, pass him up, careful now, that's it. There! How's that?'

'Super, darling. Where shall we put his skin?'

'In front of the fire, I thought.'

Gazing at the gloomy paper, Bea saw all at once that birds hopped here and there, amongst the cherry boughs. She hadn't noticed that. She

217

looked at the one closest to her, something between blackbird and thrush, very still, and bright of eye. He gazed back at her.

'Hello,' she said, now she had found him. HELLO.

★ ★ ★

Freddie had a new name, too. He might have gone to St Peter's, the Ryehurst prep school just a walk away from the church. He might have sung in the choir, played cricket against local schools, come home every afternoon, like Bea. Like her, he might have made friends nearby, met up with them in the holidays.

'Mountford Park is my old school,' said Will. 'He'll love it.'

And now he was Sutherland, from the moment he arrived. 'Freddie' simply evaporated, as if he had never been. He too had a new house: there were four in the school, named after the points of the compass. He was in East. He had a number within East: Fourteen, and in case he ever lost his new black slip-ons in the scrum of the changing room after Games, there were little brass nails hammered into the soles: E14. The nametapes Flo had sewn wonkily into every item of his clothing before they left Melcote, and packed into Will's old trunk from India, had this information too: F. Sutherland, E14. It was stencilled on to the trunk, and on to his tuck box, stuffed with flapjacks.

He had a dorm, a long, long room with high, square-paned windows and twenty iron beds in it, painted white. You had to make your bed with hospital corners. You weren't allowed to speak after lights out. If you were a new boy, you were made by the Dorm Captain to mix twenty different squeezes of toothpaste with a bit of water in your plastic beaker, and drink it. If you were sick, you were laughed at. He was very sick.

★ ★ ★

The HQ of the Rural Landowners was in a street off Piccadilly.

London! As Will walked beneath the plane trees of Green Park, slowly turning to yellow and gold, he heard the unending rumble of traffic. As he crossed Piccadilly, dodging taxis and buses and sleek expensive cars, coughing in the petrol fumes; as he climbed the narrow stairs to his office, he thought of himself twenty-five years ago, cooped up in insurance, looking out on to Trafalgar Square, on to the light, the fountains, the pigeons rising and falling so freely while in here people opened filing cabinet drawers and shut them, and downstairs the typewriters clattered away.

India! India had saved him. And now —

Here we go again.

Of course, it was different now. A family to support, for one thing — the main thing. That gave it all meaning. And he'd done pretty well, no doubt about it: promotion, a bloody great salary hike. He couldn't have gone on for ever as Regional Sec., could hardly have paid the school fees, for a start: even now, old Fitz was helping

219

out. Up here, he had the chance to make things happen throughout the organisation, flex his muscles a bit.

'Morning, Sutherland.'

'Morning, sir.'

That was James Marshall, the Secretary, walking along the corridor to his office: always here first, with his flat in town. And place in the country, of course.

Will would be reporting to him. And there was no question, he thought, as he went into his own office, and greeted his own secretary and shorthand typist, that reporting to someone on the spot, breathing down your neck as you might say, was a damn different kettle of fish. Everything was pretty damn different. He dropped his briefcase, hung up his coat.

'Coffee, Mr Sutherland?'

'That would be marvellous.'

* * *

Bea and Flo set off for school together. Bea swung her new satchel and Flo pushed her bicycle alongside. *I've bought a bike!* she wrote to Vivie, soon after their arrival.

Will found it in the *Surrey Mirror*. It was a great big old green thing, with a basket and a rusting bell, and never had she imagined she would ride a bike again, but —

I couldn't do without it! The house was a good mile from the town. The bike was a huge help with shopping. And then she could spin home again once she'd dropped Bea at school.

'How are you finding it, darling?'

'I like it.'

They walked along Rushbrook Road, the bike ticking, the railway line screened by trees, the leaves beginning to fall. By the station they waited for the traffic lights to change on the busy main road: another route, up Ryehurst Hill, to London.

'Over we go.'

They crossed and turned down into Summers Road, where the school lay, and here everything was really rather nice, solid Edwardian houses set within large gardens, the hills rising behind. The school, a few hundred yards down, was in two such houses, connected by a glassy modern corridor. The Head was called Miss MacArthur.

'I wonder why it's called Micklegate,' said Flo, as they came to the gates.

'It's Scottish. It means Little Gate. Bye, Mummy.'

'Bye, darling. See you this afternoon.'

And as the bell rang out and Bea — *Oh, I can't get used to it, Vivie! We keep calling her Baba and she gets so cross* — hurried down the path to the open front door with all the other girls, Flo swung the bike round and hopped on. 'Bye!' she called again, and rang the bell, but Bea had already vanished.

★ ★ ★

She cycled slowly home. She unlocked the front door.

Utter silence greeted her. No Will in his office,

talking away on the phone, swearing at the inky old Gestetner, wondering when a cup of coffee might appear. No companionable little lunch. No geese, honking away in the orchard.

The day yawned ahead.

No Freddie, at the end of it, coming home from school with Baba, racing in to hug her round the middle. Oh, how was he getting on, all that long, long way away?

They'd seen him off at the London station with his trunk and his tuck box and grey flannel suit, his little white face. One of the masters on the platform had looked sweet: young and handsome. 'Don't you worry, Mrs Sutherland. I'll keep an eye.' Mr Ward. She thought that was it. So kind.

She walked into the kitchen.

'Snowy?'

A little sound answered her. There he was, stretching and yawning.

'Hello, my darling. How are you getting on?'

He was getting on better than she was, that was a certainty. He'd licked all the butter off his paws, he'd explored the garden. He'd put his nose round every door in the house, found a nice warm Rayburn in here, the one thing that linked them all to happy Melcote days, and settled down. She'd write and tell Freddie that, in her weekly letter. The boys were only allowed to write home once a week.

Darling Mummy and Daddy, I hope you are both very well. I am very well. I am learning Latin. On Friday we watched our First XI play the First XI from Southbrook. We won. I am looking forward to seeing you all again. How is Snowy? Lots of love from Freddie.

In the first letter there had been dozens of kisses at the end. Now there were none. All their letters were read. He must have been told.

'Oh, Snowy.' Flo kneeled down beside him, stroked his ears. Autumn sun shone weakly through the dusty windowpane, still uncurtained. There was nowhere here for him to sit and let the morning sun shine through his ears, as it had in the cottage dining room. And this window at the side overlooked not a green, and a lane, but a concrete passage. She got up stiffly, went to the garden window, moving past a heap of boxes, still unpacked. What was *in* them all?

'Oh, Snowy,' she said again, and then the phone rang. She raced to the dining room.

'Hello? Vivie! Oh, darling, how lovely, I was just feeling a bit — '

They talked for twenty minutes, something that would have been impossible in Melcote, unless Will was out on a Call. She heard all about Hugo, starting on his A levels, she heard about the Paying Guests, had words with the parent-birds, put the phone down feeling a hundred times better.

★   ★   ★

The school was enormous. Simply huge. When you walked back from the playing fields, you

223

could see it went on for ever. Masses of chimney pots. Creeper all over it, turning red. One or two masters lived out here in the grounds: nice Mr Ward, for instance, who taught Geography, and seemed to like him. Inside were the Dorms. Classrooms. Changing Rooms. Matron's Room. Headmaster's Office. That was Mr Campbell-Davies.

Deputy-Headmaster's Office: that was Mr Lansdowne, very tall, with a whiskery white moustache. In a good mood he had a twinkly smile, but he did most of the beatings. There were different kinds: the cane, the slipper, the gym shoe. Sometimes a ruler on the bare hand.

Freddie hadn't had any of these yet.

What was it like, to be beaten? He couldn't imagine it.

He did know one thing: he was hungry. He was hungry from the moment he woke up to the moment he went to bed. Breakfast was porridge and toast, with an egg on Sundays, and a flapjack from the tuck box after church. Lunch was lunch: shepherd's pie, or hot pot or something: that was a proper meal, with pudding. But after that, all they had was a drink of milk and two slices of bread and butter and jam, at four o'clock before Prep. They were on the go all day: lessons, bells, breaks, running about and no mooching, lunch, more running about, lessons, games — 'Come on! Pass! Pass! *Move*, Sutherland!' Then change, then just the bread and butter and jam, then Prep, then bedtime.

He was starving. He was homesick and starving.

As for the lessons . . . At the end of each one, you went up to the master to get him to sign your ticket: that was to show you'd been working properly. If you hadn't, he didn't sign it, and you were in trouble.

Freddie had an exercise book for each subject, all stacked up in his desk, with his name on. F. Sutherland, E14, Arithmetic. F. Sutherland, E14, History. F. Sutherland, E14, Latin. It went on and on, and Latin, with Mr Lansdowne, was the worst. Sometimes he was funny and nice. Sometimes he was frightening, and his brown eyes glinted beneath the whiskery white.

'*Amo, amas, amat,*' they all chanted. 'I love, You love, He She or It loves.' It was all chalked up on the board: they copied it down. '*Amo, amas, amat,* We all love the cat,' whispered Bell Minor, next to him. Freddie giggled. A piece of chalk came whizzing through the air. It caught him right on the ear, and he yelped. 'Next time it's the board rubber, Sutherland. Understand?'

'Yes, sir.' He rubbed his smarting ear. For a moment he felt like crying, but he just managed not to.

Apart from the chalk, the first few lessons weren't too bad, but then it got more difficult, and then there were Tests. Conjugations and declensions. Cases. They'd done nouns and verbs and all that sort of thing at the Miss Beasleys, but here, in Latin, he couldn't get the hang of it. Even the stuff that was supposed to be easy.

'What does *sum* mean, Sutherland? Come on.'

'Um. Is it a noun, sir?'

225

'A *noun?*'

The whole class fell about, at the way Mr Lansdowne said it. Freddie went scarlet.

'It is not a noun, Sutherland, it's the first person singular of the verb To Be. It means 'I am'. And what are you, you dim, dim boy?'

He didn't know, he couldn't think, he was bright red and fighting back tears.

★ ★ ★

'Mummy,' he sobbed into his pillow at night. 'Mummy.'

'Is that Sutherland?'

'Is that weedy Sutherland?'

They were beside him in the dark.

'Does he want his mummy, then?'

'Is he a little weedy mummy's boy?'

They poked him and jabbed him. They pulled away the pillow.

'Stop it! Give it back!'

He leaped out of bed, his nose streaming. Footsteps came along the corridor. The pillow and the other boys were back in bed before you could say knife, lying like ramrods.

'Sutherland.' The light was snapped on. 'What are you doing out of bed?'

'I — I — sorry, sir.'

'Get back at once.'

'Yes, sir.'

He scrambled in, sniffing everything back.

'Not crying, are you?'

'No, sir.'

'Nothing to cry about.' Mr Newsome strode

over. 'Where's your pillow?'

He couldn't speak. He thought he knew which one had it, but they'd kill him if he said. Mr Newsome stood in the middle of the dorm.

'All right, boys,' he said wearily. 'Who's got Sutherland's pillow?' He made it sound funny; there were muffled sounds. It also sounded as if Sutherland was a wet and a weed, as if anyone could just come and take his pillow whenever they wanted. 'Count of five, or the whole dorm's in detention tomorrow. One, two — '

'Me, sir.'

A heavy sigh. 'It would be you, Collins. Go on, give it back. And apologise.'

Collins got out of bed and came over. He dropped the pillow on the counterpane. 'Sorry, Sutherland.'

He nodded.

'The first boy to say another word goes to see Mr Lansdowne in the morning.' Mr Newsome snapped the light off again. 'Good night.'

'Good night, sir.' It rippled down the dorm.

Then there was silence.

Freddie pulled down the pillow into his arms. He didn't dare even whisper Mummy's name, but he pulled her close and hugged her, and thought of her, all snug by the fire in the sitting room, mending something with the sewing case he and Baba had given her — doing it not very well, but doing it, while Daddy went out to put the geese to bed.

Then he remembered.

★ ★ ★

227

'Good morning, gentlemen.'

James Marshall put down a file on the gleaming mahogany table. Beside him, Miss Bell, his secretary, distributed the agenda and pulled out her shorthand pad. Will gave her a little wink, and she blushed. Middle-aged, unmarried, the perfect secretary. Little bit lonely, perhaps?

'Right,' said Marshall. 'We begin with the Common Agricultural Policy. As you all know, this is on the way . . . '

And the talk began. Subsidies, quotas, price-support mechanisms. On and on it went. No doubt about it, he had to get a hell of a lot of stuff under his belt.

And by lunchtime he was glad to get out of the place for a bit. He took his briefcase, had lunch round the corner in a little café he'd got fond of, behind Swan & Edgar, reading through a lot of bumf. Import tariffs. Ghastly stuff. Then he walked down to St James's Park.

Oh, that was better. He walked towards the lake: ducks sailing across the water, waddling along the bank, quack-quacking away. Of course, he couldn't have lunch on his own every day, wouldn't want to, and it wouldn't look good. And they seemed a good bunch on the whole, he'd make friends. But for now . . .

He leaned on the rail, wishing he had a few crusts to throw down. 'Quack, quack,' he said quietly, and he thought of the geese, of old Gander, waddling over that gorgeous bright grass beneath the apple trees. All gone now, to a chap in Sutton Bassett, and even he'd had to blink back tears when they went.

Had he done the right thing?
Bit late to ask that now, Sutherland.

★ ★ ★

Flo woke with a start, from the deepest of the deep. My God, what was the time?

She looked at the alarm clock on the bedside table: ten past three! She'd forgotten to set it — oh, how could she? Snugly beside her on the eiderdown, Snowy slept on. She turfed him off, leaped out of bed. No tea ready, and she felt as if someone had hit her over the head with a mallet. She'd thought a little nap would do her good.

She clambered on to the bike and rode away in the fresh autumn air, reaching the school gate with all the other mothers just as the bell rang. Out came the girls in their hats and blazers, Bea chatting away as if she'd been here for years.

'How was your day?' Flo asked, as they ticked along.

'The maths is hard.' Bea rattled on about algebra, and things to the power of six.

'Daddy will be able to help you,' said Flo, as they came into quiet Rushbrook Road. 'If he's not too tired.'

IF HE'S NOT TOO TIRED.

★ ★ ★

You had to make a tremendous dash for it, changing at East Croydon. And the crowds! Swarms of them, all in their bowler hats and briefcases, looking at their watches, pushing

229

and shoving to get their favourite seat: pretty pitiful, quite frankly, but nobody wanted to end up standing in the corridor.

Anyway, he'd made it, and he sat in the middle of the compartment, having a look at his fellow passengers as they pulled away. Anyone he recognised? Any pretty girls? There were usually a few little secretaries doing the commute, cheered the journey up a bit, chatting away, powdering their noses. Not today. Squashed up in his seat, looking out at the darkening countryside, the lights from all the little towns, he had a word or two with the chap next to him, who turned out to live in Dorking, and worked for a big firm of London accountants. He'd been commuting for twenty-seven years.

'Good Lord.' They must be about the same age. 'Good Lord,' he said again, and the chap smiled, and shut his eyes, couldn't blame him. Will shut his own eyes, and took himself for a moment to the trains of India: the jammed corridors, people clinging on to the roof as they pulled away, steam rising into the burning sky. He saw the smoke rising from the villages, the children waving, the bullocks hauling a wooden cart heaped up with cane. The wheels of the train rattled under him, under him: he was there as if he had never left it, young and fit and ready for anything, leaping on to old Kolynos, riding for miles.

'Redstone! Redstone! Change here for Ryehurst and all stations to Guildford.'

He woke with a start, grabbed his briefcase. Doors slammed, and he was off again, down the concrete steps and up the next lot, on to the platform where the Ryehurst train was waiting. He shook India away, looked at his watch. Six forty-five: Freddie would be in bed by now. Sounded as if it was all going swimmingly. Thank God for that — made all this worthwhile. And he stood in the corridor, stretching his legs for the last lap, looking out on to the lights of Redstone and then the dark outline of the hills.

★　★　★

Lights out. Mr Newsome prowling along the corridor.

'Mummy,' sobbed Freddie into his pillow, as quietly as he could.

2

There were Outings. For Freddie this meant a week of churning anticipation and so much nervous excitement on the day that he could hardly touch his breakfast, famished though he was. It meant a Saturday morning of the usual prep but then the unusual gathering in the hall as car after car pulled up over the gravel.

'Darling! Gosh, you look well.'

In came the mothers in hats, and the boys shrank into manly embarrassment, brusquely allowing a kiss, shaking hands with their fathers, following them out to the car.

'We've found a super place for lunch.'

One after another they peeled off, and those boys whose parents, like Freddie's, lived at some distance, hung hungrily about.

'Not here yet, Sutherland? Go and kick a ball about with Fletcher.'

They went outside, ran up and down in the cold, stopping to look every time a car drew up at the gates.

For Will, Flo and Bea, Outings meant getting up as early on a Saturday as on any other day, a flaming nuisance for Will and a huge effort for Flo, who had spent the day before baking new supplies for the tuck box. They had a good breakfast to sustain them for the journey, and then: 'In the car!' They piled in.

'Got the map?'

Flo shut her eyes. Map-reading was hell, and they got lost every time.

'Right here.'

'Jolly good.' Out went the yellow indicator, tick tick tick, as Will pulled out into the road. 'We're off!'

The journey was a hundred miles. All the way up to London, all the way through it, and out into Hertfordshire, where Will's father, oh so long ago, had had a parish before the Norfolk days.

'It was a marvellous time, tip-top school. Got me into Shrewsbury — not that I enjoyed that much.' Will looked in the mirror. 'You all right there, Bea?'

'Fine, thanks.' She was gazing out of the window, giving marks to all the houses. To those she liked best she gave a little wave, like the Queen.

They came into London.

'Traffic's building up a bit. What happens after Wandsworth?'

Flo didn't know. She gave him a Glacier Mint from the glove compartment. He snaffled it up.

Then: 'Is this Hammersmith Bridge?'

She thought it was. They followed the traffic over it; seagulls cried.

'Now then. Right or left?'

She hadn't a clue.

'We'd better stop and ask.'

Stopping and Asking was always a feature: indicating, slowing, then frantically winding the window down as some sensible-looking person came walking along —

'Excuse me!' Will leaned across Flo. 'I say! Excuse me!'

The sensible person looked startled.

'Sorry to bother you, we're just wondering — '

At last they were sailing along pretty country roads, with the trees in autumn colours and really nice houses for Bea to wave at, a duck pond here and there.

'I know this bit like the back of my hand,' said Will, and then, as the school gates came into view, 'At last, at promised last, I see a promise of my fair one here.'

'Well done, darling.' Flo patted his hand.

'Nothing to it. Tell you what, why don't we take him out to the zoo?'

★   ★   ★

The zoo was thirty miles from the school, up the B486, a road number none of them ever forgot.

'What did you say it was?' snapped Will, as Freddie sat ashen-faced beside him, the window wide open, everyone getting cold.

'The B486,' chorused Bea and Flo from the back.

Flo leaned forward and stroked Freddie's shoulder.

'All right, darling?'

He nodded infinitesimally as Will saw the sign, put his foot on the brake, then the accelerator, then the brake again. Freddie put his hand to his mouth.

'We'll have a lovely time when we get there.'

When they got there, paying a fortune at the gate, Flo flung open her door and rushed to fling open Freddie's, just in time. He was sick all over the grass.

'Poor darling. Mummy's here.' She wiped his face with the flannel she'd brought specially, gave him a drink of water, took him on her lap. 'Next time I'll give you a Kwell.'

'Poor old chap,' said Will, getting the picnic basket out. 'Well done for not doing it in the car. Now, then, here we are, you'll feel better when you've had something to eat.'

'I need to go to the toilet.'

'The *toilet*?' Flo looked at Bea over Freddie's head. 'Never, ever say 'toilet'. The lavatory. The lav.'

'WC,' said Will cheerfully, and then, 'I'll take them. Come on, kiddos. We'll have an expedish.'

Lions and tigers roared in the distance. Off they went, and Flo put her head in her hands. Out of the basket, when they returned, she brought hard-boiled eggs with tiny twists of salt in tissue paper, ham and lettuce sandwiches, the Thermos. The lettuce had gritty little bits in it.

'Sorry — I was sure I'd washed it. Freddie, darling, have some lemon barley water, that'll perk you up.'

Will drained the Thermos cup of coffee. 'That's better. Can you hear the sea lions?'

They could. He did an imitation, and everyone laughed.

'I knew this would be a good idea,' he said, breaking up Fruit & Nut chocolate. 'Bloody expensive, but still. Jolly good show, Sutherland. Now, who wants to see what? Freddie? This is your treat, old chap.'

Freddie looked down at the tartan rug. 'Can I just stay with Mummy?'

'After we've come all this way? I suppose so. Come on, Bea, let's see what's what. Take my hand.'

They set off towards the shrieks and roars.

'Penguins first? It might be feeding time. Gosh, this is fun.' It was clouding over. He squeezed her hand. 'You warm enough?'

'Yes, thanks.'

A great roar sounded in the distance.

'Did I ever tell you my story of The Tiger of Tulsipore?'

'I think so.' She turned to look back at the others. Freddie and Flo were climbing back into the car.

'Ough, ough, ough!' said Will, being a sea lion. People turned round. Bea took her hand away.

★   ★   ★

An hour or so later, after the penguins, the terrifying tiger, gorgeous giraffe, and the sea lions, after the baby elephant — 'Mummy'd love that,' — they made their way back to the car, beneath a darkening sky.

'Now what?'

They stopped. Through the open window they could hear Freddie howling. Will frowned.

'Stay here.'

But as he walked over the grass Bea saw Flo waving him away. Then she put her arms round Freddie again. He strode back, his face like thunder.

'I don't know. I don't bloody know.'

And they stood there in silence, as Freddie's dreadful howling went on and on. Bea looked at

236

Will, and then away. He looked terrifying. She didn't know what to say, she didn't know what to do. So she just swallowed, and did nothing. The picnic remains were still there on the tartan rug. They sat down. 'I don't know,' Will said again, and unscrewed the Thermos. 'Ugh!' He spat out cold coffee. It started to rain.

'Right, that's it. Come on.'

They threw the remains into the basket, bundled up the rug, full of crumbs, and raced to the car. Will flung open the boot, hurling everything inside. Flo and Freddie, wrapped round one another in the back, jumped a mile as he banged it shut. The howling stopped abruptly. Bea scrambled into the front. Will came round, got in, and slammed his door.

'What's going on?'

'Poor Freddie's homesick, that's all,' said Flo, wiping his face with her hankie. 'There you are, darling, better now?'

Will shut his eyes. 'I don't know,' he said for the hundredth time. He looked in the mirror. 'You'll soon settle down, old chap. Always a bit difficult at first. We'd better get back now — want to come in the front?'

Bea turned round. Freddie shook his head.

'We'll be all right with the window open,' said Flo. 'If you could just try not to stop and start so much.'

'Stop and start?' He turned on the ignition. 'Can't even drive the bloody car right.' He pulled out. 'Sit back, Baba.'

'Bea,' she murmured.

'Shut up!'

They were off. Bea closed her eyes, hearing Freddie's sniffs from the back and Flo's sweet soothing noises.

★ ★ ★

'I've done my best,' said Will that evening, when at last they reached home. They had left white-faced, tear-stained, silent Freddie with nice Mr Ward, ticking off everyone's names as they returned.

'I know what it's like, Mrs Sutherland. Don't worry, he'll be all right, won't you, Sutherland?'

Freddie gave a struggling smile.

'Well done.'

And he and Mr Ward were off together, into the noisy throng of boys, making their way into the dining room for milk and bread and jam.

'That sounds all right,' said Will, as they dashed back to the car in the rain.

'He says it's all they have until breakfast,' said Flo, trying to keep up. 'Didn't you think he looked thin?'

'Thin?'

Now it was after six, dark and wet, Bea half-asleep in the back.

'I've done my best,' said Will again, turning off the engine. 'He'll settle down, you'll see.'

HE'LL SETTLE DOWN, YOU'LL SEE.

★ ★ ★

There were Test Papers. The words came to Bea like snarling animals: Test Papers growled, hid in waiting, were frightening and impossible. With

238

them, the words 'Eleven-plus' hung before her — as all words did, but larger and darker.

ELEVEN-PLUS.

'Non-verbal Reasoning,' said Miss Walters, giving out the papers. She looked at the wall clock. 'You have thirty minutes.'

Bea's class had been practising Non-verbal Reasoning all last year. At The Rookery no one had ever mentioned it. Verbal to her bones, she gazed at the paper before her.

In the following questions, there are three or four shapes in boxes on the left and then a space followed by another shape in a box. Each box on the left has a pair of letters in it which are a code for the shape in that box. You need to work out the code that applies to the shapes on the left and then choose which pair of letters should be given to the shape on the right. There are five possible answers, but only one is correct and must be marked on the answer sheet.

What were they talking about? What on earth were they *talking about?*

'If you get stuck on one question, move on to the next,' said Miss Walters, at her desk beneath the blackboard.

Bea moved on.

A line of little black shapes, doing things. A circle in a box balanced on a square and then tipped sideways. A triangle without a box rested on a circle and then fell over. So it went on. There were arrows.

One of these five shapes is related to the shape before the arrow in the same way as the two shapes in the box are related to each other. Choose which one and mark it on the answer sheet.

The wall clock ticked, the windows shook in the November wind. All around her, girls were bent over the papers, ticking and circling away. Bea held her pencil over a box.

★　★　★

She walked home from school with Flo, the bicycle ticking beside them. Leaves blew about.

'What sort of a day?'

'We did Non-verbal Reasoning.'

'What on earth is that?'

'You have to work out how things are connected to other things. I think.'

'And how are they?'

'I don't know.'

★　★　★

'I can't do this,' she said to the bird on the cherry bough. He listened attentively, just as Squeaker used to do. 'I don't know what they're talking about,' she said. Deep in the old dark leaves, he watched her with his beady eye.

Darling Mummy and Daddy,
  I hope you are both well. Thank you for a super Outing. It was nice at the Zoo. We are

*working for end of term Exams. The weather
has been very cold. We lost against Belfield
last week but we won against Markham. I
am still in the Fourth Eleven. I am looking
forward to seeing you again soon.*

With love from Freddie
PS. Please give my love to Bea and Snowy.

It was waiting on the mat when Flo cycled home
from Micklegate. She'd kissed Bea goodbye as
always.

'Good luck, my darling, and try not to worry.
Soon be Christmas!'

'Christmas is weeks away.'

'You don't *have* to pass it.' She kissed her
again.

'I *want* to pass it. Everyone's going to pass it.'

'But if you don't, you can go to Dolphin
House — you'll probably go there anyway.'

'There's Fiona!' And she was gone, looking so
pretty in that grey felt beret, but much too pale.
Oh, school was ghastly, ghastly. Flo weaved the
bike through the Other Mothers. What a smug
lot they were. She gave the bell a vicious little
ring.

And here was this stilted, pitiful little letter,
beautifully set out, perfectly spelled and
punctuated, with sadness in every line. She sat at
the uncleared breakfast table, reading it again.
Nice at the Zoo. Hell at the Zoo. Those howls in
the car, as she held him close.

'What is it, my darling? Tell Mummy.' It was
everything, everything: that was all he could say.

She poured out the last of the stone-cold tea;

241

she pictured the prep room, the boys all writing their weekly letters after chapel, longing for Sunday lunch. He *was* thin, how could Will not see it? She saw them all dipping their brand-new pens in the inkwells, saw the master up at the blackboard.

'First, you hope that your parents are well. Always. Then you thank them for their last letter. This week you thank them for the outing. Say something about it, remember! Yes, Harris?'

'Sir, how do you spell 'grateful'?'

'Good boy.'

Squeak of the chalk on the board.

Oh, poor little Freddie, what could she do? She cleared away breakfast, went into the sitting room and opened the bureau. There amongst a heap of lists and muddle was her wedding-present writing case, so worn now, the zip broken, stamps poking out. *For my darling Flo,* Will had written, on regiment paper. 'Rajputana Rifles' was embossed at the top in shiny black. *Delhi, 1946.* She still had that little note tucked inside.

Traffic went past. She heard herself give an enormous sigh, and pulled out the Basildon Bond.

My darling Freddie, Thank you so much for your letter. What a good speller you are! And your writing is simply beautiful...

★ ★ ★

On Sundays, before church, Harris, the Dorm Captain, did a locker inspection. You had to have everything lined up. Spongebag, slippers, brush and comb. Bible. Library book. Before Lights, you had to read a chapter of the Bible, and then you could read your library book: they chose them on Wednesday afternoons.

Freddie gazed at the library shelves. A lot of the books were History: the masters were always on about people called Rosemary Sutcliffe and G. A. Henty, but he wanted something like the kind of books they used to read in the cottage, something with country things in it, like the Speckledy Hen bringing eggs in her basket, or Walter Duck on Blackberry Farm, quacking away in his scarf. Of course, he was too old for that kind of thing now.

The Bumper Book for Boys, *The Boys' Book of Adventure* — like *Biggles*, those went in a flash. Then he found something: *Down the Bright Stream*. He opened it, turned the pages. There were pictures of very old gnomes, sailing a little boat along. It made him think a bit of the canal in Melcote: he took it up to the desk, and got it stamped. He tucked it into his locker and longed each day to read it.

'Sutherland, your spongebag's on top of your Bible,' said Harris. 'Don't you know that nothing should ever go on top of a Bible?'

He knew; he took it off. How had it got there?

'What are you reading?' Harris pulled out the gnomes. 'Dodder and Sneezewort? *Cloudberry?*'

'It's jolly good,' said Freddie, blushing.

Harris turned the pages, and read out a bit. A snigger ran all down the dorm.

Freddie blushed deeper, and he felt his face go

funny. 'You're making it sound silly,' he said. 'It's jolly good really.'

Harris read a bit more. 'It's weedy,' he said, and put it back in the locker. 'Hello, what's this?' He fished out a picture of a baby koala, clinging on to its mother with a happy smile. Beneath, threaded through with blue ribbon, hung a tiny calendar.

I got it in Woollies! Flo had written. *You can cross the days off, darling* —

He had crossed them off. There were twenty-three to go, and no more Outings.

'A baby koala!' Harris swung it by the ribbon. 'With his mummy!'

Freddie made a grab for it. 'Give it to me!'

It went spinning through the air. Collins caught it.

'It's mine! My mother sent it!'

'His mummy sent it!'

Freddie kicked his shin. In moments, they were all upon him. Then Mr Newsome came in.

★ ★ ★

Flo stood on a chair, draping silver balls on green satin ribbons through Panther's gaping jaws. His yellowing teeth were perfect for the task. She slipped the ribbon over his red plaster tongue and through the bottom molars, got down to see if both balls were evenly balanced, reached up and tugged down the right-hand side. There!

Upstairs, Freddie and Bea were still in their nightclothes. Oh, thank God the boy was home.

She'd feed him up, she'd send him back fit and strong. And she carried the chair back to the dining room and stood there, working out where to put the tree.

Freddie and Bea sat on the carpet in the empty playroom, not a stick of furniture in here yet, only the gramophone and a few old toys.

'Yes, We Have No Bananas' — the record wound slowly down, and the needle went scratching away.

'Play it again,' said Freddie, pulling his dressing gown round him. He sat by the window, looking down at the wintry trees across the road as Bea cranked the handle once more.

'I'm so glad you're back,' she said.

'So am I.' Up here at the top of the house it was just as cold as school, but it didn't matter. There were three whole weeks before he had to go back.

'Tell me what it's like,' said Bea, when they'd sung along with 'No Bananas' for the millionth time. She lifted the needle off.

'There are different kinds of beating, but I've only had the cane.' He felt his face begin to tighten, and stretched his mouth wide.

She frowned. 'Don't do that. What was it like?'

'Awful. We all had it, for making a scrum in the dorm.'

'Poor Freddie.' She wrapped her arms round her knees, watching him. Then, after a moment, she said: 'It sounds like one of the records at Auntie Agnes's.' They loved her records. 'Sort of Stanley Holloway. 'There's different kinds of beating, but I've only had the cane.'' She got up and sang it, making up the tune.

They sang it together, marching down the stairs.

★ ★ ★

The tree, with its lovely coloured lights, stood in front of the French windows, the presents piled up beneath. Red barley-sugar candles, clipped to the boughs with little metal holders, leaned at mad angles towards the floor.

'Never, never, never leave a candle unattended,' said Flo, as the children stood gazing at it all.

'Burn the bloody house down,' said Will, bringing in a couple of pegs. Four days out of the office, four days without commuting — my God, he deserved this. He handed a glass to Flo.

'My darling. It all looks splendid.'

She gave him a kiss. 'I *love* Christmas!'

'But can't we light the candles at all?' asked Bea.

'No need,' said Will, as he and Flo clinked glasses. 'You've got the fairy lights. And never leave those unattended, either, do you understand? It only takes one to blow a fuse and the whole tree's in flames.' He sipped his whisky. 'Burn the whole house down,' he said again.

★ ★ ★

On Christmas morning Freddie took his stocking up to Bea's room, and they opened them both in the dark, pulling out tiny packages wrapped in newspaper: packets of Polos, Woollies notebooks, Fry's Turkish Delight, walnuts and an orange, right at the bottom. They poked about, feeling to see if there was anything else. Then they sucked Polos together, tucked up in Bea's bed.

After breakfast, Will put the Bird in the oven, quite a performance, and then they had the presents. At last! He produced a clipboard from his briefcase, and wrote down in columns what everyone had had, from whom, so they could do their thank-you letters without making awful mistakes.

'To Will, from Flo,' he said aloud, writing away. 'One box of Black Magic chocs.'

'Darling, you really don't need to write that down.'

Nothing could stop him. He looked up from the column. 'Freddie, do stop making those faces.'

'Sorry,' said Freddie, covering his mouth. He didn't even know he was making them, half the time.

The surprise was the present Will gave to Flo. He pulled it out from beneath the tree, something large and soft and exciting, wrapped — dear Will — in Woollies paper, shiny and awful. Never mind.

'What's *this?*' She unwrapped it slowly, rustling away.

'Mummy, go *on!*'

Will was brandishing the ballpoint. 'To Flo, from Will . . . '

Out came a soft fluffy dressing gown, in duck-egg blue. For once, even the colour was right.

'*Darling!*'

'Got it in Swan & Edgar,' said Will happily. 'Like it?'

'I love it!' She pulled it on, over her new red cardigan.

Bea and Freddie stroked it.

'You look lovely, Mummy.'

Kisses all round.

Then the children were fumbling under the tree, pulling out Agnes's brown paper parcel, which had arrived excitingly three days before Christmas. They read the labels, handed out four packages.

'To Will, from Agnes,' said Will with his clipboard. 'Save that string,' he added, as Flo reached for the scissors.

'I really don't think you need to write it down,' said Flo, as he unwrapped a bilious green hand-knitted pullover, flecked with bilious yellow. 'You won't forget that in a hurry.'

'She does her best. Poor old Agnes.'

'She's not poor now she's got Neville. Now, then, what have you got, Freddie?'

'A book,' he said flatly.

'Quite a big book!'

He shrugged, tearing the paper. And then —

A bear in red jumper and cheerful yellow checked scarf smiled joyfully up at him, suspended beneath a vast green balloon, on a seat with an engine and propeller and huge springy feet.

'Rupert! A Rupert Annual!'

They positively had to haul him away from it, when it was time for church.

Will took them both, while Flo did the sprouts, laid the table and watched over the Bird, a task so awful she could hardly think. Huge great thing. All that *stuffing*. She checked the roasting time again and again. 'Don't even think of basting it,' said Will, as he corralled the children. 'I'll do it when we get back. Right, kids, we're off!'

Church was lovely, the bells ringing away, a great big tree, holly in all the windows and the crib with its tiny light shining in the corner, just like Melcote. They sang 'Hark! the Herald' until they almost burst, and then they went home for Christmas lunch, starving.

★ ★ ★

'Marvellous,' said Will. Bea had found the sixpence in the pudding, they'd passed round his Black Magic chocolates. 'Marvellous,' he said again, snaffling an orange cream. 'Couldn't have done the whole thing better myself. My darling.' And he and Flo got up and hugged one another, as the tree lights shone sweetly away — on even at lunchtime; it was Christmas, after all.

Freddie got down from his chair. Where was Snowy? He found him in the sitting room, flat out on Panther's skin in front of the fire. He bent down and stroked him, and wished him Happy Christmas. Then he straightened up. It was lovely and warm in here, with cheerful cards all along the mantelpiece, amongst the ivory elephants. One caught his eye. A pheasant was walking through a snowy field, his plumage glossy and bright against the blue-white countryside, the field gate trimmed with snow, the misty sky.

He gazed at the card, picked it up and opened it. *Best wishes to all of you from Mike.*

Mike had helped on the farm: he couldn't remember him, but that wasn't the point. The point was how that picture made him feel, as he put it back and stood there, looking and looking. It made him ache with longing, so badly that he wished he'd never seen it. There was the country, there was everything they'd left.

'I want it back,' he whispered. Firelight flickered. He stood there making one of his faces, a horrible one, he could feel it, but it didn't matter: no one could see. He shut his eyes, and willed himself into that field, that snow.

3

When Bea was eleven, and had comprehensively failed the Eleven-plus, not once but twice on the re-sit, — 'It doesn't matter, darling, you can go to Dolphin House,' — she was allowed to walk to and from Micklegate by herself. Flo took her for the last time as term began in September, that butterflies-in-your tummy, back-to-school feeling palpable in both of them as they walked up Rushbrook Road.

'You promise you will always look both ways,' she said to Bea, walking along in her new (second-hand) grey blazer.

'Promise.'

'And never, never cross the main road except when the lights are red.'

'I've *said*, Mummy. Stop fussing.'

Lorries roared down Ryehurst Hill.

'Leave me here. Watch me cross, then you'll know I'll be all right.'

Flo swallowed. 'Go on, then. Bye, darling.'

'Bye!' And she was over in a flash, turning on the other side and waving. 'See?' she shouted as the lights went green and the traffic began to move.

Cars of Other Mothers turned into Summers Road — all those women at the wheel. How on earth did they do it? A girl in one of them waved to Bea and she waved brightly back. Then she hurried on, without a backward glance.

Now what? Flo cycled slowly home.

A year after moving here, she still knew almost no one. Oh, there were plenty of people she knew by *sight*, people to say hello to down the town, or after church — when she went, which wasn't often. She'd been to tea in one or two Other Mothers' houses, when Bea was there after school with one of her friends, and she'd had them back, of course, but somehow she couldn't connect. Just couldn't get a purchase. There was always the business of Where do you live? and always that silent, infinitesimal but clear-as-the-nose-on-your-face reaction: Croydon Road. Oh. There.

She unlocked the front door on to the empty hall.

India — oh, beloved India — was everywhere before her. The elephant table in the corner, Panther on the wall, his ears still tufty and his snarl not such a bad thing, really: he knew them all so well now. There were the photos: Will in uniform, Will hung with garlands, smiling into the sun as Panther and his rifle lay before him on the baking grass, all the dear Indians in white standing gratefully round. Panther had been a horrid beast when he was alive.

I was quite a nice beast when I was alive, Flo felt herself write in her non-existent diary. Oh, that diary! What the hell was there to write about now?

She went up to the photo of Will in his army uniform: that heavenly khaki shirt and jacket, that sweet loving smile. Such a darling man, really. *Always*, he'd written in the corner.

Always. Will. That was soon after he'd proposed.

Flo stood before the photograph and it all came flooding back. She saw herself up on deck, as the steamer moved slowly into Bombay harbour, through the hot sea breeze, all her dear friends from the RWVS around her. What fun those girls had been! Darling Rhoda, longing for her chap still out in Burma, demanding from her bunk as the voyage and her waiting went on and on: 'How long, oh Lord, how long?' Darling Ann, striding about on deck in her linen dress and scarlet lipstick, a G & T in hand. 'We're going to have a marvellous time, you wait and see.' Sweet funny Judy. 'Haven't got a gasper, have you, Ann? I seem to be completely out.' Deck quoits and sparkling sea and dinner at the Captain's table. All of them laughing their heads off at nothing.

Where were they all? Darling Rhoda had died of a broken heart when the chap from Burma left her. They said you couldn't, but she had. Ann sent Christmas cards from Hong Kong. Judy and her gaspers had entirely dropped from view.

And now? *Always Will* was out of the house from morning to night and quite often difficult when he was in it. Vivie, the only woman she could really talk to and laugh with, was a hundred miles away, with her bridge parties and her Paying Guests, not to mention looking after the parent-birds and Hugo.

And here am I, thought Flo, as the emptiness of the house pressed all around her, with another yawning bloody day ahead, not a single person I

253

want to have coffee with, or tea with, or ever set eyes on again, quite honestly, and not even needed to pick up Bea from school.

Well. That did mean an extra half-hour in bed with Snowy.

'Always a silver lining,' she said, as he came wandering out of the kitchen, and burst into tears.

★ ★ ★

Funnily enough, once the whole dorm had been caned together, things got a little bit better. He was one of them, now, and the bullying turned more to ragging, things you could laugh at. Mummy's Boy became Silly old Sutherland when he dropped a ball or got too close to the Bunsen burner in the lab, and singed his eyebrows.

'Watch out!'

'You stupid boy!'

'Silly old Sutherland,' said Collins, as the bell rang. 'You OK?'

But making friends didn't stop him feeling sick with nerves before some of the lessons. Nor crying his eyes out at the end of the holidays. Up in his bedroom with Mummy, holding him close as he howled.

'I don't *want* to go back! I *hate it* there.'

He could hear the sitting-room door slam downstairs.

'Tell him not to make me go back. Tell him I *hate it!*'

'Oh, darling Freddie.'

254

At last he made himself stop, and she kissed him and went slowly downstairs and opened the sitting-room door. He could hear Daddy asking, 'What's going on?' and then the murmur of their voices, Mummy trying to say something, Daddy growling away.

'No son of mine — ' he said, and then the door was shut.

Freddie turned over his wet pillow and lay there, frowning.

No son of mine —

What was he talking about? Of course he was his son.

★ ★ ★

Flo stuffed the tuck box to the brim, but they only had tuck on Sundays, and the rest of the week he was starving. They all were. He lived from Outing to Outing, and the prospect of a picnic or a decent lunch, and then he spent the whole day crying and couldn't eat a thing.

'Freddie, for God's sake.' Will flung down his napkin. 'This is supposed to be a treat.' All around them in The Duck Garden other families were tucking in. But even the name of the restaurant, all white tablecloths and shiny glasses, was enough to set him off.

'It makes him think of Melcote,' said Bea, as he ran from the room and Flo ran quickly after. 'It reminds us of the geese.' She put down her knife and fork and looked at the tablecloth.

Will gave an enormous sigh.

'I've done my best,' he said. 'I can do no more.'

255

Bea didn't know what to say. They ate in silence, waiting for the others.

'How about a knickerbocker glory?' he said, when they reappeared, Freddie white and tear-stained, Flo holding his hand. 'Would that cheer you up, old chap?'

It helped, though Will had to finish it.

'Marvellous. Want a bit, Flo?'

★ ★ ★

Darling Mummy and Daddy, Thank you so much for the Outing, and espeshly — crossed out — *especially the nikerboker glory...*

'I knew he'd like that,' said Will, laughing. 'The master must have left the spelling deliberately. Got a sense of humour, those chaps.'

'Will, I really do think — '

'Think what?'

She took a deep breath. 'He should come home,' she said. 'He could go to St Peter's. Everyone says it's so good — '

Will's face darkened, and her stomach rose and fell. 'Don't be ridiculous. It's my old school, I loved it. He'll be all right in the end.'

★ ★ ★

He seems at times to be mentally paralysed, Mr Lansdowne had written at the bottom of his end-of-year report. That sounded awful. Will frowned, read it out to him.

'What on earth does he mean?'

Freddie looked down at the dining-room carpet.

'I don't know. Sorry, Daddy.' He felt his face give a tight little twitch, and clenched his hands. The twitch got stronger. He opened his mouth wide, to stop it.

'What are you doing?'

'Nothing. Sorry.' The French windows were open on to the summery garden. He could see Snowy, washing under a bush. 'Can I go now?'

'Oh, Freddie.' Will gave one of his enormous sighs. 'I don't know,' he said, and swivelled round from the roll-top desk. 'Come here.' Freddie inched forward. 'For God's sake — you aren't afraid of me, surely?' He held out his arms. 'We're friends, old chap. We've always been friends. Come and give Daddy a hug.'

Freddie let himself be hugged. He leaned against Will's scratchy tweed jacket, smelling pipe smoke and leather from the elbow patches that Mummy sewed on, poking through the great big needle and huffing.

'You know I love you, don't you?' Will murmured above him. He nodded. 'And you love your old daddy too, don't you?' He nodded again. He felt he was going to cry, but please, please no, he'd cried enough, it was driving everyone mad. He sniffed, and Will kissed him. 'Run along. Go and see what Mummy and Bea are up to. I think I can smell lunch, with any luck.'

★　★　★

Now here he was, back once more, in his second year, feeling sick and looking at his Latin book as Mr Lansdowne came into the form room.

'Good morning, boys.'

'Good morning, Mr Lansdowne.'

Twelve wooden chairs scraped back as everyone rose to their feet.

'Sit down.'

Today was a Test. They were now on the Fourth Declension. The First had been pretty good, really: *Terra, terra, terram, terrae, terrae, terra.* Anyone could do that. Then the plurals, shouted out with gusto: '*Terrae, terrae, terras, terrarum, terris, terris!*'

Terra meant Earth, it was part of Mediterranean, the sea that went round the earth. A bit of the earth, anyway. Southern Europe. North Africa. Nice Mr Ward was taking them through all the seas in Geography, Freddie's best subject. They coloured in maps, they traced outlines of countries, they learned rivers and capital cities and crops. It was interesting. And Mr Ward was never cross. That was the main thing.

But now. The Fourth Declension: lots of nouns. Any one of those they'd learned could come up. His stomach was in knots, and they hadn't even started.

'Open your exercise books.' They opened them. 'Decline in the singular and plural in all its cases the noun *Genu*. Meaning what, Richardson?'

'Is it a kind of animal, sir?'

'An *animal*?'

Richardson was a bit of a favourite of Mr Lansdowne: up at the Master's desk he was smiling tolerantly.

'Yes, sir,' said Richardson boldly. 'The one in the song.'

'Ah. You mean 'I'm a Gnu'. And Mr Lansdowne said it with such an amazingly funny emphasis, just like Michael Flanders, that they all burst out laughing. ''I'm a Gnu,' he said again, making it even funnier, and then, as they rolled about: 'All right, boys, settle down. Thank you for your contribution, Richardson, and no, Genu is not any kind of animal, it's — what is it, Sutherland?'

He was still streaming with tears of laughter. Mr Lansdowne could be so nice, that was the thing, and it reminded him of Daddy humming the tune at breakfast, or putting his head round the door when you weren't expecting it, and just coming out with it: 'I'm a Gnu,' and disappearing.

'Well?'

'Oh, gosh, sir.' What was it? All he could see were gnus, their long bony faces and glinting eyes. 'Sorry, sir.'

Mr Lansdowne sighed elaborately. He shook his head. 'Harris?'

'It means knee, sir.'

'It means knee. Thank you. And what is the ablative plural?'

'*Genibus*, sir,' said Harris, without a flicker of hesitation.

'Good boy. Meaning, Bell Minor?'

'By, with, or from the knees, sir.'

A ripple ran round the form room.

'That's enough,' said Mr L. again, and they knew he meant it. 'Singular and plural, in two neat columns.' They dipped their pens; they started.

He got through it, he knew at least most of it, and as they all put Latin away and got out Religious Knowledge, he breathed a great sigh of relief. Religious Knowledge was all right. He'd known half the Old Testament stories before he even got here: Jacob and Esau, Jacob and the Angel, Cain and Abel, Abraham and Isaac. 'My brother is an hairy man,' Daddy pronounced now and then, for no particular reason. That was Jacob, talking about Esau.

They had to learn the names of all the Books of the Old Testament, in order. Genesis, Exodus, Leviticus . . . Then all the Books of the New Testament, the Gospels, all the Epistles, and the Acts of the Apostles. The Epistles were written by St Paul: he'd written masses. They had to learn verses by heart, and recite them. Today it was from Corinthians 2.

Because of the Latin test, he'd hurried through this last night, so hungry anyway that none of it meant much, and the Latin was more important, because it was Mr L. He'd muffed his verses last week, and had a ticking off, but now, as the Reverend Arthur Wells came limping in, he thought: it'll be OK, I sort of know it.

'Good morning, boys.'

'Good morning, Mr Wells.'

'Sit down.'

They sat. Mr Wells put his Bible on the Master's desk, and put his hands together. They saw him every Sunday, in his flowing white; now, in his tweed jacket and fawn jumper, he looked like any other master, except for the dog collar. On the whole he wasn't too bad — people said he had sciatica, that was why he limped sometimes, and he could get really mad, but Freddie had never seen him in a bate. He was droning on now about St Paul, how after his conversion he'd travelled from Jerusalem to Rome. Freddie's mind began to wander. He was starving: soon it would be break, and the little bottles of silver-topped milk.

'So, boys. Remind me of what you were asked to learn by heart.'

'Corinthians 2, sir,' everyone chorused. 'Chapter vi, verses 1–6.'

'Very good. Now, then. I should like you to take verses in turn.' Mr Wells ran his gaze ran over the boys. 'Ballantyne, you begin, then Sutherland, then Collins . . .'

Freddie swallowed. This meant he had verse 2, the really awful one, the one he'd just skipped last night, thinking, I'll come back to it, but he hadn't, he hadn't.

'Right, then.' Mr Wells was walking towards the desks, his open Bible in hand. He'd be able to check every comma.

'Stand up, Ballantyne. Off you go.'

Ballantyne got to his feet behind his desk, and cleared his throat. ' "We then, as workers together with him," ' he said clearly, ' "beseech you also that ye . . . that ye . . . that ye receive not the grace of God in vain." '

'Well done. Sutherland?'

He got to his feet, his knees almost knocking together. ' "For he saith," ' he began, and came to

261

a grinding halt. ''For he saith . . . ''

''For he saith, I have heard thee,'' prompted Mr Wells.

''For he saith, I have heard thee.'' Freddie heard his voice in the silence all around him, heard Mr Wells come up closer, limping heavily. He fixed his eyes on the blackboard. ''For he saith, I have heard thee,'' he said again, and stopped, and just stood there.

It was no good, there was no use in even trying. 'Sorry, sir.'

'You haven't learned it,' said Mr Wells, right beside him now. 'You simply haven't learned it.'

'Sorry, sir.' He was about to turn round, and look at him, and just hope he'd go on to Collins, but a blow from Mr Wells's Bible suddenly caught him across the side of the head, and he dropped to the desk.

'For the second week running, you haven't learned it!' A second massive blow came again, this time so hard that he shouted out in pain. He put his hand to his ringing ear, then put his head on the desk. He could hardly breathe. Dimly he heard Collins, and then the others, pick up the recital.

''For he saith, I have heard thee in a time accepted . . . behold, now is the time of salvation . . . ''

Lights flashed before him, the ringing went on and on. He felt himself go hot and cold, hot and cold, and then felt most horribly sick.

'' . . . in much patience, in afflictions . . . by kindness, by the Holy Ghost, by love unfeigned.''

It was over. He raised his head. The room

went round and round.

'Sutherland? You will write out those verses this evening, and I will hear you again next week. You will write out fifty lines: *I will learn my work by heart*. Is that clear?'

'Yes, sir.' He put his head back down on the desk.

'Sit up.'

'Sir — '

'Sit up.'

He sat up, as Mr Wells limped up and down, wincing, firing questions about St Paul, until the bell rang at last for break.

'You OK?' whispered Collins, as they all poured out into the hall.

'Not really.'

'Wells is a pig. Shall I take you up to Matron?'

He nodded. They went slowly up the stairs. Matron put her kind beaky nose out of the linen cupboards.

'Well, well, what have we here?'

Collins explained. Matron shook her head, and took Freddie's hand. 'You come with me, Sutherland, have a little rest. Off you go, now, Collins, no need to hover.'

He lay in the San all afternoon, a sick bowl beside him, light just chinking through.

★ ★ ★

There was one terrific thing about being up in London, and that was having a secretary. A proper, trained, efficient woman, all to himself. As it were.

'Morning, Miss Fisher!'

'Good morning, Mr Sutherland.' She rose from her desk in the adjoining office, always here before him. 'Coffee?'

'That would be marvellous.' He hung up his hat and coat, gave her a smile. 'When you're ready.'

Down she sat before him, as he lit his pipe, ready to go, with her spiral-bound notebook and pencil. Nice-looking woman — might have been pretty once. Funny how some of these girls missed the boat; he'd have thought she'd make some chap very happy.

'We'll get the letters done now, then I'd like to spend the whole afternoon on the Grand Plan, if you don't mind.'

'Of course.'

She had it all next door, in a bloody great box file. They'd have fun with that.

The Plan had been tried out with huge success last year. You had to have a pilot for a thing like this, test the water. The RLS should have its own show, he'd suggested: not just stands at the Royal, and the County shows, but something funded by them, something terrific to really put them on the map.

'I'd suggest calling it the RLS Country Sports Fair,' he'd said at a meeting, and a little murmur ran round the mahogany table.

'Bit of a mouthful,' said Roger Hale, he of Forestry and Woodland.

'Tells you exactly what it is, though,' said James Marshall, up at the head of the table.

Will said he had thought of calling it Fish, Fur

& Feather. 'Thought it had quite a ring to it.'

No one thought it had the kind of ring they wanted. In the end, they settled on the RLS Country Fair. Miss Bell wrote it down in the minutes.

'It'll become the RLS Fair before you know it,' said Marshall. 'If it takes off.'

'It'll take off,' said Will. 'I'm pretty sure of that.'

And, my God, it had. The punters had come pouring in. His idea was to hold it each year in the grounds of a stately home. They'd take it round the country, from Longleat to Chatsworth, from Castle Howard to Blenheim Palace. Harewood House. Ripley Manor. You name it.

David Bone, Heritage department, nice chap, had suggested they run the pilot in a place called Hetherington Hall, up in the Peak District. Sounded perfect. Gorgeous grounds, dreadful death duties, house falling apart, needed something to attract new visitors. They went through all the possibilities: gun dogs, clay pigeon shooting, target shooting, field archery, falconry.

'Hold a Hawk,' said Will, as the meeting ended.

'Terrific,' said David Bone.

So, there it had begun, with three nights up in the Peaks last June, weather terrific and a huge success all round. Worth all the outlay, brought in twice what had been predicted, and a pat on the back for Sutherland.

'Jolly good show,' said Marshall, at the end. 'Really splendid.'

There'd be a rise, with any luck at all.

And now they were planning the next show, Miss Fisher getting out the box file after lunch and a call to be made to Sir John Kavanagh, he of Bickland Hall, down on Dartmoor, keen as mustard to get the RLS Fair on board next summer.

'He's on the line now, Mr Sutherland.'

'Jolly dee.'

★ ★ ★

They were spending half-term in Wimbledon with Auntie Agnes. And Uncle Neville, of course. And Tinkerbell, their big fluffy tortoiseshell cat, whose tail had once caught fire from a spark on the hearth. Every time they went there, Bea and Freddie hoped this would happen again.

'Lunchtime!' called Auntie Agnes. 'Come and wash your hands.'

They washed them in the downstairs lav, slithering the soap about between them. Uncle Neville coughed outside the door.

'Quick!' whispered Bea. 'He needs a widdle.'

HE NEEDS A WIDDLE.

Uncle Neville had to widdle a lot, because of the pills he was on, for his Heart. Out they came, and in he went. They crossed the dark hall to the dining room. It was light in here, overlooking the wintry garden.

'Something smells yummy,' said Freddie, taking his place.

Auntie Agnes took the lid off the dish and the most gorgeous smell wafted over the table. Chicken casserole, in a scrumptious sauce, with mashed potato, green beans and carrots: he was absolutely starving, waiting for Uncle Neville to be served first because he was Uncle Neville, then Bea, because she was a girl. He felt himself begin to make a Face, stretching his mouth really wide, and covered it with his hand. No one seemed to notice.

At last they could all tuck in.

'You *are* a hungry chap.'

'What are your school meals like, Freddie?' asked Uncle Neville.

He shook his head. He didn't want to say how awful they were, because that would be disloyal to Daddy, who wasn't here, and anyway Uncle Neville was helping with the Fees. He'd heard Daddy once, swearing over a bill and muttering, 'Thank God for old Neville.'

'They're not too bad,' he said, finished before anyone because he was so hungry.

'You look to me like a boy in need of feeding up,' said Auntie Agnes. 'Second helping?'

'Yes, *please!*'

Everyone laughed.

After lunch, Uncle Neville went slowly upstairs for his rest, and Auntie Agnes went to do the washing-up. Bea and Freddie went into the sitting room.

'Tinkerbell!'

They bent down and stroked her, edging her hopefully closer to the fire.

Then they listened to gramophone records: Kathleen Ferrier in her amazing soupy voice singing 'Blow the wind southerly, southerly, southerly . . . ' while Bea gazed soulfully into the mirror, watching herself cry; and then Stanley Holloway's dreadful story of how Young Albert had been taken to the zoo by his parents and got eaten by a lion.

Completely eaten!

Auntie Agnes came in. Freddie got up. You should always get up when women came into the room, they told you that at school. 'Would you like my chair, Auntie Agnes?'

'No, thank you, darling, I'm fine here.' And she settled down with her knitting on what she called the settee, though Mummy said you should never, ever call it that, it was always the sofa.

The coals glowed in the fire, Tinkerbell turned over, people went past in the street, where every morning they still gave sugar to the milkman's horse. School was a million miles away. Sometimes he even forgot it.

*   *   *

But then half-term came to an end.

'Hello, Sutherland, how are you getting on?' Nice Mr Ward ruffled Freddie's hair as he went past in the hall.

'Fine, thank you, sir.'

'Well done. You must come and have tea with me one day. Bring a friend.'

'Thank you, sir!'

Then Mr Ward strode away, into the Map Room, as the bell rang for the end of break, and Freddie followed everyone else into the form room for maths.

'Mr Ward's asked me to tea,' he said under his

breath to Collins, sharing the double desk, as Mr Freeman wrote decimals up on the board. 'He said to bring a friend.'

Collins wasn't too bad these days: sometimes at break they walked up and down together, talking about Rupert Bear and all his friends in Nutwood: Algy and Podgy Pig, and Rastus Mouse. 'D'you want to come?'

'Maybe.'

Then it was all copying off the board, and heads down, and sums, and then it was French. But at lunch break, when they were out in the grounds, Freddie asked Collins again. It was a lovely day, clouds whizzing over the school in the wind, and sun playing over the grass. Mr Ward's cottage was at a little distance from the main building, quite a nice place, with white-painted windows. Freddie had heard about his teas.

'No, you haven't.'

'What d'you mean?'

'You don't know what goes on there.'

'What d'you mean?' Freddie asked again, mystified. What could go on with jam sand-wiches and slices of cake? He'd love a good tea.

Collins called over to Harris, kicking a ball about with Bell Minor. Both of them came over.

When they told Freddie about nice Mr Ward, he felt his mouth fall open. He simply couldn't believe it.

'You mean — '

Harris laughed. 'It goes on all the time. But the teas are good, it's almost worth it.' Then he told Freddie something simply disgusting, and added, 'No tea's worth that, though.'

Freddie looked at him. Then he looked at the sun and shadow racing over the muddy grass and felt sick. It was as if the whole place had changed completely. Well, not just the school. Sort of everything.

'Have you — have you all — '

'Most of us. He goes round all the boys in turn.'

'Well he's not going to go round me,' said Freddie, and everyone laughed. Then the bell rang.

'Why didn't you say?' he asked Collins, as they walked back.

Collins shrugged. 'I don't like thinking about it, I suppose. I wish it hadn't happened.'

'Have you told your parents?'

He shook his head. 'I don't think they'd believe me. They like him, all the parents do.' Then he ran on ahead, and in through the door where everyone was swarming.

That night Freddie lay in bed, thinking about it all. Was this one of the Facts of Life? Mummy hadn't mentioned it at all. He thought about kind Mr Ward welcoming new boys on the platform on the First Day, getting to know them, ruffling their hair. He thought about Harris and Collins and Bell Minor, all of them, going over to the cottage for tea, knocking at the door, going inside to a super spread on the table, eating till they were stuffed.

'Come and sit on my knee, Bell Minor. I expect you miss being at home sometimes, don't you?'

'Yes, sir.'

'Of course you do, we all do sometimes, I remember what it's like. But you know, if ever you feel a bit mis you can always come over here and talk to me.'

'Thank you, sir.' Tears welling up.

'You can run along now, Collins and Harris. Bell Minor and I are going to have a little chat.'

Off they went, saying thank you, sir, thanks very much, closing the front door behind them.

And then —

'Let me give you a hug, Bell. There, that's better, isn't it? Come and snuggle up.'

And then —

'Is that nice? Do you like that feeling?'

And then —

It was disgusting, it was horrible. And frightening.

Freddie lay in the dark. He could sort of see why you wouldn't tell your parents, but he could tell Mummy, and she'd tell Daddy. He'd do something.

*   *   *

'The old bugger,' said Will, after the next Outing, and roared with laughter. 'Ought to be sacked.'

'It's not funny, Will, it's not funny at all. Honestly. You must write to Campbell-Davies.' Flo shuddered. Freddie, her darling, her boy. The very thought of it. And she had been so taken in! '*Don't you worry, Mrs Sutherland, I'll keep an eye.*'

'Write tonight,' she said.

'I'll see,' said Will, passing his cup for more

tea. 'One has to be careful. Don't want to stir things up too much. It does happen.'

Flo looked at him over the teapot. 'Did it happen to you?'

He dropped in a couple of sugar lumps. 'I can't remember now.'

⋆ ⋆ ⋆

On her way home from school, Bea told herself stories. She didn't start until she'd crossed Ryehurst Hill at the traffic lights, but once she was in Rushbrook Road she was away. Often, she was carrying on with the one she'd begun in bed the night before, falling asleep as she walked down the long steep hill to a farmhouse in a valley. The farm was in Shropshire, a place made vivid by Malcolm Saville and *The Lone Pine*, which she was reading at Rest Time in school.

Now, walking slowly home, she said hello to the Shropshire sheepdog in the yard, and hung over a stable door, greeting her rough-coated pony. Wind blew from bare hills, and lapwings called. It was going to rain. She opened the heavy front door into the farmhouse kitchen, where someone had laid High Tea. She could hear the cows filing out to the field as she drank a glass of creamy milk and ate freshly baked bread and ham cut from a ham hanging down from the ceiling.

Then what happened?

If anyone had asked Bea what these stories were about, she would not have been able to tell them. There were no other characters, only

272

herself, and different houses in the country. The feeling it gave her — the lost, blissful feeling of looking at each place, a connection as strong as rope binding her to each one: that was why she did it. It wasn't to make things happen, it was just about being there.

Yet there was always something to continue, and now, at the end of Rushbrook Road, with the Croydon Road traffic buzzing along, she turned round, and walked slowly back again, swinging her satchel, hearing the lapwing cry, seeing the great dark rain clouds move slowly over the hills.

'Where on earth have you been?' asked Flo, when she finally rang the doorbell: three times, the family ring. 'I was beginning to get really worried.' She'd set the alarm to wake her from her nap, come down to get everything ready. Then waited and waited, while Bea dawdled home.

'Sorry. Sorry, Mummy. I'm starving. What's for tea?'

WHAT'S FOR TEA?

They had it together, on either side of the fire. Flo sat on the sofa, and Bea in an armchair opposite, a tea tray on one of the little Indian tables beside her.

'What sort of a day, darling?'

'Fine, thanks.' She helped herself to a banana sandwich, and reached for her book. At school it was Malcolm Saville, here it was *Good Wives*, with Jo married to the lovely professor and Meg spending too much money on clothes, and she and her husband having their first quarrel.

'Always got your nose in a book,' said Flo, pouring tea. 'Couldn't we have an actual conversation?'

'Sorry. Sorry, Mummy.' She put it down. 'What sort of a day have you had?'

'Oh — ' Flo heard herself give an enormous sigh — 'all right, I suppose. I went down the town this morning, saw Mrs Thing.'

Bea reached for a ginger biscuit. 'Which Mrs Thing?'

They both laughed. 'Mrs Whatdoyoucallit,' said Flo. 'You know, that woman with specs in Rushbrook Road.'

'Mrs Mason.'

'Mrs Mason. Mrs Mason bought a basin. God, what a dreary woman. Oh, look, here's Snowy.'

'Snowy! Come here!'

He came, he settled down on Panther's skin. Bea leaned forward and stroked him, and didn't go back to her book. The hideous emptiness of Flo's day began to fade.

★ ★ ★

'And how was your day, darling?' she asked Will, as they all had supper, Bea's homework out of the way. No maths tonight, thank God, and Non-verbal Reasoning banished for evermore.

'Splendid.' He tucked into very dark brown shepherd's pie. Flo hadn't burned it, so it must be an overdose of gravy browning. Sometimes it was almost black. 'Getting going on the next RLS Fair,' he said. 'Down in Dartmoor.

274

Bickland Hall — beautiful spot, apparently. I'm going down to have a recce next week, spoke to Sir John this afternoon.'

'Half of what you think is right, darling,' Flo said to Bea, as she took an enormous mouthful, and then, 'Lovely, Will. I'm so glad.' So good for him, getting out and about.

'And what I thought,' he said, polishing off watery tinned peas, 'was that we might all go down there for the Fair, have a little summer holiday. What do you think? It's not that far from old Fitz — we could drive over at the end.'

'And visit the family on the way down,' said Flo.

'Do that, too, why not?'

He *was* in a good mood.

'Stay in a caravan, perhaps.'

'A *caravan?*'

'Or a tent. We could camp in the Bickland grounds.'

'*Camp?*'

Bea burst out laughing. 'Honestly. You two.'

'What did you have in mind?' asked Will, as she and Flo cleared away.

What Flo had had in mind was a lovely old inn, with beams, and no cooking for a fortnight, and a romantic bedroom looking down on to a gorgeous garden. She said so, bringing in a Pyrex dish of raspberry blancmange.

'We'll see,' said Will, and that was the end of that. After supper he went to watch the news, while Flo washed Bea's hair in the bath.

'Poor Mummy,' said Bea, as the shampoo went on. 'All these lovely things you want.'

'I am *not* Poor Mummy,' said Flo, rubbing it in. 'Lean back, mind it doesn't get in your eyes. Never, never call me Poor Mummy.'

★   ★   ★

On her way up to bed, Bea said good night to the bird. 'I failed the Eleven-plus,' she said. 'Everyone says it doesn't matter. I'm going to go to Dolphin House. Everyone says it's a really good school.'

The bird sat unblinking on his bough. 'But I think I must be stupid,' she said.

I THINK I MUST BE STUPID.

The bird listened quietly, as always. He gave her the same kind of feeling as her stories did: he was something steady and true. She leaned forward, and kissed his cold wallpaper face.

4

Summer 1959: the tent in the boot, Snowy in the cattery, countless Indian stories. 'Have I told you the one about ploughing with bulls? They were going for slaughter, but I had a marvellous idea ... ' Down they drove to Bournemouth.

'Vivie!'

She stood at the open door in a pretty belted frock and clip-on earrings, looking more like Vivien Leigh than ever. 'My darlings!' She held out her arms. 'Come along in!'

In they went with their cases, and there were Granny and Grandpa, getting up slowly from their chairs in the conservatory, where great big grapes hung down.

'You two seem to have grown,' said Grandpa.

The pencil marks on the kitchen wall at home had gone up and up.

'Taller than Granny!' Bea gave her a hug: what a tiny thing she was, in her little blue dress and horn-rimmed spectacles.

'How old are you now, Freddie? Twenty-one?'

Freddie laughed. 'I'm ten, Grandpa.'

'Ten? Almost old enough to join the army.'

'Where's Hugo?' Bea's stomach had been full of butterflies for days. Now it was in knots.

'I think he's helping Daddy upstairs with the luggage.'

Mummy and Vivie had disappeared into the

kitchen: they could hear them chatting and laughing away.

'Where's Whoopoo?'

Whoopoo was up on the kitchen shelf as always, next to the Kelloggs Cornflakes. Sunny Jim seemed to have disappeared. Bea still wasn't tall enough to reach up and rub Whoopoo's head with hers; she tried to lift Freddie and let go at once. He might look skinny but he weighed a ton.

'How are we getting on?' In came Will, all smiles and jolly dee, and there was Hugo behind him, taller than any kitchen shelf and so handsome that Bea almost fainted. He was eighteen now, he'd Left School. *Eighteen!*

'Hugo!'

'Hello, Auntie Flo.' He blushed, crossed the kitchen and kissed her. 'Nice to see you again.'

'And you, my darling. Gosh, you do look gorgeous.'

GOSH, YOU DO LOOK GORGEOUS.

He blushed to the roots of his curly dark hair. 'Thanks.'

'Hello, Baba.'

She let him. It didn't matter what he called her, it would be all right. And anyway, when he said it, her stomach went flip-flop. It was as if he knew her inside out.

'Hello,' she said, and didn't know what to say next. 'How are you?' she said at last.

'Fine, thanks.' And then he was helping Freddie up on a chair, and they both rubbed foreheads with Whoopoo's furry head and laughed. Will did it too.

'Marvellous. How's lunch coming on? Want a hand?'

Freddie scrambled down from the chair. 'Can I ring the gong?'

★ ★ ★

By the time lunch was over it was as if they'd been here for ever. There were the same old deck chairs out in the garden, where Flo and Vivie sat and chatted all afternoon, and the babies in the Home next door went on crying, just as always, though they must be new ones, now. Granny and Grandpa went for their rests, Daddy smoked his pipe and fell asleep in the conservatory, Bea and Freddie went upstairs to look at Hugo's railway, which was still there, up in the attic. Hugo showed Freddie the switches.

'I remember,' said Freddie. 'Thanks.'

Then Hugo said he'd better do the washing-up.

'I'll help you,' said Bea at once, not quite so tongue-tied with some lunch inside her, and they went downstairs, just the two of them.

'I have a system,' said Hugo, running the taps. 'First I do the glasses in really hot clean soapy water.' She began to pass them carefully. 'Then I do the plates, and rinse them, and put them up in the rack. Then I do the silver in fresh water.'

Helping, passing, watching, Bea knew she would always wash up like this, always love the sight of gleaming glasses set out on a tea towel to drain, and the sparkling china plates set one by careful one in the wooden plate rack. They dried all the silver together, laying it out on a tray in groups of forks and spoons, big ones first, then dessert, then serving spoons.

Hugo picked up the tray and carried it through to the dining room. Together they put everything into the canteen, lined with green baize, each tiny coffee spoon with its own tiny place.

'Do you do this every day?' Bea asked, as he snapped it shut. At home they just had a drawer in the dresser, and although there were sections it was often an awful muddle.

'In the holidays,' said Hugo. 'My mother does it in term time.' It felt so funny to hear Auntie Vivie being called 'my mother'. 'But of course I've left school now.' He smiled at her, and her stomach went flip-flop again.

'And what are you going to do?' she asked, as if she was at a cocktail party, or something. Lots of people had cocktail parties in Ryehurst, and though Will and Flo hardly ever went to them she knew there was a lot of talk about what people Did. In Ryehurst they were mostly boring accountants, Mummy said.

'I'm going to university,' said Hugo. 'I'm going to read Physics at Bristol. Shall we go and see how Freddie's getting on?'

Then he and Freddie spent the whole afternoon playing trains, and Will came up and joined in, making puffing and tooting noises. She could see Freddie wished that he wouldn't.

★　★　★

'Hello, old chap. Like a toffee?'

He smiled shyly. 'Thanks, Grandpa.'

Grandpa patted his eiderdown, and Freddie sat on the bed, watching him open the Coronation tin. There was a picture of Queen Elizabeth on the top, smiling away in her crown. He gazed at the toffees inside.

'Some of them are mint, said Grandpa, shaking them about. 'That's one, I think.'

Freddie preferred the plain ones, but he took the mint and unwrapped it carefully. It was so nice in here: a little room down a passage from the hall, with the window open on to the garden and books by the bed. A single bed: Grandpa didn't sleep upstairs with Granny, for some reason.

'How's school?' Grandpa asked, as they sucked away.

'Fine, thanks.'

'Best subjects?'

'I like Geography.' Not quite so much, now he knew about Mr Ward.

'Worst?'

'Latin.' And as he said it he could feel a Face coming on, even with his mouth full of toffee, and he looked down and sucked it as hard as he could. 'I'm pretty good at Maths,' he mumbled.

'Like Hugo,' said Grandpa. 'He's a clever chap, too.' And then, as Freddie flexed his hands, 'You probably don't want to talk about school in the holidays. I never did.' He reached out and gave him a pat. 'I do remember,' he said. 'I was away at school, too. That was before dinosaurs walked the earth, of course.'

Freddie laughed, and looked up. Through the open window he could hear the birds, singing away in the apple trees, and the babies, crying away in their prams in the garden of the Home.

'Whose babies are they, next door?'

Grandpa shook his head. 'I tried to count them once, but it's like counting sheep, and you know babies — they all sound the same. Like sheep.' He held out the tin. 'Have another toffee, and don't tell a soul.'

Freddie took a plain one, and they sat sucking companionably. It wasn't for a long time afterwards that he realised that Grandpa hadn't actually answered his question. It was Auntie Vivie, at teatime, who said the mothers were all Disgraced.

★ ★ ★

After that it was all trips to the sea on the trolley bus, and everyone saying what a strong swimmer Freddie was now.

'But, darling, I can see your ribs,' said Auntie Vivie. 'Don't they feed you there?'

He gave a little sort of smiling shrug, rubbing his wet hair with the towel, turning away to keep the Face private.

There were ice creams on the prom, and a lot of looking at shell boxes in the shops. There were walks with Will and sometimes Hugo in the Chines, with the same sand filled with pine-needles getting into your sandals, the same sweet heavy smell of pine and the glimpse of the blue, blue sea.

Mummy and Auntie Vivie didn't come for walks: they sat in their deck chairs and talked and talked. They took out their Lizzie Arden compacts and powdered their noses, they put on their bright red lipstick. They talked all the time at home, too, getting beach picnics and meals together, and they were always laughing. There was lots of 'How quaint!' and 'My dear! Did you ever hear anything so priceless?' And, 'No! What a hoot! What an absolute hoot!'

There was lots of singing, too: Auntie Vivie was mad about *West Side Story*. She played all the songs in the drawing room after supper.

Granny stayed up! Sometimes, just because Bea liked it, she wore her fur tippet, even though it was really for going out. It was a kind of fox, long and thin and glossy, with fierce glass eyes and lots of little feet and tails, sewn on all the way down.

'Did Grandpa shoot that?' asked Freddie, sitting on the pouffe.

She laughed. 'No, darling. I bought it in Bourne & Hollingsworth.'

Sometimes they listened to records on the hi-fi, with someone new called Tom Lehrer singing what seemed to be rude songs, and Will laughing more than ever. They played Snakes and Ladders, learning how to be Good Losers, everyone shrieking. On the last night they stayed up late.

'Time for bed, you two,' said Will at last.

'We don't *want* to go to bed.'

He shooed them up the huge staircase, saying hello to a Paying Guest coming down.

'She's a pretty girl,' he said, rushing to open

283

the front door. 'Where's she off to, I wonder.'

'You're leaving tomorrow,' said Grandpa, coming out of the drawing room, and they both laughed.

And next day all the luggage came downstairs again, and Flo shook sand out of sandals, and Bea wore her hair very soft and loose and stood in a corner of the hall, waiting for Hugo to say goodbye to her.

He came in from helping Will put everything in the car.

'Hello, Bea, what're you doing hiding away?' He smiled at her, and her knees went weak, and then everyone was coming downstairs or along the hall, and there was endless hugging and kissing, and Mummy in tears.

'Goodbye, my darling.' She and Auntie Vivie just hugged and hugged.

Then Hugo stepped forward and put his hand on Bea's shoulder and bent down and kissed her. 'It's been super having you here.'

'You too,' she said, like an idiot, because of course he was here all the time, and then she turned and ran down the path as Will called, 'Bea! In the car!' and began to toot.

*   *   *

As they crossed into Devon after a picnic lunch — 'One of Vivie's best, if you ask me' — everyone started to talk about the farm. Freddie couldn't remember it at all, but he felt as if he did, with all the stories: the goats snatching the dusters off the washing line, the hen in the pram, Daddy wringing Brownie's neck by mistake. And the cows with half their bottoms hanging out, when they'd had calves. Bluebell. Guernsey Noo.

'All right, Bea, that's enough.'

'Can we go there? Can we go back and see it? *Please* can we?'

Will didn't answer. Then: 'We haven't got time. Flo? Got the map?'

They rolled over the river Axe, where fishermen were standing absolutely still and swallows skimmed the water.

'Like the swallows in Melcote,' said Bea, and then she looked out of her window, and thought about Hugo again. She hadn't really stopped for a second since they left. If he was eighteen now, and she was almost twelve, that meant that when she was seventeen he'd be twenty-three. He'd have finished Reading Physics and be ready for proper life. Could you get married at seventeen?

* * *

At six o'clock that evening — 'God, what a hell of a drive' — they came into Bovey-on-the-Moor — 'Sweet little place' — and saw, as they came out of it, white marquees in the distance.

'That's it! That's Bickland! They've done their stuff!'

'There's a sign!'

So there was: a proper AA sign with RLS Country Fair on it, up at the side of the road, with a great big arrow.

Tired as everyone was, they all began to feel excited. Will had talked about this for weeks: his great idea; how wonderfully the try-out had gone, up in the Peak District; how this was the big one, this would put the RLS on the map for ever. So much to see and do. Gun dogs, sheep dogs. Falcons, fishing, clay pigeon shooting, you name it. Lunch in a marquee. Strawberry teas. And the kids could sell programmes, if they wanted; that would be fun. All they had to do now was put the tent up.

Flo had done her best to forget about the tent. As they drove along past more AA signs and then through the tall iron gates, wide open, with an RLS Country Fair banner across the top, she went on trying to forget it. She put the map in the glove compartment — oh, thank God for that — and gave an enormous sigh.

'What's the matter, Mummy?'

WHAT'S THE MATTER, MUMMY?

'Nothing.'

'What a gorgeous place,' Will was saying now. 'See it, kids? I knew this would be right as soon as I saw it.'

They gazed out of the windows at the dark green summer trees, the rolling moor, the river glinting as the sun went down. Snow-white marquees were spread out everywhere and in the distance stood Bickland Hall: grey stone, tall windows, a huge front door. A couple of black Labradors were drinking from a bowl outside. Imagine living there!

'And there's the camp site!'

Flo shut her eyes. They bumped over the grass towards it.

★　★　★

'Come on, Freddie, old chap. This is a man's job.' Out of the boot came the great big army tent in its bag, out came the tent poles and the bag of pegs. 'Where's the groundsheet?' There it was, spilling ancient grains of sand. 'Last time I had this tent up was in the desert.' Out came all the Kit.

'Bea, you and Mummy can blow up the Lilos. Now, then.'

Will and Freddie hauled the tent out of its bag and spread it on the grass. Bea blew on the Lilo pump and watched them fiddling about with guy ropes. If Hugo was here he'd have it all up in a trice, he was so practical and clever. Look at his system for washing-up. Look at all that Meccano, still up in his attic room. Cranes. Pulleys.

At last the thing was standing. All around them people were putting their own tents up, or cooking their suppers on Primus stoves. The smell of sausages hung in the air. Dogs ran about.

At a safe distance, Flo and Bea had been puffing until they almost burst. The Lilos still lay limply on the grass.

'Honestly, Mummy, they're hardly filled at all.'

'Leave the wretched things. Help me with this Primus thing.'

They gazed at the Primus thing; they fiddled with little bits of steel.

'Don't light it!' called Will from inside the tent. 'I'll be the one to light it!'

Flo had no intention of lighting it. The whole thing looked terrifying.

'I'm *starving.*'

'Where's the tiffin?' Will came crawling out. He stood up, rather too quickly. The tent pole caught him right on the brow.

'Oh, fucking hell.'

OH, FUCKING HELL.

★ ★ ★

At last they all settled down. 'At last, at promised last, I see a promise of my fair one here,' said Will, feeling better, like everyone else, with some hot food inside him. 'Nothing like a fry-up.'

He'd gone over to the house to let Sir John know he was here. He'd puffed up the Lilos. 'That'll do, I think. That'll have to do.' They still felt a bit squashy. Bea and Flo had done the washing-up in a communal washing-up place, next to the toilets.

'*Not* toilets. Lavatories.'

'I know, I know.' At last they were all snuggled, up in their sleeping bags, undressing by the light of a Tilley lamp, hung from the middle tent pole.

'Whatever happens,' said Will, blowing it out, 'if it rains, don't touch the canvas.'

Everyone immediately reached out and touched it.

'Why?'

'Because that lets the rain in. So long as you don't touch it, we're all right.'

He crawled past Bea and Freddie towards Flo. They all said good night in the dark. Then they lay there on their lumpy pillows, listening to other campers laughing, still staying up. After a while, all anyone could hear was Will's snores. They were deafening, they filled the whole tent.

'Mummy! I'll *never* get to sleep!'

'Put your fingers in your ears.'

The next thing they knew it was the middle of the night. Rain beat steadily down.

'I've touched the canvas!'

'Idiot.'

Rain dripped steadily through.

★ ★ ★

But next day the sky was a fresh rinsed blue and the sun was out. 'Thank God!' With breakfast inside them, much the same as supper, they walked over the soaking grass towards the show ground. Already a huge queue of vehicles was forming at the gate. Lots of Land Rovers. And then it all began.

First stop was the RLS tent itself. James Marshall was there already, with Sir John, and the Regional Secretary for Devon, who Will had got on board from the beginning. Alec Anderson, nice chap. There were introductions all round.

'My wife, Flo. The kids, Bea and Freddie.'

Smiles and handshakes and best behaviour. 'Never, ever, say 'Pleased to meet you',' the children had been instructed. 'The grown-ups say, 'How do you do?' and you answer just the same: 'How do you do?'' They answered it, over and over again.

The tent had trestle tables heaped with programmes and leaflets, with girls in jodhpurs and velvet Alice bands smiling behind them.

'Now, then, who wants to sell programmes?'

Bea did. She was given a tray slung round her neck and a tin of loose change, called the Float. Other people were queuing up for their trays, but she was the youngest.

'How's your maths?' Sir John asked her kindly.

'Not very good, I'm afraid.'

'Never mind, I'm sure you'll manage.' He smiled down at her, and she was sure she would. The nice bit was smiling at everyone and being polite. 'Would you like a programme, sir?' 'Madam? May I offer you a programme?'

From now on, Will was going to be occupied all day. He'd meet them for lunch in the Refreshments Tent.

'So you all have a marvellous time, and I'll see you at one o'clock, all right? No wandering off. Stay in Mummy's sight all the time, understand? Bea? Got that? Ah, there's David Bone. David, old boy! Come and meet the family!'

David Bone, the Heritage officer who'd been such a support from the beginning, came in smiling away. He was tall and lean and handsome, Flo noted, something Will hadn't mentioned. They all shook hands and said 'How do you do?' again. Was he camping, too? No, he was staying in a nice little B & B. Unfortunately his wife had gone down with something just two days ago, or she'd be here too, of course.

'I see you're going to be busy,' he said, smiling down at Bea with her tray of stacked programmes.

'May I offer you one?' she said, and everyone

290

laughed. What was so funny about that? He bought one straight away, though she realised afterwards that of course he'd have one free.

'Right, then,' said Will, as people came into the tent: possible new members, picking up leaflets and asking questions. 'Off you go!'

Off they went, Bea in her summer frock and cardigan, the wet grass getting into her sandals, holding her tray carefully before her. Flo and Freddie, also with wet feet, held hands as they went to see what was what.

Clay pigeons were whizzing through the air on the far side of the ground, next to the rifle range. The sun was rising, the grass drying out a bit, everyone in a good mood. They craned their necks to see the clay pigeons explode, they watched keen young farmers at target practice, they stood by the beautiful shady river watching fishermen cast their flies and haul in gasping trout.

Then it was time for lunch, with more huge queues, and Will nowhere to be seen until at last he pitched up saying everything was going splendidly. The Beer Tent was next door, with a lot of fat farmers and tweedy landowners crowded in, and dogs lying panting on the grass outside.

'Enjoying yourselves?'

'Yes, thank you, Daddy.'

'I've sold thirty programmes.'

'Splendid. Got all the money safe? And how are you, my darling? Everything all right?'

Flo nodded. She wouldn't say no to a nice little rest in the tent, with everyone out of the way, but so long as the sun stayed out she could manage.

'It's lovely, darling. Well done.'

'I'm going to get more programmes,' said Bea, wiping her mouth with a paper napkin — 'Not a serviette!'

'Hello,' said David Bone, there in the RLS tent as she went in. 'How are you getting on?'

'Fine, thanks.'

'Well done. That's such a pretty frock.'

'Thank you!' She flashed him a smile.

THANK YOU!

There were three whole days of this. Gun dogs. Sheep dogs. Archery. Hold a Hawk. Fondle a Ferret. On the second night, they were invited into the Hall for drinks at six o'clock. Everyone changed into their unironed best, Flo in the candy-striped frock that she'd had since Melcote days, but it would just have to do.

'My darling. You look gorgeous.'

She put on her lipstick, got out her scent. The damp smell of the tent was transformed to something heavenly.

'What's it called?' asked Bea, drinking it in.

'Never, ever, tell anyone the name of your scent, darling. Otherwise they'll copy you.' With her Coty-varnished feet in peep-toed sandals, she felt ready for anything.

'Right, then.' Will stood at the entrance, untying the flaps. He retied them as they came out one by one. 'We're off!'

Inside, the house was gorgeous: an airy stone hall, a fabulous broad staircase hung with portraits. 'No better than ours,' Will said under his breath, as they climbed and climbed. The party was in a drawing room on the first floor, where pretty girls, out of jodhpurs now, were circulating with drinks on trays. Champagne! And orange squash for the children: Bea and Freddie were the only ones. They stood there sipping, looking polite, while Sir John and Lady Helena went graciously round, and people greeted Will with, 'Congratulations!' And, 'You even managed the weather!' He beamed from ear to ear.

Flo followed in his wake. All the women were dressed up to the nines and the Melcote frock felt suddenly completely inadequate. Her peep-toe sandals, stuck with bits of grass, looked worn and second-best.

'And you're Will's wife,' people kept saying, over and over again, and she kept saying she was, and smiling, and wondering what to say next. It felt as if they all knew each other, that she was the new girl, a fish out of water even here. Furthermore, it seemed they were the only RLS people camping. She tried to make this sound fun. She tried fluttering her eyelashes at one or two of the chaps, whose names she'd heard for ages — James Marshall, Roger Hale, of Forestry & Woodland — but their wives came quickly into view. And some of them, it seemed, were working: had nannies, ran things. Chaired committees.

Flo had never wanted to be on a committee in all her life. She had another glass, listened politely, sipping away, to talk of beagles, and volunteer groups, and preserving hedgerows.

'How fascinating,' she said. 'How absolutely fascinating.' After a while she realised she was drunk.

Trays of vol-au-vents were coming round. Through the roar of the room came the dignified slow chime of a grandfather clock. Flo took two vol-au-vents and tried to count the strokes.

'Was that eight or nine?' she asked the room. No one answered. She swung round to look for Bea and Freddie and almost fell over, grabbing the nearest arm.

'I say, are you all right?'

David Bone. It would be him, someone so important to Will, and she almost making an ass of herself. Gosh, what a handsome man he was.

'I'm fine, thanks,' she said, with a trilling little laugh. 'Super party. Just had a tiny bit too much. Wondering where the children have got to.'

They both looked round. She had to do this very carefully. There they were, standing by one of the tall mullioned windows, the setting sun lighting Bea's fair hair and Freddie's best white shirt.

'Lovely children,' said David Bone.

'It's time I got them home to bed.'

But as soon as she'd said it, and he'd turned to talk to someone grand, Will was beside her, saying that Sir John had invited them to stay on for supper, just a few people, just something simple, but a super idea.

She shut her eyes and the room spun round.

'I don't think I can,' she said quietly, opening them with enormous care. To sit over supper, to try to sound intelligent in this setting? Drunk?

'Say I'm not well,' she said, and was flashed back to Melcote, when he'd had to say it a hundred times.

His face fell. 'Oh, darling, please. It means so much to me.'

'But the children — '

David Bone was at their side again. 'I'm just off,' he said. 'Well done again, Will.'

And before she knew it, Will was asking him to see the children back to the tent, would you mind, old boy, that would be such a help, and beckoning Bea and yawning Freddie over, and before you could say knife it was all arranged.

★   ★   ★

They walked over the shadowy grass towards the camp site. Pigeons beat their way to the trees as the sun sank down, the last visitors went bumping away from the field car park, the air was warm and still.

'Having a good time?' David Bone had asked them, as they came out of the huge front door on to the terrace.

'Super, thanks.'

They stopped to stroke one of the Bickland Labradors, getting up to greet them, wag wag wag. 'We've got a dog like that at home,' he told them, and then they were off, hearing all about the dog, called George the Second. 'I'm sure you can guess why.'

'And have you got children?' asked Bea, taking the hand he held out to her as a Land Rover came slowly past.

295

Two boys, he told them, giving her hand a squeeze. 'Away at school, like Freddie. Do you like your prep school, Freddie?'

'Yes, thanks.' Freddie gave another enormous yawn. He hadn't made a Face since they got here, he suddenly realised.

And here they were at the camp site, with the delicious smell of sausages and smoke rising into the air, and there was their tent, which Daddy had had in the War, Bea told Mr Bone, and he laughed, releasing her hand.

'Right, then, old chap,' he said to Freddie, untying the flaps. 'You'd better go in first as you're so weary. Need any help? Got your toothbrush?'

'I'm fine, thanks.' He went into the tent, all ship shape as Will made them keep it, just like being in the dorm. Perhaps the Faces had gone for ever now.

'Do you want to come for a little walk, Bea? Just while Freddie gets undressed?'

'OK.' She'd seen Freddie get undressed a million times, but perhaps she shouldn't have done, perhaps if you had two boys at boarding school you knew how things should be done.

'Back in a tick!' Mr Bone called into the tent. Then he held out his hand and led her towards the river bank, where the last of the fishermen were packing up their things. 'Bit cooler there,' he said. 'Tell me about your school. What are you best at?'

And she told him about English, where she'd come Top, and about reading at rest time, but not about the stories she told to herself all the time.

'Clever as well as pretty,' he said, squeezing

her hand again. Cool air rose from the glinting water, the last of the fishermen was making his way up the bank. 'You'll drive the boys wild when you grow up, do you realise that?'

Bea didn't know what to say. Hugo flashed into her mind, and then he was gone. There was only the river, quietly flowing along, and the birds beating into the trees.

'We'd better get back,' he said softly, and then, 'May I kiss you good night?'

MAY I KISS YOU GOOD NIGHT?

The words hung before her in the dusky air.

He bent down towards her, and she lifted her face for his kiss on the cheek, as she did every night to her parents. To Hugo, saying goodbye. But Mr Bone didn't do that. He pulled her to him, and he kissed her right on the mouth, where no one had ever kissed her, and then he sort of bit her lips, quite hard, and thrust his tongue inside.

Quick as a flash, it was over. She put her hand to her mouth, and he laughed, and said, 'Sorry, Bea, you're just irresistible,' and then he led her away from the river bank and back towards the camp site, saying, 'Don't tell your father, will you? There's a good girl. Let myself down there for a moment.'

She didn't know what to think. She wasn't even quite sure what had happened. People were all around them as soon as they got back, cooking, playing catch, or walking over to the toilets. Lavatories. She needed to go there now.

'Good night, Freddie!' Mr Bone called outside the tent, but there was no answer: when they

297

looked inside he was fast asleep. 'Good night, Bea,' he said, running his hand down her hair. Then he turned and strode away, looking just like any other grown-up.

★ ★ ★

Next morning, when she woke, Flo was still asleep, and Will and Freddie were boiling the kettle on the Primus. Bea lay in her sleeping bag, feeling strange. She had a tummy-ache, and she felt a bit wet Down There, as Auntie Agnes called it, when she was having a bath in Wimbledon. She put down her hand, pulled it out again, had a look.

'Mummy,' she said to the sleeping form. 'Mummy!'

'Now what?'

'I've got the curse.'

★ ★ ★

And of course there were no STs, as Flo called them. They had to walk all the way over to the First-Aid Tent to get some. The St John Ambulance lady gave Bea an aspirin and a drink of water, and then she and Mummy went slowly back to the tent, holding hands, and Mummy put the packet of STs into her case, and Bea had a little lie-down.

'I'll have one too,' said Flo, lowering herself to the big double sleeping bag. She still felt hung over. 'Poor darling,' she said, looking across to Bea. 'Are you feeling ghastly?'

298

'The aspirin is helping.' She lay on top of her sleeping bag, the hard ground beneath her. The Lilos were all completely flat by now. 'Mummy?'

'Yes, darling.'

'Mummy, don't tell Daddy this, but Mr Bone kissed me.'

MR BONE KISSED ME.

Every time she thought about it, she felt so strange. She tried to imagine Hugo kissing her like that. Would she like it then? But surely he wouldn't. Nobody nice would actually put their tongue *in your mouth*.

There was a silence, then Flo sat up. 'What do you mean?'

Bea tried to explain. 'But don't tell Daddy,' she said again. 'He specially asked me not to. I'm just telling you.'

'Darling — ' Flo began, then stopped. 'I think you'd better try to forget about it now,' she said at last, her mind whirling. 'We'll talk about it another time. Have a little sleep now.'

And Bea turned over, and had a little sleep.

★ ★ ★

'Will,' said Flo that night, when both the children were asleep, and they were in the double sleeping bag, so uncomfortable, and he was yawning like mad, worn out with it all, but pleased as punch. 'Will, I've got to tell you something.'

She told him.

Will was silent, for the first time in days. Then: 'The wicked old bugger,' he said. 'I'll have a word.'

Within moments he was snoring.

★ ★ ★

Next morning was cloudy, threatening rain. They had to pack up and get the tent down quickly, otherwise it would be Hell.

'Our last outdoor breakfast,' said Will, tucking into fried bread.

'Thank God for that,' said Flo.

'But it's been fun, hasn't it?' he said, looking round. 'Enjoyed it all, kids?'

'Yes, thank you, Daddy.'

'Right, then.' He polished off the last bit of crust. 'Fitz next. Action stations.'

It took them an hour, and how the rain held off was a miracle.

Will slammed the boot down on everything. It began to pour.

'In the car!'

They piled in. Bea tucked herself into a corner, looking out at the rain.

Freddie moved up beside her. 'Shall we play I-Spy?'

They played it half-heartedly, as the rain came down in buckets and the windscreen wipers went back and forth and Will told the story about how Kolynos once got stuck in quicksand. He'd had to leap off in a hurry, and no mistake. He'd had to haul and haul.

★ ★ ★

They bumped up the lane to Fitz's house just in time for tea, racing through the rain to the front door where she stood waiting for them, just like Vivie.

'Hello! Hello! Willie! How did it go?'

Hugs and whiskery kisses, and the table laid with fresh scones, strawberry jam and clotted Dorset cream. Eleanor poured tea from the great big silver teapot into bone-china cups.

'Tell us all about it.'

So Will told them all about it, as the rain beat down on the garden, and Flo kept an eye on pale Bea, and hungry Freddie, helping himself to a third scone. He'd put on weight this summer, he'd grown. Thank God for that. As for her, all she wanted was to sink into a soft clean bed and sleep for a week.

'Can we get down? Can we play the piano?'

'I'll come and play it with you,' said Fitz, getting up slowly, and sitting down again. 'Oh, my poor old back. I did something to it yesterday, just cutting roses.'

Will let out a snort, and turned it into a cough.

* * *

'Darling?' said Flo, as they got ready for the night in such a pretty bedroom. 'Did we really not have time to go back to the farm? The children would have loved it. I'd have loved to see it again.'

Will pulled his shirt over his head. 'To tell you the truth,' he said slowly, 'it would have broken my heart.'

* * *

They stayed with Fitz and Eleanor for three days, going down to the Cobb when the sun came out, having a swim or a paddle. Not as much fun as in sandy Bournemouth: here the beach was hard grey pebbles. Will took Freddie out mackerel fishing in a little boat that heaved and tossed all afternoon. Freddie hung over the side, being sick.

'Bad luck, old chap,' said Will, when at last they came back to shore. He held up two fat glistening mackerel. 'We'll give these to Fitz for supper, eh?'

Freddie was sick again, all down his front.

'Flo? Flo!'

  ★ ★ ★

More parlour songs, more 'Op-pop-pop-pop-poposite the ducks' at the top of their voices. More honeycomb for breakfast and pegs on the terrace. On the last day they were off bright and early.

'In the car!'

They waved and waved.

'Right, then. Got the map?'

'When are we fetching Snowy?'

  ★ ★ ★

The phone was ringing when at last they got home and went wearily into the house.

'I'll get it,' said Will, striding into the dining room.

He came out after a few minutes, looking somehow different.

'That was Agnes. Poor old Neville's died.'

302

5

'My uncle died in the holidays,' Bea said in the changing room, looking down at her new lace-up shoes. Did that make her sound important? Were uncles important? She couldn't really remember much about Uncle Neville, except for him putting out the fire in Tinkerbell's tail, and looking ill. But he and Auntie Agnes had loved one another, and now she was all alone.

'I'm so sorry,' said Fiona Barlow, sitting on the bench and putting her gym shoes on. 'Did you go to the funeral?'

Bea shook her head. She had never been to a funeral: children didn't. Will had gone, all by himself, just as he'd gone to the wedding. Flo had had to stay to look after her and Freddie on the farm then, and she had to look after them now. And anyway, she didn't really like Auntie Agnes, you could tell. She wouldn't want to go.

'I went to my grandfather's funeral,' said Fiona, as they all filed into the gym. 'I saw the coffin.'

'Gosh.'

And then Miss Billington was blowing her whistle, and they all ran to sit down on the changing mats, and Gym began.

★　★　★

Poor Agnes. Poor old thing. Standing beside her at the service, listening to her voice tremble

303

bravely through the hymns, Will had felt as sad as he'd done for years. It brought back Mother's funeral, it brought back Norfolk, and all the poor girl's uncertainties and tears. Not much of a life, if you thought about it.

Back at the house, helping her with the sherry, talking to the vicar, to Brian, Neville's brother, last seen at the wedding, and Jean, his pretty wife, and the handful of friends from the church, he knew that Neville had saved her. There he was, in a studio photograph, sitting on top of the desk that had once been Mother's, smiling kindly. And what would become of Agnes now?

'Don't worry, Sis, I'll always keep an eye,' he said that evening, Brian and Jean gone back to Chichester and the two of them on either side of the fire, the cat on the hearth between them. At least there was the cat.

'I know you will, Willie.'

She was in Neville's chair, not knitting or sewing, just sitting there, looking white. And thin. She'd lost a hell of a lot of weight. Looked after old Neville till the end.

'Got any plans?' Even to him it sounded crass.

★   ★   ★

On Bea's way back from school, deep in a story, something happened. She was just walking along as usual, taking herself to the farmhouse smothered in ivy, the one set back in empty winter fields, when suddenly she just wasn't there any more. Not at the farmhouse, not in Rushbrook Road, not anywhere. Everything went blank.

She stopped, felt herself breathing quickly. Then it was over: she was back. How strange.

One or two cars went by, a train rattled through to Redstone. Everything was just as usual. She shook her head. By the time she came to the junction with Croydon Road she'd forgotten all about it.

Left, right, left: it was a busy road, and she always looked carefully. All clear, and she ran across the road. Snowy wasn't allowed out at the front at all, not ever, just in case. She clicked open the garden gate and rang the bell three times. She rang it again. At last Flo came.

'Sorry, darling, just having a little nap. What sort of a day?'

★ ★ ★

The autumn term was always the worst, because you went Up, and everyone expected you to remember everything from the year before. If you failed your end-of-year exams, of course, you stayed Down, which had happened to Bell Minor, and was really awful, but so far Freddie had always passed. Now he was in Form Four, only two years to go, and quite senior, really, though still not a prefect, of course. You were only a school prefect in Form Six.

The new boys all looked tiny now, coming into breakfast with red-rimmed eyes. He could remember crying like that. Now he only did it at home. He tried not to, but as the term approached, he couldn't help it, lying in bed, counting the days.

'Mummy? Mummy, can you come up?'

Up she came, slowly climbing the stairs.

'What is it, darling?'

'I don't want to go back.' He began to cry. 'I really don't want to go back.'

He howled and howled, the door shut tight, her arms around him. It went on night after night.

⋆   ⋆   ⋆

Bea stood talking quietly to the bird, as Freddie sobbed beneath her.

'What can I do?' she asked him. 'What can I do?'

WHAT CAN I DO?

The bird didn't know. He just perched there on his dark bough, listening. She went up to bed. The sobs went on and on.

⋆   ⋆   ⋆

Will had read his report at the start of the holidays. 'Listen to this, Freddie. 'He is doing very well now, seems much less anxious, and is making a good contribution to his Form.' If Lansdowne says that, he means it.' He felt in his pocket, pulled out half a crown. 'Well done, old chap, really terrific.'

Freddie made a Face. He just couldn't help it, stretching open his mouth till his lips went tight, screwing up his eyes. He stretched out his fingers as far as they would go, then pulled them in again.

'Oh, don't start that again.'

'Sorry.'

Mummy said it was a Nervous Tic, and he would grow out of it. But when? The main thing was never to do it at school. As soon as he felt it begin — before a test, or just any time he was feeling frightened — he clamped his mouth shut and covered it.

'Take your hand away from your mouth, Sutherland, you're not hiding anything in there, are you?'

A ripple of laughter.

'No, sir.'

Autumn wind blew across the grounds. There were lists of matches with all the other prep schools pinned up in the hall, as usual: the best thing about them was the teas afterwards. He was still starving hungry most of the time. New boys swarmed round him. He would warn them about Mr Ward.

For a long time he hadn't been able to look at Mr Ward in Geography, though he loved the maps, he loved learning capital cities, and rivers, and all the seas. He loved learning about crops, and trade routes. When they did India — cotton, tea, sugar — it made him think of home, and all the stories. He pictured the jungle, the chattering monkeys and shrieking birds, and the tiger of Tulsipore coming out by moonlight to drink in the nullah, Daddy up a tree very quiet, and watching.

He saw the wicked old crows in every town and city — Lucknow, Delhi, Calcutta, Bombay, he knew them all, knew exactly where they were.

He came top in the India test, way above everyone.

Darling Mummy and Daddy, Guess what!

One other nice thing about this term was that once he'd got used to being in Form Four, and everything being harder, he had a good group of friends. And the funny thing was that Collins was his best friend, when at first he'd been so horrible, ragging him in the dorm, snatching his pillow when he cried: all that. They were about neck and neck in tests — he was better at Geography and French, Collins was better at Maths and Latin, but on the whole they were about the same. They were both in the Second XI and knew they would never be in the First. Collins had been the one to take him to Matron when Mr Wells hit him that time with his Bible, and asked how he was when he came out of the San.

But most of all, they both loved Rupert. They both got annuals at Christmas.

When they walked round the grounds at break time — 'Sutherland! Get your hands out of your pockets!' — they talked about Nutwood, and all Rupert's pals, and their favourite adventures. Some of them were so funny.

'Rupert and the Hazel Nut!'

'Honestly,' said Freddie, as Mummy would say.

The bell rang out, and he and Collins turned round and followed everyone pouring back into the school.

'See you at lunchtime.'

'See you, Sutherland.'

Of course, he had quite a few pals on the train now, after all this time. Robert Pike, a solicitor, Andrew Hall, an accountant — as Flo said, this was all these chaps ever did in Ryehurst, all they'd ever done. Anyway, they were perfectly good company, but it was mostly the girls, quite frankly, who made the commuting bearable. All of them secretaries, as far as he knew, all bright as buttons, and all good fun. Pretty, too, most of them.

When he pitched up on the platform first thing in the morning there they all were, waving away, and when the train to Redstone pulled in he raced to get them their own carriage. It had become a bit of a joke.

'Well done, Mr Sutherland!'

As the train pulled into Victoria, and they all poured out, he was in a pretty good mood these days. A rise on the way, no question about it, and he was dug in at the office now, felt he'd been part of it all for ever sometimes. Overall, of course; the commuting was bloody tiring. He usually fell asleep on the train home, and always after supper; once or twice he did wonder if he should see the doc: not getting any younger, and his blood pressure still went up now and then, he could tell.

But on the whole — on the whole, with the kids nicely settled at school, Bea at Dolphin House now and Fitz helping with the fees again, and Flo with a jolly good holiday under her belt, things weren't bad at all.

The only thing he hadn't done anything about was having a word with David Bone.

Somehow — as with that filthy man Ward — somehow he just hadn't.

★ ★ ★

Now what, Flo asked herself, as another day began. Freddie was gone, poor little chap. Will was gone, and nothing she could say would persuade him to take Freddie away.

'When he's just starting to do so well? Don't be ridiculous, darling.'

Bea was gone, and always had her nose in a book when she was here.

Now what?

Letters fell on to the mat. Still in her fluffy blue dressing gown, she went to pick them up. One from Vivie — lovely. All about Hugo and Bristol, now. The rest were circulars: the Conservative Party Autumn Fair, something from Christian Aid. The parish magazine. She threw it on to the old oak chest. Agnes was delivering the parish magazine, she'd told Will in their Sunday phone call. She was thinking of doing Meals on Wheels. 'I must keep busy!' Flo was trying not to think about Agnes, her newly lonely life, those reproachful calls.

'Any chance of having her for Christmas?'

They should, they should. She couldn't face it.

She made a shopping list, she cycled down the town and shopped. Then she came back again, and put it all away: the cod from MacFisheries, tinned veg, the crème caramel that Green's made and that everyone loved. Green's was saving her life. Tea things for Bea, who was always hungry when she came in. A new little notebook from Woollies, to keep an eye on the milkman.

She made a cup of coffee, she took it into the sitting room. Snowy put his nose round the door.

'Hello, my darling.' She patted the sofa cushion. 'Up you come.'

Up he came, as she sipped her coffee, and tried to remember how many pints they'd had yesterday. She fished out her pen, wrote 'Tuesday' in the notebook.

Something stirred within her. She'd been keeping track of different milkmen for as long as she could remember, even in Melcote, when blue tits used to peck at the silver foil tops and take the cream off, so why today, why now, should just writing 'Tuesday' set something off?

Flo sat back, and looked at the bureau. All her old writing was in there, all her old exercise books, all tied up with string. She hadn't looked at them for years, not since that dreadful time. Unpacking everything when they moved here she'd just stuffed them all into the middle drawer and closed it.

Now she got up, and opened it.

★　★　★

'Mummy? Mummy, can we save the milk bottle tops for the guide dogs? They're having a collection at school. A hundred milk bottle tops are worth a pound!'

'All right, darling, I'll try and remember.'

Snowy was stretched out on Panther's worn old skin. He was almost three feet from his nose

311

to the tip of his tail: Freddie had measured him.

'And, Mummy, I keep forgetting to tell you. Sometimes I have these funny turns.'

Flo put down her teacup and looked at her.

'What sort of turns?'

'I don't really know. I had one today, at lunchtime. One minute everything's just as usual, and the next I've sort of vanished. Everything goes blank.'

EVERYTHING GOES BLANK.

'Blank or black?'

'Blank, I think. Then I come back.'

THEN I COME BACK.

Flo shook her head. Freddie and his tics. Now this.

'It's probably because you've started the curse,' she said at last. 'Everything changes then.'

'Soon I'll need a bra.'

'So you will. I'd better measure you. We can have a little shopping expedition, can't we?'

Bea nodded, taking another Mr Kipling cake. 'What did you do today, Mummy?'

'I bought a new exercise book,' said Flo.

It was scarlet, and shiny. She couldn't wait to begin.

★ ★ ★

'Sometimes I'm not really here,' Bea said to the bird on the bough that evening. 'Don't you think that's strange?'

'I just go blank,' she said. 'Something goes blink in my brain. I've told my mother, but she

312

says I'll grow out of it. That's what she says about everything.'

The bird gazed at her, in his thoughtful way.

'Perhaps I'm just tired,' she said. 'Like my mother. She's always tired.'

SHE'S ALWAYS TIRED.

★ ★ ★

Mr Lansdowne had his favourites, everyone knew that. He had one or two in every year: boys he made jokes with, or teased, or gave top marks in Latin to now and then, even if they hadn't actually got everything right. When all the masters filed out of chapel each morning, Mr Campbell-Davies, the Headmaster, first, then Mr Lansdowne, so tall and handsome with his snow-white hair and whiskers, he'd give a wink or a smile as the organ sounded and everyone stood up: to Winterton, who was Head Boy now, who he had always liked; to Mortimer in Year Five, who had curly hair and was an ace cricketer; all the way down to some little new boy — this year it seemed to be an eager beaver called Finch.

'Morning, Finch! How are we getting on?'

'Very well, thank you, sir.'

Now and then the favourites were given special jobs — sweeping the classroom, clearing up the changing rooms — and extra sweets on Sunday when they'd done them. Sometimes they were invited to Mr Lansdowne's room for tea. Of course, nothing ever happened there, nothing like Mr Ward, it was just toasted buns by the fire, but the fact was, Mr Lansdowne did his beatings in there. If you went, you were always nervous, even though he liked you. Freddie knew this, because in Form Four Collins was the favourite. It used to be Richardson, but now it was Collins.

The thing about Collins was, he was jolly good-looking. He had fair hair and blue eyes and was tall and straight. He had a really nice smile. He could be funny — sometimes he had them all in stitches. And he was a good all-rounder. Not top in everything, but reliable — that was what Mr Campbell-Davies had said last year, on Prize Day, giving him the Best All-Rounder cup. You could see why the masters liked him, and of course Mr Ward had liked him a lot, though Collins had always managed to get out of going back to his cottage in the grounds.

'Sorry, sir, I've got extra prep. Sorry, sir, I've got cricket practice. Thanks very much, sir, but I'm afraid I can't.'

After a while, Mr Ward gave up. He was on to a new lot now.

★   ★   ★

It was after the first Outing that the worst ever beating took place. And the awful thing was, it was given to Collins.

They'd all pretty much got the hang of Form Four: the start-of-term nerves had died down and there weren't any tests till half-term. In Latin they were on to the subjunctive and the pluperfect, and today Mr Lansdowne seemed in a tip-top mood.

'Good morning, Form Four.'

'Good morning, Mr Lansdowne.'

'Had a good breakfast?'

The thing about him was, he could be the nicest person in the world. The mothers all thought he was marvellous, and at home Daddy was always saying what a good chap he was. He twinkled, he told funny stories, and his wuffly white whiskers made you think of a kindly animal. Everyone knew his beatings were bad, but afterwards he always shook your hand and was nice.

'Don't let it happen again, will you, Sutherland?'

'No, sir.' He swallowed back his tears, turned round and walked out, very straight. That was in Form Three, after he'd fluffed two tests in a row, and he hadn't been beaten by him since, in fact he was doing pretty well with beatings this term. Only the gymshoe, so far, from Mr Morley.

Now Mr Lansdowne was up at the board, writing up the subjunctive active of *Audire*, to hear.

'Note the double s, boys.' The chalk squeaked as he wrote up *audivissem*, *audivisses*, and all the rest of it, and he made a little hiss as he said 'double s', so they'd remember. He sounded like a snake.

And something got into Collins, who could be the class joker when he felt like it. Everyone was in a good mood, and he put his hands together and made a snakey movement. Ballantyne sniggered.

'Settle down.' Mr Lansdowne didn't turn round, he just moved a bit further along the

315

board, and Collins's snake turned and followed him. Fisher spluttered. 'Snakey,' whispered Collins, and they all put their hands to their mouths. That kind of giggling — you just couldn't stop once you'd started. Freddie could feel himself going scarlet. Mr Lansdowne moved to the left: so did Snakey. He moved to the right — off went Snakey, his head going up and down and his tongue out, ready to hiss. Harris exploded.

Mr Lansdowne swung round. Collins's tongue went back in his mouth quick as anything, but not quick enough. Mr Lansdowne's eyes narrowed — as a snake's might, Freddie thought a long time later, but now he could hardly think at all. Everyone froze.

'Are you making fun of me, Collins?'

'No, sir.' He went red to the roots of his soft fair hair.

'I think you were.' Mr Lansdowne stepped out from behind the desk, his eyes very dark. 'I'm surprised at you, Collins. I thought you were a cut above the rest. It seems you're a very rude boy.'

'Sir, I — '

'That's enough! Poking your tongue out? How dare you?'

Everyone sat stiff as ramrods. Freddie felt his heart begin to pound. He was going to make a Face, he knew: he could feel every muscle in his mouth working, wanting to stretch out hard, as if in a silent scream, and he clamped his lips together, so hard his teeth almost went through.

'You will come to my room at five o'clock. The rest of you will be there, too, is that understood?

Now copy this down. I don't want to hear another word.'

Leaves blew past the window. From the drive came the sound of the milk crates for break being unloaded and carried indoors, rattling. Pens chinked on inkwells. These things felt enormous in the silence of the room.

★ ★ ★

Never had a day been so long. Everyone kept looking at Collins, who was pale and quiet, though he kept saying it would be all right, Lansdowne would probably have calmed down after tea. At five to five, excused by Mr Whistler from Prep because Mr Lansdowne said so, sir, Form Four walked in file along the hall and down past the turn in the stairs. 'Good luck, Collins,' whispered Richardson, Form Prefect now, and then he knocked on the door.

'Come in.'

Inside, Mr Lansdowne stood waiting by the fire, his cane in his hand. Everything looked so nice in here: the armchairs, the hunting prints on the walls, the table piled with books and marking. Mr Lansdowne didn't look nice at all. Freddie swallowed.

'Shut the door, Ballantyne.'

It closed with an awful click.

Then everyone was made to stand round the room, which wasn't very large, so they were all pressed up against each other, and you could feel the wet palms of the boy next to you. Somehow everyone knew this was going to be bad.

317

'Over there, Collins,' said Mr Lansdowne quietly, and pointed to a place on the carpet. Collins went there, white as a sheet. 'Bend over.' He bent. Everyone had said he should scrounge some newspaper from the kitchen and stuff it down his shorts, but Collins said old Lansdowne could tell when you'd done that, and it would put him in even more of a bate. Now they could see him clamping his lips hard together, as he clasped his knees.

Then Mr Lansdowne walked slowly to the other end of the room, running his cane through his hand, and bending it. He flicked it hard, and it whistled through the air. He turned round. He ran.

He ran at Collins, the cane held high, and then, with a terrible swish, he brought it down so hard that Collins screamed. It wasn't a yell or a yelp, it was a scream, and Freddie shut his eyes. He gripped his hands into fists to stop the face he was desperate to make. He could hear Mr Lansdowne run back to the other end of the room, he opened his eyes, saw him turn round, and run at Collins again. He was tense and glittering and terrible and now no one could look. Down came the cane, and Collins screamed, even louder. There were four more times. Then it was over.

Everyone was shaking. Collins was kneeling, almost collapsed, just howling and howling. Mr Lansdowne had sweat streaming down his forehead; he was trembling from head to foot.

'You may go.'

Above the dreadful sounds Collins was

318

making, you could hardly hear that. Freddie saw him kneeling on the floor, sobbing uncontrollably. He saw Mr Lansdowne look down at him, sweating and trembling and panting in a way that Freddie knew, all at once, in a horrible way, was because he was excited. He liked it, it did something to him. He liked the beatings, he liked beating Collins especially. He put the cane back by the fire, and his hands shook.

'I said you may go.'

Freddie and Richardson walked over to Collins and helped him up. No one had ever cried like this, in all the time they'd been there. He just couldn't stop. They put their arms through his and helped him through the door, everyone following mutely in file.

'Poor old Collins, poor old Collins.' Outside, they all said it, over and over. The howling and sobbing was a dreadful thing, uncontrollable, hysterical, tears and snot and sweat pouring out. Doors opened. Matron appeared at the top of the stairs, Mr Whistler came out of the prep room and frowned. He was young, he had only just started. People said he was going out with Miss Young, the Assistant Matron.

'What's up?'

'Sir, sir, Mr Lansdowne, sir — '

'Fetch him a glass of water.' Mr Whistler put his arm round Collins and led him to the detention bench outside the prep room. 'Sit down, old chap, it's over now.'

Collins sat down and leaped up again, yelling. Then they saw the blood.

'Matron!'

She came running down, she took Collins slowly up the stairs, still howling. Then they all went in to prep.

Miranda Marshall had never wanted to go to India, but when the chance came, at the end of the War, she was thrilled! Her heart had been broken by a passionate love affair, and now she could make a fresh start...

Flo sat at the open bureau, and it all came pouring out. This time she could concentrate, this time she would get it right. Two days ago, she had felt so nervous she didn't think she'd be able to do it. After all these years: how could she pick it up again? She leafed through all the old exercise books from Melcote, all her diaries from Devon. How had she managed to write a word there, with hens in the kitchen and the children always up to something, and Will and Mike needing proper men's meals twice a day? She got quite lost reading it all. Gosh, they'd been happy: frantic at times, but happy — until Will got his blood pressure, anyway.

When she looked through the Novel, it gave her awful feelings.

'*I can't do it, I can't do it!*'

That had been the start. That dreadful time. They never spoke of it now, she hardly thought of it, really. But now — if she started to write again, would it stir it all up?

She'd shut the books, shut the bureau, gone to get tea ready. Bea would be home in a minute; perhaps she should leave it alone.

But today — this morning, when she'd thought: I'll try it just once — it was going really well. A much better opening, she could tell at once, and India all came rushing back: she was practically *living* it.

The heat was intense: she had never known anything like it. And the noise! As they drove away from Bombay harbour, with its tall green palm trees, they could hear people shouting, traffic hooting, army trucks rattling, the cries from the bazaar...

Cars went past on Croydon Road. The carriage clock on the mantelpiece struck one. Good heavens, where had the morning gone?

★ ★ ★

'And what have you been up to today, my darling?' Will passed his plate for a second helping. Outside it was pouring with rain, in here warm and cosy, coke sifting down in the Rayburn, the gingham curtains drawn, *The Archers* over.
'Well, actually,' said Flo, feeling better than she had for years, 'I did some writing.'
He frowned. 'Sure that's a good idea?'
'It was fine, honestly.' She scooped out the last of the mince. 'I really enjoyed it.'
'Why shouldn't it be a good idea?' asked Bea, tipping her plate to finish the gravy.
'Tip the plate away from you, darling, always.'
'Why?'
'Don't argue!' said Will, and she swallowed. A

321

Mood was on the way.

'Anyway,' Flo said brightly, 'I've done a Crème Caramel.'

But where Will would usually say 'My darling,' or 'Splendid,' now he said nothing. Bea helped clear away the first course.

'Why's he in a mood?' she whispered in the scullery.

Flo shook her head. 'He's not. Don't take any notice.'

She gave her the pudding bowls, picked up the Crème Caramel, slipping about in its dish. There came a sudden screech of brakes from the road, then an awful yowl.

'What on earth was that?'

They carried everything through to the kitchen.

Then: 'Where's Snowy?'

Everyone looked. He wasn't in his basket. Bea ran down to the sitting room. He wasn't by the fire. Out in the hall, she flung the front door open, on to the dark and wet.

'Bea!'

She ran to the gate. There he was, white and limp, and soaking in the gutter. Cars swished by.

'Is it him?' They were both behind her. Then they saw. Flo burst into tears.

'I'll get him.' Will strode out through the gate.

'Be very careful! He might not be dead.'

'I know what I'm doing.'

Hands to their mouths, they watched him bend down, scoop up the long white body as cars went by, rain glittering in the headlights. He carried him into the house, kicking the door shut behind him. 'He's alive.' Then into the sitting room, down by the fire. 'Gently, gently.'

Snowy's eyes were wide and dark and his mouth was open. A trickle of blood came out as he panted.

'He didn't stop!' Bea kneeled down, stroked the soaking wet head. 'He just drove away!'

'It's dark,' said Will. 'It's raining. Cats and dogs, if you'll pardon the expression.'

'*Will!*'

'*Daddy!*'

'Sorry. But you know what I mean — you hit a cat in the rain, you drive on before you cause an accident.'

'But it's *Snowy!*'

'I know. Poor old thing. I'll go and call the vet. If he's open. Where's the number?'

Flo fetched the address book; Will went through to the dining room.

'Hello? Hello? Will Sutherland here. Sorry to trouble you, but there's been a bit of an accident — '

Flo and Bea kneeled by Snowy, stroking him softly as Will went on. Snowy's wet fur was drying in the warmth, but his eyes were still dark with pain. Then he closed them, and died.

★ ★ ★

Bea lay in the dark in her bedroom. 'Our cat was killed last night,' she heard herself say in the morning, as they all went into class. 'He got hit by a car.'

How could she be thinking about how to tell

it? Already. When Snowy was lying dead in his basket, Mummy in floods of tears. Why wasn't she in floods?

She relived the moment: the rushing outside, the sight of his darling white body in the rain. Hadn't she felt something then? Of course, of course she had.

But now — within such a short time she was distanced from it all, putting it into a story: not one of her private ones, but something to tell people. Putting herself at the centre of things: that was the worst bit of all.

There's something the matter with me, she thought bleakly, hearing Will lock all the doors downstairs, and follow Flo up to bed.

Raining cats and dogs, if you'll pardon the expression.

How could he? How could he, with Snowy gasping by the fire, about to die? There was something wrong with him, too.

Mummy's the only real person in this house, she thought, hearing her blow her nose in the bathroom, and say, as Will joined her: 'Things will never be the same again.'

'My darling. We'll give him a little funeral.'

Mummy made him human, she made everything all right for all of them. That was her life.

'His body went stiff very quickly,' Bea said in the darkness, taking her place in class.

⋆   ⋆   ⋆

*Darling Freddie, I'm afraid I've got something awfully sad to tell you...*She stopped, put her pen

324

down. No, she couldn't do it. If he'd had a bad day it might be the last straw, might upset him terribly. Who knew what really went on when he was away?

Traffic went by, the carriage clock chimed the half-hour. It was almost time for lunch, and almost every day, for as long as they'd been in Ryehurst, she and Snowy had gone upstairs together after lunch. He purred, she yawned, she sank into one of those deep, deep sleeps —

Now, it just wouldn't be the same.

Well, she'd stop doing it. Poor Snowy. Perhaps this was a Sign. She'd get a Mrs Thing to do the housework in the morning, she'd save up the money from the housekeeping. She'd do all the shopping, and then — then she'd sit down and write.

★　★　★

Agnes came for a visit. Poor, poor little thing. She'd shrunk, and beneath that dreadful hat her dark eyes looked almost black. She had great shadows under them, in that pale sad face.

Will fetched her from Redstone station. Flo embraced her in the hall. She would make an effort, she really would.

'I'm so sorry.'

Agnes gave a little shrug. 'Oh, well. There we are.'

Flo took her coat, and her horrible hat.

'Come and have a drink,' said Will. 'Come by the fire.' He called up the stairs. 'Bea! Bea! Auntie Agnes is here!'

Bea came running down. 'Hello, Auntie Agnes.'

Another hug, warmer on both sides. Then it was sherry and Twiglets in the sitting room, and everyone saying how sorry they were again, and Agnes saying, Perhaps it was for the best, poor Neville, he was so ill.

Flo went to finish off the lunch.

'Take another glass with you, my darling.' Will filled it to the brim.

He and Bea stayed by the fire and heard about Agnes's journey from Wimbledon, which had been long, and talked about whether she was going to stay there now. Perhaps she should move to a flat.

'What do you think, Willie?'

He poured her another glass, too. He didn't know. A bit of him wanted to say: Come and move near us, Sis, why don't you do that? Be part of the family. We'd love it. Another bit, much larger, knew it wouldn't work, they wouldn't love it. She and Flo: they were doing their best today, but — chalk and cheese, no two ways about it. Perhaps she could move to Chichester, be near Neville's brother and his wife. He might suggest it later.

'I don't think Tinkerbell would like a flat,' said Bea, drinking squash. 'She likes going in the garden, doesn't she?'

Agnes sipped her sherry. 'I'll stay for Tinkerbell, then. For now.'

And then they finished off the Twiglets, and talked about Snowy, and how awful that had been, and then Flo was calling them into the dining room for lunch, where Will sharpened the steel — 'Mind your backs!' — and set vigorously about the lamb.

'You're such a good cook, Auntie Agnes,' said Bea, passing the gravy.

'So's Mummy, of course.' Agnes was flushed from the second sherry.

'Ha, ha,' said Flo, likewise, and buoyed up with several good days with the book. 'I wouldn't care if I never cooked another meal again, quite frankly.'

Agnes gave a nervous little laugh. 'You don't mean that, Flo.'

'Oh, but I do.'

It was the kind of exchange that in Bournemouth, between Flo and Vivie, would have had everyone in fits. Now: it was just a little thing, but it was the first sharp moment, and it felt like battle lines.

'Well, anyway,' said Will, shovelling great thick slices of lamb on to her plate, 'here we are, Sis, that'll keep your strength up.'

They got through it all by talking about school: Freddie doing so well, really settled in, and all that dreadful Eleven-plus stuff behind Bea now, thank God. In her last term at Micklegate she'd won the Composition Prize.

'English is my best subject, really.'

'What do you write about?'

'We're given different subjects. Sometimes it's description, like An Autumn Day, and sometimes it's things where you have to discuss, like A Woman's Place is in the Home.'

They all agreed that it was.

Of course, Agnes said, she was keeping busy outside the home, too, now she no longer had

Neville to cook for. Doing the flowers at church, though other people did them much better, of course. And she'd joined a prayer group.

'What about you, Flo?' she asked, with a bit of an edge in her voice. 'What do you do all day when Bea's at school?'

Flo took a breath. 'I'm writing a book,' she said.

Will gave a little cough.

'A book! Good heavens, I thought you'd stopped all that.'

Will coughed louder.

'Are you all right, Daddy?'

'What's this one about?'

'Still about India.'

Agnes gave a mirthless little laugh. 'I hope I'm not in it.'

'Not exactly.'

Miranda was sharing her billet in Bombay with a rather plain girl called Annette. She was nice enough, but they didn't really have anything in common. Miranda had had lots of love affairs, and even though her heart had been Broken in the War, at least something had happened! When she was nursing, the patients were always making eyes at her, and she went out with various young medics. Annette had been an Assistant School Matron. Then she had worked in Great Ormond Street Hospital, but...

★ ★ ★

'Any chance of having Agnes for Christmas?'

'Do we have to?'

'Darling, she's all on her own.'

'I know, I know. I just can't face it.'

Bea watched his face get that tense look.

'What am I going to say to her on Sunday?'

'I don't know. I'm sorry.'

On Sunday, when he rang her after church, he shut the dining-room door. When he came out, he said: 'She's going to Neville's family — Brian and Jean.'

'Thank God for that.'

★   ★   ★

And now it was the Christmas holidays, and Freddie home!

'Where's Snowy?'

He went very quiet when they told him. Bea took him out into the garden, and showed him where the grave was, under a rose bush.

'Why didn't anyone tell me?' he said at last.

'Mummy said it might upset you too much.'

It was freezing out here. They went back indoors, and up to the sort of playroom, up at the top of the house. They settled down on the floor.

'How many beatings have you had?'

He counted on his fingers. 'I had the cane only twice. I had the gymshoe three times. And the slipper.'

'But what do you get beaten *for*?'

He tried to think. 'I don't know, really. Ragging about. Forgetting dates in History. Not learning stuff properly.'

'Poor Freddie.'

'I had quite a few Narrow Squeaks,' he said, and she laughed. When he told her about them it all seemed so far away, and her laughing made it seem funny.

But he didn't tell her about Collins and Mr Lansdowne. Somehow he just couldn't.

6

There was masses of homework at Dolphin House. Each morning when she left the house Bea's satchel was almost groaning with the weight of it. Now they had proper Science, with a lab and a Bunsen burner and Dissection at A level. She would never do A level in any of the science subjects, she knew.

Top in English, bottom in everything else. One of those. You could do Extras: she'd wanted to do piano, but Flo said Elocution was more important, so she did that, in a little room with a gas fire, on Wednesday afternoons. Mrs Roberts told them how to put in Expression. They stood up one by one, and recited mournful poems:

'Toll no bell for me, dear Father, dear Mother,
Waste no sighs . . . '

'Beautiful, Bea.'
It was the highlight of the week.
The rest was pretty hard going, but outside the classroom no one ever talked about work. In the cloakroom, at break, at lunch, it was all pop, pop, pop. And the *New Musical Express*, though no one called it that, of course: it was the *NME*, bought every Saturday, the same day you watched *Juke Box Jury*. Who was going to get to Number One? That was all anyone really cared about. And stiff petticoats, for doing the Twist.

Even at home they could play pop now. For Christmas, Will had bought a record player!

'To everyone, from Will,' he intoned, writing away on his clipboard, as Bea and Freddie unwrapped in amazement. 'One Dansette record player.' He put down the biro. ' "Thank you, Daddy." '

'Thank you, Daddy!'

They talked about boys at school, too. Not that they ever saw any. Once a year, the Sixth Form had a dance with the Grammar School Sixth: they were the only boys in Ryehurst, apparently, and Bea saw them on the bus, in their black blazers and long grey trousers. Freddie was still in shorts! Some of the older ones had slicked-back hair. But she never actually spoke to any of them, and anyway the bus ride was short, and anyway —

Boys were for later. And anyway — there was Hugo. He made the boys on the bus look like babies.

Every morning, she kissed Flo goodbye and walked down to the main road. She waited at the bus stop. When the 406 arrived, she sometimes sat next to Carolyn Joyce, who came all the way in from Buckhurst. But if she was late — turning over in bed for ten minutes more as Flo stood at the bottom of the stairs in her dressing gown calling, 'Bea! Bea!' — then she was on her own. She got off three stops later, crossed the road, and walked up the hill to school.

Now they were in The Favoured Tall Trees Road Area: that was what the estate agents called it, and that was how Will said it, with his funny emphasis. The houses were large and double-fronted, with big front gardens, and it all felt quiet and rich. Cars whizzed past her: the mothers who Drove. Sometimes, if it was pouring, they stopped and gave Bea a lift. She clambered in with her satchel, saying 'Thanks awfully,' and saying it again when she got out. When she left Micklegate she'd been given the Courtesy Cup.

At the top of the hill, girls were walking nicely through the big double gates and down the wooded school drive in their grey felt hats and royal-blue blazers.

They all piled into their cloakrooms. ''Only the Lonely',' sang Rosemary Reed, hanging her hat up.

''Dum-dum-dum-dum-ah-doo-wah',' sang everyone, being the Backing Group.

★　★　★

His report at the end of Form Four said he was developing Leadership Qualities. Will gave him another half-a-crown.

'You're doing splendidly, old chap.'

And as soon as they got back, and went up to Form Five, he was made Form Prefect, something he'd thought would never happen.

'Thanks, sir. Thanks very much.'

He pinned the badge on to his jumper.

And now he'd pretty much got the hang of it all; really, they all had. He knew what he was good at: Geography, French, Science, perfectly good at English and Maths. Even with his Latin, he knew he'd pass the Common Entrance. He was good at cross-country running, just as Will had been. And that got you out of school, of course, into the countryside, panting up hills and down through muddy woods: you felt terrific when it was over.

And then there were all his gang, like the Bash Street Kids in the *Beano*: Ballantyne, Harris, and Richardson, and still friends with Bell Minor, who'd come Up now, all of them ragging about, but knowing when to stop, always keeping an eye out.

'Psst!'

Back to their desks in a flash.

'Cave!'

Sitting up in their beds with their books as if butter wouldn't melt in their mouths. 'I was just sitting up in bed reading my Bible, sir, when all of a sudden it just flew out of my hand and hit the light bulb.' That was one of Will's stories, from his time here.

The only thing that was awful, of course, was missing Collins.

He hadn't come back.

★ ★ ★

The pages were piling up and up. To hell with exercise books: she was using a big white pad now, which for some reason made her feel much more like a real writer. And no more Running a Home without Help! She had help now. And she'd taken that wretched book out of the kitchen and stuffed it into the drawing-room bookcase. There! Away with it!

And now, on the two days a week when she'd let in Mrs Thing — oh, what joy to have her, straight out of the *Surrey Mirror* and in through the front door — Flo opened the bureau and settled down. The sounds of the Hoover, and Mrs Thing huffing and puffing and sloshing through the house, the smell of the polish on Tuesdays, and on Thursdays the lovely warm smell of the ironing — all this faded, like the cars going past and the leaves swirling down from the trees across the road. Within moments of starting, she was There.

In the afternoons she rested, while her husband, back on a sugar cane station after the War, went out to Supervise. They had moved up to the borders of Nepal, and they were expecting a baby!! He came home in time for drinks on the veranda, brought on a little brass tray by their bearer. He took her in his arms.

'My darling . . . '

A tap on the door. Another.

'I'm done now, Mrs Sutherland.'

She wrenched herself back to Ryehurst. Tuesdays and Thursdays were perfect, the house all in order, ironing in piles, only supper to think about. And Bea, of course, coming home at four.

'What's for tea?'

'Go and have a look in the larder, I'll be with you in a minute.'

Back to the bureau, just a few more lines.

'Mummy? Mummy, I can't find *anything*.' Bea

335

came down the hall, still with her grey felt hat on. 'I've been through all the tins. I found one ginger biscuit.'

'Oh, darling, there must be more than that. Let me come and see.'

'I'm *starving*.'

Sometimes it was Will who was starving. That wasn't funny. Key in the lock, six forty-five on the dot. The two-note whistle.

He was the most attractive man she had ever seen! She'd thought it when she first saw him, that boiling hot afternoon in Delhi, and she thought it still, moving into his embrace as the sun sank low, and the shadows lengthened.

Now he was here, wanting supper.

'How about beans on toast? With an egg.'

'Anything.' He was pouring himself a whisky. 'I've had a hell of a day. Want a peg?'

'Thank you, darling. Supper in two ticks.'

He grunted, carried his glass through to the sitting room, saw the open bureau, the heaped-up sheets of paper.

Not again. Every blasted day.

'I don't bloody know.'

'Mummy?' Bea was on the landing. 'How long till supper?'

'Two ticks!'

Perhaps she went off the boil a bit on Mrs Thing days. Took her eye off the ball, as Will would say. Did say, eating his beans on toast in the kitchen, looking exhausted.

336

'Surely you haven't been writing all day?'

She gave a little laugh. 'No, no, of course not. Just a few hours.'

He shook his head. 'So long as it's not, you know — '

'It's not. Honestly.'

'Not what?' asked Bea, poking her knife in her egg yolk.

NOT WHAT?

'Not anything, darling. Don't let that drip.'

Poor hungry Will. She felt dreadful. On Friday she made a Green's Lemon Meringue Pie.

'That's more like it.'

★ ★ ★

'In the car!' Crack of dawn on a summer's day, Flo in a flowery hat, Will in a linen jacket, his cricket bat tucked in the boot. 'Got the map?'

'Darling, we really don't need the map now.'

'Better to have it.'

She fed him with Glacier Mints. And at last —

'Well done, darling, that was a super drive.'

There were the tall school gates swung open, other cars pouring through, the sun shining, the grass cut, boys in their white shirts and cricket things, already down at the nets. As soon as they parked and got out they could hear the thwack of the balls, the cries of 'Well done!', the smell of the grass and all the parents greeting one another, everyone in a good mood, fathers especially. Today it was Parents' Day, 1961, with a Father's Match and special tea.

'Darling!'

There he was, coming shyly over, brown eyes lit up with happiness.

'Freddie, old chap!' They shook hands, he kissed Flo politely and nodded to Bea.

'Hi.'

'Hi, Freddie.'

And here was twinkly Mr Lansdowne, striding over.

'Mrs Sutherland. Lovely to see you again.'

Flo blushed beneath the flowery hat. 'And you, Mr Lansdowne. Aren't we lucky with the weather?'

'Always sunny for Father's Match. Will, how are you?'

'Absolutely splendid, thanks. Good to see you.'

Hearty handshakes. Then Mr Campbell-Davies, the Headmaster, came over, his gown flying, more handshakes, all the other parents milling about and pigeons cooing in the chestnut trees.

First they were going to have lunch in town, back to The Duck restaurant with its snow-white linen and winking glasses. A treat, only once a term, and no tears from Freddie. He hadn't cried on Outings for a long time now.

'So, old chap, how's it all going?'

'Fine, thanks.'

That was all you ever got out of him. Will shook out his napkin.

'Any Narrow Squeaks?' murmured Bea, as the waiter came for their order.

He shook his head and smiled, and then they both had to be quiet while Will read out the menu and gave the order. 'What'll you have, my darling? The chicken?' He took off his glasses. 'My wife will have the chicken,' he told the waiter, so loudly that the family at the next table all looked round. He put his glasses on again, looked at the menu. 'Now, then, you kids . . . '

After lunch, they went back to the school, and when they'd walked off the chicken and roast potatoes and ice cream with wafers, and Will had talked to a million masters and parents, and Flo had talked to one or two Mrs Things — 'Darling, I can't help it, I can never remember their names' — and Freddie had gone off with his friends and Bea had just sort of hung about, a bell rang out and at last it was time for the Match.

'Right!' said Will, galvanising himself, and went to get his bat.

'I need the lav,' said Bea, and she and Flo walked over to the creeper-smothered house and into the echoing hall. From somewhere came the sounds of chinking china being set out for the tea. This was where Freddie spent his life: was signed up for matches, went into his form room for lessons, and up the huge winding stairs to his dorm. The form rooms all looked quite ghostly now, with no boys inside, and just mothers in summer hats and flowery frocks, putting their heads round the door to have a little look, going to the lav and saying, 'My dear!' and 'Where did you get that frock?' and 'The holidays are hell!' Bea and Flo had a laugh at that.

Out on the cricket pitch they found things hotting up. This was the only time in the whole year when Will played cricket. He was a runner, and in India he'd done a lot of wrestling, drinking buffalo milk to get himself strong, and he was a great walker, of course. 'I'll do my best,' he said now, striding up and down and swinging his bat about.

'He'll hit someone in a minute.'

They sat down in the shade.

Then all the fathers got into teams, and all the boys sat down in rows in their forms to watch, with their Form Masters keeping an eye. Mr Campbell-Davies made a little speech, about how good it was to see everyone, and how this, like Prize-giving, was a highlight of the year, and he knew all the fathers would distinguish themselves. 'Ra-ther!' said Will. A polite little ripple of laughter ran through everyone.

But actually it wasn't too bad. Harris's father, Dr Harris, was captaining Will's team, and the father of a top-form boy the other. It all had a civilised air, and Will was not the only father to shout out 'Howzzat!' and in fact was fitter than lots of them; looked pretty good when he ran. Some got really red in the face.

Quite soon Bea stopped watching, and lay back on the grass, hearing the firm click of bat on ball and the cries of the fathers, while the mothers chatted all round her. She covered her ears when Flo called someone Mrs Thing again, or kept saying, 'How fascinating,' to everything anyone said.

Why were her parents so different? Listening to everyone talking away about their husbands and children, she had the impression of lots going on, lots of friends and things to do. Of course, many of the parents were local, they'd be bound to know each other a bit, but even so —

Very few visitors came to their own house. That was how it felt, on the whole: just one or two people from church, or the RLS, passing through, like Jonathan Gibbs, the Regional Sec for Surrey, who was tall and good-looking, so Mummy didn't mind him coming, even though he was Living in Sin, apparently. Will saw people at the office all day, and when he went out and about to farms and showgrounds and things. When he came home he fell asleep on the sofa. Bea had all her friends at school, but she rarely brought them home. She never quite felt she could say to Lizzie Moore, or Rosemary Reed, or any of them: Come and have tea, just like that, on the spur of the moment; she never had. All those empty cake tins.

As for Freddie: when he came home to Ryehurst in the holidays, he didn't know anyone. It was just him and her, really. If she went to play records with Lizzie or Rosemary at their houses, she felt guilty, leaving him alone, though he never seemed to mind. The only regular visitor to the house was Auntie Agnes, and that was usually awful.

Whack went the cricket bat, and she could hear fathers panting up and down, doing their runs, and the mothers calling out, 'Well *done!*'

She sat up.

And there it was again: the cricket and the pigeons in the chestnut trees and all the chat around her — they were gone, she was nowhere, as if something in her brain had just been

341

switched off. Blink. Blank. Nothing. Then:

'Darling? Are you all right?'

'Just had one of my funny things, that's all.' She shook her head. 'I'm fine now.'

I'M FINE NOW, said the words in the hot summer sky.

★　★　★

The match ended at half-past four, with Dr Harris's team — Will's team! — the winners, and then everyone trooped in for tea in the enormous dining room, where tables were laid with linen cloths and vases of summer flowers stood about, arranged by Mrs Campbell-Davies and Matron. There were cucumber sandwiches, egg-and-cress sandwiches, tiny iced cakes, strawberries and cream. Bea noticed Freddie and his friends simply wolfing it all, even after that enormous lunch. All around them mothers were talking to the masters about their own boys, and how they were getting on, and the fathers were talking about the cricket, or their work, or the Cuban Missile Crisis, which had had Will glued to the News every night.

Then Mr Campbell-Davies and Mr Lansdowne were all going round saying how marvellous it had been, and you could tell it was time to go.

'Goodbye, my darling.' Flo drew Freddie to her, and he shrank back, just as all the other boys were doing when their mothers tried to kiss them in front of everyone. 'See you very soon,' she whispered, and he nodded, longing to hold her tight.

'Bye, Freddie.'

'Bye, Bea.'

'Goodbye, old chap, you're doing splendidly.'

'Thanks, Daddy.'

He stood in the drive with his little group of friends, like Rupert and his pals in Nutwood, waving and waving as they drove away.

'I told you he'd settle down.'

★　★　★

As Form Prefect, he had duties after the match, and he swallowed back all the old feelings at saying goodbye, and went into the form room to check that none of the visitors had moved the chairs, or left anything behind: it was amazing how parents treated the place as their own. Someone had opened a window in here, and the smell of cut grass outside mingled with the usual dust and chalk. He went to close it, seeing masters chatting away to one another, everyone in a good mood.

He turned back, saw a handkerchief under a desk and picked it up. It was a little flowery thing, the kind of hankie Auntie Vivie sent to his mother for her birthday — *Something else to iron!* Mummy would say, tucking it into her sleeve, or dabbing it with scent on special occasions. *Never, ever tell anyone what scent you use...*

Freddie stood in the warm quiet form room, lit by the sinking sun, and pressed the little hankie to his face. Was it hers? Could he smell her, could he conjure all that love and warmth?

The flowery cotton smelled of nothing but itself. A bit dusty, perhaps. But as boys went past in the echoing hall outside, and as he thought, This has nothing to do with me, and put it in his pocket to take to Matron, he suddenly knew something, in the most horrible way. In the sunlit room it made him go icy cold, but it made everything about his family and his years away from them make sense.

No son of mine...

That was what Will had said, down in the firelit sitting room, banging the door shut on all those tears.

He'd lain upstairs in the dark, wondering what he meant. Now he knew.

Part Four

The Chalk Path

1

It was done! It was finished! Flo sat at the bureau numbering the pages, reading it all again. It was good! So much better than that first attempt in Melcote: this read like a proper book. Now all she had to do was get it typed.

'What I need is a good woman,' she said aloud, skimming over Pets and Articles for Sale in the *Surrey Mirror*, making for Office Services. And then she found one. Within moments she was on the phone, announcing with enormous happiness to Miss Mabel Hunt (65 words per minute), 'I've written a book. It's about our time in India.'

★ ★ ★

What luck! Miss Hunt lived on a road by the Common, just five minutes' bike ride away. Flo was cycling up there next morning, the manuscript in her basket, as soon as she'd finished breakfast. It was bright and sunny, the grass on the Common thick and lush, the white-painted sails of a windmill like a picture-book against the summer sky.

As she cycled down the unmade road, she saw a row of modest little places with nice front gardens, and already she could hear Miss Hunt through an open window, tapping away like mad. And Flo was, she knew, as soon as she saw her, in her sensible blouse and specs, in the hands of a professional.

It would take her most of the summer, said Miss Hunt, leafing through the pages in her tiny front room. Partly because of reading the — er — handwriting, partly because she already had quite a lot on. A book by a local historian, most interesting.

'My book has quite a lot of history in it,' said Flo. 'Well, personal history. It's set just after the war. The period leading up to Indian Independence. My husband was in the Indian Army.'

Miss Hunt leafed through a few more pages. The words 'love', 'kiss' and 'forever' were liberally sprinkled. Her charges, she said, were quite competitive, but Flo almost fainted.

'Two and six a *page?*' It was more than the hourly rate for Mrs Thing. 'I'll have to think about it,' she said, as firmly as she could, knowing that somehow she would find a way. Father would find a way.

And she got on her bicycle and rode home, doing sums, as larks sang over the Common.

* * *

The summer holidays. Freddie home, lunch for three every day. Most mornings he and Bea spent in the sitting room, one in the armchair, one on the sofa, on either side of the empty fireplace, listening to records on the Dansette.

'This is Cliff Richard and the Shadows,' she told him, as the 45s dropped down. She spent all her pocket money on them, off down to Rhythm, the record shop, every Saturday morning. 'Fall in Love with You', 'I Love You', 'Please Don't Tease' — Freddie listened dutifully.

'What are you thinking about?' He seemed to be in a dream these days.

'Nothing.' But his strange new knowledge churned around inside him.

'Do stop making those faces.'

Sometimes Flo prised them out and sent them up to the shops beneath the railway bridge to get things for lunch. Oh, thank God for fish fingers. There, put it on the table, done it. Done, done it, done it.

How was Mabel Hunt getting on?

After lunch, she went upstairs for her rest, and then Bea and Freddie went down the town.

'You've gone awfully quiet,' said Bea, as they left the house.

'Sorry.'

But he couldn't think of anything to tell her now. He wasn't in trouble so often; his report, on the whole, had been tiptop. 'A good strong year in most subjects, an excellent runner, and a useful, sensible boy to have in the school.'

'Marvellous,' said Will. 'I knew you'd settle down.'

'Thanks.' He knew it sounded curt, but he was trying not to use the word 'Daddy', now he knew. 'Mummy' was different — he just couldn't stop himself.

Bea wasn't that interested anyway, as they walked along. She was thinking about the school play. She was quite settled at Dolphin House: so good at English, not so bad at French, close to the bottom in an awful lot of subjects, but a lovely singing voice, said her Music report, and good at Drama.

Every year Mrs Roberts, of Elocution, put on a Shakespeare play on the terrace, for the fifth and sixth forms. This year it had been *The Taming of the Shrew*, with two prefects, Jessica Connolly and Patricia Banks, playing Petruchio and Kate. Mrs Lambourne, the music mistress, said Bea should audition for *Twelfth Night* next year, for the part of Feste. He sang beautiful sad songs.

'Never heard of him,' said Will. 'But then, I don't suppose he's ever heard of me, either.'

She and Freddie had come to the High Street. And there was Julia Charters, gazing into the Rhythm window. Bea raced ahead.

'Is that your best friend?' asked Freddie, when at last she came out.

'Julia? No, I've got lots. Who's your best friend?'

He hesitated. 'It was Collins, but he left.'

'Why?'

'Don't know.' That was something else he couldn't talk about.

The town clock struck the half-hour. Still only half-past three. They mooched into Woollies, and then down Abbey Street and into the bookshop, which was very old, with beams and bare floorboards and just a nice feel about it. It was almost all grown-up books, but there was a children's section at the back, and they hovered over Enid Blyton, *Rupert*, *Anne of Green Gables*, *The Railway Children*, *Down the Bright Stream*.

'I remember this,' said Freddie, taking that one down. 'I got into trouble for reading this in the dorm, soon after I started.' He turned the pages, feeling a Face begin.

'You shouldn't be doing that *still*.'

'I know.' But it was a part of him now, had been with him for years, much longer than his new knowledge about himself. The Faces were almost a friend, or like something extra inside him, egging him on. *Go on, stretch those muscles till they hurt, that's it, isn't that better? Now do it again.*

'Don't you have things you can't help?' he asked Bea, closing the book as the town clock struck four.

'Sometimes I go blank,' she said. 'Sometimes I'm just not there. I never know when it's going to happen. Then it's gone.'

'What does Mummy say?'

'She says I'll grow out of it.'

'That's what she says to me.'

They walked out of the murmuring bookshop, and home through the town for tea. It was just like any boring old day in the holidays, but when they got back, and did the three rings, it took ages for Flo to answer.

'She can't *still* be asleep.'

They rang again, pressing their faces to the frosted glass.

'There she is!'

And here she was, opening the door and looking sad and different.

'Come in,' she said slowly, and then she told them.

351

★ ★ ★

'Oh, no! Not Grandpa. I really loved Grandpa.'
'So did I.'
He'd died really peacefully in his sleep.
'The way we'd all like to go,' said Will at supper. He put his hand on Flo's. 'My darling.'
She sat there, her chin in her hands.

★ ★ ★

After supper, Freddie went for a walk by himself. Not very far, just down to the little green at the end of the road, where a huge cedar tree stood. He climbed up the couple of steps, walked over the grass and sat on the seat beneath it.
'Grandpa,' he said aloud.
He thought about the Coronation sweet tin, the smell of toast at breakfast, grapes in the conservatory, endless twinkling kindness.
I was away at school, too. That was before dinosaurs walked the earth, of course.
Above him the boughs of the cedar rose and fell. How strange it was to think that someone he'd loved so much hadn't been related to him at all, not really. It *felt* as if he was related, they all felt like that, he'd been with them so long. But none of them was a real relation at all. Grandpa had been just a kindly friend.
The evening breeze stirred the tree. He thought about Grandpa's apple trees, of the great big garden behind the house, where you could hear all the babies crying from the Mother and Baby Home next door. 'Who are all those

babies?' he'd asked, and now he realised that Grandpa hadn't answered him. Not properly. That was because he'd been a baby like that, hadn't he? A baby who had to be given away.

Adopted.

So somewhere in the world were his real parents, living quite apart from one another, probably. There weren't any fathers in the Mother and Baby Home, that was the point: the mothers were all on their own, and they couldn't possibly keep their babies, because they were Disgraced. Somewhere in the world his real mother might even now be wondering about him, all by herself and lonely.

He swallowed. This was almost too sad to think about. And all this time his parents had been keeping up the pretence, not wanting to upset him, wanting to make him feel he was one of theirs but deep down, actually, wanting time without him. Sending him away so they could be with Bea, just the three of them, all close.

So why had they taken him in, in the first place?

He got up, he walked up and down beneath the tree. There was only one person he wanted to talk to about all this, and of course he couldn't. He couldn't go home, and say: 'Mummy, I know I'm not yours.' That would upset her terribly.

He'd just have to keep it to himself for ever.

2

Father had left her and Vivie a handsome sum each. Dear, dear Father. They were still waiting for probate, of course, but things were going to be easier: she could help out a bit with the school fees; she could — at last! — put down a new carpet in the hall. Best of all, she didn't have to worry about paying Mabel Hunt that fearful sum.

'Here it all is, Mrs Sutherland.'

There it all was! Stacked up so neatly in a box, with a carbon copy for Editing, and her original Manuscript stacked up neatly, too. The bill sat on top.

'And did you — did you enjoy it?'

'It reads quite nicely,' said Mabel Hunt.

That would have to do. She put it all into carrier bags, put the bill in her handbag. 'I'll settle this very shortly,' she said, feeling at last like a proper writer, with a typist, and Editing to be done.

It all weighed a ton in the bicycle basket. She rode home slowly, took it inside — gosh, what a weight — and opened the bureau. She called out to Mrs Thing, banging away with the ironing board, 'I shan't be long!' got on her bike again, and rode down the town. She'd seen an advertisement in the *Telegraph*: she knew what she needed now.

In the lovely old bookshop — and why didn't

she come in here more often, the children were always saying how nice it was — an assistant looked up from the till.

'Can I help you?'

'Yes,' said Flo firmly. 'I'd like a copy of *The Writers' & Artists' Yearbook.*'

★ ★ ★

Will came home, turned the key in the lock, gave his little whistle. Evenings drawing in already: soon be lighting the fire again.

House felt awfully quiet.

'Tik hai?'

A little gasp from the sitting room. He put his head round the door.

Flo looked up from the bureau. 'It *can't* be seven o'clock!'

Pages were everywhere: all over the sofa, in little piles on the floor, heaped up in the bureau.

'What on earth are you doing?'

'Editing.'

'What?'

'Editing the book. I got it back from the typist.'

He frowned. 'Well, jolly good, but where's supper? Come to that, where's Bea?'

'She's having supper with Lizzie Moore: she rang, I said she could. Let me get you a peg, darling, food won't be a minute.'

What was she going to give him? She practically ran to the drinks cupboard, as he dropped his briefcase, went to hang up his coat.

'I've had a hell of a day.'

355

'Sorry, darling, sorry, sorry. Here you are.' She gave him his peg, she cleared off the heaps from the sofa. 'There, settle down and I'll call you in two ticks.'

Fish fingers? Not after a hell of a day. She gazed at the shelves in the larder. All those tins. Got it — Fray Bentos steak-and-kidney pie. He loved it; it only took twenty minutes. She found the tin opener, struggled with it, put the thing in the oven. In moments, as she scrubbed the potatoes, the smell of it went wafting through the house.

'My darling.'

★   ★   ★

She'd got away with it that time. But Editing was all-consuming: she'd had no idea. It took her two days just to read it all through, lost — completely and utterly *lost* — in it all: the war, her broken heart (oh, Guy!), the excitement of India, the falling in love — properly, loved properly back — for the very first time in her life.

And now: now she still had masses to do, she could see how much work was needed. *The Writers' & Artists' Yearbook* listed every literary agent and publisher in the country. It gave advice on the Presentation of Manuscripts. Every day she decided on something new: a chapter should end here, not there; this scene needed more description, that one less . . . She crossed out furiously, she marked what went where. It was a full-time job!

'Tik hai?'

'Two ticks!'

The whole thing might have to be retyped!

★ ★ ★

'My mother is always writing,' Bea said to the listening bird. 'I think she cares more about writing than us.'

CARES MORE ABOUT WRITING THAN US.

From amongst the gloomy cherry boughs, the bird regarded her. It was ridiculous, really, at her age, to be talking to him still. Like Freddie's faces — she should have grown out of it a long time ago.

'She gets carried away,' she said. 'I don't even know if it's any good.'

★ ★ ★

The evenings drew in, the clocks went back. It felt like seven: it was really six, everyone hungry as hell, Will coming home in the cold and dark. Then came the showdown.

She'd had quite a good run last week: supper on time, done some proper shopping; even, on Friday, made a curry!

'My darling!'

'Why do you always put in marmalade?'

'You're supposed to.'

'Are you sure?'

But keeping it up . . . keeping it up, when Chapter Six should probably go completely . . .

Bea on the phone. Gone to tea with Julia

357

Charters; they'd asked her to stay for supper.

'Mrs Charters will run me home. You don't mind, Mummy, do you?'

Truth was, she didn't. It would give her another hour.

After the wedding, they went to live for a while in Lucknow, a beautiful old city where once there had been a terrible Massacre...

Key in the lock, no whistle, bang of the front door. She almost leaped out of her skin. And now she could hear the rain: it was pouring out there.

'Will?'

No answer. Briefcase dropped, furious foot-steps up to the coat rack, hanger wrenched off a hook and dropped.

'Darling?' She went to the door, saw him turn with the hanger in his hand, trousers soaking, his face like thunder. 'What is it?'

'Just a fucking awful day. And don't tell me there's no fucking supper.'

She swallowed.

'God Almighty, Flo!'

He strode into the dining room, wrenched open the drinks cupboard. Chinking. Muttering.

'Where's the whisky?'

Where was the whisky? Had she been supposed to get it? He always got it.

'Isn't it there?'

'No, it bloody isn't.'

He came out, he pushed past her, he banged his way into the sitting room. Chapter Six, in its new order, lay all across the sofa. He swept it to the floor.

'Will!'

'Get me something to eat.' He sat down heavily. Some of the pages were still on the cushions.

'Will, you're sitting on — '

'Get me something to eat!'

She fled, she broke eggs into a bowl, her hands shaking. If she put cheese in an omelette it would make it more substantial. She opened the fridge.

No cheese.

She scrabbled about. A box of Dairylea, with two triangles left. Could you cook with Dairylea? She could only try. And there was a tomato!

'Here we are!' She carried it through on a tray.

'Thanks.' He was sitting by the fire. 'What is it?'

'Cheese and tomato omelette.'

'*Omelette?*' He poked at it. Melted Dairylea oozed out of the edges. He took a mouthful.

'What are you having?'

'Nothing. I'm not hungry.'

He shook his head, as she stood there, pages all round her feet. She bent to pick them up.

'I work all week,' he said slowly, above her. 'Up and down on that fucking train, summer and winter, tired out, worn out, blood pressure probably going sky-high again, Marshall saying the last show was over budget, we might have to think again — I come home and there isn't even a decent meal. You've got the whole bloody day here, and all you can think about is that fucking book.'

Flo stood up. 'Have you finished?'

'No, I bloody haven't!' He picked up the tray; for a moment she thought he was going to hurl it. 'I'm sick to death of it,' he said. 'I come home, in the pouring bloody rain, all I can think about is a whisky and a good hot meal, and all you can dig up is a fucking omelette. Which tastes like muck, quite frankly. What's the matter with you, Flo? Is it so much to ask?'

And that last bit quite broke her: she burst into tears. It was true, it was true, what had she been thinking of? He did everything, he always had.

'I'm sorry,' she wept. 'You're right, it's all my fault, I'm so sorry.'

He grunted, got to his feet. 'I'm going to have a bath,' he said, and went slowly up the stairs.

Flo stood weeping, looking down at the heaps of paper. The rain poured on and on.

★ ★ ★

Late autumn, windy and cold. Down on the lacrosse field Bea shivered in goal, where she was always put because she was so hopeless. The strangest game: in the hands of those who were good at it, she could see it was swift and graceful — racing down the field with your stick, lifting it to catch the ball thrown to you — there! Into the net! Racing on: 'Pass! Pass!' from Miss Miller on the touchline, hurling it on to the next girl in a great strong throw.

But she — she just couldn't get the hang of it, always had to change hands, picking up with her left, throwing with her right: it made her feel like

360

left-handed Freddie, not that anyone ever even thought about that now, he'd coped so brilliantly.

'Pass! Pass!'

At last it was over, everyone walking up through the woods as dusk approached, she with Rosemary Reed, damp twigs underfoot and an earthy smell everywhere. She supposed Games must be good for you, in a way.

And she'd got the part of Feste! All those lovely songs.

On to the crowded bus, with all the Grammar School boys, not looking at any of them, off at her stop and calling out, 'Bye! See you tomorrow!' Crossing the main road, and walking past the cedar tree, walking faster in the cold and home to the light in the hall behind the frosted glass, and tea by the fire. If there was any tea.

Three rings.

Come on.

Three rings!

At last she came.

Oh, God.

'What's the matter? Mummy, what's the matter?'

But Flo couldn't speak. Bea shut the door behind her, followed her into the sitting room, where tea was laid and the fire was roaring. Really roaring.

'Mummy? What is it?'

Flo opened her mouth to speak. She howled. She howled and she sobbed and she cried and cried —

'Stop it! Stop it! What's happened?'

361

At last —
'I've burned it.'
'What?'
'My book — I've been neglecting you all — I threw it on the fire — ' She sat on the sofa and cried so hard the whole road would hear her in a minute. Beside her the paper-fed flames went roaring into the chimney. Little black pieces blew on to the hearth.

'Oh, Mummy — ssh, ssh. You can write it again, I know you can.'

'Never,' said Flo. She leaned back exhausted, covered her eyes. 'That was my best version, I know it was. I'll never write it again.'

Bea sat down in the armchair. A lovely tea was beside her on the little carved Indian table: a sandwich cut in four, a glass of milk, a Mr Kipling chocolate cup cake, a pot of Ski raspberry yoghurt, her favourite.

'Thank you so much. Poor Mummy.'

Even as she said it, she knew —

'I am NOT Poor Mummy!'

She started to cry again. Bea got up and sat beside her and hugged her.

'Darling Mummy, I love you, I'm so sorry.'

But even though it was true, even though she meant it, here it came again, that hard little splinter of ice, that distance and coldness. Someone was suffering. Look at that.

★   ★   ★

'Something is wrong with me,' Bea said to the bird. 'I don't feel things. Not as I should.'

362

How dark was all the fruit around him, how dark he was, except for that cold yellow eye.

'There's nobody else I can talk to,' she said. 'Not like this. Sometimes I feel as if I haven't got a heart at all. I just watch things, from a long way away.'

The bird listened gravely.

'I wasn't always like this,' she said.

I WASN'T ALWAYS LIKE THIS.

* * *

Oh, how long were the days again now. Autumn turning into winter, dark before you knew it. Bea came back with her homework, went straight up to do it after tea. Letters arrived from Freddie that seemed — she couldn't put her finger on it — rather formal and stiff. He was getting older, he was growing away from her: it was natural, but it hurt.

As for Will: just exhausted, most of the time. Exhausted and distant. Home for supper, off to the television, snoring in moments. The day gone, and nothing to show for it except a pile of washing-up, and even that she sometimes left overnight. Awful.

Every morning the alarm went off in the darkness. Every morning Will turned it off and went down to make the tea, and she lay there, thinking: Not another day.

In came the tray with a rattle of cups.

'Flo?' Not 'My darling.' He put her cup down beside her.

'Thank you.' Then she made herself — forced

herself — to sit up, drink her tea, get up and pull on her dressing gown, go down to make the wretched breakfast, see him off, call from the bottom of the stairs.

'Bea! Bea!'

Light breaking as she set off for school.

'Bye, darling!'

She stood in the hall. Now what?

Now nothing at all.

I'm sinking, she thought. And then, with a shiver of dread: Oh, no. Please not that again.

Sometimes, on days without Mrs Thing, she went straight back to bed. When she had the strength, she read: Somerset Maugham, H. E. Bates. Oh, if only she could have written like that! Or she slept until lunchtime, with long complicated dreams. When she woke she clung to what shreds she remembered: proof that she was alive. Once she was at a party, everyone laughing and talking around her, and she just standing there, all by herself. Someone came up to her, tall and kind —

She woke with a start, hearing sweet Roddy Byatt — that's who it was! — saying quite clearly: 'Flo, my dear. How are you these days?'

'Not too good, I'm afraid,' she said to the empty room, and she lay there, the curtains still drawn against the grey November day, thinking again, for the first time for years, of a lonely, desperate walk along the canal side, winter light fading fast.

★   ★   ★

Christmas on the way, and Flo looking like death half the time. Christmas, and poor old Agnes alone in Wimbledon and never an invitation. Every Sunday Will phoned her after church.

'How are we getting on?'

'Quite well, thank you, Willie.' The brightness in her voice was ghastly.

'We've got to have her over,' he told Flo, sharpening the steel for Sunday lunch with extra vigour.

'Oh, God.'

'Poor Auntie Agnes,' said Bea, sitting well back.

He put down the steel. 'Do you want to have her for Christmas?'

'No,' said Flo, as she always said. These days, even to get lunch for the three of them was as much as she could manage, slowly peeling the potatoes in the scullery, everything in her like lead.

'Well, then.' Will carved off a couple of slices of over-cooked lamb and passed Bea her plate. 'We'll have to have her over beforehand.' He bent to the joint once more. 'I know it's a bit of a strain.'

'She's got worse,' said Flo, helping Bea to potatoes.

He knew it was true. Where Agnes before her marriage had been hesitant, in widowhood she was irritable. Querulous, that was the word. Everything you said she contradicted, or made sound somehow wrong: 'No, Willie, that was in 1949.' 'Rest in the afternoons? Good heavens!' 'The running cup? Well, I suppose it's better

365

than nothing.' 'Fat balls for the blue tits? Oh, no, I always give them a coconut.'

But when all was said and done ... He finished the carving and sat down heavily.

'She's my sister.'

'All right, all right.'

'She's all on her own.'

'All *right!* Ask her over.'

Between them, Bea reached for the gravy boat. She could just slosh it all over the table, of course. That'd shut them up.

THAT'D SHUT THEM UP.

★　★　★

Agnes came two weeks later. It was dreadful. She talked about her journey, she talked about church. The vicar had done this, the curate had done that, the prayer group met every Wednesday: her high-pitched voice went on and on.

After lunch, Will took her and Bea bird-watching in Abbey Park, while Flo did the washing-up. Almost over, she said to the steamy little scullery. Only tea to get through now. And in a strange way the day had shifted her depression: irritation at least made you feel alive.

But then —

'What about your book, Flo?' asked Agnes, suddenly, out of the blue, as they sat by the fire with their teacups and Battenburg cake. 'How are you getting on?'

Everyone froze.

'She's stopped all that,' said Will at last,

reaching for the sugar bowl.

'Stopped it? Why?'

'It got a bit much for me,' said Flo, her stomach clenching. 'I got a bit overtired.'

'You're always tired,' said Agnes.

★ ★ ★

Will drove her to the station, waved her off, drove home. It was over: thank God for that. For at least a few weeks he had done his stuff. And Flo had made an effort, even got through that nasty little moment at the end.

'Hello-a-lo?'

He found Flo and Bea by the fire.

'My darling. Well done, that was marvellous.'

'It was ghastly.'

'I actually *like* Auntie Agnes,' said Bea. 'Freddie and I used to have happy times there.'

'I know, I know, she should've had kids of her own. Now, then, who'd like a peg?'

'I'll do supper.' Bea got to her feet.

'Darling, that would be heaven,' said Flo, sounding to Will more like herself again. God, it felt snug, just the three of them. Poor old Sis. And he went to the drinks cupboard, took in a tray, as Bea went to look in the larder.

'Cheers, my darling. How are we?'

Flo took her glass and looked into the flames. 'Not very good,' she said. 'Not very good, quite honestly.'

He sat down beside her. 'I was a brute. I never meant you to burn the wretched thing. But you know — after Melcote — that dreadful time — '

'Oh, Will.'

His arm went round her, she leaned against him. That was more like it.

'Nice little Christmas coming up,' he said gently. 'I'll organise the tree next week.'

The darkness of the last few weeks began to swim away: she could feel it, there by the fire, close to him again, everything coming slowly back to normal. Or as normal as it would ever be, without the book.

'It was all about *you*,' she said slowly. 'All about India and us.'

'I know, I know. Sweet of you.'

'Not *sweet*, for God's sake. Just . . . '

How could she explain?

'I'll make it up to you,' he said, and then Bea was back in the room saying all she could find was a tin of sardines, and they began to laugh.

★   ★   ★

And then, at New Year, the most marvellous news came through. A letter came to Will from Mr Lansdowne.

'Freddie! Freddie, old chap, come here!'

He ran down the stairs. 'What's wrong?'

'Nothing's wrong, it couldn't be better. Guess what?'

He simply couldn't.

Will led him into the dining room, picked up the letter on the desk.

'They've made you Head Boy!'

For a moment he just stood there, unable to take it in.

'They can't have done,' he said at last. 'It's only two terms to go.'

'I know, I know.' Will flourished the letter. 'But listen to this. 'The boy Harris has gone down with glandular fever and is unlikely to return until after Easter. We'd like your young Sutherland to take his place: he's shown himself to be a super chap, and I'm sure he'll acquit himself splendidly. I do hope you're pleased with this news.''

He put down the letter again. 'I'll say I'm pleased. Aren't you?'

Freddie looked out at the wintry garden. He saw himself leading the school into chapel, reading the lesson as Head Boy, introduced to new parents, his name up in gold lettering on the board in the hall when he left —

He'd got through, he'd got somewhere at last: an adopted boy made good.

'I'm very pleased,' he said.

3

Spring in Ryehurst. Nothing like spring in Melcote, of course, apple blossom everywhere, goslings hatching out, peep peep, that brilliant grass, but still — he'd planted a flowering currant by the gate and there it was, in flower. Daffs and forsythia in the garden, and a blackbird nesting in the creeper.

'Bea, look at that!'

'Lovely.' She went inside. In a few moments the sounds of Elvis came drifting soulfully out of her window. Flo thought he was gorgeous, but Will's favourite was that Frank Ifield chap. Got a bit of oomph.

''I Remember You!'' He yodelled it now, coming back into the house, Saturday morning at his desk, having a bit of a catchup, letter to Freddie, he and Flo right as rain these days.

'Here we are.' Coffee brought in, set down beside him.

'My darling.'

French windows open, sun pouring in, everything tickety-boo.

⋆　⋆　⋆

Flo sat at the bureau, empty of everything now. No writing, no editing, everything gone. Just the family letters, her snippets of this and that cut out of the paper and stuffed into pigeonholes;

370

just bills, and recipes she never cooked, and her battered old writing case.

In the empty house, she read through Vivie's last letter. It still felt so strange to think of them down there without Father.

Mother has rather taken to her bed, and I live for news of Hugo. He did brilliantly in his last exams, of course. A new girlfriend on the scene, I gather! Not that I ever meet any of them...

Flo wrote a special letter to Mother, picturing her up in bed with her rose-patterned wallpaper and heaps of satin eiderdown.

Freddie's doing so well as Head Boy. We're absolutely thrilled.

She put down her pen. Was she thrilled about anything now? Everyone's life was going on without her: that's how it felt. Oh, what had she done, last autumn? Impulsive, foolish, passionate — that's what it had been. A passionate gesture: it sounded rather marvellous, in its way.

On to the fire with you! To hell with you!

But then — what an outpouring of grief, and all in front of Bea. Terrible. They'd never talked about it since. Bea didn't talk about anything much these days, except pop and her play.

As for darling Freddie: suddenly he was growing up, all those funny faces gone, just clearing his throat in a manly way now and then, his voice on the very edge of breaking. And so much less demonstrative — of course it was only natural, but oh, how she missed those great hugs and kisses. At least there were no more tears now, going back to school, and anyway it was almost over —

He starts at St Luke's in the autumn, just half an hour away by car. No more ghastly Outings! It's a school for the sons of clergy, like Mountford Park — of course he isn't a son but a grandson, but we still get a fees reduction!

Had she imagined it, or had he gone very quiet when Will went thundering on about this on the last Outing? On and on he'd gone about his father and the Church, almost like Agnes, and Freddie so unresponsive — did he not like talking about family now?

Anyway, must go, darling Mummy. I'll write again soon!

And she wrote out the envelope and stamped it, and put it on the old oak chest to take down to the post.

Now what?

Long empty days without passion or purpose. That's what it felt like, still.

She had lunch. She climbed up the stairs to bed, she sank into sleep like a lover.

'Flo, my dear,' said Roddy Byatt, deep in a dream. She was walking by the canal, walking fast by the dank cold water, thick with duck weed. She could see him up ahead of her, walking in his winter overcoat, the rifle at his side. Then he turned to look at her, and she saw his ashen face.

'Flo, my dear.' He lifted the gun: she woke, gasping.

⋆   ⋆   ⋆

Easter on the way, the weather lovely, chocolate given up for Lent. Something to tell Agnes in his

372

weekly call after church: that and the blackbird, whizzing back and forth from the creeper with a beak full of worms: she'd like that.

'How're we getting on?'

And for once she had something new to tell him.

'She's going on a trip to the Holy Land,' he told Flo and Bea as they brought in the lunch. 'For Easter, with people from the church.' He picked up the steel and whipped the carving knife back and forth. 'Do her a power of good.'

★ ★ ★

Easter, lovely Easter. In Melcote there had been a breakfast table full of primroses, boiled eggs dyed in cochineal with little pencil faces on them, all done by Flo. Easter was like a watercolour, everything washed in pale spring sunlight, the happiest time of the year.

But before it came Good Friday.

'I can't go to church on Good Friday,' said Flo, as she said every year. 'It's just too terrible and sad.'

'Oh, darling, please.'

She shook her head, and he stopped trying. She'd gone a bit quiet again; he couldn't say why.

So it was just the three of them, Will and Bea and Freddie, home for the holidays and being all Head Boyish about everything — offering to carve, even! No thanks, old boy — walking down the road on Good Friday afternoon, as the church bell slowly tolled.

373

Jesus had died at three in the afternoon; the service began at two. They walked quietly and soberly into the shadowy church, where candles were lit on the altar. They kneeled, they prayed.

As always these days, it took Bea a while to clear her mind. By the time she had pushed away the image of herself singing on the terrace next term, charming all the parents at the play, she had barely time to begin, 'Dear God, On this tragic day, I think of the sufferings of Your Son,' before everyone was getting to their feet again.

And I'm not thinking about the sufferings of Christ at all, she thought, as Mr Barber began to intone behind the rood screen. This service is supposed to be so sad that Mummy can't even bear to come here, and I'm just thinking about myself as usual. Beside her, Freddie cleared his throat in that maddening way he'd developed. Wherever you were in the house, or out down the town, wandering about in Woollies, say, you could always tell where he was. Perhaps it was another Nervous Tic. What did he have to be nervous about now?

They stood for the first hymn. And then, as the organ sounded, and they began to sing, she felt a great lump begin to form in her own throat.

'There is a green hill far away,
Without a city wall . . . '

She was back in the classroom at the Miss Beasleys, everyone crowded round the piano, the room smelling of powder paint and daffodils in a jar, and she singing that gentle tune, imagining that grassy hill, so beautiful and sad and oh, so far away.

Freddie's voice was quite steady now as he sang beside her.

> 'We may not know, we cannot tell
> What pains He had to bear . . . '

Her eyes filled with tears: not for the suffering of Christ, but for the child she once was. *I was nice when I was little, wasn't I?* she asked herself. *What's happened to me?*

And as the voices of Freddie and her father rose, she bent her head, and tears splashed on to her hymn book. She thought of Snowy's accident, hit by a car in the dark and rain, and how half of her had been so sad and the other half just wanted to tell her friends at school all about it. It was Freddie who'd really been upset: he could hardly speak when he came home, and they told him. She thought of her self-importance when they heard about Uncle Neville: 'My uncle died in the holidays.' As if that made her someone special.

But above all she thought of her mother, sobbing her heart out in front of the fire, where the last blackened pages of her book had turned to ash.

I'll never write it again.

Bea had tried to comfort her — *I am not Poor Mummy!* — but actually, in her heart, she had simply sat and watched her, cold as ice.

'You've gone awfully quiet,' Freddie said to Bea after lunch. They were washing up in the scullery, as they always did together when he was home. 'Why were you crying in church?'

Bea shook her head. 'Sometimes I feel I'm just not a very nice person.'

I'M JUST NOT A VERY NICE PERSON.

He dried the fish forks carefully. 'Yes, you are. I don't know what I'd do without you sometimes.'

'Do you mean that?'

'Yes. In the holidays, I mean.' And as he watched her rinsing the plates, he thought that this might be the hardest part, one day, telling her she wasn't really his sister at all, that their parents had concealed the truth from her, as well.

Silverfish swam about on the wooden draining board.

'I do love you, Freddie.'

He cleared his throat. 'Me too.'

★ ★ ★

And then, as soon as the holidays were over, and Freddie had gone back to Mountford for the last time, there came a thing and a half.

'Agnes has met a chap!'

'No!'

He was a vicar, of course. A widower, a Scot, with a parish in Dumfries, so not at the back of beyond, in the Hebrides or somewhere. Just over

the border, plenty of trains. And of course
Mother had been half-Scots, they'd have that in
common. They'd met on the trip to the Holy
Land, lots of different church groups coming
together, staying in some affordable hotel outside
Jerusalem. Supper all together, love at first sight.
    'No!'
    'That's what she said.'
    'Well, thank God for that.'
    'Pass the gravy. I wonder when we'll meet
him.'
    'Do we have to meet him? Can't they just get
married and go and live in Scotland?'
    'Honestly, Mummy.'

★　★　★

The school play: suddenly it took over everything. It got her out of Games, it even got her out
of Maths. As the time drew near, there were
rehearsals in every spare moment, the costumes
arriving from London in enormous boxes, everyone trying them on and having hysterics, Julia
Charters as Sir Toby Belch stuffing a cushion
under her doublet to make her really fat.
    'You look pregnant!'
    Bea had special singing lessons with Mrs
Hemming, the music mistress, after school in the
empty ballroom, sun pouring on to the worn old
parquet, the piano striking up and she with her
invisible audience:

'Come away, come away, death,
    And in sad cypress, let me be la-ai-aid;

377

Fly away, fly away, breath,
I am slain by a fa-ai-ir cru-el maid . . . '

'Lovely,' said Mrs Hemming. 'Stretch out those
vowels a little more gently, Bea. That's it, much
better.'

The make-up arrived! Boxes and boxes of it!
'You are coming, aren't you, Mummy?'
Other Mothers. But she'd have to do it.
'You don't have to come if you don't want to.'
'Of course I'll come. Daddy too. You're so
clever, darling.'

★ ★ ★

Bea stood in her jester's harlequin and cap at the
corner of the terrace, by the urn brimming over
with geraniums, and her voice floated out over
the audience, all gone quiet.

As the trio played softly in the corner by the
grass, and everyone's eyes were at last upon her,
she forgot to feel guilty, or ashamed at showing
off, she forgot she was shallow and cold. She was
just there where she should be, holding them in
thrall.

'Not a flower, not a flower sweet,
On my black co-ffin let there be
strow-oh-own . . . '

Even though it wasn't done, to clap in the
middle of the play, everyone did.

★ ★ ★

The last week of term. Everyone was gathered in the gym. There was a stage there, used for House plays in the autumn, used for Prize-giving now. The windows were open on to the gardens, the scent of roses and cut grass drifting in, the staff up on the stage in their best clothes and everyone wanting to know which House had come top in the year, and who had won what.

Miss Hawthorne was in her linen suit.

'Good afternoon, girls. Sit down.'

Everyone sat. Then it started: the announcements, the clapping, as girl after girl went up, bobbed and thanked, and came carefully down the wooden steps, clutching her book or her cup. Bea held her breath. There was a Drama Cup. Would she — could she —

It went to Vanessa Grant. Well, of course it would; she'd been such a brilliant Orsino. It didn't matter, there'd be another chance next year, and perhaps it only went to Sixth-formers anyway.

And she clapped away with all the others, as Rosemary Reed murmured, 'Bad luck, you were super,' beside her. But then, all at once, as she looked up at the stage, dust motes dancing everywhere in the sunny hall, it came again: something went black in her brain, and she just wasn't there any more.

4

Autumn. New school uniform because you were growing so fast, new fountain pen: all that. But now it was a completely different uniform, a grey suit with long trousers, a whole new school.

Will would drive him over, just the two of them, chaps together. A fresh start, any little unhappiness at Mountford left behind. He'd bought him a camera, to mark it: a splendid new life coming up. Made him think of leaving for India, in a way: out of insurance and into the big wide world at last.

Fred, a bit white round the gills, had his bags all waiting in the hall.

'Bye, Mummy.' His voice was really breaking now; he cleared his throat.

'Goodbye, my darling. I love you so much. You look gorgeous!'

'Bye, Bea.'

'Your voice sounds so funny! Bye, Freddie. Fred. See you soon.'

'In the car!'

They had a new car now, a Morris Traveller. It was low on petrol and spun along nicely: got them to St Luke's in Brockwood in no time.

'Here we are!'

There was a master, waiting on the steps, as all the boys arrived.

They'd been here once, in the summer holidays, had lunch in Brockwood, then met the

Headmaster, had a bit of a look round. More of the same, as far as Fred could see: tall gates, grey stone, creeper. But built round a quad, with a war memorial in the middle: that made it feel more grown-up, somehow. He and Will got out his bags from the back, carried them up the steps. Then there was all the usual stuff with the master, all the splendids and jolly goods, and then they shook hands.

'Goodbye, Freddie, old chap. Fred, I mean.'

'Bye.' Here he was, packed off once again. He swallowed, as boys came streaming past them. 'Thanks again for the camera.' He would not say 'Dad'. He would not.

★   ★   ★

They were all working really hard this term: the autumn of 1962, the start of their O level year. You had to take it seriously. She did, she was really trying. Sitting up at her desk in the evenings she did grammar and comprehension, précis and essays as if she'd been born to do them: A or A-minus every time, should do really well. Nothing else came so easily, except Religious Knowledge, which was sort of in her bones, as it was for Freddie. Fred, as he said he was now. Eight subjects altogether. They weren't going to let her take Maths, or Physics and Chemistry, just Biology.

'The Reproductive Organs,' Miss Leaming wrote up on the board. 'Of the Rabbit,' she added firmly. They tried to stifle their giggles. Miss Leaming was a tall, gaunt woman who people said belonged to the Plymouth Brethren. Very strict, apparently. It was hard on her, teaching Reproduction.

'Thank you, Miss Leaming.' They got to their feet as the bell rang out.

'Thank you, girls. Have a nice weekend.'

Oh, the weekends. Somehow Bea seemed to be spending a lot of them with Will. Nothing to do on a Saturday night, *Juke Box Jury* over, supper over, Flo slowly climbing the stairs.

'Mummy,' Bea had said, at the end of last term, over tea after school. 'Mummy, you know those sort of blank things that happen sometimes?'

'Blank things?'

'You know, when I'm sort of not there. Or here.'

'I'm often not here,' said Flo, pouring another cup.

'Mummy! I'm trying to tell you something. I had quite a big one in Prize-giving. I just went completely blank.'

Flo looked at her. 'Have you got the curse?'

'No. It's not due until next week.'

She shook her head. 'Perhaps Dr Hughes should have a look at you.'

But somehow he never had, and then, in the whole holidays, it only happened once or twice: out walking with Will, listening to his Indian stories. 'I remember once . . . ' Keeping him company because she felt she must: Flo never went with him, ever.

'Going up already?' he asked her now, as she yawned after supper. 'You snuggle down. I'll be up shortly.' He went into the sitting room, turned on the television. 'Bea? Coming to watch?'

They sat on the sofa, he tried to take her hand. 'My darling.'

MY DARLING.

She moved away.

'Arden House . . . '

Dr Finlay's housekeeper picked up the handset on an ancient telephone. Handsome Dr Finlay, crusty old Dr Cameron, Janet the housekeeper: drama in the Scottish hills, the heather.

'I wonder how Auntie Agnes is getting on with her chap. A few other widows with their eye on him, I gather.'

'Oh dear. Poor Auntie Agnes.'

Dr Cameron and Dr Finlay were clashing over a diagnosis, Janet was getting the supper.

Was this what a weekend was supposed to be?

★   ★   ★

Within a week, he knew it was going to be OK. For a start, they had proper food: proper meals, three times a day. Porridge and some kind of egg, with toast and marmalade for breakfast; meat and two veg and pudding for lunch, piping hot; sausages and baked potatoes for supper, with fresh fruit. Within a fortnight, he had to ask Matron to loosen the waistband on the long grey trousers (two pairs).

He slept better, too, no pangs of hunger, and not much of the new boy stuff to contend with, either. There were people he liked the look of, who liked the look of him, straight away: they all knew the ropes from prep school, and they just sort of got on with it, really.

And he could do the work. He didn't go straight to the top, like some of them, but he held his own in everything, right from the word go. And there was lots of stuff to do apart from work: lots of societies, the Combined Cadet Force, as well as all the sport, of course. An indoor swimming pool.

Dear Mummy and Dad — how else could he begin? — *I hope you are both well. I'm settling in well here, and like it very much . . .* Good to be able to write the truth, for once. *There are four Houses: I'm in Wellington. They've put me in for trials for the Cross-Country Running Team next week, and I've signed up to the Photographic Society . . .*

Of course, there was one thing they hadn't had at Mountford: fagging.

'Where's my kit? Sutherland! Where's my kit?'

'Right here, Collingwood. And I've done your boots.'

Collingwood was in the Upper Sixth, a prefect, Captain of the First Eleven. Tall and dark and full of himself, with a name that was close enough to Collins for Fred to feel a pang when he first heard it. Collins: where was he now? But he didn't spend much time asking himself that: there was too much to get on with. He had to clean Collingwood's rugby boots, polish the brass on his CCF kit. He had to sit on the seat in the lavatory cubicle to warm it up, early on a winter morning, before Collingwood lowered his own, Upper-Sixth rear end.

'OK, Sutherland. Off you go.'

Prefects could beat fags if they wanted but so far he'd avoided that. So far, he hadn't been beaten by anyone, boy or master. He spent Wednesday afternoons outside with his camera, taking photographs — snaps, as Will always called them. You could make anything interesting, if you looked hard enough. He learned how to develop the negatives, Mr Simmonds presiding over the darkroom, full of plastic trays and chemicals. To lean over with your tweezers, submerge your ghostly film and see it all turn into a proper black-and-white photograph, hang it to dry up with little pegs on a line: it was completely absorbing. Fascinating, as Flo would say.

All in all: life was looking up.

Turning over in his new dorm bed, he thought of the misery of Mountford Park, the endless hunger, the sick fear, the beatings. Collins's beating. Collins's parents had taken him away — he must have told them. But Will — he'd just left him there, even though everyone went on about how thin he was, even though Flo had told him about Mr Ward, and the disgusting things that went on in his pretty little cottage in the grounds.

But then — Will wasn't his real father. Why should he care?

★   ★   ★

385

'Mummy? Are you all right?' Saturday afternoon, Will out for a bird-watching walk with Harold Beamish from church, Lizzie up in London with her parents, Flo in bed as usual.

'Just a bit tired.' She patted the eiderdown. 'Come and snuggle up. I hardly ever see you these days. What have you been up to?'

'Nothing much.' Bea pulled up the eiderdown, picked up Flo's book. 'Somerset Maugham — you're always reading him.' The book was a Reader's Digest compendium, three novels bound fatly together between red boards: *Of Human Bondage*, *The Moon and Sixpence*, *The Painted Veil*.

'Which one's the best?'

'*The Painted Veil*, I think, but they're all good — completely draw you in. So vivid! I wish I could write like that. And H. E. Bates.' He was lying underneath Somerset Maugham, with such a pretty dust jacket. 'Lovely country stories,' she said.

'Mummy — do you think you'll ever — '

'No,' said Flo. 'I don't. Let's not even think about it.' She patted Bea's hand. 'Now you, my darling, you've got to go on the stage.'

Bea put the book down. Did she want to go on the stage? She didn't know what she wanted to do. She lay there looking at the room, at everything she'd known all her life: Will's chest of drawers, with the three embroidered Indian cloths on top; Flo's varnished wood dressing table with its triple mirror, so you could see yourself from every angle, going on and on for ever.

Downstairs the letter box banged.

'Probably the parish mag.'

Probably, but worth just having a look.

And yes, a letter. For her! She ripped it open, pulled out an invitation, with a little note.

Dear Bea, Hope you've had a great half-term. Hope you can come to this — there are going to be boys!

Lizzie was giving a party, for her fifteenth birthday.

★ ★ ★

Fred came home at half-term. He seemed to have grown six inches.

'My darling! You look about seventeen!'

Heaven to have him home again. That sweet shy smile. Gradually unwinding, as the week went by.

'Dad?' He had to call him that. It stuck in his throat, but he had to.

'Yes, old chap.'

'You know the boxroom?'

'I know it well.'

'Do you think we could turn it into a darkroom? For all my photography stuff?'

'Don't see why not.'

★ ★ ★

Of course, one of the boys at the party would be Lizzie's snooty big brother, James. He was away at school, but she'd get him back for the weekend, of course she would, and probably he'd bring his friends. No one at school could talk about anything else.

What was she going to wear?

Flo took her down the town. 'It's time you had a clothes allowance, darling.'

Was it really? All sorts of possibilities opened up. Flo sat on a chair in Penny's Boutique, while Bea tried things on. Really, of course, she'd rather be on her own, or with a friend, but then how would she pay for things? Couldn't she just be given the allowance and —

'I like to come with you, darling.'

Out and about for once, clothes shopping with Bea, mother and daughter, thinking about boys and parties. A bit of fun at last.

'What do you think?'

Bea came out of the changing room and stood before her. Flo hardly recognised her. A nifty little black dress with two rows of big white buttons down the front. Was it common, or was it the height of fashion?

Bea twirled in stockinged feet in front of the full-length mirror. 'I'd need shoes. Heels, I mean.' She stood on tiptoe.

'Darling, you're much too young for heels. They throw your pelvis out.'

They came home with heels and the dress.

'Will? Darling, do come and look.'

'Oh, Mummy! I don't want him to look.'

'Why on earth not?'

Like her mother so often, she simply couldn't explain.

On the night of the party it poured and poured. Will ran her up to Lizzie's house. It wasn't remotely like theirs: it was in a long road behind Micklegate, where the houses were simply enormous, set in great big gardens with tennis courts.

'That's it.'

'Good Lord.' He pulled up, peered out as the windscreen wipers swished back and forth. 'Well. Have a marvellous time. I'll collect you at half-past nine.'

'Ten. Daddy, please. No one's going home at half-past nine.'

'All right, ten. Bye, darling.' He leaned across to kiss her; she already had the door open. Flo's umbrella went up in a trice. 'Bye!' he called, but she was running off into the wet in her high heels.

'Oh, I don't know,' he said, as he drove away.

Inside the house, Mark Wynter was singing 'Venus in Blue Jeans' on the huge great hi-fi, and Lizzie's father was offering everyone fizzy drinks, in the great big hall. It was only lime juice and soda, or bitter lemon, but it looked really glamorous in champagne glasses. Bea put Flo's umbrella in the stand.

'Bitter lemon, please. Thanks awfully.'

'Which one are you?' asked Mr Moore.

'I'm Bea.' She laughed. 'I've been here lots of times — you know me!'

'Bea? Good Lord. I'd never have recognised you. You look super, I must say.'

'Thanks. Where's Lizzie?'

Lizzie was with her brother in the huge great drawing room, wearing make-up and earrings. Parquet flooring ran through from the hall, so the space felt even more enormous. The doorbell was ringing like mad. Bea took her drink and went to say Happy Birthday.

'Thanks, Bea. You know James, don't you?'

'Yes, of course. Hello.'

'Hello, Bea.'

She hadn't seen him since the summer holidays, and he seemed completely different now: even taller, and even more deep-voiced, and even more impossible to talk to. She tried.

Get your boyfriend to talk about himself. That was what Evelyn Home advised in *Woman*, which Flo said was common but which she still read now and again, when Mrs Thing left it behind.

'What are you doing for your A levels?'

'Physics, Chemistry and Maths,' said James, looking down at her from his enormous height. Like Hugo!

'This is Alex,' he told her, as a boy in a suit came up.

And he was gone, and she and Alex were left standing there, and now it all had to start all over again. Actually he looked quite nice, fair-haired and smiley, with lovely blue eyes. A dish, in fact. She started to ask him about himself, and then 'Let's Twist Again' was pounding out from the hi-fi, and in seconds everyone was twisting, you simply couldn't help it, it had been Number One for months, and even Mr Moore was twisting, pulling Mrs Moore on to the floor, though she could see Lizzie wished that they weren't.

Now it was Cliff, 'Do You Wanna Dance', another one you couldn't keep still to, and she and Alex were bopping away, not really looking at each other, but smiling when they did, and then it was 'Hit the Road Jack'. Lizzie must have spent ages choosing the order, and now everyone had sort of unwound, so they were all singing 'Hit the Road Jack!' in the chorus, having a really good time. Then they all had more drinks, really thirsty, and Alex told her he couldn't remember what he was doing for A levels, and that made her laugh.

Then all at once the lights went down, and there was Cliff, soulfully singing 'The Young Ones', which really did feel as if he knew them all, understood just how they were longing for everything to happen at last, and before she knew it, Alex had drawn her into his arms, and they were dancing close as anything, and then it was 'When the Girl in Your Arms Is the Girl in Your Heart', so slow and romantic, which she was always singing to Freddie, and suddenly she was being kissed.

For a moment it felt like that awful kiss from David Bone, down by the darkening river at the RLS show, but now — now she was with someone young, and dishy. Alex seemed to think she would know what to do, just as he did, and of course she didn't, but she just sort of followed him, and then she began to like it, and went on, until the music stopped, and she and Alex moved apart, and smiled at one another, and looked away.

Darling Vivie,
  Bea's got a boyfriend! Still on the scene

after two or three months! Of course (a) they hardly see each other, since he's away at school and doesn't even live in Ryehurst, he's just a friend of the brother of one of Bea's school friends, and (b) Will and I both think she's much too young for a boyfriend, really. There's a pop song she keeps playing, one of those really catchy ones, called 'Sweet Sixteen'. She won't even be sixteen until next summer!

But still — we've met him, for all of two minutes (!) when he took her out to the flicks on an exeat, and I must say he's absolutely gorgeous! I can quite see why she's fallen. And though they don't see each other much, they write all the time: I see her little face when she comes home from school, looking out for a letter, and the way it lights up when one comes. Of course, she's got to concentrate on her O levels, but as she says herself, no one can revise all the time!

Anyway, darling, Happy New Year! 1963 — how on earth did we get here?! I hope it's a really good year for you all, and to see you in it! Thank you again for that heavenly bath stuff. I wallowed, all over Christmas!

Ever your loving Flo.

PS. We were all so sorry to hear about poor Whoopoo. Such a darling cat.

She sealed up the envelope, licked the stamp. There. Written at top speed — incredible how she had a spring in her step these days. It was having Bea all lit up, much less mopey, much more *here*. And something proper in common: if there was one thing she knew about, it was love and love affairs.

She sat at the open bureau. A January afternoon, a few flakes of snow drifting down past the window. Snow always lifted your heart. Bea writing to Alex upstairs and Fred doing clever things in his darkroom. So much happier these days.

Now a New Year beckoned, and she must do something with it. Sitting at the bureau, her pen in her hand, she reached for a blank sheet of Basildon Bond. Something was stirring again, she could feel it. Will wouldn't mind if she wrote just a bit — surely he'd rather have her lit up and happy like Bea than crawling into bed all the time. And the children were older, hardly needed her, really, perfectly capable of getting their own lunch once in a blue moon. Their own tea. Today, for instance.

Something was happening. Her pen hovered over the page. Not about going out to India, falling in love, but about coming home. Home with a new husband, a baby on the way. Starting a new life *here*.

She took a deep breath.

In January 1950 Miranda Marshall and her husband, who had been an Indian Army Officer, moved with their two small children to a ramshackle old farm in Devon. It was up a mile-long lane, and miles from anywhere...

She'd got it. She'd got it! The children, when they were small: the perfect subject. What a lovely word 'ramshackle' was. Ryehurst just melted away.

5

In the summer Bea got her eight O levels, with As for English Language and English Literature and nothing very exciting for anything else. Failed Latin. When they went back in the autumn, Miss Weaver told her she'd have to take it again if she wanted to do English at University. Was that what she wanted?

My mother thinks I should go to drama school, she had written to Alex when her results came through. *I wish you could have seen me in Midsummer Night's Dream.*

She wished a lot of things.

She sat in the library, where they had their English lessons, pale December sun at the windows, her head bent over *Paradise Lost*. Miss Weaver was going on about the Doctrine of Free Will. She tried to concentrate.

At home in Fitz's desk, a little bundle of letters from Alex was still crammed into one of the pigeonholes. He'd taken her out, he'd met her parents — 'Darling, he's absolutely divine!' — he'd kissed her until they were breathless, he'd written from his school in Sussex. She skimmed down the stuff about rugby and cricket to *All my love*, at the end. She told him about playing the part of Lysander, and wrote *All my love, Bea*, with enormous care, so he could see how much she meant it.

Then, almost as soon as she got her O level

results, and was longing to see him again, the letters had stopped. Just like that. Every morning she'd run down for the post, found only Christian Aid things, or a letter from Auntie Vivie, or Auntie Agnes, happy with her Scottish vicar now.

Nothing from Alex.

'Darling, don't look like that. I'm sure there'll be something tomorrow.'

'Darling, he's probably having a little holiday. After his A levels.'

Nothing. Not once, all summer. Not even on her birthday. That was it, she knew. She sat up in bed crying, and Flo came up in her dressing gown and told her how sorry she was, but she'd get over it, honestly she would.

'Darling, you should have seen me, when Guy broke my heart in the war. I thought I'd never recover.' She held sobbing Bea in her arms, remembering how awful it had been. It was Father who had suggested India — *Go on, darling, take a deep breath and have an adventure. Be brave!*

'And then I met Daddy,' she said, stroking Bea's hair, 'and really fell in love. With someone who loved me with all his heart. It'll happen to you, my darling, I know it will.'

★ ★ ★

There'd been a hell of a lot of changes since he'd joined the RLS. The Common Agricultural Policy had finally come in: to all intents and purposes they were part of Europe now. A more stable income for farmers had to be a good thing. But a lot of them were expanding at a fearful rate.

It wasn't just hens cooped up in batteries, it was hedges ripped out to increase the crop yield, chemical fertilisers, new animal breeds: everything under control in a way he couldn't have imagined, down in Devon all those years ago.

And the wildlife was affected, of course: horribly affected. Fewer hedgerows to nest in, birds and butterflies dying from poisons on crops they'd been feeding on for ever. Dreadful, a lot of it.

'We have to move with the times,' James Marshall said in the boardroom. 'But we have to be vigilant, too. We're getting reports of a few farms going bust already: too much expansion, too soon.'

Out and about last summer, Will had seen a bit of that. Saw a thing or two he didn't like the look of. Calves crammed together in sheds without a chink of light. As for the poor old pigs: sows farrowing in stalls so cramped they couldn't turn round. Stretched out on concrete, suckling a dozen piglets, in pen after pen in those great big barns. It meant more pigs to the floor space, more productivity — but that didn't mean it was right.

'I'd like to raise the issue of farrowing stalls,' he said at a meeting just before Christmas. He told them about a pig farm in Suffolk, making a fortune. So far.

And at what cost.

Nobody took much notice.

★ ★ ★

Almost the end of the holidays.

'And where did *that* year go?' Flo asked everyone, at supper on New Year's Eve. 'What happened to 1963?'

'A pretty good year,' said Will, carving the last of the turkey, and the ham from Fitz. 'Bea's got her O levels, Fred's settled in at St Luke's. Old Hugo's done his National Service.' He passed her plate. 'RLS Show broke all records.'

I had my heart broken, said Bea to herself. Apart from that it was a fabulous year. She bit her lip.

'You all right, my darling?' Flo passed her plate, and Bea nodded. Brave little thing. Plenty more fish in the sea. And Fred so settled now, thank God.

Best of all, she had finished her book! That was why the year had gone so quickly; just whizzed by.

Pages were heaped up in the bureau: three chapters for Devon, one for Market Hampden, four for Melcote. Nothing about Ryehurst: what was there to say? But all the children's little doings and sayings — she'd relived it all, so happily. It wouldn't mean anything to them now, of course, but one day —

'Now what are you up to?' Will had asked one Saturday in the spring, coming in from giving the lawn its first cut.

'Just — just a little book about the children. Watching them grow.'

'What a sweet idea.'

No fuss at all — but then, she hadn't let this one take her over.

'Why can't we all live on pills?' she asked now, watching him dig out the very last crumbs of the turkey, wondering what they were going to have tomorrow. Would the ham do another meal? 'Why can't we all live on pills?'

There was simply no answer to that.

★　★　★

I'd love you to read my book one day! Flo wrote to Vivie a couple of weeks later, the children back at school and the house to herself once more. *Once I've got it typed. And honestly — I know it's just about our little family, but tell me if you think it would have a wider appeal. Don't you think people might like to read about a family starting a new life after the War?*

Strangely, there was no answer to this letter. There must be a new lot of Paying Guests. All those beds, all that welcoming. Then one evening, while she was getting the supper, and Bea glued to *Top of the Pops*, she heard the phone ring.

'Get that, will you, darling?' she called. It was probably for Bea anyway; she was always on the phone, it drove Will mad. 'Bea!'

'All right!'

She tore herself away and ran to the dining room, as the phone rang on and on.

'Bea. Bea, it's Hugo.'

She almost dropped the receiver.

'Hugo! Gosh. How are you?'

'I'm fine, thanks. Is Auntie Flo there?'

'Yes, yes, of course, I'll just get her.' She ran to the scullery. 'Mummy! It's Hugo!'

Flo turned down the potatoes. Bea went back to the sitting room. Now gorgeous Pete Murray was announcing the Supremes, but for once she hardly heard them. Hugo! Just the way he said her name.

'Darling? Darling, switch that off for a minute.'

She turned it down, seeing her mother's face at the open door. At the same moment, Will's key sounded in the lock.

'Vivie's terribly ill,' Flo said, as the Supremes sang silently on. She said it to Bea, and she said it again to Will, as he came in with his briefcase. She put her hands to her face.

'She's been in a nursing home for over a week. I'm going to have to go.'

★　★　★

Hugo met her at the station. It was pouring with rain.

'Thanks so much for coming, Auntie Flo.' He took her bag, he put up his umbrella as they crossed the car park. So calm and measured, even in a crisis.

'How is she?'

'Not very good, I'm afraid.'

She felt suddenly sick with anxiety. A rare kind of blood disease, they'd told him. Had they told Vivie?

'Let's go straight there.'

And he turned off at the roundabout, and after a few minutes they were in a quiet leafy street. The nursing home looked familiar, somehow, even in the fading light, and then she remembered.

'This is where you were born!'

'Good heavens.' He gave his slow smile and pulled in.

A glass-panelled door led into a porch, another one into Reception, where a jug of Christmas roses stood on the desk. They signed their names, and the girl on the desk looked hesitant.

'I'm not sure if Mrs Leiden is having visitors.'

'She's having me,' said Flo. 'I'm her sister. What room is she in?'

'Room six, on the first floor. I'll let her nurse know.' She picked up the phone.

'You go on up, Auntie Flo,' said Hugo. 'I'll wait here.' And he sat down in a leather armchair and reached for a magazine.

Never had a house full of people sounded so quiet. It was almost deathly up here. Flo walked along the thickly carpeted corridor, looking at the numbers on the solid, cream-painted doors. Six: she knocked, and entered.

Vivie, a nurse sitting beside her, lay in a white bed with a white quilt and the snowiest white linen. Against it, her pretty permed hair was flat and lifeless, her face a sickly yellow-grey. Her eyes were closed, a drip-stand stood above her, the tube leading into her grey-yellow hand. The nurse got up, and pointed to a buzzer. 'If you need me,' she said quietly, and then, at the door,

400

quieter still: 'You're just in time.'

Flo sank on to the chair. 'Vivie?' she whispered. No answer. 'Vivie, it's me.' She got up again, leaned over the bed. 'Darling, I'm here.'

Vivie's chest rose and fell.

'Darling,' said Flo again. She took the hand without the drip in hers. Never had anything felt so thin. 'I'm here,' she said softly. 'Right beside.'

The faintest smile. Then a whisper. 'Hugo — '

'He's downstairs. I'll go and get him.'

But Hugo said he would see her tomorrow, he didn't want to tire her.

'He'll see you tomorrow, my darling.'

No answer.

'Vivie?' The rain was beating against the window, as if it knew. Vivie's breathing was long and slow: every time she breathed in, Flo held her own breath, waiting. Then she breathed out, and Flo with her.

'Vivie? Can you hear me?' She squeezed the thin hand, she started to talk: about Hugo, waiting downstairs, and how much he loved her, how much they all did. About how it was pouring with rain today, if she opened her pretty eyes she'd see just how much. About how —

Vivie opened her eyes. They were cloudy and unfocused.

'Darling.' Flo got up, leaned over her, so she could see. 'Here I am.'

Vivie's eyes cleared, just a little. She smiled. After a moment she murmured something.

'I need a lion.'

'A lion?'

It must be the drugs.

'A line,' said Vivie faintly. 'To bring me back.'

For a moment Flo could not speak. Then: 'Sweetheart. I'll be your line.' She stroked her sunken cheek, limp hair. 'Back you come.'

Another thin little thread of a smile. Then, as Flo released her hand, she whispered something else.

'What did you say?'

She mumbled it, something about families.

'Just once more, darling, I didn't quite catch — ' And she leaned again over the bed.

'Families,' whispered Vivie. 'All families disappear, and become one.'

Then her eyes closed, and her breathing slowed.

Flo waited, but she didn't speak again. She buzzed for the nurse. She went to fetch Hugo: he wouldn't come. When she got back, it was over.

★   ★   ★

Perhaps it was her mother's unutterable sadness that did something to melt Bea's sliver of ice. Not completely, but —

'Do you know what she said, before she died?' Flo was sitting at the supper table, on her first night home. 'She said she needed a line, to bring her back. I thought she said 'lion'.' She bit her lip. 'And then — then she said that all families disappear, and become one. As if — as if she knew something now.' She began to cry again.

Will put his hand on hers. 'My darling. What a — what a beautiful thing to say.'

'Nothing will bring her back! There wasn't a lion to save her!'

'Oh, Mummy, please. I love you so much.'

She had loved her aunt, too: hadn't been close to her, but had loved her prettiness, her vitality, the way she welcomed them all with open arms, the way she made Flo laugh, chattering away with her for hours on end, playing the piano, singing songs from musicals. And she was Hugo's mother. He must be feeling terrible.

I wish Fred were here, she thought, climbing up to her room one evening. Flo had gone early to bed as usual, and sobbed into her pillow. Now, with a sort of sick, closed feeling, Bea could hear her father locking the doors downstairs. All of them. Every night. As if anyone ever got robbed in Ryehurst.

Something was going wrong between Will and her. When he came into a room she went out of it. When she went in again his hearty, 'My darling! Come and sit down!' made her shrink. If Fred were here, she thought now, she'd have someone to share it all with. He could help comfort her mother. They could laugh about Will together, take the edge off his heartiness or moods.

She stopped, halfway up the stairs. There was the bird among the boughs. The cherries had faded over the years, but he was still there, dark and true. She hadn't talked to him for a long time, had forgotten all about him when Alex was around, and anyway — it all felt faintly ridiculous now. A wallpaper bird.

And yet —

He had kept all her secrets. Somehow, because she had confided in him for so long, he had a beating life.

'My mother's so sad,' she said quietly.

MY MOTHER'S SO SAD.

He listened gravely. She touched him, she felt the words sink into him. Then she went up to her desk.

Perhaps she should write to Hugo again: he'd answered her stiff little letter of condolence — what did you say? — with one that was almost as stiff.

Dear Bea, Thank you so much for your very kind letter...

He might have been writing to a stranger — but then, they'd hardly seen each other for ages. Perhaps she could write something a bit more human now, just to see how he was getting on.

She heard her father's heavy footsteps climb the stairs, and stop at the foot of her own.

'Bea? Switch that light out!'

She was going to be seventeen next birthday! She sat up quickly, filled with irritation, and as she did so a blackout hit her, hard. Only for a moment, but it left her shaking. Then: 'Just finishing my essay!' she called down, and heard him grunt, and make his way to the bathroom.

★　★　★

How was Hugo coping now, in that great big house? They still had their wonderful char, of course; and the Paying Guests, and old bridge

404

friends of Vivie's, who popped in to see her mother — but still. It must be so lonely for her, and it wasn't a proper life for a young man. He was working for a branch of a big London company, something to do with radio communications: was that much fun? And where were the girlfriends? Perhaps she shouldn't ask: he probably smuggled them in, and up to the attic. Perhaps he smuggled up a Paying Guest, and who could blame him?

On a spring afternoon, Flo picked up her book once more and leafed through the pages in her scribbled Biro. One or two lines caught her eye. Darling Freddie, in Melcote. Going white at breakfast: 'Anyone want to come outside and watch me be sick?' A terrible commotion, and then: 'Just dealing with a rhinoceros.' Even now, in the midst of all her sadness, that made her smile. One day it might make him laugh.

Oh, what should she do with it? What would Vivie say? She'd always been so busy, so admirable: abandoned by that wretched man and just getting on with things.

'Vivie? What do you think?'

The curtains stirred in the summer breeze. She hated net, hated it, but what could you do on a main road?

'Type it up,' said Vivie. 'Type it up, darling, and see what it looks like.'

★　★　★

After all the ghastly business with Vivie, the next thing was Agnes. Poor thing, it almost broke his

405

heart to hear her bleak voice on the phone.

'It's all over, Willie. Someone else has got him.'

'Oh, Sis, I'm so sorry.'

He'd thought it was too good to last. Chap on his own, nice-looking widower: there were always half a dozen widows and spinsters ready to pounce. Especially with a vicar, so much in the public eye: they'd have been clucking round the manse, cooking him little dishes, inviting him for tea. This chap could have been stringing any number of old biddies along, keeping his options open, raising poor Agnes's hopes.

'Bluebeard of the Glen,' he said. It didn't make her laugh.

'I'm so sorry,' he said again. 'Dear old Sis, shall I go up there with my gun? Turn up at the church and declare a Just Impediment?'

He could hear her violently blowing her nose.

'I only hope I haven't made too much of a fool of myself.'

'Of course you haven't. Of course not: you're being splendidly brave.'

She sniffed, blew her nose again. 'I'll have to go back to my lonely life now, I suppose.'

'Oh, Sis.' It turned his heart over, as Flo would say. 'You know I'm here. We're all here. You're always welcome.'

If only it were true.

At teatime he rang Fitz, and told her all about it.

'Oh dear, poor Agnes. I know what it's like having your heart broken.'

Did she really?

'I thought you and Eleanor were — er — well, you know, pretty happy.' It still stuck in his throat, acknowledging that set-up.

'Oh, we are, Willie. I'm thinking of a long time ago.'

Well, well. Old Fitz was a dark horse. He must have been in India when all that was going on. Whatever 'all that' might have been: frankly he couldn't imagine.

★ ★ ★

'All in all,' he said to Flo that evening, 'I think we can call this year pretty much of a wash-out so far, don't you?' He took her hand. 'How are you, my darling? Feeling half a degree up?'

'A quarter of a degree,' said Flo. They were having their pegs in the garden, the grass cut yesterday, everything brimming and fresh. A blackbird with his beak stuffed to bursting point made a beeline for the ivy on the wall at the end, and disappeared.

'Look at that,' said Will. 'Must be a second brood.'

'My book,' Flo said carefully. 'I so wanted Vivie to read it.'

'Of course you did.'

She took a deep breath. 'I've taken it to be typed.'

'Good idea.'

Honestly. You could never tell what he was going to think.

407

6

Fred came back from school, and knew no one. He did not know a soul. Of course, he was used to that: for years, he'd come home from Mountford Park and spent all the holidays with only Bea for company. As she got more dug in with her friends she'd been out and about more, but they'd still spend all those hours listening to records together, one on either side of the fireplace, Bea mooning away over Cliff or Bobby Vee.

'Take Good Care of My Ba-a-by,' she sang, and he'd thought it was about a real baby, whom someone had given away.

'Honestly, Fred. Of *course* it's not!'

He almost told her, then, his secret knowledge, but he just couldn't make himself, and afterwards he was glad. Much better that she shouldn't know. When she went out to help get the lunch, he put on one of Will's Concert Hall Classics, a Special Offer from the *Reader's Digest*. He sat listening to Beethoven symphonies with his eyes shut, filled with the kind of feelings he hadn't known he had.

'Turn it *down!* We've been calling for ages.'

After lunch, when she'd gone out with yet another friend, he went up to the boxroom, his darkroom now, and spent hours developing his prints. They were bird or landscape photographs, taken on walks with Will or out by himself in the week — who else was there to go walking with?

Last summer it hadn't mattered so much: it was only the first summer holidays from St Luke's, and it just felt like more of the same old Mountford thing. But now: now he was fifteen, with nothing to do for months.

'Fred!' Bea had come running out to meet him at the gate as the car drew up, all his stuff in the back, his bags and cricket things. 'Gosh, I'm so glad to see you again!'

'Fred! Fred my darling!' Flo came down the hall as they all piled in through the front door. 'You've grown *again!* Give me a hug.'

She wasn't so sad about Auntie Vivie now, said she was writing her book again, as Vivie would have wanted her to. 'Thinking of getting it published!'

They all sat in the dining room having a welcome-home lunch, the French windows open on to the garden, birds all singing away, everyone in a good mood.

And of course it was great to be back in the first day or two, everyone laughing as Will went droning on about show grounds, and pig pens, and how this or that put him in mind of the war, or India. 'I don't think I've told you about the time . . . ' And doing the washing-up with Bea, picking at bits of the Sunday joint, taking it in turn to sing notes of *Swan Lake* or *Sleeping Beauty*, another Special Offer.

'He's on to Negro Spirituals now. Gosh, Fred, I've missed you.'

'Me too.' And again he thought, looking down at the knives and forks in his hand, drying them carefully: How am I ever going to tell her?

But within a couple of days it was back to being on his own: Will up in London or out and about at some show or farm visit, Flo either writing or asleep, and Bea on the phone all the time, or —

'Just going over to Rosie's!'

Rosemary Reed was Rosie now, and had cut her hair short in a bob, like someone called Mary Quant, apparently. He hardly ever saw any of these girls, except down the town; Bea never brought them home. She went to their houses, where it was all pop music, or parties on Saturday nights, and he ended up watching television with Will.

'Great to have you home, old chap.' He yawned, and fell asleep.

Fred got up quietly and went back up to the boxroom.

Weeks of the holidays stretched ahead.

I don't really have a place here, he thought, unscrewing a bottle of developing fluid, pulling down the blind. Tiny points of evening sunlight pricked the dark blue like stars. He stood there in the little room, doing nothing for a moment.

'I don't belong,' he said, his voice quite broken now. It shocked him to hear himself speak the truth aloud.

Dear Hugo,

Thanks so much for your lovely letter. It's so nice to be in touch again, but it feels like such a long time since we saw each other that it's almost like writing to a pen friend!

Sometimes I can hardly even remember what you look like!

That wasn't true: she could remember every-thing: his dark curly hair, his gorgeous eyebrows, that slow sweet smile. That *voice*. How could she have wasted all that feeling on Alex, when all the time Hugo was living and breathing and being so clever, and surely just waiting for her to grow up?

Footsteps on the stairs.

'Bea? What are you doing?' In came Fred, at a loose end as usual.

She turned to look at him, so tall and lanky now in his holiday shirt and trousers. A bit old-fashioned? 'He's at that in-between stage,' said her mother. 'He's going to be simply gorgeous.'

'Actually,' she said, 'I was writing to Hugo.'

'Again?'

'Yes, again.' It was like having a proper boyfriend, someone much older and more interesting than any of the boys she ever met at parties — even James, Lizzie's stuck-up brother, who rarely bothered to speak to her now. He hardly came home at all these days anyway, always up in London with his friends.

'Do you want to go for a walk after lunch?'

'I'm going over to Lizzie's.'

'Oh.' He wandered across the room, looked out of the window on to the garden. She heard him sigh. Poor Fred.

'Sorry.'

'It doesn't matter.' He wandered back again, stood looking at the books on her desk. Half of

411

her was writing to Hugo and half revising. *Everyone's applied to university,* she'd written in her last letter, *and I've put down York as first choice.* It sounded so certain and organised, but in fact she might just as well have stuck a pin in.

'Where do you think I should go?' she'd asked her parents, and neither had had a clue. York was Miss Weaver's idea.

Fred had picked up a book. She turned over her letter.

'Don't peer.'

'I wasn't.' He leafed through the book: *Selected Early Twentieth-century Poetry and Prose.* Looked dreadfully dull. Or soppy. 'Charlotte Mew. Never heard of her. But then, as Dad would say, I don't suppose she's ever heard of me, either.' He flicked the pages. 'What's this about?'

Bea had a look. ''The Changeling' — oh, that's good, we did it in Elocution in the Upper Fourth. I can quote great screeds.' She stood in the middle of the room, and struck a mournful attitude. He sat down on the bed. Somewhere a lawnmower started up.

''Toll no bell for me, dear Father dear Mother,'' Bea recited above it, with immense slow feeling.

'Waste no sighs;
There are my sisters, there is my little brother
Who plays in the place called Paradise.'

She spread her hands expressively.

'Your children all, your children for ever;
                But I, so wild,
Your disgrace, with the queer brown face,
                was never,
      Never, I know, but half your child!'

She put her hand to her breast, and stopped. Fred felt himself go very still.

'Go on.'

'Oh, it goes on for ever. It's all about a child who feels out of place in his family, and doesn't know why, and one dark night he's snatched by the fairy people, who come to claim him.' She speeded up dramatically.

'All night long they danced in the rain,
Round and round in a dripping chain.
Tried to make me scream and shout . . .'

She dropped her voice. 'And then they take him. And it ends: 'I shall never come back again.''

She spread her hands again. 'That's it. Poor changeling.' Then she saw his expression. 'Fred? What's the matter?'

He bit his lip, and for a moment she thought he was going to make one of his awful faces. She'd almost forgotten about them. Then he looked straight at her.

'Don't you know?' he said, and his voice was very strange.

'Know what? What are you talking about?' WHAT ARE YOU TALKING ABOUT?

His eyes filled with tears — she hadn't seen him cry for years, and she went quickly over and

413

kneeled beside him on the bedside rug.

'Fred, please. What is it?'

He took an enormous breath. Then he got up quickly and said, 'Nothing,' in a dreadful croaky way, and then, 'I'm going out for a walk.'

And he ran down the stairs, past Mrs Thing coming up with her cleaning stuff, past the sitting room where Flo was going through her typescript. In a moment the front door banged.

Fred never banged doors. Never. He never shouted, or got cross, and these days he certainly never cried. He was quiet and smiling and polite, and —

Not entirely natural, Bea thought now, as Mrs Thing banged about in the bathroom below. Certainly not like her.

* * *

He flung the front gate open, stood for a moment on the shady pavement. Which way?

Not down the town; he was sick of the town. And he waited for a car to go by and ran across, turning into Rushbrook Road and striding down it, past the railway line and up to the crossing with Ryehurst Hill. He stopped at the traffic lights. To the left the road ran into the boring old town, with its bookshop and park, and nothing else, unless you wanted to spend all your time in Rhythm. He didn't. And he crossed into Summers Road, which led past Micklegate, Bea's old school, which he, away all the time, sent out of the family, had never visited.

It was all shut up now for the holidays, and he

strode by. This was a pleasant road, full of substantial houses, beneath the line of hills. It was quiet now, with no schoolgirls about, not that he'd have known what to say to any of them. He slowed down a bit, approaching the tennis club, where he supposed he could meet people if he wanted. If he played well, which he didn't. Nor did Bea, and as he heard the thwack of balls across the courts, and the cheerful cries of 'Bad luck!' or 'Well done!', and glimpsed them all racing about in their whites, he realised there was a whole life going on in Ryehurst that he knew nothing about, where everyone knew one another, played tennis, had cocktail and dinner parties as Will and Flo never did.

'Now when we were in India . . . '

Sometimes it seemed as if India was the only place in the world that mattered. India was what brought Will alive, with all his stories; India was what Flo spent years writing a book about — then throwing it on to the fire and sobbing her heart out. That was what Bea had told him. And they didn't fit in here, not really; had come too late to get dug in. Will would talk to anyone, but Flo wasn't a digging-in kind of person.

'They're all *accountants!*' she always said, as if you could sink no lower.

He didn't really know what was so awful about accountancy, just knew he wouldn't want to be one. He didn't know what he wanted to be, or who he was: he just knew that on a beautiful summer morning he was lonely and pent-up and miserable as hell.

'Poor changeling,' Bea had said brightly.

415

He'd come so close to telling her — but then what would happen? She would look at him in horror. Everything would change. No one in the family would ever feel easy with one another ever again. His parents — his adoptive parents — had kept up such a good front all these years, he'd just be tearing it all to pieces.

He'd slowed down, stopped to draw breath outside a block of flats.

'You lost?' asked a chap who must be the caretaker, raking the gravel.

'Sort of,' Fred said wryly, and then, 'No, I'm fine, thanks.'

Almost opposite the flats a pretty tree-lined road ran up towards the foot of the hills. Birds were singing their hearts out. He crossed, and began to walk.

★   ★   ★

Flo went through the typescript of her new book for the third and final time. There.

Surely it was ready now. And surely this was something people would enjoy: country life in the fifties, the dear old farm, that lovely village, with all those little stories, all those funny little sayings. They'd been such darling children.

Now then. She pulled *Writers & Artists* out of its pigeonhole, ran her finger down the lists of publishers. Should she just stick in a pin? Or should she send it to an agent first? Should she, ha ha, send it to the wretched Michael Lewis, he with the specs on the end of his nose, and affair in London?

416

For a wild moment, sitting there on a summer morning, Flo thought: I'll do it. After all these years, I'll show him. And all her old spirit flared up. The spirit that all those handsome young officers had found so irresistible in the war — they had!

Bea was running downstairs. Wanting lunch, of course. What were they going to have?

'Had a nice morning, darling?' Flo asked, making her way to the larder. She'd better do a stock-up tomorrow. 'Where's Fred?'

'Didn't you hear him go out?'

Flo shook her head. She hadn't heard a thing.

★ ★ ★

The road, which he realised after a while was private, was called Pilgrims Way, but the Way itself, a long broad path, ran along the foothills, west to east, towards Canterbury, he supposed. A railing marked the end of the road, and he went round it and into the real shade of the path.

It was nice here. The earth was baked hard, though here and there he could see hoof prints and droppings, and a sign said 'Bridleway'. One or two walkers went by with their dogs, and he could hear a pony whinnying from a field. If you shut your eyes, you could be in real country.

He shut them, he listened to the birds. Thanks to Will he could distinguish quite a few: robin and thrush and chaffinch, and blackbird, of course — anyone would know that. He breathed in the smell of earth and horse and sun-warmed grass on the hills, rising high behind a line of

417

trees. Then from somewhere came a sweet familiar sound. He opened his eyes. Hens — they must be in somebody's garden. And at once, unstoppably, he was back in Melcote, hens calling through the village, laying an egg and telling the world about it.

Thinking this was horribly painful. It had been great there, everyone at home and people to play with whenever you wanted. The Gibson boys, peeing over the nettle bed. Shy little Nancy Byatt, coming to play with Bea, so frightened of the geese. But the best thing, of course, was that he hadn't known the truth then. Hadn't realised.

He swallowed. Ahead through the trees was another little railing, running up beside steps cut into the chalk, before the hill proper began. Coney Hill, he remembered now, though he had only ever walked along the top from Ryehurst Hill, having a half-term picnic, years ago. He walked up the steps, he began to climb.

★   ★   ★

'But where has he gone? Where's he got to?'

'I'm sure he'll be back soon, Mummy, don't fuss.'

'I'm not fussing, I'm just concerned. It's not like him, just to go off like that.'

It wasn't. Bea washed up the lunch things.

'I'm sure he's all right,' she said, as Flo went upstairs for her nap. 'And I'm going over to Lizzie's now.'

'Again?'

'Again.'

He climbed up the hill in the sun. The grass was short, and smelled earthy and warm. Chalk land: the kind of thing Mr Parris from CCF would always tell you when you arrived at a new place for manoeuvres, making sure you knew everything about the terrain. Clumps of little blue flowers he thought were probably harebells grew all the way up, butterflies were dancing everywhere. If Will were here he'd be pointing them out — 'That's a Meadow Brown, old boy. And I'm pretty sure that's a Chalkhill Blue.'

It was very hot. Ahead, the turf had been cut quite away, and a broad path led up to a kind of memorial or something, of polished pink granite. He climbed up the last of the grassy hillside and then he was on to the grey-white chalk, his shoes scrunching on stony little bits that had flaked away. He was really sweating now, and he stopped at the war memorial and stood there panting.

Far below he could see the outskirts of the town, the expanse of the Abbey Park, with a gleam of the lake, and in the far distance the hazy line of what must be the South Downs. A little light aircraft crossed the sky, with a peaceful, contented sound: up in the blue, nothing to worry about, just having a look at the world. How great that must be. He shaded his eyes and watched it putter away.

He'd got his breath back, though he was really thirsty, and he climbed on up the chalk path until he had reached the summit. Then he flung

419

himself down on the turf. When was the last time he'd been up here? He remembered that half-term from Mountford, quite early on in his time there, sitting down with one of Flo's picnics — gritty bits in the lettuce sandwiches, and hard-boiled eggs with salt in a little twist of paper — but she hadn't come with them, she'd stayed at home as usual. 'I'm just not a walker, darling. Off you go, have a lovely time.' So it had been just the three of them, him and Bea, and Will going on about natural history, and the great big Roman snail shells you could find up here.

All that had been in another lifetime: that was how it felt now. It was in the days when he couldn't stop crying, as the time to go back drew near — in a half-term you hardly had time to do anything before it was time to go back — calling his mother up to his room and howling, night after night. Still being sent back, term after term.

It was before he'd understood why.

No son of mine...

And he remembered, on this picnic, Will getting out his binoculars, and looking out over the town spread out below.

'That's it, I can see our house! Clear as anything. Have a look, kiddos.'

He'd peered through, the binoculars so heavy then, the horizon rising and falling until — yes, he could see their very own house, his home, and imagine Mummy resting, in the shady quiet.

He sat up, and looked out once again at the view. From up here you could see the whole town: and yes, even without binoculars he could make out the main road running out to Redstone, and, just, the length of Croydon Road: if he screwed up and shaded his eyes he thought he could see their house, such a long way away. Bea and Flo would be having lunch, wondering where he'd got to.

I shall never come back again.

It was like the changeling, looking back on the place that had once been his home, snatched by the goblins on a dark wet night, taken back to the place where he really belonged.

And where was that?

Should he seek out his real parents one day? How did you do that?

He got to his feet. He turned and walked along the broad length of the hill, and struck out west, towards what he knew from his CCF maps was Box Hill, with Dorking below and what he supposed, in the end, would be Brockwood, and St Luke's, where he was making a decent life now.

The sun-warmed turf was springy beneath his feet. It was beautiful up here. Everything felt summery, fresh and alive, and the walking began to soothe him. He nodded to one or two people coming the other way, out with their own binoculars, and then a rabbit quite suddenly went racing down over the hillside and into a hole. Must be a dog about somewhere.

And yes, he could see ahead a family stop and call out, 'Here, boy! Here!' as a black Labrador went hurtling after it. There was a stile in a hedge before the next flank of the hill, and they stood there and waited, calling again. 'Tinder!'

Fred observed them as he approached: parents in their fifties, he supposed, looking nice enough, and a boy about his own age, tall and sandy-haired, laughing as the dog finally came panting back up towards them. Everyone made a fuss of him, and then they had to help him go over the stile — 'That's it! Over you go!' By now, Fred was almost at the stile himself.

'Morning!' said the father, as the dog finally scrambled down on the other side. He had a canvas bag slung over his shoulder. 'You look hot,' he said. 'Like a drink?'

'Gosh, thanks, I'd love one.'

Out came a Thermos of ice-cold water, and he drank and drank.

'Thanks so much.' He wiped the rim of the plastic mug and handed it back. 'Saved my life,' he said, and the father smiled, and put it all back in the bag, and then he and his wife climbed over, following the Labrador, far ahead now in the sun. The sandy-haired boy gestured at the stile, as if to say, 'After you,' in polite public schoolboy fashion.

'Go on,' said Fred. 'You were there first,' and followed, jumping down after him. And then, as the parents went striding away, there they were together, two boys out and about on the hills in the summer holidays, much of an age and quite a bit alike. Fred could sense this almost at once, as they left the stile behind, knew that this was another boy home from boarding school, out with his parents because he didn't know anyone else, not really.

'That's a great dog,' he said.

'He's bonkers,' said the boy. 'Have you walked far?'

'Just up the hill from Pilgrims Way.' And then, as if he had to justify being out by himself, no friend, and not even a camera or binoculars slung round his neck to show that he had a purpose, he said, 'Family getting on my nerves a bit,' with a little laugh.

A smile. 'I know what you mean. Where do you live?'

'Oh, just on the other side of the town,' said Fred. 'In Croydon Road.' He knew that Bea and his mother felt everyone looked down on Croydon Road, but this boy hadn't even heard of it. 'What about you?'

'We live on the Heath,' said the boy, squinting into the sun. A hawk was poised in the blue above them, hovering over the hillside.

'Kestrel or sparrow hawk?' Fred wondered.

'I'd say kestrel.' The boy was squinting up. 'My name's Piper, by the way.'

'Sutherland,' said Fred. He'd been saying it since he was eight. Who knew what his real name was?

* * *

Flo woke in the empty house. A summer afternoon, the curtains drawn over the open window, everything peaceful and still. She yawned, and looked at the bedside clock. Quarter to four: perfect. And she lay there for a few minutes longer, in the best time of the day: Bea and Fred out, a good couple of hours before

423

she had to think about supper, and that she didn't have to worry about really, with Will off on some Shropshire pig farm. She had nothing to do except make a pot of tea and bring it back to bed. And her typescript all ready to go! What a happy thought.

She reached for her book. *The Darling Buds of May* — it didn't matter how many times she read it, it always made her laugh. Such a clever writer, even Will loved it, and he never read a thing except the *Reader's Digest* and the *Telegraph*. Sometimes an old John Masters, when he was in the mood. Now then, where had she got to?

Two things came to her as she found her place.

The first was that she should send her book to H. E. Bates's publisher. Of course that was what she should do! If they liked him — and who couldn't? — they'd be bound to like her own little story of country life. And she checked the spine.

The second, in this quiet house, was that she still didn't know where Fred was. Bea was over at Lizzie's as usual, probably with an eye out for that super-looking brother, even if she was always writing to Hugo these days, but Fred —

'Mummy, he did actually slam the front door. How could you not have heard that?'

Slam the door? Fred?

'You know me, darling. When I'm writing — '

When she was writing, the sky could fall in.

She put down *The Darling Buds*. Where was he? Why had he gone slamming out of the house?

424

'Don't fuss, Mummy, I'm sure he's fine. Is there anything except fish fingers?'

There wasn't. The larder was low again, and she, buried in her book, thinking about agents and publishers, hadn't even heard darling Fred —

Oh, God, where was he? Of course, he was fifteen, he could look after himself, but —

It was just not knowing. She looked at the clock again. She thought of all the years of separation, the sobbing his heart out in the school holidays, the years of sending him back there, thin and white-faced and trying to be brave, and how super he was now, so confident and happy.

Except that it seemed that he wasn't.

Where was he?

Half-past four. She got out of bed. She thought: If anything happened to you, I'd die.

* * *

'Do you want to join us for lunch?' Mrs Piper asked him, as they came down to the bottom of the hill.

'Well. Gosh.' He was starving, now, but should he say yes? Weren't they just being polite?

They stood there in the shady lane, the dog nosing about in a ditch and a couple of riders making their way up towards them. Coney Hill Riding School, said a sign on an open gate, and they all stood back as the horses clip-clopped through, the riders raising their hats. Ahead, the main road roared with traffic: they were quite a

425

long way out of Ryehurst now.

'We'd love to have you,' said Mrs Piper.

Would they really? He tried to imagine bringing home someone he'd just met, with Flo miles away with her book, or tucked up in bed, nothing in the larder and Will, if he was there, being all hearty, so you could hardly get a word in.

'Come on,' said Piper, and he smiled and said well, gosh, again, and everyone laughed.

'Thanks a lot. I'd love to.'

And Mr Piper put the dog on his lead as they approached the busy road, running to Ryehurst one way and Dorking and Brockwood the other. He'd only ever been along here by car, going to and from St Luke's. Now, as they finally found a gap in the traffic, and hurried across, he saw the huge expanse of the Heath properly, for the first time.

A windmill stood on the horizon, and golfers were striding about in the distance. A lot of the place was thick with gorse, but there were ponds here and there, shining in the sun.

'We live over there,' said Mr Piper, letting the dog off the lead again, and he went racing away, nose down, towards a line of trees. As they approached, Fred saw that they shaded an unmade road, more of a track, really, and a few big houses set back from it.

'The third one along,' said Piper, as they came into the shade. 'God, I'm hungry, aren't you?'

'Starving. This is so nice of you.'

And it was so nice here, dappled shade falling on the soft mud track, and another horse coming slowly up behind them, then trotting away, kicking up clouds of dust. Riding. Another Ryehurst world he knew nothing about.

Mr and Mrs Piper were opening their wooden front gate, more the kind of thing you'd see in a field, letting the dog run through and up to his bowl in the porch.

'What a lovely house.' He heard himself sound like Bea, or Flo, but it was: creeper-covered stone, double-fronted, with a garden that ran all the way round.

And he felt at once at home, and then realised why. It made him think of his grandparents' house. And as the dog flopped down into his basket, Fred stood in the broad airy hall, doorways off it leading this way and that, almost expecting to see the great brass gong he loved to strike, but seeing instead a table cluttered with books and papers, the staircase rising behind it lit by a leaded landing window, so that light fell everywhere.

'Lunch in ten minutes,' said Mrs Piper. 'Richard, why don't you show — ' She stopped, and smiled. 'We don't even know your name,' she said, and Fred smiled back, and told them, and then all at once felt so happy and alive that he almost said that actually it wasn't his real name, but stopped himself in time.

'Do you want to phone home?' she asked him, gesturing at the phone on the cluttered table. 'Just to let them know where you are?'

He shook his head. They wouldn't care, Bea going off to that Lizzie girl, Flo sleeping all afternoon. Anyway, it felt so wet to be phoning home at his age: Here I am, Mummy, fifteen years old and out by myself. Having a nice time for once.

I shall never come back again.

* * *

'But where *is* he?' asked Flo, when Bea finally came back, ringing three times and hopping about in the porch, singing 'Yesterday' under her breath.

'For God's sake, Bea, it's after five and we don't even know where he *is*. Do stop singing that wretched song. Come and sit down. Tell me again why he slammed the door.'

'Honestly, I don't know.' They went into the sitting room. 'I was just reciting a poem,' she said.

'A poem?' Flo gazed at her. 'What poem?'

'"Toll no bell for me, dear Father dear Mother,"' intoned Bea, standing in the middle of the room and loving the sound of her own voice as usual.

'Waste no sighs;
There are my sisters, there is my little brother
Who plays in the place called Paradise . . . '

Flo burst into tears.

Footsteps along the road, the click of the front gate.

Three rings on the doorbell.

'There you are,' said Bea. 'I told you he was all right.' And then, as Flo leaped to her feet,

'Honestly, Mummy, surely we should have our own keys by now.'

Flo ran to the hall and flung the door open. There he stood in the evening sun, her boy, her darling.

'What's the matter?' he asked her, seeing her tearful face. Now what had happened? Another book bitten the dust?

She drew him to her. 'My very own,' she murmured, into his sweaty shirt. 'Thank God you're home.'

Oh, why did he pull away?

7

Was it possible that a single day could turn your life around? That was how it felt to Fred, that summer. He had a friend. He had someone to do things with. Above all, he had the Piper household, so different from his own that it felt like another country.

'Just going over to the Pipers,' he could say after breakfast, Flo in her dressing gown, Bea deep in her *NME*. He pushed his chair back.

'When will we see you, my darling?'

'Not sure.' And he was gone before she could say another word.

He caught the bus out to the Heath, rumbling through town past the market hall, past Boots, and MacFisheries, where Flo bought the cod for their fishy-milk suppers, and Budgens, where she went for their fish finger and tinned peas lunches. Then she went upstairs for her nap.

Mrs Piper didn't have naps in the afternoon. Like her husband, she was energetic, tall and kind. Like him, she was a teacher, and like Auntie Agnes she actually liked cooking. There all resemblance ended, as Will might say, laughing about some old girl in church.

The Pipers didn't go to church: they were Quakers. They didn't read the *Telegraph*, or even *The Times*: it was the *Guardian* that came to their house each morning, a paper he had only seen in newsagents, and then not looked at much. Later in the summer they were all going to France, where no Sutherland had ever been.

He'd never been abroad! Will had lived for thirteen years in India, not to mention all the places he'd been to in the war — Palestine, North Africa. Even Flo had been adventurous enough to go out to India, too. But he and Bea: it was pathetic, really. Bournemouth. Dorset. His CCF and photography trips took him here and there, but that, apart from his years at Mountford Park, was about it.

One day he'd travel the world. One day he'd find his real parents: his mother, anyway — he was pretty sure most babies given up for adoption didn't have fathers, not really. But for now —

Now the bus had left the town behind, and he could see the rise of hills on his right, and soon, on the left, the great spread of the Heath. He jumped off at the stop, and struck out along the path, smelling the gorse in the morning sun, his camera bumping against him. Richard was keen on photography, too, and was good on natural history, as he was, though Fred could tell after just one or two meet-ups that, unlike him, Richard was seriously clever. But it didn't seem to matter, he was so nice.

And he knew about boarding-school life: houses, cross-country running, all that. They had lots in common, though his school was different, a Quaker school, down in Kent, with no houses, and something called Meeting, instead of chapel. It sounded OK, but he thought it was pretty odd that parents like the Pipers would send their son

431

to boarding school at all.

'It's because I'm an only child,' Richard said, out on one of their walks. 'They thought it would be better for me, than just stuck at home with them all the time. Especially as they have to stay late at school quite often.'

'Didn't want you to be a latch-key child,' said Fred, thinking of Flo, and her scorn of working mothers.

'Exactly,' said Richard, as they walked along Pilgrims Way, Tinder up ahead nosing at everything, wag wag wag. It was great having a dog to go walking with. They stopped to give an apple to a lonely pony in his field, then they climbed up the long chalk path on the side of the hill and looked down on the town, and out to the shimmering horizon. They talked naturally and easily, had done so from the beginning. Sometimes, Fred thought now, approaching the beautiful line of trees, the dusty path, it felt like being with Collins again.

★ ★ ★

Of course, there were things they didn't talk about. Girls, for a start.

'What's your sister like?' Richard asked once.

It must be so strange, being an only child. What could he say?

'She's all right. She's — you know. Boys. Pop music.'

But they didn't go on to talk about her, they talked about rock, which Richard was really into. Fred was still more into classical music:

Beethoven, Tchaikovsky. All Will's Concert Hall LPs, with hands clapping down at the bottom of the sleeve.

But Richard went on about the Stones, and Bob Dylan, and said he would play him some stuff. Bea, and the whole idea of her — a girl, someone quite different — dropped from view. It was sort of understood between them that girls were in another world, that they didn't really know any, had been just with boys all their lives. They wouldn't know what to say to a girl, not in that way.

But it wasn't just girls they didn't talk about, as they whistled for the dog, and walked on. Fred kept his secret knowledge to himself, buried deep.

★ ★ ★

'Tell us about your family, Fred,' said Mrs Piper — Mary, apparently, and Mr Piper was David. They said he could call them by their first names, but he just couldn't. And how could he talk about his parents — hearty Will and his landowners, his county shows, all shooting and sheep-dips, his church-going, his time in India, which he still went droning on about? How could he talk about Flo and her books and old boyfriends and sleepy afternoons, to people who taught history and maths, Mr Piper at a school in Dorking and Mrs at the secondary modern in the Abbey Park?

'The *secondary modern?*' he heard Flo say. '*Quakers?*'

433

On Sundays they all sat in silence in Meeting. 'But what do you actually believe?'

They believed in peace, apparently. Mr Piper had even been in prison in the war, as a conscientious objector — he could see Will's face if he told him about that.

But Quakers also believed in everyone being equal — Mrs Piper had a great-aunt who'd been a Suffragette. Fred didn't even know what a Suffragette was, until she explained, in the nicest way, saying, 'As you know,' though he didn't.

When they talked, they sounded the same as his parents, pretty much, but they simply weren't. And anyway, those people, with their pegs, and their elephant table, and Panther's head on the wall — they weren't his real parents at all.

'Well,' he said, over supper in the garden, when Mrs Piper asked him again about his family. 'Well, um, I — ' And he ground to a halt.

Everyone laughed. But the way the Pipers laughed was so warm and understanding, you couldn't imagine them heaping scorn on things. For a second he even thought about telling them the truth.

'More salad?'

'Great. Thanks.'

'Another slice of bread?'

'Please.'

The bread was home-made, crumbly and brown and not like any bread he'd ever tasted, really. The salad was all from the garden. He thought of tinned peas, tinned carrots, if you were lucky. Of course in Melcote days they'd had home-grown veg, but all that had gone when they moved, like that funny old pressure-cooker thing, steaming its head off on Sundays, Will shouting, 'Careful! Careful!'

That had felt like a real home.

'You've gone very quiet.'

'Sorry.' He bent down and patted Tinder's head.

'Nothing to be sorry about. Everything OK?'

'Fine, thanks.'

And then Mr Piper said he could see a bat, just the kind of thing Will would say, and everyone followed his gaze and talked about pipistrelles, peering through the dusk.

The garden was fabulous, running right round the house, with vegetable beds, a fruit cage, apple and plum trees out here at the back, which had a nice raggedy feel. There was even a quince tree, something else he'd never really heard of, though he could tell you quite a lot about a peepul tree, and the village women leaving offerings beneath it, making *puja* to its spirit, to give them babies. The little yellow quince — which would get huge, apparently — were like something out of a fairy tale, or legend or something, glowing like lanterns now, as the moon began to rise.

'I'll tell you one thing,' he said, getting up to help clear the plates. 'This house reminds me of my grandparents' house. I think it's the same period,' he added, stacking stuff on a tray, hearing himself sound knowledgeable.

'And where do they live?' asked Mrs Piper.

'Bournemouth,' he said, 'but my grandfather's dead now, unfortunately. And my aunt. But

435

we're going down there next month, to see my grandmother. We quite often go down there in the summer.'

★ ★ ★

'In the car!'

August, and they were going on what everyone knew would probably be their last family holiday.

'Hugo,' said Bea to herself.

But Hugo had other fish to fry.

'I bet he has,' said Will.

'Darling, don't be so insensitive,' said Flo, seeing Bea's face.

'Insensitive? Me?' He had two weeks off work, and he needed every day of it. The last RLS show, up at Castle Blakeney, had almost done him in.

'In the car!'

They were going to see Granny, all on her own while Hugo went off to Italy. Who was he going with? Nobody knew.

'He's a dark horse, old Hugo.'

'Stop it!'

'Stop what?'

Granny had someone coming in each day to cook her a nice lunch, and their Mrs Thing, of course.

'Poor Granny. She's longing to see us.'

They were going to spend two days there, and then they were going to Dorset, but not actually staying with Fitz.

'I'd love to have you all, Willie, but I'm just not at my best.'

It was too much for her, he knew: four people, two of them teenagers — probably getting a bit much for him, quite frankly. He showed Flo an ad in the *Telegraph*, booked the guesthouse for all of them: nice place on the cliffs, bit of a walk down to the sea.

But Bournemouth first. How strange it felt: that great big house, with no Grandpa, snipping at his grapes in the conservatory, no Vivie running to the front door to greet them, arms open wide, no big black Whoopoo up on the kitchen shelf, rubbing his furry head against yours. No Hugo, Bea thought bleakly, carrying in her case.

There was only Mrs Thing, come to answer the door in a pinny that was just like the one their own Mrs Thing wore all the time, and tiny little Granny, her specs on the end of her nose, tucked up under her slippery eiderdown in her bedroom with rose-patterned wallpaper. Carpeted steps led down to her very own carpeted bathroom: as always, to Bea, this felt like luxury, but the whole house so sad, and pointless, really, without Hugo. Did he really have to go to Italy, just as they were visiting?

'How are you, Granny?'

'All the better for seeing you, darling. How pretty you look these days.'

'Thank you.' But what was the point of looking pretty, all on your own? 'How's Hugo?' she asked lightly. Even at a distance, you should never sound too keen.

'He works dreadfully hard — but still, there's always a girlfriend about somewhere! I expect

437

you have lots of boyfriends now.'

'Sort of.' She felt her stomach do a nosedive. Girlfriends? He never mentioned girlfriends. A dark horse, old Hugo — oh, horrible, horrible men.

'Anyone special?' asked Granny, smiling away. ANYONE SPECIAL?

'No.' She got up, and went to the open window. Down in the garden Will and Fred were getting the deck chairs out from the conservatory. You could still hear all the babies crying away next door in the Mother and Baby Home. She saw Fred stop and listen for a moment, then get his finger trapped in the deck chair and shout.

'They're awkward buggers,' said Will. 'You all right, old boy?'

'Here we are!' sang Flo at the open bedroom door. In she came with a lunch tray.

'Darling, that's so sweet of you,' said Granny, though Bea could tell from here it was just tinned soup and cheese. Edam. Flo knew three kinds of cheese: Edam, New Zealand cheddar and Dairylea. But she'd put on a snowy tray cloth, and a rose in a pretty little vase, the kind of thing she was really good at.

'I'll leave you to it,' said Bea. 'I'll get our lunch going, shall I?'

'That would be heaven.'

★　★　★

For two days it was cooking for Granny, washing up in the great big kitchen where Hugo had

438

taught her how to do it. It was seeing Flo pick up Vivie's photograph, and bite her lip. It was looking at the big family photograph taken of them all on Grandpa's eightieth, Hugo holding Whoopoo, everyone smiling away in the garden; and the photos of Grandpa and Hugo as a little boy, walking home from school, playing ping pong out in the garden.

'What a rotter that man was,' said Flo, meaning Vivie's handsome husband. There was a photo of the two of them, just engaged, so happy. Then he'd scarpered. Nobody knew why.

'Leaving a boy without a father, dreadful thing,' said Will, and then, 'You all right, Fred old chap?'

'Fine, thanks.'

For two days it was Granny coming down for tea in the garden, going back up again for supper on another little tray. It was playing all the old records on the hi-fi, 'I'm a Gnu' and 'There Was an Old Lady who Swallowed a Fly', but Will's roars of laughter sounded a bit hollow, even to himself.

'Still,' he said, as he and Fred loaded up the car again, 'we've done our stuff, that's the main thing. Poor little Granny.'

She came shakily down in her dressing gown, and kissed them one by one in the sunny drawing room.

'Goodbye, Fred darling. So lovely to see you again.'

Fred went out to wait in the hall. If the Piper house reminded him of this one, the great staircase rising above him, now he could see only the past: everyone together, walking through the pines, swimming and running about on the beach, smothered in Nivea cream; throwing the dice for Ludo and Snakes & Ladders, watching the Hornby train up in the attic run round and round on its endless journey. Striking the gong for mealtimes.

'*My turn!*'

He stepped forward, lifted the leather-headed stick, quietly struck the brass. It sounded through the hall, as loved and familiar, as deep and full, as someone he had known for ever. Then it slowly faded.

★　★　★

'In the car!'

Dorset, and it rained and rained. Every time it stopped, Will suggested a walk, but there was always some reason for people to cry off: Flo reading in bed, Bea slumped in an armchair in the guest lounge, humming some wretched pop song under her breath.

'What's the matter with her?' he asked Fred, the one person he could usually dig out. They looked at seabirds and fishing boats through their binoculars, took photographs, walked down the cliff path and along the pebbly beach, where smugglers used to haul stuff up into the caves.

'I think she's thinking about Hugo.'

'Oh, for God's sake.'

And even old Fred was hard to talk to these days. Cormorants and guillemots, and that was about it. Not that he wanted to talk about much else, but it was a feeling he had, couldn't put a finger on it, something not quite as usual.

'Everything all right, old chap? Had a good summer on the whole?'

'Very good, thanks.'

'Expect you're glad to have a local friend.'

'Very glad.'

And that was that, though he seemed to have spent half the summer with this new family.

'What are they like, the Pipers?'

'Very nice.'

He gave up. Once or twice they had a swim, but the sea was rough and the flag often flying to warn of dangerous currents. They climbed slowly back up again, holding their swimming towels over their heads as the rain came down once more. When they got in, Bea was nowhere to be seen.

'I think she went out for a walk.'

'But — ' He was exasperated. This was a family holiday: what was she doing out there by herself? Frankly, he was a bit hurt.

* * *

She walked along the cliff top in sun and wind and rain. If the rain got really heavy, she ran to a concrete shelter, full of cigarette butts and graffiti: names and hearts, swear words and crude drawings. She gazed at them, had a flash of Miss Leaming, and the reproductive organs of the rabbit, but it didn't make her laugh. None of it seemed to have anything to do with her. The rain blew away and she walked on, breathing the

441

smell of wet turf and the sea. Gulls wheeled overhead, shrieking.

Dear Hugo, I was so sad not to see you last week. We're down here in Dorset with nothing to do! I wish you were here. I know you're much older, and I must seem like just a child to you, but I'm seventeen now, in case you hadn't noticed, and I'm not a child at all...

She wasn't anything very much. That's what it felt like, stuck down here.

'You'll be going to university, I expect,' said Eleanor in her graceful voice, when they all went up for supper.

'If I pass my A levels.'

'My dear, of course you'll pass them. I'm sure you'll do very well.'

'Sit up, Bea,' said Will suddenly. 'Don't sit there slouching like that.'

'Sorry.' She sat up, and her eyes filled with tears. Seventeen years old, and her father could still make her cry. She would not, she would not. She looked away, eyes brimming.

'Where have you applied?' Fitz asked kindly.

She couldn't speak.

'I think she's applied to York,' said Fred.

Everyone admired his lovely deep broken voice.

'I don't suppose you'll want to sing those funny old songs any more,' said Fitz, passing the runner beans.

He smiled. 'I might.' He helped himself. 'Bea? Want some?'

She took the dish. Tears splashed into it. Everyone noticed. She ran from the room.

442

'For God's sake, what's the matter with her now?'

FOR GOD'S SAKE, WHAT'S THE MATTER WITH HER NOW?

★ ★ ★

Upstairs, she lay weeping on Fitz's bed. She didn't know what was the matter with her, any more than they did, she was just — all churned up, wanting everything to change.

'Hugo,' she sobbed into the pillow. He'd make everything right. He'd take her in his arms, that was all she wanted —

After a while she stopped crying. She could hear the clatter of plates in the kitchen, her mother calling her from the foot of the stairs, then going back to join the others. Piano music came drifting up from the drawing room, and Fitz's sweet old voice.

'Op-pop-pop-pop-poposite the ducks
Is the spot where I unbend,
And among my flow'rs after bus'ness hours,
I am glad to see a friend . . . '

She could hear Will singing along, op-pop-pop, and everyone laughing. How could she go back down?

'Bea?' A tap at the door, then Fred put his nose round, just a twitching bit, and she had to laugh. 'You OK?'

'Oh, Fred.'

He came in. They sat on the edge of the bed.

443

'It's just . . . ' She spread her hands. 'It's just sort of everything,' she said.

He nodded. 'I know. Me too.'

She looked at him. 'What do you mean?'

He took a breath, as he'd done all those weeks ago, up in her bedroom at home, as if he wanted to tell her something really important. 'Don't you know?' he'd asked her. Then he slammed out of the house.

'Fred?'

He shook his head. 'Nothing. It doesn't matter.' And then: 'Come down now, Dad's in quite a good mood.'

She washed her face at Fitz's basin behind a lovely screen in the corner, dark green, painted with splashy leaves and flowers. The house was full of such beautiful things, and she and Eleanor so calm and happy together, though everyone said it was awful, really.

★　★　★

The last day of the holidays.

'Did I tell you I'd sent my book off?'

'I think so.' He was sitting on the lid of the trunk, his back to her. She kneeled down and fumbled with the locks. There. Done it! They got to their feet.

'You've grown again!'

He tried to smile. He was taller: he was torn in pieces.

'Come and give me a hug.'

He came round and hugged her, there in the middle of his parents' bedroom, clouds blowing

444

past the window and the first leaves swirling over the garden. Flo put her head on his shoulder. Oh, how good that felt.

'My very own,' she murmured, for the millionth time, and as always felt that little tug away. In a second, the hug was over. 'Fred?'

'Mmm?' Already, he was halfway to the door.

'Darling?' Should she have it all out in the open? What was there to have out? He was growing up, he was growing towards manhood, it was all only natural, but —

'Sometimes I wonder,' she began. 'Sometimes I feel — '

But Mrs Thing was hoovering along the landing, and he smiled and shook his head, unable to hear what she felt or wondered, and then he was up in his dark-room, packing up his stuff, the door tightly shut against the light.

★ ★ ★

He'd said goodbye to the Pipers, had a last walk up the chalk path, Tinder racing ahead as usual. As usual, they stopped by the memorial, panting, and looked down on the town spread out below. The air was damp, a band of yellow marking the trees at the foot of the hill, just beginning to turn. Mist clouded the far horizon, but the roads and houses were still pretty clear, the dark spread of the Heath beyond.

'All those different lives,' said Fred.

'Each with their own little drama,' said Richard drily, as if he were quoting. He did that, you could tell, to avoid a cliché.

445

'Your family doesn't have a drama.'

'Of course it does. In the past, anyway.' He blew his nose. 'My father in prison in the war. All that.' He stuffed his handkerchief back in his jacket pocket. 'What about you, Fred? I still haven't met your family — have they got two heads or something?'

'Just the one,' said Fred. Tinder had come bounding back to join them. He put his hand on the sleek dark head. 'You must come over one day.'

'So you keep saying.'

They stood there, two boys and a dog — sort of timeless, really, if you stepped back and looked at the scene. Fred found himself stepping back more and more these days. He found himself remembering something.

All families disappear and become one.

That was what Auntie Vivie had said, apparently, just before she died. He said it to Richard, half wanting to get off the subject of families altogether, half wanting to impress. It was mysterious, that line. 'What do you think she meant?'

Richard shook his head. 'We all get swept up in the great tide of history, perhaps,' he said after a moment, sounding like a headmaster all of a sudden. Perhaps that was what he would be, one day, but you felt he could be anything he wanted, really, he was so bright. This term they'd be starting their O-level year: already he'd begun revising.

'Swot,' Fred had said, seeing the heap of books on his desk one weekend.

446

'Idle bum,' said Richard, sifting through a pile of LPs. 'Listen to this.'

He listened — to the blues, as Richard called it, looking at the poster above his desk. Ban the Bomb. At Easter, he and his parents had gone on a march. They'd go again, next year.

'Come on,' he said now, and they turned, and climbed up the long chalk path to the top, a dog and two boys, and one with something to hide.

Will I tell you one day? Fred asked himself, kicking away flinty pieces of white. Will I tell you I'm not who I seem?

8

Fred was gone, and his letters fell on to the mat. Rugby. CCF. Photography. All the usual stuff. What did her mother keep looking for, reading them over again? And then came a letter from Hugo.

Dear Bea, Thanks for your postcard. I was so sorry to miss you when you came down to see Granny...

He was so sorry! He'd missed her! He'd had a great time walking in the Italian lakes — who with? — and now he was back at work, doing something brilliant with electronic communications, whatever they were, with the possibility of working abroad.

> *So not much chance of meeting up with you at the moment, I'm afraid, but I do hope we'll manage it one day. Good luck with your A levels. I know this is the big year, but I'm sure you're going to do well. Please give my love to everyone, and lots to you, of course!*
> *Hugo*

She read it again, she kissed it, she held it to her breast. She carried it to the window, and looked down on the garden, where Will was doing a last cut of the grass. Up and down, up and down, boring, boring, boring. But she knew what she was going to do.

She was going to work like mad, show Hugo his faith in her was justified. And then, though of course she could go to university if she wanted, she wouldn't. If Hugo was going to work abroad, he wouldn't wait for her, not for another three years, no one would. But she would be free to go with him! And already she could see their life together, after a whirlwind wedding, she the young wife in some nice hot country, having cool drinks in the shade, being so proud of him.

Down in the garden, Will was coming back towards the house, on the last push. He looked up and saw her, and lifted his hand with a smile, and she smiled back absently, already a thousand miles away, so happy.

What did this all make her think of?

It made her think of her mother, and India, that was the truth. Long cool drinks in the shade of their beautiful garden in Tulsipore —

'*Expecting you, my darling! That's where you began.*'

Was she, deep down, just like her mother, with all her talk of love and romance and boyfriends and then, at last, The Real Thing?

No, this was different. Surely it was. She didn't want to be someone who spent her whole life writing about the past, sleeping away the present. She wouldn't! She'd have a completely different kind of life, and already she felt it coursing through her, felt filled with purpose and excitement.

Dear Hugo, What a lovely long letter!

She sat at her desk.

'All I Have to Do Is Dream,' sang the Everly

Brothers, on the Dansette. So romantic and sad.

She put her head on her arms, and her brain did one of its blinks.

★   ★   ★

'I don't feel well,' she said to the wallpaper bird. 'I go blank,' she told him again. 'Sometimes I just disappear.'

I JUST DISAPPEAR.

The bird thought that nobody could do that.

★   ★   ★

The next letter was from York. They wanted to see her for interview. She almost fell off her chair.

'Well *done*, darling. I'll come up with you.'

Bea looked at her mother, still in her dressing gown. She couldn't imagine it: not the interview, not her mother being with her — it felt almost outlandish. Her mother was here, yawning away, making toast every school day morning, writing or making the same old meals, not suddenly appearing on campus in a hat. She couldn't even remember why she'd put York first, and anyway — she wasn't going to go.

Still. It was nice to be asked. And she wrote back, saying she'd be delighted to attend.

And then something happened, and everything changed.

★   ★   ★

450

October: down on the lacrosse field, on a cold grey afternoon. It had rained, and the ground was muddy — you could easily slip and fall, racing from one end of the pitch to the other, your stick held high.

'Pass! Pass!'

Bea wasn't racing about. She was so useless, they still always put her in goal, and she was useless there, too, making a wild dash to defend as Mary Cheever, taller than anyone, came hurtling down and shot the ball straight past her.

'Goal!'

'Wake up, Bea Sutherland!' shouted Miss Miller.

'Sorry.'

'Sorry won't win a match.'

She stood there shivering as they all went racing back again, waiting for the hour to be over. Wind blew over the muddy grass, the shouts of the girls came and went. Everything came and went: she was used to that now, but this felt more powerful, somehow; it must be the cold. The whistle shrieked from the touchline. Blink, went her brain, and she went with it. She put out her hand. It went nowhere. Blink blink.

Bang.

*　★　★*

She came to on the grass, cold and wet, with people gazing down at her. They looked terrified. She tried to speak, but her tongue was clamped to her teeth, and felt thick and swollen. Her head ached as if someone had put it in a vice. She

451

tried to move her legs. They felt like lead. Her games shorts were soaking: was the grass really so wet? She opened her mouth again, felt a frill all round her tongue, where her teeth must have —

'You're all right,' said Miss Miller, pulling her sweater off. She laid it over her, and Lizzie and Rosie quickly did the same. 'You're all right, Bea, you just — '

Just what? She'd wet herself, she knew. And she could taste blood. Slowly she put her hand up to her mouth.

'Girls, go back to the house. Mary Cheever, you run ahead, you're the fastest. Vanessa, run with her. Tell them to call an ambulance, tell Matron to give you blankets. Fast as you can!'

★ ★ ★

Late afternoon, the sky above Piccadilly already darkening, and a heap of stuff on the desk to deal with. He'd got the new pig pens through in the end: next year they were going to show them at the Royal. Well done, Sutherland: have a pat on the back. Princess Alexandra was scheduled to open it: marvellous.

Meanwhile —

Meanwhile he was fifty-two, and there were days he was so dog-tired he could have been seventy. A twelve-hour day, if you counted the commute, and working at full tilt for most of it. It was different in spring and summer: out on the show grounds, out on the farms, chatting to everyone. Now: as winter approached, he

452

sometimes felt as if he were on a treadmill.

'I don't know,' he said to the shaving mirror in the mornings. He said it now, reaching for the next letter, as the phone on Miss Fisher's desk began to ring. 'I don't bloody know.'

'Mr Sutherland?' She put her head round the glass partition. 'Your wife's on the phone.'

Flo, ringing the office? Unheard of. He picked up his receiver.

'My darling. What's up?'

He listened, and he felt himself go white.

★ ★ ★

'Up we go,' said the ambulance man, covering Bea in a blanket.

'We're off,' said the other one, taking the handles. 'Ever flown before?'

She smiled weakly. She was dazed: by what had happened, by the strange bumpy journey up through the dusky woods, the flash of the torchlight ahead. Lying on her back, Matron and Miss Miller marching on either side, she thought she could see the first faint prick of stars, but perhaps they were inside her head. A lot of things were inside her head, apparently. It was pounding away. Then they all heard an owl, and everyone talked about it, whether it was a screech or a little owl. It might be a tawny, thought Matron.

'I saw a barn owl once,' said the ambulance man behind her. 'When I was a kid. Never forget it, great big white thing. Gorgeous.'

'My father knows about birds,' said Bea, and

then she shut her eyes because she couldn't keep them open any more, though she was afraid of what she might see behind them. It was all right. It was only darkness.

★   ★   ★

All the way down on the train he thought of her. He saw her on his knee on the old farm tractor, bumping away down the track to the fields, past the bleating goats, the blue smoke puffing through the funnel on a summer's afternoon. He saw her racing about the farmyard, chatting away from dawn to dusk, riding Guernsey Noo home for milking, holding Freddie's hand as they came in to the milking parlour. Wrapping that poor bloody hen in a cardigan, tucking her up in a box in the kitchen, wailing when he'd wrung her neck.

'*She's gone to heaven, darling.*'

'*You bloody fool!*'

He saw himself perched on her bed on a cold spring evening, telling her it was all over, he'd have to sell up, poor old Hatpeg would have to go, and she flinging her arms round his neck.

'*Poor Daddy.*'

He heard her singing 'All things bright and beautiful' beside him in church, swinging his hand, hopping and skipping, as they walked back across the Green; he saw her running through the garden, running all through his life, until —

When had it ended?

'*That's Grey Fluffy Yellow Toes! That's Grey Fluffy —* '

Hopping up and down in front of the larder door, seeing the goose hanging limp and heavy, just in time for Christmas, save a penny, your own bird on the table, what was wrong with that?

'Wrong bloody bird,' he said aloud, and then coughed, as the woman across the compartment looked up. Half-empty carriage, the rush hour not begun, but he'd left the office the moment he heard, grabbing his coat and briefcase, running down the stairs and out into the roar of Piccadilly.

'Taxi!' To hell with the expense.

His little Bea.

When he went into a room she went out of it. No good pretending.

'Come in and shut the door, my darling.'

She didn't want to.

'Oh, I don't bloody know,' he muttered again, remembering a snow-white cat flung down in the gutter, dying in the pouring rain.

'*Raining cats and dogs, if you'll pardon the expression.*'

'*Daddy!*'

Was it then? Was there ever a single moment you could point to, when your child began to leave you?

'Blundering oaf,' he muttered, and the woman across the compartment got up and went out into the corridor. He leaned back, shut his eyes as the train rattled onward, remembering the game they used to play with the kids on train journeys, before they'd had the car.

'What are the wheels saying now?' You could make them say almost anything you wanted

— bacon-and-eggs, bacon-and-eggs, happy-little-hol, happy-little-hol —

Ep-i-lep-tic, ep-i-lep-tic. That was what he heard now. He tried to change it to Daddy's-little-Bea, Daddy's-little-Bea but he couldn't make it work.

And when he thought about the hospital —

He put his head in his hands.

★ ★ ★

They were going to keep her in overnight, under observation. 'I'll see about a bed,' said the Casualty doctor, drawing back the cubicle curtains. 'We'd just like to keep an eye.'

'Of course,' said Flo. She looked dreadful.

'Poor Mummy,' murmured Bea, and they both smiled, and said it together.

'I am *not* Poor Mummy!'

'You sound happy,' said a nurse, coming in with a paper cup of water and a pill in a dish. 'That's nice. And this is phenobarbitone, I expect the doctor told you. Calms everything down. I expect you'd like a nice cup of tea,' she added to Flo.

'That would be heaven.'

When she had gone, Bea lay back on the bed and she and Flo looked at each other. It was strangely quiet in here. You'd expect Casualty to be all go and drama, like Dr Kildare, but the doctor had told them it was always quiet on Wednesdays. That made them laugh, in a mad sort of way.

'Oh, darling.' Flo took her hand. 'Poor darling.'

456

'Were you asleep when they rang?'

'I'm afraid I was.'

Deep in the deepest, and the phone coming into her dream, someone ringing and ringing her, trying to get through. In the war? Back in Melcote?

'Roddy?' she said. 'Is that you?' No, it was Freddie. Freddie! 'Where are you?' she asked. 'Tell me where you are!' Then she woke in a panic, and grabbed the receiver, hearing Miss Hawthorne announce herself in her calm headmistress way.

'Poor Mummy,' said Bea again.

'Never seen two people so cheerful,' said the nurse as they laughed, coming in with two cups of tea on a tray. Four little packets of sugar were on each saucer.

'Four?' said Flo faintly.

'Good for shock. You'd be surprised what hot sweet tea can do. I'll let you know as soon as we've got a bed.'

Bea drank, and felt tea in the frills all round her tongue.

'What can you remember?' the doctor had asked her, but she couldn't remember anything, just being on the pitch and then not being there. Bang. She'd come in to hospital in her games kit, all muddy and wet. 'I should have brought a nightie,' said Flo. 'I should have thought.' But they gave Bea a hospital gown, said not to worry.

'Daddy's on his way,' she said now, putting her cup down. 'I don't know what time he'll get here.'

'Oh, Mummy. Did you have to tell him?'

'Darling, of course I did. Don't worry.' She leaned over and kissed her. 'I'll keep him at bay.'

Bea gave her the teacup. She felt a bit better, and sleepy. 'You've kept him at bay all your life,' she said. 'You've done everything.' She shut her eyes. 'All those Glacier Mints.'

★　★　★

He couldn't help it: walking down the endless corridor towards the ward — a children's ward, they told him on the desk — it all came horribly back: locked doors, wandering women, Flo slumped in a chair. He hadn't even recognised her.

God, what they'd been through.

He saw himself bringing her home again, months later, out of that hellish great place, holding her hand in the taxi as she looked out at wintry trees and fields, not saying a word.

Get a grip, he told himself now, and he stood there for a moment, taking a great big breath. Then he saw the white-painted swing doors to the ward, and a teddy bear with a bandage smiling on the glass.

'I'm looking for my daughter,' he said to the girl on the desk. 'Beatrice Sutherland.' Better keep it formal.

And there she was, halfway down on the right, past a lot of sick-looking kids with their mothers, and Flo beside her.

'My darling!' He strode down the ward.

'Ssh!' Flo put a finger to her lips.

He slowed down, he stopped at the end of the

458

bed. Fair hair spread out over the pillow, white little face. Fast asleep.

'My darling,' he whispered, and heard his voice break. He wanted to say, 'Daddy's here.' He wanted to tell her that everything was OK, he'd look after her for ever. But he knew it would only drive her away, and anyway, he didn't trust himself to speak. He looked down at the honeycomb hospital blanket, and tears fell on to it, unstoppable. Flo got to her feet. He dug out his handkerchief, he blew his nose, she said, 'Ssh, darling,' and then the supper trolley came rattling down the ward, and Bea opened her eyes.

'Hello, Daddy.' A flickering smile.

He didn't say a word. He went round beside her, he took her hand. She let him.

★ ★ ★

When they had gone, when the ward was dark and quiet, just the lamp on the nurse's desk shining, she lay there and tried to think. 'Will you tell Fred?' she'd asked them, but they said probably not, it would only upset him, they'd tell him at half-term, when they knew a bit more what was what. Will said he'd let Agnes know.

'Will you tell Hugo?' she asked her mother. 'Will you ring him?'

'Yes, darling, if that's what you want.'

Now she lay on the pillows and imagined it all: the telephone ringing in the great big hall, his frown of concern. Those gorgeous dark eyebrows, that slow measured voice. 'Do give her my love,' he would say, and then: 'No — tell her I'm on my way.' And he threw things into a bag.

Somewhere along the ward a little boy was crying. Bea saw the night nurse get up from the desk. It was so funny being on a children's ward with all the dolls and teddy bears, but this was the first bed they had.

'Mummy,' the little boy was sobbing. The nurse was being kind, but he didn't stop, and she thought about Fred, all those years ago, crying in the dorm, trying not to be heard; crying in the holidays, night after night. Hard to imagine it now, he was so tall and self-contained, and yet — something was going on.

Something was going on with her, too, something had been building up for years. Blink. Blink blink, and you just weren't there any more. Then you came back. That was called *petit mal*, the nice doctor had said, down in Casualty. What had happened today was a *grand mal* attack. Sometimes you never had another one, but they'd like to keep an eye on her tonight.

The little boy stopped crying. Bea turned her head on the pillow, slowly, as an experiment. Was another attack on the way? Her tongue still felt frilly and painful, but the headache was gone. The phenobarbitone calmed everything down: there probably wouldn't be another. But if not tonight, then when? Supposing she had one tomorrow, when Hugo was here?

Perhaps it was the pill, perhaps the horrible fit had ended something, but she knew then: he wouldn't be here. He wasn't going to pack a bag and race off to the station, he simply wasn't.

He'd send her a card, go on working.

And meanwhile — she'd have to be on guard. All the time. If she'd been crossing a road, when it happened —

My life is going to be different now, she thought, as the night nurse walked back to her lamp-lit desk, and the ward fell quiet again. MY LIFE IS GOING TO BE DIFFERENT NOW.

9

Lamplight shone on the panther skin, and the watercolours above the sofa: an Indian lake, and the distant domes of a palace; the huge gateway to an Indian city, people and bullock-carts swarming through, vultures hanging in a hazy sky. Edwardian stuff, Great-Aunt Whatever-her-name-was, some tough old Sutherland bird —

'I'd better tell Fitz,' he said.

Flo slowly sipped her whisky. 'Was there something in your family?' she said at last.

He shook his head. 'Nothing. Yours?'

'Nothing at all. Of course — ' She hesitated. 'Of course I had that dreadful time, but I don't think that's anything to do with — '

He got up out of his armchair and went to sit beside her.

'Oh, Will.' She put down her glass.

He drew her to him. 'You're my very own.' He almost told her, then, about what it had been like, today, walking down the corridor to the ward, remembering it all. But he didn't. Why upset her, why stir it all up?

'Remember our honeymoon?' he said. 'Remember how that baby was made with love?'

'Oh, Will,' she said again.

Firelight played over the hearth. Traffic went by. They sat there talking about it all: making love on baking afternoons, sun filtering through the shutters; jungle expeditions with that darling

462

dog, sailing home on the troopship, expecting their first baby, all the men flinging their topis out across the sea as the siren sounded; everyone down at Southampton to meet them: the parent-birds, Vivie and little Hugo, serious even then . . .

'And then we had Fred,' said Will, remembering Norfolk, and living with Mother and Agnes in the Rectory, going to agricultural college, boning up on crops and livestock and machinery, bounding in to class one morning to say, 'We've got a little boy! Born last night! Super little chap!' Everyone pleased as punch: they were all in together, pulling new lives together after the war. A few of them from India, of course.

'We must tell Fred,' he said now.

Flo wanted to say there was something so upsetting about Fred these days, but she didn't. They'd been through enough for one day, had enough to think about. And Will looked shattered; she must think about supper. What was there?

'I do love you,' she said, turning to kiss him.

'I'll always love you,' he said, and then, suddenly realising: 'Left my fucking briefcase on the train.'

★ ★ ★

They were going to tell Fred at half-term, but he wasn't there: he was off to a CCF camp in Berkshire, quick-march, quick-march, att-en-*shun!* Maps. Orienteering. Survival. Tents in the rain.

463

A letter came from a London hospital, calling Bea up for tests. She'd rested at home for the rest of the week, tucked up on the sofa with lunch trays, taking her pills and reading her Get Well cards: from Fitz, from Auntie Agnes, with an awful rhyme inside, from Hugo, with lots of love; from everyone in the Upper Sixth, signing in every inch of space. Then she went back, and was told not to push herself, she'd soon be feeling stronger.

Now: 'We've got to do it, darling. Better to know.'

It was their first time in London together, something Flo had always imagined would be such fun, shopping in Fenwicks or Debenhams, a treat after A levels. Having a nice little lunch.

Instead: 'This is it,' said the taxi driver who'd brought them from Victoria, pulling up now in a garden square. The hospital specialised in nervous diseases. One or two people were walking stiffly up the steps to the hospital; a nurse came out with a young man on sticks. It was windy and cold.

'Taxi!'

All change: Flo and Bea got out and the trembling young man was helped to climb into the cab. They walked through the huge main doors. Inside, a woman in a hospital dressing gown was walking jerkily across the hall with a desperate-looking husband. She grimaced, she gestured, she started to shout.

Flo swallowed.

'It's all right, Mummy,' said Bea.

They were directed to their clinic. They sat

464

and waited, turning ancient pages of *Woman*. None of these people know anything, thought Flo, abandoning bright encouragement to cook, to coordinate accessories.

'Beatrice Sutherland?' A nurse with a clipboard came through a dark swing door.

Flo's legs were like jelly as they got to their feet. 'Soon be over,' she whispered, and Bea nodded, almost as pale as the young man in the taxi. 'Paw in paw,' said Flo, and they held hands as they walked through the door, the nurse smiling away as if it were nothing, what was going to happen.

What happened was that Flo was asked to sit on a hard plastic chair beneath a window, and Bea to get up on a couch. Equipment was everywhere, with the nurse rubbing thick smelly ointment into Bea's scalp and the white-coated doctor explaining that he was just going to put some electrodes on, and take readings on the machine beside her.

Then he put them on, one by one, all over her head, and as Bea put her hand up, and was asked to take it down again, something in Flo began to stir.

It was something she hadn't allowed herself to think about for years, would have said she couldn't even remember, but she remembered now: climbing up on to a couch in her nightdress, lying down — being held down, even — as someone clamped things on to her head. Then someone reached for a switch.

'Excuse me.' She got up from the chair. 'Darling,' she said to Bea. 'I'll be back in a

465

minute — ' And she pushed past the machine and the doctor and nurse, and through the swing door, and ran: out of the clinic, out through the echoing hall with its wandering jerky patients and on to the pavement, gasping.

People went by. One or two cast a glance — a middle-aged woman in a hat, looking a bit strange, but a lot of strange-looking people came and went along here. Nobody stopped.

Across the road was the garden square, and its iron gate stood open. Flo hurried shakily over: a taxi screeched, and the driver shouted. 'Sorry,' she said to the open gate. 'So sorry.'

Pigeons were pecking away at a few bits of bread on the grass, and a gardener was sweeping up fallen leaves along the paths. Flo sat on a bench beneath bare trees and struggled to collect herself.

It was over. It happened a long time ago, and it was over.

And somewhere, deep within her, it was all there still.

★　★　★

They were on a route march: heads down in the pouring rain, sodden kit weighing a ton, left-right, left-right, five more miles to go. Why had he ever thought it would be good to sign up for this? Partly because the Pipers were going away for half-term on some Quaker camp, and coming on Corps Camp was for Fred partly a way of showing that he wasn't just going to sit around at half-term, either, even though he felt

466

embarrassed as soon as he'd said it, coming down the hill with the dog at the end of their last walk. The only marches Richard went on were the Ban the Bomb ones.

'At least you'll get fit,' he said, clipping on Tinder's lead. 'And maybe you can come to Aldermaston next year.'

'Maybe.' He could just see how that would go down at home.

Anyway, he was here, with Tom Hall, whom he liked, tramping in silence beside him in the rain.

'Left-right, left-right!'

Mr Parris — Sergeant-Major Parris — was marching along beside them now, and the one thing you could say about all this was that it stopped you thinking.

★   ★   ★

The test results came on a Saturday morning, in a letter addressed to her parents.

'Well, now,' said Will, at the breakfast table, and Flo, in her dressing gown, said brightly: 'At least we'll know what's what.'

'Absolutely.' He picked up a clean knife, and Bea saw that his hand was shaking: just a little, but it was. 'Well, now,' he said again.

She wanted to say, 'It's all right, Daddy,' just as she had tried to reassure her mother in the hospital, even though it was she herself who had to go through this thing — even though her mother had fled from the room, and been gone for ages, something she still hadn't explained. 'I don't know what came over me, darling.'

467

She saw Will's anxiety, the tremor as he slit open the envelope, the frown as he ran his eyes down the page, but she couldn't speak, couldn't reassure him — partly because of her own nerves, now, everything hanging on this letter, but it wasn't only that.

Her father talked: she listened, or pretended to — that was what they all did, that was the pattern of things. He was irritable: he made her cry. He reached for her hand, she took it away: it was how things were. Only in hospital had that been different: she was weak, she was ill, he looked so upset. But now —

'For God's sake,' said Flo. 'Put us out of our misery.'

'It's not too bad,' he said slowly, putting the letter down. 'Not too bad at all.'

'What does it say?' asked Bea, and then: 'Can I read it?'

She was seventeen, it was her illness, yet she had to pluck up courage to ask.

'Of course you can.' He passed it to her, across the toast rack and crumbs. 'Daddy's little Bea,' he said, and she ignored that, reading quickly.

She wasn't epileptic. Not in a full-blown, life-changing way. Though she suffered from *petit mal*, there was no indication that another great fit was likely. She would need to stay on phenobarbitone, perhaps for a couple of years. No alcohol. She mustn't get overtired. She wouldn't be able to drive for a good three years, and then with a special licence.

Lizzie was having lessons already. She was going to have a Mini for her eighteenth birthday.

Until today this had been neither here nor there, just one more rich Surrey thing to notice. Now it felt like a marker. She put down the letter. Flo picked it up.

'Well,' she said, skimming it fast. 'Who cares about driving? Your boyfriends can drive you.'

'Of course they can,' said Will, passing his cup for more tea, his hand quite steady now. 'I've driven Mummy all my life.'

'Driven me up the wall,' said Flo, as a wintry gleam of sunshine came in at the garden window.

'My darling.'

Bea got up. Both of them immediately asked her if she was all right.

'I'm fine,' she said. 'Just going to — '

Just going to what? She climbed up the stairs to her room. The wallpaper bird took no notice, and she took no notice of him. He belonged to a different person. She lay on her bed, with the little brown bottle of pills beside it.

She knew that she'd had a great escape: that if she were careful her life needn't be that different, not really, she could just carry on. But something had shifted: she'd had a glimpse of something more serious than she'd ever imagined. Illness. Darkness. She'd had a reprieve, but she felt set apart: only a little, but it was there. Winter sun came and went in the room. She was changing.

★　★　★

Then came the interview.

'My darling. What are you going to wear?' Flo had asked, longing to take her shopping, to do

469

sweet mother-daughter things together. They went down to Penny's Boutique, and chose a nifty little suit, with a skirt that Will said was much too short, though at least it wasn't a mini-skirt. Not that he minded mini-skirts, he thought they were rather fun. But not for an interview.

'All right, darling, all right, all right.'

'Did I say something wrong?'

This was the night before, everyone a bit keyed up and he back in full hearty mode again. He tapped the barometer. 'Glass is going up!' He wished Bea luck and told Flo her new hat was gorgeous. Then they went to bed and he went round locking all the doors.

'Is this hat really all right?' asked Flo, as the train pulled into York.

'It's fine, Mummy.' Bea pulled their overnight cases down from the rack. She'd put in her copy of *The Four Quartets*, which Miss Weaver had got them all reading even though it wasn't on the syllabus, saying that they should be able to show they knew something about modern poetry.

'And you're sure you've got your pills,' said Flo. They were staying in a B&B that Will had found through the Yorkshire Regional Secretary. That was going to be the best bit, as far as she was concerned.

'Certain,' said Bea.

'Are you nervous?' She had no idea what a university interview might be like, simply couldn't imagine such a thing.

'Oh, Mummy. Stop going on.'

They walked up the platform with their bags.

The campus was windy and very modern, and swarming with students in duffel coats and polo-necked sweaters, the striped York scarf flung round. Some of the boys had long hair.

'They look like beatniks,' said Flo, shuddering. A cheerful young lecturer showed them round. She noticed Other Mothers with their sixth-form children, none of them wearing a hat. The lecturer wore no make-up. Some of the Other Mothers looked like blue-stockings: that was what she and Vivie would have called them. '*My dear, she's a frightful blue-stocking. The men run a mile!*'

The interview was at half-past two. They had lunch in a student canteen where Beatles songs were belting out from somewhere. 'How can they bear it so *loud?*' Flo could hardly hear herself speak. Then they made their way to the English Department building, passing a sign to a theatre.

Bea left Flo sitting in her hat on a bench in the first-floor corridor.

'Don't disappear.'

'I promise I won't. The best of luck, my darling. I'll be thinking of you every minute.' Then she pulled out the *Telegraph*, and Bea walked away in her little suit, past posters of Wordsworth and Shakespeare and writers she'd never heard of. Who was Allen Ginsberg? Who was Ted Hughes?

Yes, she was very nervous. But also — excited. It was exciting here. She knocked on the door.

'Come in.'

471

The lecturer was young, like the one who had showed them round the campus. He wore jeans and a baggy sweater and Buddy Holly glasses, and he gave her a friendly smile and introduced himself, getting up from a desk heaped with papers.

'Mark Foster. Do sit down.'

As far as she could remember afterwards, when the whole thing seemed like a dream, he was very nice to her.

He asked her about *King Lear*, and if she'd seen the production with Paul Schofield at Stratford last year, and didn't seem to mind when she said that she hadn't. He asked her to explain the conceit in a George Herbert poem and seemed to think she knew what she was talking about. Then he asked her what else she was reading, what modern authors, just as Miss Weaver had said he might, and she said *The Four Quartets*.

'I'm not sure if I really understand them properly, but they say something to me, even so.'

Mark Foster said that a lot of people felt like that when they began reading Eliot, and it was a mark of his power. He asked if there was anything in particular that spoke to her, and she quoted the lines about time and the bell having buried the day, the black cloud taking the sun away. He nodded.

'What do they mean to you, those lines?'

Bea hesitated, sitting on a low modern chair as clouds whipped past the plate-glass window. She said: 'Perhaps it's because I was ill for a while — I had a sort of insight. I don't know how to explain.'

He looked at her. 'And are you better now?'

'I'm fine,' she said, and then, in a sudden rush, 'And I really want to come here.'

AND I REALLY WANT TO COME HERE.

The words hung in the air beyond the plate-glass window. It was true: had she ruined it all by saying she'd been ill? Would they think she wasn't strong enough to do a degree?

He smiled. 'That's good to hear.'

THAT'S GOOD TO HEAR.

Then he got to his feet and said it had been very nice to meet her, and she'd be hearing from them soon, and before she knew it she was out in the corridor again, walking on legs that felt like water towards the bench where her mother was waiting, as if in a doctor's surgery.

'Darling! How did you get on?' Flo got to her feet. 'Was it ghastly? Did your mind go blank the moment he asked you a question? That used to happen to me at school all the time.'

'Mummy, please. It was fine, I think.' They went down the concrete stairs and out on to the campus again. There was the sign to the theatre. 'Can we have a look?'

A poster for a play called *The Caretaker* was pinned up outside.

'Who on earth would want to see a play about a caretaker?' Flo was longing for a cup of tea. How much more tramping about? They peeped in at the door. Students were rehearsing, all in black. They shut the door again.

'But you could have a lovely time here, darling,' Flo said, as they made their way to the porters' lodge, where they'd left their bags. 'All your acting — you could be a star. Just don't go out with a beatnik, that's all I ask.'

★　★　★

The letter came from the Admissions Department two days later. It offered a place with two Bs.

'Only two Bs!' said Flo, who knew A from B if nothing else. 'They must have loved you, my darling.'

'Of course they did,' said Will that evening. 'Splendid,' he added, wondering about grants, and if Fitz or Agnes could help.

I can get that, Bea said to herself, walking up the hill to school, swinging her bag as people in cars whizzed past. I can get that easily if I work.

She walked on, past the quiet solid houses and in through the open gates. And work, which had once seemed like something you just had to do, something you got out of the way before you phoned a friend, and made plans for a party, felt now like her closest friend.

★　★　★

Agnes had taken to going on trips. She went with her prayer group to Canterbury, and then to Winchester. Then to Wells. Then Notre Dame, on a special one. She sent postcards. Then she came back.

'We've got to have her over,' said Will, putting the phone down after the Sunday phone call. Exhausting. How she went on. And now the

474

poor bloody cat had died. But it had been months — and not once for Christmas, not once. All these years with poor old Neville's family.

'We really must,' he said, sharpening the carving knife. 'Time we did our stuff.'

'I can't,' said Flo. 'I can't have her going on and on about nothing, poking about in the kitchen, telling me how to make the gravy. Asking why I need rests. And all those ghastly presents.'

He dug about in the lamb. 'The kids can help. You can help, can't you, Bea?'

She nodded. She could do anything now. 'And Fred.'

'Oh, I can't wait to see Fred again.' Flo took her plate. Now Bea was settled, she didn't have to worry about her, as long as she took her pills; she could concentrate on making everything right with him again. That was what she was longing for.

'She could come on Christmas Eve and go home the day after Boxing Day.'

Will had served Bea and was carving his own thick slices. He was always hungry as a horse after church. 'We can take her out for walks while you have a rest, my darling.'

'And I'll get the tea, Mummy.'

Flo shook out her napkin. Something rose within her. 'I am not,' she said, slowly and clearly, 'having Agnes. For Christmas. Full stop.'

Will flung down the carving knife. Bea leapt.

'Then we've bloody well got to have her over beforehand. Is that clear?'

IS THAT CLEAR?

Come home, Fred, Bea said softly to herself. I need you. Come home.

★   ★   ★

Agnes came on the following Saturday, gaunt as a stick and firing on every cylinder. Was this the aunt who had been such a darling when they were little? Who had knitted and cooked and run out after them into the street in her curlers when they fed the milkman's horse? Who had nursed poor Uncle Neville without a murmur, loved and been loved by him?

'How are you, Auntie Agnes?'

'Oh, I'm very well, thanks.' She took off her awful hat. 'Very busy, of course. Never a dull moment in our parish! What about you, Bea? No more funny turns, I hope. That was terribly strange, nothing in our family at all. Still, I'm sure it won't happen again, if you're sensible.'

She had brought her Christmas presents with her: they sat in the hall beneath Panther, in a bulging carrier bag. Bea, in a last-minute panic, had gone round Boots after school yesterday, wrapped Yardley's Lavender in the shiny Woollies paper that Will bought in bulk every year.

Sipping her sherry, Agnes told them at length about when she was going to Jean and Brian's, and how, and which of them would meet her at Chichester station. 'Of course,' she said, 'I'll open my presents from you on Christmas Eve, to save carrying them down on the train.'

The thought of her doing this, the thought of

476

anyone opening presents alone, made Bea suddenly so sad she didn't know where to look. Not even Tinkerbell, now, to watch her unwrap.

'Lunchtime!' said Flo, coming in at last.

In they all went to the dining room, and talked about the birds on the bird table. Then Bea answered a hundred questions about university, and whether she was sure she really wanted to go, and why York, and why English, and what exactly was a degree anyway. Then Agnes asked about Fred.

Oh, Fred, Bea said to herself again. When he got home she would go through this visit line by line, over the washing-up. She saw his slow smile, heard his laugh. He'd understand every moment.

'And how is your family, Flo?' asked Agnes over coffee, back in the sitting room, when they'd wrung every last drop out of Fred and his Corps Camp and photography and subjects for O level.

'Well,' said Flo, passing her cup, 'I haven't so much family left, now, as you know.'

'So sad about your sister.'

'Yes, yes, it was.'

'What did she die of again?'

Flo took a breath. It was like a darning needle, a great big thick darning needle, poking and stabbing away.

'Does it matter?' she said, before she could stop herself.

Bea froze at her tone.

'My darling,' said Will, and then said nothing.

Agnes was flushed and bristling. 'I'm only taking an interest.'

'Well, don't,' said Flo, her heart racing now, and then all hell broke loose.

'Mummy — ' said Bea, as Will's face began to darken.

Agnes put her cup down. 'Of course,' she said, 'you don't want to talk about your family. It's understandable.'

'What on earth do you mean?'

'Well, you know. Your father being in trade. I know it must embarrass you.'

Flo's mouth fell open.

'Now look here,' said Will, as Bea put a hand on her arm.

'I mean I'm sure it must have been nice having all that money, but still. Biscuits. Not exactly — '

'Auntie Agnes — '

Flo leaped to her feet. She made wildly for the bookcase, grabbed the first thing she saw and threw it. *How to Run Your Home without Help* went hurtling through the air, and landed in Agnes's coffee cup.

Splash. Outrage. Everyone on their feet.

'Never,' shouted Flo, almost incoherent. 'Never, never, never again.' She ran from the room, and everything shook as she slammed the door.

There was a ghastly silence.

★   ★   ★

'Don't speak to me,' said Flo, when Bea went up later. 'Just don't.'

'Don't speak to me,' she said to Will, back from the station and climbing the stairs as if a dozen sacks of animal feed lay across his

478

shoulders. He shouted. Then he shut the door and went into Fred's room. Then he shut that door, too.

Downstairs, the washing-up done and everything put away, Bea stood in the kitchen, twisting a tea towel this way and that. No wonder she'd had a fit.

NO WONDER I HAD A FIT.

★ ★ ★

'I'm sorry,' said Flo that night, as Will rose to his feet from his prayers. He kicked off his slippers, sat heavily down on the bed.

'She's my sister,' he said, for the millionth time.

'I'm your wife.'

'She's all on her own.'

'I know. But even so — ' She reached for his hand. He didn't take it. He climbed into bed, switched his light off. After a moment, she switched off hers. They lay there in the dark.

★ ★ ★

And then Fred came home. Thank God, oh thank God. Mid-morning, and he was here, home on the bus from Brockwood, with his height and his smile and his bags in the hall, where Flo, her nerves still on edge, but rallying, had put up the decorations. The old silver balls, on the green and red ribbons, dangled from Panther's jaws, a sprig of holly sprang from behind every picture frame.

479

'My darling!' She flung wide the door when he gave the three rings. 'Give me a hug.'

He hugged her. The house smelled of polish and a fishy lunch and the pine of the Christmas tree. He couldn't deny it: great to be back.

'Come and tell me everything,' she said, taking his hand. 'Come and sit by the fire. I want to hear every *detail.*'

'Fred!' Bea came running downstairs. 'I've got so much to tell you,' she said, and over the top of Flo's head she mouthed, 'It's been *awful.*'

He laughed. 'Back in a tick. I'm bursting.' And he went into the downstairs lav, hearing Will mutter, 'I don't know,' as so often in here, and seeing his poem on the wall. All the old things.

> Out of Burma, out of Burma,
> By the long and dusty road,
> By the bullock, by the steamer,
> Thousands came and bore their load . . .

Poetry was Bea's thing, but he could see, washing his hands and reading it through again, that a poem that had always been just part of the background was in fact rather a good one, and that if anything could make a link between this house and the Pipers' it might be this, with its images of refugees pouring over the border, their struggle and hope.

> We shall go and watch the paddy,
> Growing bright green in the rain . . .

480

It was good. Something to be quite proud of, in a way. And then, as always, as he made his way into the sitting room where Flo and Bea were waiting with the Indian coffee tray, he slammed a shutter down. No more of that. It was good to be back, but he mustn't let himself lose his guard. You couldn't love people you were going to have to leave.

★ ★ ★

The fire was bright, the house was quiet and Christmassy, Flo resting upstairs, and he out of school uniform. Everything was as it always was, the two of them in the sitting room, all ivory elephants and watery old paintings of India.

'I had a fit,' said Bea.

He frowned at her. 'What do you mean?'

'Remember my funny turns?'

'Sort of. Tell me.'

She told him: about the great bang in her head, right in the middle of lacrosse; the ambulance men carrying her up through the woods; the hospital, Will striding down the ward calling out, 'My darling!' Then London, the tests, Flo fleeing from the room —

'I don't know what all that was about,' she said. 'I thought she'd just gone to the lav or something, but it was ages. Anyway — then there was York.'

'What? Hang on a minute. What about the tests?'

She took a breath. 'I'm OK,' she said slowly, putting more coal on the fire. 'So long as I'm careful, I'm OK.'

'What does that mean?'

'No drinking, no driving. Not yet. Pills. Early nights.'

'Sounds like fun.' He sat there in Will's armchair, trying to take it all in.

'But a-ha!' she said, and looked just like her old self again. 'I'm going to York!' And then, having shocked him — really, he'd had no idea all this was going on — she made him laugh till it hurt, imitating Flo's face as they tramped round the campus, shuddering at everything but doing her valiant best.

'And then Auntie Agnes came.'

By the time she'd finished that one, the whole of last term had pretty much vanished.

'Biscuits? What's wrong with biscuits?'

He'd never really wondered where that lovely Bournemouth house, and all that comfort, had come from.

'God knows,' said Bea. 'Anyway, it's all a bit awful still between Mummy and Daddy.' The carriage clock chimed four amongst the Christmas cards. Time to take Flo her tea tray. 'But now you're home everything will settle down.' She leaned across the fireplace. 'Honestly, Fred, I don't know what I'd do without you. What would I do if I didn't have a brother?'

'Don't be silly.' He gazed into the fire.

★ ★ ★

At the weekend Will was home, and it was all Splendid to have you home, old boy, and What have you been getting up to, and How was

482

Camp? It was Let's have a look at your photos, and Those are jolly good.

'I can hardly get a word in edgewise,' said Flo.

'Nobody can.'

'What do you mean?'

They were hardly talking to one another. On Monday he went back to the office and the house fell quiet again.

'Now where are you off to?' asked Flo, as Fred pulled on his jacket after lunch.

'Just going down to the Pipers.'

'Already?' She felt a little rush of irritation. 'You've only just got home.'

'I've been here all weekend.'

'Yes, but — '

But what? But where were the lovely long talks they were going to have? Was she being unreasonable? He talked to Bea, he listened to Will, he went up to his darkroom, he did anything, it felt, rather than settle down with her. And who were the wretched Pipers anyway?

'What's so special about them?' she asked, as he made for the front door, and wished at once that she hadn't, it sounded so petulant and sharp.

He hesitated. Then: 'It's just — you know, having a friend,' he said, and was gone, without even a kiss goodbye.

Well, of course he wanted a friend, of course he did. Bea had a million, was out at Julia's now, or was it that Rosie Reed girl, who looked like a tart these days when you saw her down the town, all black eye-liner and black tights, like one of those beatnik-y people in York.

Was that what Bea would turn into, if she went?

'Oh God.' Flo stood in the holly-sprigged hall, and suddenly saw herself utterly alone.

She relived the dreadful scene with bitter old Agnes — daring to ask about her sister's death, daring to set herself and her awful churchy life above darling Father, the kindest man in the world — and Will's withdrawal since, all that loving after Bea's illness vanished. She saw herself running from the London hospital, into the wintry garden square, that terrible time come back to haunt her; walking across York's freezing campus, feeling like someone from another age, another country, almost, as all those bright clever people whipped past. And she saw Bea gone, become someone she'd never be able to laugh with or cuddle again, and above all she saw Fred, to whom she had once been everything —

The doorbell was ringing.

The doorbell was ringing, and it was almost Christmas. Flowers from Hugo. Wine from Fitz. Some Special Offer for Will. She opened the door, took the brown paper parcel from a young thing in a woolly hat, doing the Christmas post.

What have we here? She peered at the postmark.

Her book. Her typescript.

Dear Mrs Sutherland...

In the sitting room, where she had written her heart out, she tore it open.

We regret to say that we do not find Flowers Unfolding *suitable for publication on our list.*

'What is it?' he asked her, back from a walk across the Heath with Tinder racing after every cantering rider, from an afternoon of John Mayall and the Bluesbreakers, up in Richard's room, and home-made fruit cake in the kitchen, everything calm and quiet and happy. He looked at her awful, swollen red eyes. 'What's happened?'

'Oh, Fred. It's just — just my silly book, that's all.' She put her head on her arms on the kitchen table and began to cry again.

This must be like that scene years ago, with Bea: coming home from school and finding the last book flung on the fire, her mother beside herself. What had she said then? What could he say now?

'I'm so sorry,' he said, as kindly as he could, standing beside her. He put his hand on her shoulder, and she wept and wept.

'It's not just that — it's you — '

'Me?'

He listened, as it all came out: he was leaving her, they had nothing to say to each other now, of course it was only natural, but she loved him so much, and —

'Sometimes I feel you just don't belong to me,' she said, and with those words a great sea of fear and darkness welled up inside him, and he knew that this moment was unstoppable, and his heart began to pound.

He said, 'Mummy.'

He said, 'Mummy, look at me.'

And then he told her.

485

10

How could you explain that an idea so bizarre, so outlandish, so — so bonkers, really — could take such a hold on your mind? How could you say that for years you had lived with it, against all reason, all common sense? Was every boy sent away to boarding school cast out of the family because he was adopted? Had the Pipers sent Richard to his Quaker school because they didn't want him? It was all absurd: brought out into the open, the words said at last, he could see that, of course he could. And yet — how deep those thoughts had lain, how they had gripped and held him. How they gripped him still.

'Prove it,' he said. 'Prove it's not true.'

They were in the sitting room, she was scrabbling in the bureau. Even by the fire he was cold and shaking.

'I know it's in here,' said Flo. 'I know it is.' Everything in the world was stuffed into the pigeonholes: bills, vaccination certificates, the milkman's notebook, letters from Vivie, letters from the parent-birds, all those stiff little letters from Mountford, bundled up in years.

Darling Mummy and Daddy...

She burrowed, she dug about. The carbon copy of *Flowers Unfolding* was stacked on the baize, recording his baby steps on the farm, all his little sayings in Melcote — wasn't that proof enough?

'*Just dealing with a rhinoceros* — '

'I *know* I put them here.' The most precious documents in the world, without which you were nothing — where else would she have put them? The flap was a sea of papers, and she turned to look at him, sitting so tense in Will's armchair, like a stranger, almost, like someone who'd come to visit. Now she knew what he'd been thinking, believing, suffering, all these years, he looked quite different, somehow. They'd been living with someone they didn't know at all.

'But, darling,' she said, helplessly. 'Darling, I swear — '

There must be something she could do, something to make him understand, to know. To unfreeze that terrible look.

An ivory elephant was poking its trunk out from amongst the Christmas cards. With a sudden rush of strength and inspiration, she marched across the room. She was the head of the herd: she grabbed it, and cards fluttered down.

'I swear,' she said fervently, standing before him. 'I swear by this ivory elephant that you are my child, and Daddy's child. You were born in Norfolk on the twelfth of April 1949, Frederick William Sutherland, and somewhere in this wretched house is the certificate to prove it.' She kissed the smooth ivory dome of the elephant's head.

'He knows,' she said, as if she were talking to Freddie in his cot, Freddie snuggled up in her arms. 'Elephants know everything, and they never forget.'

He got up, he began to laugh. She looked just like Bea, standing there in the middle of a drama, reciting, declaiming, relishing every moment.

I shall grow up, but never grow old . . .
I shall never come back again.

That was the changeling, out in the wild wind and the rain, out with goblins and fairy people, unable to return. But he was returning: he was coming back, he could feel it now, as Flo kissed the silly old elephant once more, and held it out to him, with its missing tusk. No one but your real mother would go on like this.

'I love you,' she said, seeing his face begin to soften, hearing him laugh, and all her own sadness and loneliness and anger and distress ebbed away, as he came towards her, took the elephant, put his arms round her, and told her he loved her too.

★   ★   ★

'Birth certificates?' said Will that evening, dropping his briefcase in the hall. 'They're in the safe. What on earth do you want them for?'

★   ★   ★

'Adopted?' said Bea, home from Rosie's and perched on his bed beside him. 'Are you mad?' She sat there listening, trying to take it in. All his old books were up on the shelf, with his swimming cups and Head Boy shield.

'Rupert and the Changeling,' she murmured, after a moment.

They laughed till they fell off the bed.

*   *   *

'Adopted?' said Will, listening to Flo talk on and on beside him. He lay against the pillows, unable to move. 'How could he — how could he possibly — '

'Children,' said Flo. 'They can think all sorts of things.' And then: 'We — you — should never have sent him. If anyone went, it should have been Bea.'

'She's a girl!'

'She'd have loved it. A different kind of child.'

Will was silent. 'Oh, I don't bloody know,' he said at last.

But at last he took her hand.

*   *   *

Christmas. Christmas and a surprise for Will, sitting there by the tree with his clipboard. Still. Honestly, Daddy. Everyone in a good mood now, all together in church for once. 'This year I have to come,' said Flo, though it was a hell of a thing, getting the bird in, getting off on time. But she had to do it. She tucked her arm into Fred's as they walked up the path and the bells rang out. Books. Publishers. What did they matter now? Who cared?

'Now, then,' said Will, as a large box was put on his lap after lunch. 'What have we here?' He picked up his Biro. 'To Daddy, from Bea and Fred.' Everyone watched as he tore off the wrapping. 'Something from Boots,' he said happily, and then, 'A tape recorder! What am I going to do with that?'

'Talk to it,' said Flo. 'Give us all a bit of peace.'

'It's for your bird walks,' said Bea. 'And for your Indian stories. Fred and I thought we'd like to have a record, didn't we, Fred?'

'For when I'm dead and gone, you mean.'

'We didn't mean it like *that*.'

He opened the box, he pulled it out. Quite a neat little thing, with its microphone and a tape already inside.

'And we got you an extra box of tapes,' said Fred, pulling a package from under the tree.

'Well, well. What a super idea.' He picked up the Biro again. 'One tape recorder. One extra box of tapes. My darlings. Thank you both very much. Most thoughtful.'

They weren't really sure if he liked it.

'What do you think?' whispered Bea, as he fell asleep on the sofa, when Queenie had given her speech.

'You wait and see,' said Flo. 'It'll be his best friend before you know it.'

★　★　★

Before they knew it, it was back to school. 'I've got something to tell you,' Fred said to Richard, on their last walk with the dog. January, a new year, a freezing afternoon. Freezing, but exhilarating: everything now felt charged with new life.

And he told him, walking along the ridge of
Coney Hill, looking down on the long chalk path
where other winter walkers whistled for their
own dogs, or took out their binoculars.

'I knew there was something.'

'You sort of saved me from the worst.' Fred
pulled up his collar, put his head down in the
biting wind.

'How did I do that?' Richard's dry tone was an
antidote to all the emotion of the last few weeks:
it was hard to imagine high drama, or tearful
scenes in the Piper household — or being
helpless with laughter, come to that.

'You just did,' said Fred. He didn't know how
to explain what it had felt like: having
somewhere to go, having a proper friend again.
'You're a great family, that's all.'

'Thanks.' Richard dug his hands into his pockets. 'And how does your own family look now?'
he asked. 'Now you know it's your real one.' Again,
there was that bit of the headmaster, as if he were
years older. In some ways perhaps he was.

'They look OK,' said Fred, and then: 'They
look like themselves.' He didn't know how else to
put it. All that agonising about how different
they were from the clever liberal Pipers — his
father's colonial heartiness, his pig pens and
Telegraph and endless Indian stories; his
mother's frailty and endless writing, which got
nowhere, her endless hours in bed — it didn't
matter, really, it was just how they were.

'My sister's been ill,' he said, as they came to
the stile. 'I suppose quite a lot's been going on,
really.'

'Am I ever going to meet her?'

'Maybe. She was a bit of a party girl, but she seems more serious now.'

'I wouldn't mind meeting a party girl,' said Richard, and then they both laughed, and heaved Tinder over the frosty stile, and watched him race ahead.

★ ★ ★

I understand it now, Bea said to the wallpaper bird. She stood before him for what she knew was the last time. He looked at her with his faded yellow eye. What did she understand?

All that coldness, she said, murmuring into the dark cherry boughs. All that distance and coldness — I know where it began.

And where was that, he asked her, and she began to cry.

When Fred went away, she said. When he was so desperate, so unhappy. I used to hear him crying — and there was nothing I could do about it. Nothing!

And so —

How dark and still he was, how grave.

And so I switched off, she said. I buried it all, I just shut my feelings for other people away.

And now —

I'm coming alive again, she told him, hearing her mother climb the stairs to bed, and, far below in the hall, her father locking the sitting-room door.

COMING ALIVE AGAIN.

11

Spring, and he was out running with the team, panting in shorts and singlet over field and stream, singing in the showers with everyone afterwards, getting down to work on Monday, feeling fit. Ten exams: he made lists of every single thing he had to do.

Then came a call to the Housemaster's study.

'Come in, Sutherland. Sit down.' Mr Bradbury cleared his throat. 'Sorry to say I've a bit of sad news.'

'Sir?'

Dad, he thought at once: he's had a heart attack. But that would have been Very Bad News: he knew that at once, as the morning sun shone through the leaded windows, the bell rang out for break, and he heard it was Granny who'd died.

'Your mother rang. I believe it was very peaceful. But they'd like you to go home for the funeral: I've given permission, of course.'

'Thank you, sir.'

'Take some work with you: see your subject masters.' Bradbury got to his feet. With what was clearly an effort, he asked if Fred had been close to his grandmother, and Fred, standing up too, said no, not really, it was his grandfather he'd been fond of.

'But it's sad for my mother, of course.'

'Of course. Please give her my condolences.' Bradbury nodded that the interview was over, and the world of women, of mothers and daughters and human feeling, was at once dispatched, as Fred closed the door with a click.

⋆ ⋆ ⋆

They drove down to Bournemouth on the journey they'd made so many times as children: quiet in the back there, you kids; sixpence for the first person to see the sea. Rides on the trolley bus, ice cream on the prom. And all those happy times in that house, Vivie flinging wide the door as they arrived, holding out her arms. *'Hello! Come in, come in!'*

Now the front door opened, and there was Hugo: dark suit, black tie, impossibly good-looking. Bea walked slowly up the path in her new black coat, following her parents.

'Hugo, old chap.'

'Hello, Uncle Will. Auntie Flo. I'm so sorry.' That slow sweet smile, that heart-stopping voice. 'Hello, Bea.' He bent to kiss her cheek.

'Hi.' She'd had butterflies about this moment all the way down, checking her reflection surreptitiously in the driving mirror, until Will asked what she was looking at. Did fair hair against black look pretty? 'Hi,' she said again to the tiled hall, as Fred, in his first black tie, came up behind with their cases. How silent and echoing everything was around them.

Hugo was greeting Fred, asking Will about the journey, offering coffee, which their Mrs Thing was making in the kitchen. She was going to get the lunch on, too.

'The hearse will be here at eleven.'

'Poor Hugo — you've had to organise it all.'

'It's all right, Auntie Flo.' He flashed her the sweetest smile. 'I'm pretty good at organising.'

You're pretty good at everything, thought Bea, as they all went for a wash and brush-up and made their way to the drawing room. Do you never get upset? Are you upset now? Even a tiny bit?

★ ★ ★

Perhaps because it was just a small family service, with one or two shaky old friends in fur tippets, but the funeral was nothing like as terrible as she used to imagine it would be. The saddest thing was seeing Flo cry, the only one there who did. They had Granny's favourite hymns, 'The Lord is my Shepherd' and 'Lead, kindly Light', and the service was conducted using the King James Bible — thank God for that, Will said afterwards. He hated all the New English Bible stuff. Bea knelt next to her mother to recite the Lord's Prayer, hearing Hugo's steady voice from the other side of Fred.

Did he still believe in all this? Did she?

I don't think I do, she thought, getting to her feet again, and this felt like another marker in her life, another step away from childhood, and skipping home from church with Will, who still never missed a Sunday. He was following the service now, with his *Book of Common Prayer and Hymns*, bound in olive wood from the Holy Land, as poor Auntie Agnes still called it.

'We meekly beseech thee, O Father, to raise us from the death of sin unto the life of righteousness . . .'

The vicar was reading the last lines of the service, and everyone murmured 'Amen'. Then the door of the church was opened, and a draught of cold spring air blew in. Will and Fred and Hugo and one of the undertakers all stepped quietly forward, and lifted Granny's coffin and bore it slowly out, and along the path to the graveside. Bea took her mother's arm, and now — yes — she was full of emotion for her, stroking her black-gloved hand, walking slowly up behind the others to where Grandpa and Vivie were buried.

The March wind blew over the fresh spring grass and daffodils, the heavy dark branches of the yew tree rose and fell. There were their names on the headstone, with a space for Granny. Now they were all together again, and now they had disappeared, as all families do — that was what Vivie had said, when she died — becoming a part of every family that had ever been.

★ ★ ★

Back at the house, Hugo poured everyone sherry, with bitter lemon for Bea. They sat in the drawing room again, the smell of lunch wafting through from the kitchen, and it was just like old times, except that it absolutely wasn't.

'Well, well,' said Will. 'I thought that went off splendidly.' He took his glass. 'Thanks, old boy.'

Bea sat next to Flo, stroking her hand again, and they listened to Hugo ask Will about work, and Fred about school, and O levels. He was charming, polite, attentive, the man of the house where he'd grown up without a father, an only child sending messages to himself on a Meccano tray, being good and clever. And somehow he managed even now not to talk about himself at all, not really.

'And what about you, Bea?' he asked, as Flo leaned back on the sofa and closed her eyes. 'Are you quite better?'

'I'm fine, thanks,' she said, thinking of how she had lain awake in that hospital bed, imagining Hugo dropping everything to come and be at her side, then knowing he wouldn't. She told him about going to York, and could see that this at once put her into some sort of league with him, made her someone interesting, not just his little cousin, as he asked her all about it.

'Of course, I've got to get my A levels,' she said. 'Two Bs.'

'Of course you'll get them,' said Hugo, and gave her a heart-stopping smile.

'Thanks.' And with that smile she saw all those dreams again, all that romantic longing: their heavenly wedding, their life together. You were my love, she thought — and then, as the gong rang out in the hall, and everyone got up, I could love you still, and that is the truth of it.

And Fred, behind her, straightening his tie, listening to the sonorous notes of the gong begin to fade, thought: I did belong here, I wasn't an outcast, this was my real true family.

Even on a sad day like this, it was such a good feeling.

★   ★   ★

Within a month, Hugo rang to say he'd put the house on the market. And there was something else: he was getting married.

'Married?' said Bea, when Flo told her this after school. '*Married?*'

'Darling, sit down. You've gone quite white. Where are your pills?'

She shook her head. This had nothing to do with pills. Slowly she hung up her hat and blazer, slowly she went into the dining room. A lovely spring day, the French windows open on to the garden for the first time for ages, the young grass splashed with sun.

'Darling?' In came Flo with the tea tray. 'Poor little Bea.' She put the cup before her. 'I don't think I quite realised — '

'It doesn't matter. I was just being silly.'

She sipped at the scalding tea. How could she have let herself love him, all over again? She didn't even know him, not really — none of them did.

'He's selling that lovely house.' She looked at her mother. 'It's where you grew up. It's where — ' How could she put it? She couldn't bear to think of it gone. 'It's *our* house,' she said.

'Not any more,' said Flo.

★   ★   ★

'Married?' said Will, when he came home that evening. 'How splendid. Just what he needs. Tell him to bring her home.'

But he didn't. He had a register office wedding, just the two of them with a couple of witnesses, and then, he said on the phone, in his calm deep voice, they were off to New York, where he'd been offered a fabulous new job. The house had been sold to a developer. It was going to be made into flats.

'*Flats?*'

* * *

Flo stood looking at the locked drawer of the bureau. No one to write to now, no book, no diary. Will chatted away into his tape recorder, stories from the show grounds, all the old wartime and Indian stories, but for her — what was there to say, as the days went by? The vitality of those early family years, something happening every minute, the river of life within her demanding to be recorded — it was gone, like the family home.

Upstairs, the Hoover ran soothingly in and out of the bedrooms. Inside that drawer lay her typescript. Take no notice of rejection, said *The Writers' & Artists' Yearbook*. Books that are now bestsellers have been rejected twenty times. Keep going!

Had she the heart for twenty more rejections?

She had not. She didn't feel now as she had done at Christmas, with Fred restored to her and nothing else seeming to matter. Books! Publishers!

Who cared? she'd thought gaily, as he helped her up the steps to church and the bells rang out.

But like poor little Bea with Hugo: she did care still. How could she not? Writing, and thinking about writing, had sustained her for almost twenty years.

And made you ill, she told herself, turning away from the bureau. Leave it. Leave it for now.

A great sense of calm came over her. But then she turned back. Of course she had someone to write to, still. And she sat down, pulled down the flap, and pulled her old writing case towards her.

Darling Fred, It's the most beautiful day here today! The birds are just singing their hearts out! How are you getting on?

★ ★ ★

He saw her smiling face behind each line: he always had done. For years at Mountford he'd looked forward to her letters — until he went a bit mad. That was how he thought of it all now. Then he'd read them with a horrible sort of double feeling, loving all the news about home but telling himself it wasn't his home at all, not really.

April wind blew across the quad. Next weekend the Photographic Society were going on a trip, the last before they all got down to O levels in the summer. He could tell Flo about it. Of course, it was really Will's kind of thing, out and about with his birds and his camera — and tape-recorder now: 'A marvellous thing, old chap. I must play you my recordings.'

Fred wasn't sure if Flo knew which way was up on his own Brownie Box, and she certainly never came up to the darkroom. But he knew she would love to hear about the boys he was going with, the hostel where they were staying, with its stream and daffodils — he could find a nice postcard or something, to cheer her up after Granny, and the house being sold. He couldn't believe it, really. He'd have liked that gong, if anyone had asked him.

★ ★ ★

They piled off the train in the sun. No kitbag to carry, no tents to put up and shiver in half the night: he thought he'd probably chuck CCF in at the end of the year. They just had their grips with their overnight things, and their cameras, carefully packed, and they walked up the platform to where Mr Simmonds was ticking them off on his clipboard. Someone had scarpered, once, apparently, stayed on the train and got off at Windsor to meet a girl. Got expelled for it, when he got back.

But he was looking forward to this, out in the country again. Landscape pictures, with a long lens. Close-ups of plants. And for a moment, looking out of the window on the train, he'd had a flash of the Nature Table at the Miss Beasleys, and of growing a bean in a jam jar.

'What are you laughing at?' asked Tom Hall, sitting across from him.

'Nothing.'

They swung their bags up to the exit. The

place was pretty crowded: Friday afternoon, people coming home for the weekend, or having a spring country break. 'Wait just outside, boys. The bus should be there.' They made their way to the entrance hall.

Through a gap in the tiled roof a shaft of sun poured into the shady interior, dancing with dust motes, almost as if in a church. It struck the heads of the people in front, the other boys, the people spilling out into the car park; it struck, in particular, the fair hair of a slender girl in a long dark coat, surely too warm for this weather, walking just behind her parents, a pretty woman in what Flo would call a fetching little jacket, and a big tweedy man in a cap.

There was something about this girl, her slenderness, her frailty — yes, that was the word, she was pale and sweet-looking, but frail, thought Fred, and his mind was suddenly racing as he tried to place her, to think of who she reminded him of, as she turned towards her mother. Someone he hadn't seen for years. And then he knew.

'Nancy,' he said. 'Little Nancy Byatt.'

★ ★ ★

'All right, boys, follow me.'

'Sir? Sir? Could you wait just a moment? There's someone I — '

He dropped his bag and dashed after the family, walking in the sun towards their car. Nancy was behind her parents still, and he called out her name, and she turned.

'Hi,' he said, reaching her, standing before her. Gosh, she was pretty, brushing her pale hair back from her face and giving a little frown. 'I'm sorry,' he said, and felt himself blush. 'I don't know if you remember me — from Melcote. Fred Sutherland — Freddie. We were all at Miss Beasleys, we used to go in the car together.'

The frown melted, she looked at him in astonishment.

'You used to come and play with my sister.'

'Baba!' she said, and her face lit up. 'I used to love coming to your house. Tile Cottage.'

'That's right.'

'You had geese. They frightened me to death.'

'Gander,' he said. 'Very fierce.'

And they both began to laugh, to say that neither of them knew anyone in Melcote Magna now, and it was just so lovely, so amazing, really, to see one another again.

Her parents had stopped by their car and her mother was looking towards them. Across the car park, boys were climbing into a waiting bus, and the engine started up.

'Sutherland!'

'I've got to go,' he said quickly. 'Do you live here? Will you give me your phone number or something?'

'Darling?' Her mother was coming over. She looked at him quizzically. 'And who is this nice young man?'

Mrs Byatt, he thought, introducing himself, seeing her eyes go wide. I remember you. And wasn't there something — He racked his brains. Hadn't something terrible happened?

A chorus of 'Why-are-we-waiting, wh-y-are-we-waiting?' rang out from the bus.

'Sutherland!' Mr Simmonds was nodding politely towards them all, but Fred could see he was in a bate.

'I must go,' he said again. 'I'm at St Luke's, in Brockwood. Write to me. Please!'

'Well!' said Mrs Byatt, and with that charm, that flirtatious intonation, he saw his father pulling up at the Byatt house on the school run, laughing away with her, while pale little Nancy clambered in at the back, to hold hands with Baba, not saying a word. 'Who could resist such an invitation?' Mrs Byatt said now, and Nancy bit her lip, and blushed, as he did.

'Your lovely parents,' she went on, and perhaps he'd got it wrong, perhaps there was nothing terrible at all, they'd just moved. But this wasn't the Mr Byatt he remembered, coming towards them now: he'd been tall and thin, and —

'How are they? *Where* are they?' Rosie, he remembered now, that's what her parents had called her. 'Your father was such a super chap!' she said with a little laugh.

The bus was sounding the horn, moving slowly towards the road, Mr Simmonds on the steps. Fred ran, he turned and waved. 'Write!' he mouthed to Nancy, and then batey old Simmonds was ushering him on to the bus, and every single boy on it let out a revolting cheer.

'You're a dark horse, Sutherland! Who's that?'

'Shut up!' He flung himself down beside Hall.

The letter came just before the Easter break. He knew it was from her as soon as he saw the envelope, waiting in his pigeonhole with one from Will. That was all about end-of-term arrangements: did he mind getting home on his own again, there was a show coming up, and he might be away —

He stuffed it into his pocket, he took Nancy's letter outside, and away from everyone milling about in the quad at lunch break. Out by the cricket nets, Fourth-formers practising, sun dancing over the new-mown grass, he tore it open.

Dear Fred,

It was such a lovely surprise to see you again. I still can't quite believe it — all those happy times when we were children just came rushing back. Please give Baba my love, she was such a good friend. I don't think we ever even said goodbye.

Why? Why was that?

After my father's death we went to live with my grandparents in Rugby, but then my mother remarried, and now we live in Cookham Hatch, not far from where we met. I'm a weekly boarder in High Wycombe — they were picking me up that Friday. I'm taking my A levels this summer, I expect Baba is, too. Unfortunately I've been ill rather a lot, so I'm only taking two. What is St Luke's like? I expect you're taking a million O levels!

Anyway, I hope this reaches you, and one day I'd love to see you and Baba again. Where are you living? My mother says to send her love to your parents.

With love from Nancy

PS. My mother's name is Winterton now, but I've kept my surname.

PPS. You could write to me at school, if you like: here's the address.

PPPS. Do you still keep geese?!

He read it again, walking away from the boundary, out to the deep. Behind him came the thwack of bat on ball, and shouting, but down here beneath the trees he heard the honking of the geese, pit pat paddle pat, over the emerald grass, saw a pale little girl being left to play by her laughing mother, shrinking away from the great big birds, clutching her doll as he ran manfully after them with a stick. He saw himself swinging on the garden gate as she went home at the end of the afternoon, shadows falling into the lane.

'Bye, Nancy!'

Now she was back.

★   ★   ★

'Nancy!' said Bea, as they had tea in the garden. 'I don't believe it. What does she mean, she's been ill? Give me her address.'

'The Byatts,' said Flo quietly, and said no more.

'Nancy Byatt?' said Will, who came home

506

earlier than expected from the showground, and had supper with them all, shaking the salad cream over Flo's lettuce and tomato and tinned ham. 'Good God.'

'Something happened,' said Fred. 'Her father died. I remember something.'

'So do I,' said Bea. 'I remember you both looking awful, and not saying anything.'

'He shot himself,' said Will, screwing the top on the bottle of salad cream, and then, as Bea gasped, and Flo bent her head, 'Well, they might as well know now, don't you think? Not kids any more. Shocking thing,' he added, slicing into the ham. 'Not surprised Rosie's remarried, though. Gorgeous girl.'

Flo put down her knife and fork. Fred and Bea looked at one another. Fred's mind was whirling. Shot himself? Leaving that little girl behind?

'All I can say,' Flo said to Will, slowly and deliberately, 'is that you are the most extraordinary mixture.'

He opened his mouth and closed it again.

They finished their supper in silence.

★   ★   ★

She lay awake as he snored beside her. She turned, she turned again, she pulled down her pillow. At last she slept.

'Flo, my dear,' said Roddy Byatt. 'Do you remember me?'

Dusk was falling. They were walking by the canal, thick with duckweed.

'I do,' she said, turning to look up at him, and

507

she felt her whole being light up. 'Oh, I do!'

'The strangest thing has happened,' he said. 'Nancy has come back to me. Look — there she is.'

He pointed to the darkening water, and she saw a white-faced child, her fair hair spread out upon the duckweed, slowly swimming towards them.

'But, Roddy,' she said, 'is she safe?'

And then there was the most terrible sound, like a gun going off in her head, and she woke up, shouting.

'What is it?' Will was awake, sitting up beside her. 'For Christ's sake, what is it now?'

And for both of them a hideous, long-ago night came flooding back, as she sobbed into her hands and could not say what it was, just a dream, just a nightmare about the Byatts, but if only, if only he —

'You can be so brutal,' she wept. 'It was awful, what happened, you know it was, and you made it sound like — like — '

He drew her to him. 'I'm sorry,' he said, and he was. He lay there with Flo in his arms, looking into the darkness. Sometimes he just came out with things, a brute beast with no understanding, and no wonder Bea still shrank away. As for Fred — had he really thought, all these years, that he'd been sent away because they didn't love him? Because he wasn't one of them? He still found it hard to believe.

'I don't know,' he said, for the millionth time. He stroked Flo's hair. 'Perhaps it's the army,' he said. 'Perhaps it was the war. I've had to be bloody tough in my time.' He had, and he'd had to keep going: all through India, through the war, through coming home and starting all over again. Twice. 'But deep down . . . ' he said slowly.

Flo shook her head and drew a long deep breath. 'I know.' She'd been saying it to them all, for ever. 'I know.'

They lay there in silence.

'I think it's what they call a Protective Mechanism,' he said at last, and he switched on the light, and she began to smile again, as he straightened the pillows and made it all snug again, as best he could.

12

Summer, summer, summer. Up on the chalky hills the turf was bright and springy, the trees in full leaf and butterflies dancing over the sunlit slopes, where tough little harebells bloomed.

Exam time. At St Luke's the hall was filled with fold-up desks and chairs. The boys came filing in.

Fred thought: I can do this, I know I can. French was first: he'd got through the oral with its *Comment s'appelle-vous?* and *Je m'appelle Frederick*, not a name he often used or thought about, but which gave him then a moment's thought about his namesake, the grandfather he'd never known, dropping dead at the Rectory breakfast table, all those years ago.

'*Et quel âge avez-vous?*'

'*J'ai seize ans.*'

Two years younger than Nancy. Did it matter? Did being eighteen, or almost, make a girl light years older? Bea wouldn't give a sixteen-year-old a second glance, he knew that, still had her eye on James, Lizzie's older brother, now Hugo had faded away, though she told him to shut up whenever he said so.

'What do you think?' he'd asked Richard at half-term, walking up the chalk path in the sun.

Richard thought about it, watching Tinder go bolting after rabbits as usual. He said he didn't think he'd have a chance with Fred's sister, not from what he'd heard. 'But perhaps — perhaps you and Nancy are different.'

Fred thought it was true. When you'd known someone all those years ago, when you'd felt as soon as you saw each other that something was — well, special, it did make it different. Her letters were all bundled up in his locker, and she said she was keeping his. Once all the exams were over, he was going to go and see her.

'Turn over your papers.'

They turned them over.

★ ★ ★

Hot June days, the classroom windows open wide to the scents of grass and roses, blinds dropped down, notices all through the school. Exams in Progress: Quiet Please.

'Just do your best, my darling. No one can do more. Have you taken your pill?'

Bea took the cap off her pen. Her head was swimming with tiredness: she'd been working late every night, until Will called up to turn that bloody light off, she'd make herself ill again if she wasn't careful. Tonight she would go to bed early, she knew that she must, but now —

English was first. She had twenty quotations by heart.

'Turn over your papers.'

Concentrate. Concentrate.

'You may begin.'

She began. She was going to York.

★ ★ ★

Summer nights: party time again. One or two people had a proper boyfriend now, like Rosie Reed, with her black eyeliner. She'd met someone in the holidays, a languid boy called Julian. This was going to be a big end-of-school party at Lizzie's house. It was going to be late, late, late, with a DJ. Bea heard her parents discussing it: whether she should go, whether she was getting enough rest after all the exams.

'Take your pills with you, darling, just in case.'

'Take this,' said Will, handing her a small brown envelope. He'd written the initials 'VM' on the front. Bea gazed at it. It was about the same size as a Christian Aid envelope.

'What is it?'

'Virginity Money,' said Will, and roared with laughter.

VIRGINITY MONEY.

Inside the envelope was a ten-shilling note. 'So you can get a taxi, if Needs Be.'

'Honestly, Daddy.'

HONESTLY, DADDY.

She looked at him, just back from the barbers, his hair cut too short, as always, to save a penny, standing there in the hall in his old tweed jacket. Amidst the maelstrom of her feelings about him, she had to laugh.

'Lovely to see you happy, my darling,' he said. 'And you never know,' he added, as she slipped the little brown envelope into her bag. 'Better safe than sorry.' And he gave her a key. At last, at promised last, she had a key. 'For God's sake don't lose it.'

He ran her up to Lizzie's. The sun was sinking

behind the hills, lights were strung through the trees in the Moores' enormous garden.

'You look gorgeous. Have a super time.'

'Thanks, Daddy.'

He patted her hand; she let him. Then he was off, exhaust puffing out from the timber-framed car, and a little toot-toot on the corner.

'Hi, Bea!'

'Hi, everyone!'

The record-player was out on a table in the garden, the flex on an extension lead running through the grass. The DJ turned out to be a crinkly-haired cousin from London, called Jeremy. He had piles of LPs. A trestle table was laid with a long white cloth, Lizzie's mother putting out cold chicken and potato mayonnaise, her father serving the drinks, tonic with a splash of gin, quite a good splash, and soft drinks if people wanted them. Nobody did, except Bea. Everyone was in dead straight shifts, like her; everyone wore black Twiggy eyeliner and mascara so thick you could hardly open your eyes.

Music throbbed through the garden as the sun sank low. People were dancing beneath the strings of lights: Rosie and Julian, Carolyn Joyce and a boy from the grammar school who Bea had seen on the bus. That was a new development: she must have been thinking so much about revision that she hadn't even noticed them chatting each other up. Lizzie and Julia were making do with one another for now, swaying away as Marianne Faithful sat watching the children play in the evening, and tears went huskily by.

Where was James?

She walked with her bitter lemon through the garden. The last big party here had been when she'd met Alex: that seemed light years ago, and she a different person, just a teenager having funny turns now and then, someone whose school work meant nothing, really. Not someone who had to take pills all the time; not a serious student who couldn't wait for her results. But still: perhaps now she was about to leave school, now she looked pretty sophisticated, really, snooty old James might condescend to do more than glance in her direction.

Wherever was he?

This was such a huge garden, the music fading as she walked along the path, the ground sloping away past the boughs of a great fir tree, so you could hardly see what was going on down there.

She saw what was going on down there. She stopped.

Two boys were kissing one another in the shadows. Bea stood there stock still, her heart pounding. Their arms were tight round one another, their eyes closed, they were kissing and kissing, as she and Alex once had, as she'd longed to do with Hugo. A light summer breeze blew through the garden, and the strings of lights swayed, splashing the grass with yellow and rose and violet. The shadowy corner down beyond the fir tree was suddenly lit by a gleam of emerald, then it was all dark and soft again. But in that brief moment she'd heard the boys murmur, and seen their faces properly, as they drew apart.

One was someone she'd never seen in her life.

The other was James.

'Are you all right?' asked his father cheerfully, as she walked slowly back to the party. 'You look as if you'd seen a ghost.'

★　★　★

Summer weekends: tea in the garden on long afternoons.

'Look at this, my darling.'

'Look at what?'

He passed her the *Surrey Mirror*. 'A little something there that might interest you.'

Flo gazed at the folded page. He'd ringed an advertisement, as he'd done all through their life together: for henhouses, goose sheds, cars, bicycles — you name it. Now what?

Writing classes in Buckhurst. Renowned local author offers expert tuition in the art of writing: short stories, novels, memoirs. Small friendly classes. Tea.

There followed a phone number.

'What do you think?'

'I'll see,' she said. Buckhurst was two or three miles on the bus, out towards Dorking. Quite a pretty ride.

Will held out his cup for a refill, rattling it away. 'Do you good, my darling. Anyway, think it over.' He sat there, looking out over the garden, as a blackbird started up somewhere, the perfect sound of summer. The flowerbeds were brimming with golden rod and stock and late roses, all the stuff he'd put in over the years. Looked pretty good, quite a good-sized garden for a main road, though he'd never kept a pig at the end, of course.

'*Don't be so silly, Willie!*'

Poor old Agnes. Poor old girl. He'd give her a ring after church tomorrow: got to keep it up, even if she and Flo —

Well. That was families for you. He'd ring Fitz afterwards: that would cheer him up.

'*Willie! How lovely to hear you.*'

He yawned, put his cup down. Flo cleared away.

'Have a little zizz, my darling,' she said. 'You need it.'

'I might do that.' He took off his glasses, leaned back in the chair. 'Not getting any younger,' he murmured, closing his eyes. 'Sometimes the old ticker doesn't feel too good.'

She stood there with the tray; she looked at him properly. Weary as hell: that was how he would put it, and that was how she put it now, just to herself. She'd get him to the doctor, make an appointment on Monday, make him go. And as she carried the tea things in through the French windows she felt a little shiver run through her, and turned to look back at him, at his head fallen on to his chest already, his hair so grey.

'Oh, Will,' she said aloud, into the shadowy room. 'Oh, my darling.'

But later, when they had had their pegs, and as she was getting the supper, just something easy and light — thank God for cold meat and summer salads — she heard him with his tape recorder, settling down at the dining-room table,

516

the microphone before him.

'Testing, testing, testing. One two three four five six seven eight nine ten. Over and out.'

He sounded just like the Indian Army officer she'd fallen in love with, such a long time ago: brisk and organised, one two three, spit-spot, but underneath —

I want to look after you for the rest of my life.'

And she came out of the dark little scullery, the kind of place she had never imagined she would have to cook in, ever, and stood in the passage and listened.

'This story is about our return from India,' said Will commandingly, into the microphone from Boots. 'And I'm calling it 'The Troop Ship Home'.' She could hear him clear his throat, then he went on.

'This was coming up to Independence, in 1947, and the British flag about to run down everywhere. Quite right, of course: we'd done our stuff, though I was sad to leave, can't pretend I wasn't. Anyway, Flo and I had got married in September '46, and after a spell in Lucknow we were living up on the edge of the Sutherland sugar plantation in Tulsipore, just on the border of Nepal, and miles from bloody anywhere.'

All around them lay the jungle, where Will took her on expeditions, down the baked earth paths, hearing the sound of water. Long before they were married, before the war, he'd stayed up all one night in a tree, waiting for a tiger to come to drink from the *nullah*, the watercourse;

517

had seen him at last, in the moonlight. He'd recorded that story, she knew, just as she had written, over and over again, about the great snowy peaks of the Himalaya in the distance, and how in the evenings on the veranda they watched the sun sink behind them, and night fall so swiftly, the sky filled almost at once with the brightest stars she'd ever seen.

'Now any soldier demobilised in India had the right to a free passage home,' Will told the microphone. 'But they wouldn't take any woman on a troop ship who was more than four months pregnant. And by March that year Flo was almost three. So I had to get weaving, because of course I had to organise her ticket, pay for her passage . . . '

She stood by the coat rack, she listened through the open door. And she saw it all again: taking the train down to Cawnpore, and then Delhi, and then to Bombay, the palm trees shimmering in the heat, the troop ship moored in the dazzling water. Off he went next day to a little white house on the pier, while she waited in the café of the Grand Hotel, writing her last letter home.

'But the little white house was locked up,' Will went on. 'No ticket wallah, no embarkation staff officer, nothing. So I said to Flo, never mind, let's get on board, and I'll sort it all out with the purser.'

Pressed into his winter coat, she could hear him begin to chuckle.

'So we got all our kit on board, and I went to the ship's purser, and said, 'Look here, I'm

518

Major Sutherland, and I'd like to pay for my wife's passage home.' And he said, 'Well, actually, old boy, it's not my pigeon, the chap you need to see is the ship's adjutant.'

He was laughing now, and she was laughing too, all by herself by the coat rack. On and on it went, this ridiculous story, and in the end they'd sailed home without paying a penny.

'I was told, 'When you get home, you'll hear from the War Office,' said Will, taking a breath. 'And do you know, I haven't heard from them yet!' He was laughing helplessly. Then he switched off, and sat quietly, and she knew he was listening to the blackbird, singing its liquid summer song.

* ★ ★

The summer holidays, and Fred was on a train again: getting out at Windsor, getting a bus.

'Don't let's meet here,' Nancy had written from home. 'My mother will only take everything over! Is Baba coming? Bea, I mean.'

She wasn't: he'd asked her not to, just this first time, and she gave him a funny look, but since he rarely asked anything of her she said OK then, have a good time, and give her my love. He heard her say something under her breath about Rupert, and give a little laugh, but he really didn't want to know; he'd done with all that now.

The train pulled in; he got off with his rucksack, in which he had packed a picnic: such a beautiful day, they should make the most of it.

A Green Line bus was waiting outside the station, and he thought of the moment he'd first seen her, had suddenly realised, and the ribbing everyone gave him.

'Hey, Sutherland! You're a dark horse! She's pretty!'

He climbed on to the Green Line now, and checked its destination, suddenly full of nerves. He'd built it all up so much in his mind: after all those letters, would he know what to say to her, when they finally met up? What did you say to girls? It had been different when they first met like that, both so surprised and happy, but now —

The bus rumbled along leafy lanes. Cattle were grazing in the fields alongside, swishing off flies, ambling into the shade. He couldn't remember the farm, had just heard all the stories about it, but every time he saw cows in the country he felt a little tug of something, just as he did when he heard hens, or once or twice on a photo trip passed a house with a couple of geese, taken straight back to Melcote: playing with the Gibson boys, listening to records in the garage-cum-playroom as rain drummed on the roof, sleeping beneath the apple trees in one of the long cane chairs from India, or just running about, being happy.

They were pulling up, the driver calling out as he'd asked him to. And now his stomach was really in knots, as he got up, and looked out of the window.

There she was, standing at the bus stop in a summer skirt, the breeze blowing it about a bit, blowing her pale hair across her face as she scanned the window. He climbed down the steps.

'Hi,' he said awkwardly, shifting the rucksack on to his shoulder.

'Hi,' said Nancy, and then he could see that she was nervous, too, that this meeting — well, date, he supposed, it did feel like a date — was really important to both of them.

* * *

Bea, in her new duffel coat, walked quickly along the platform at King's Cross, with Flo beside her. They were late, they were late.

'You're sure you've got everything, darling.' Flo peered at the numbers on the coaches, trying to keep up.

'Absolutely certain.'

'Including your pills.'

'Oh, Mummy, please.'

'I know you don't like me to ask, but I just have to be sure.'

'I know. It's OK. And I've got them.'

Here was their coach, and there were other students getting on, one or two already wearing the York scarf, so they must be second-or third-years.

'Right.' She flung her case in through the door. 'Bye, Mummy.'

'Ring tonight, just to let us know you've arrived.'

'I will.' And as she looked at her mother she tried to imagine it: no Fred, no her, just the two

521

of them, alone for the first time in years. 'I love you, Mummy.'

I LOVE YOU, MUMMY.

And then they were hugging like mad.

People were pushing past, and one or two were running down the platform now: it was almost time.

'My very own,' said Flo. 'Go on, on you get.'

She climbed on, she carried her case to the corner seat Will had booked weeks ago, and swung it up on to the rack. Just in time. The whistle blew, doors slammed, and she pressed her face to the glass.

'Good luck, my darling!' mouthed Flo, and then both were waving and waving, as the train began slowly to move.

★ ★ ★

Back to school. O levels passed, and passed well: not as good as Richard's flying colours, but then they wouldn't be, Richard was in a different league. It didn't matter: he had his own sort of league.

'Bye, Dad. Thanks for the lift.'

'Goodbye, old chap. All the very best.'

He swung his bags in through the gates, and across the quad.

'Hey, Sutherland! How was your summer?'

'Pretty good,' he said, and as he thought yet again of the photograph tucked deep inside his wallet, he felt a great smile spread all the way through him.

Part Five

Midnight's Child

1

Late November 1983. Late afternoon, and a sudden downpour, people making a dash for it across the campus — into the classrooms, into the canteen, where Bea is entertaining this week's guest lecturer. They're running a new course on the undergraduate programme, in Post-colonial Literature: it's attracting a lot of interest — from other academics, from the students for whom it's an option.

'It's not my course,' she tells the lecturer, as they make their way to a table. 'I'm just one of the tutors. But it interests me a lot.'

'And why is that?' he asks her, as they sit down. He's a charming man, an Indian novelist born in Madras, educated in London. His voice still has a light inflection of India: it's very attractive.

Dripping wet students bang through the doors, the air is full of cigarette smoke. Bea moves a brimming ashtray across to the next table.

'My father was in India,' she says. 'In the thirties and forties.' Half of her wonders if she should talk about this. But he looks at her enquiringly, from behind his wire-framed specs.

'In what capacity?'

He is leaving his coffee to cool; Bea stirs her tea. She can't drink coffee these days: like the cigarette smoke, it can make her heave. 'He went out as a sugar cane planter, and then in the war he served in the Indian Army. He met my mother soon after it ended — she was out with the RWVS.' She takes a sip. 'Love at first sight, apparently, that's what they always said.'

He smiles at her. 'And they came home at Independence?'

And with that lightly inflected voice she can all at once hear an echo of Nehru's voice, in the great broadcast speech that Will used to imitate sometimes, saying it was marvellous stuff.

At the stroke of midnight, while the world sleeps, India will awaken to life and freedom...

'Just before. In the spring of 1947. But my mother was pregnant by then, and I was born in August, two weeks after the declaration.' Again, she feels hesitant, looks down at the plastic table top. 'I hope this doesn't sound foolish, but I suppose that makes me one of midnight's children. Almost. I was conceived in India. I missed Independence by two weeks and a continent. I suppose — well — ' She looks up. 'I'm on the other side of the coin. That's what I realised, when we were planning this course.'

He is listening intently. 'The other side of midnight, you could say. I don't think that's foolish at all. But — ' He sips his coffee. Gives her a wry look. 'Sugar cane planters had quite a lot to answer for, as you know. Not so much in India, perhaps, not so much in your father's time, but in the Caribbean.' He puts the cup down. 'The sweet tooth of the eighteenth-century gentry. We know how it was satisfied.'

She knows. The canteen fills up with students,

grows noisy. She has to raise her voice as she asks him to tell her about his lecture, and says that she loved his novel.

'That's very kind, thank you. I'll be talking about Rushdie, of course — *Midnight's Children*, but also an essay. 'Imaginary Homelands'. You know it?'

'It's tonight's handout.' And then they smile properly at one another: two people at work, who know what they're doing. 'With the essay on your own books, the *Critical Quarterly* one.'

'Very good. Thank you.' And he does look pleased, a modest man, in spite of his award. 'Rushdie is the giant.' He drinks slowly. 'My own work is less ambitious — formally, I mean. Well, you know that. I am just trying to do what a lot of other people are starting to do — give a voice to the people who had no voice in colonial history. The tea-pickers, the cane-cutters, the rickshaw runners. I'll be reading from my novel, introducing a few ideas. If I tell you any more, you'll be bored in the lecture.' She shakes her head, and he looks at his watch. 'Should we go?'

'We should.' They drain their cups, and get to their feet. He picks up his briefcase.

'I'm interested in people like your father,' he says, as they walk between the tables to the plate-glass doors. The rain is really tipping down now, people racing across campus with jackets held over their heads. Outside, he puts up his umbrella. 'If we survive this monsoon, perhaps we could have a drink afterwards. You can tell me more about him.'

'He's died,' she says abruptly, though she

527

wasn't going to say that at all, and still, months later, finds it hard to believe. He looks down with sudden concern, holding the umbrella above her in the rain, and tells her how sorry he is, that to lose your father is terrible.

'He won't see my baby.' She wasn't going to mention that, either, but this man is so nice, and she does. And then, as he says that he hadn't realised, he's so sorry, what a great mixture of things she must be feeling, a sob begins to rise.

'Oh, my dear — '

She swallows hard, tries to smile. 'I'm all right, I'm all right — come on.' Quickly she walks him across the tarmac. 'Crying at work,' she says, as they reach the lit-up lecture hall. Students without umbrellas are dashing through the doors. 'This will never do.' And now it's her mother's voice she hears, as he gives her the sweetest smile.

'You're doing too much, my darling.'

DOING TOO MUCH, MY DARLING.

★ ★ ★

Firelight plays over the hearth, and over the panther skin. The black felt backing is coming away a bit, and the claws are yellowing; here and there the fur is stiff from splashes of this and that, spilled on it over the years. The stain from the coffee that flew out of Agnes's hands when that wretched book went hurtling towards her still darkens a paw. Flo hadn't the energy to clean it off then, and she hasn't now. Who cares?

Agnes's misspelled letter of condolence is

stuffed with all the others in the bureau. *Poore Willie. He coudn't have gone on ... I am praying for you...*

She doesn't want Agnes's prayers!

She doesn't want anything, except to have him back.

Over and over, as she sips her whisky — terrible to pour your own whisky, to drink it alone — she replays the last long months in hospital. 'Got to gird up my loins for this one,' he'd said, going in for the second heart op. Another new valve. 'Wonder what breed of pig they'll use this time. Gloucester Spot, d'you think? Any chance of that?'

Six long months on two wards, and she'd stayed up there for most of it, sleeping in a dreary little hospital flat, sitting by the bed each day, holding his hand.

'You two lovebirds,' said the nurses.

'When am I coming home?' He asked it over and over again. Then he stopped.

'Am I growing a tail?' he'd asked Fred, flown back to be with them all at the end.

'I don't think so, Dad.'

He'd stood at the foot of the bed. Tubes went into the thin white hand, tubes came out beneath the hospital quilt. 'I suppose it's not an unreasonable thought,' he said, as they made their way back down the ward, leaving Will asleep.

'It makes me think of Panther's tail,' said Bea, and they all had a sad little laugh.

Will was gone two days later, dying alone in the middle of the night while she and white-faced Bea — '*Are you having a baby, by any chance?*'

529

— slept in that awful flat, woken at three in the morning.

'Oh, God.' She says it aloud to the empty room, to his armchair on the other side of the fireplace, to the gas poker he always used to get the fire going. She's terrified of it, as of so many things. Rates. Gas bills. Life alone.

Bea rings every evening. Fred writes every week from Bombay. She still can't get used to calling it Mumbai.

'Bringing it all full circle,' he'd said, when he told them he'd taken this job, leaving a huge London hospital for one in an Indian slum.

A radiographer. One of her children is a radiographer! His wife — little Nancy, so strong and happy now — is a hospital administrator!

'Super, old boy.' Will shook his hand, gave Nancy a kiss. Oh, what a sweet couple they were. Never seen any two people so happy. And when she and Fred had gone for a walk after lunch, he told Flo that Fred's career had all begun here, in the darkroom. 'Bought his first camera, set it all up for him. Have a pat on the back, Sutherland.'

'Well done, darling.'

But as she lay down for her afternoon nap, she thought of Fred up there, all through the long summer holidays, all shut away in the dark. Thinking those terrible thoughts.

'*I swear. I swear by this ivory elephant that you are my child, and Daddy's child . . .*'

He began to laugh — how mad she must have looked! His arms went round her at last. Then he found Nancy, and surely that was Fate. And yet —

Had he really been able to shake it all off? If you spent years of your youth and childhood suffering as he had done — was there a part of him that still hadn't quite come home? Kept a distance? Was that why he went away?

Sometimes she wonders.

The phone is ringing. That'll be Bea, home from work. One of her children is a lecturer! In a polytechnic, whatever that might be. Surely it's time that she stopped. 'Growing a baby is a full-time job, my darling,' she tells her, but Bea just laughs.

She heaves herself to her feet, goes through to the dining room, glass in hand.

'Hello, Mummy. What sort of a day?'

'A nothing sort of day.' She must stop saying that, it must sound so awful, but who else can she say it to?

'Poor Mummy.'

'I am *not* Poor Mummy!'

They both begin to laugh.

'And you, my darling?' she asks, taking another sip. Oh, that's better.

And she listens, hearing the tiredness in that lilting voice — should have been an actress! Should have gone on the stage! — to incomprehensible things about modules and marking, and books she's never heard of. And Bea must be so careful now — she hasn't had to take pills for years, but still, in pregnancy — you never know.

'Time you had supper, darling. Go on, off you go. Is Steven cooking tonight?' Amazing to think of a man getting the supper, but that's what they do now, she gathers.

'Not tonight.'

And Flo knows that Steven's not there, that he's still at work himself. And she wonders, she can't help herself, if this marriage will last, with all this absence in it already, and a baby on the way. That'll change everything.

Bea is suppressing a yawn. 'Off you *go!*' Flo says again. 'Thanks so much for phoning. Talk tomorrow.'

'Talk tomorrow. Bye, Mummy.'

Now what? She should get her own supper, she supposes. Everyone says she must eat, must keep her strength up. But supper by yourself — oh, why can't she just live on pills?

One more peg. And she goes back to the sitting room, pours just a little one.

'*Cheers, my darling.*'

'Cheers,' she says aloud, and takes a sip — oh, thank God for whisky — and stands there for a moment, amongst the Indian watercolours, the ivory elephants marching across the mantelpiece, the bureau, all polished mahogany and gleaming glass — another Mrs Thing, rather a good one.

All the hours, all the years, she spent at that bureau.

Slowly she walks over, and tugs the top drawer open. God, what a sight, what a muddle. She lets down the flap. All those condolence letters, all those little cuttings of this and that stuffed into the pigeonholes. Even the children's medical records are still there. Even a ration book!

A sheet of paper is poking out through the broken zip of her old writing case, the first thing

Will ever gave her. She can see 'Rajputana Rifles', embossed in black. How handsome he looked in his uniform.

Men look so gorgeous in khaki! They all said that on the troop ship — Ann with her scarlet lipstick, lovely fair Judy with her gaspers, poor sweet Rhoda, who died of a broken heart. *Men look so gorgeous in khaki!*

Something stirs within her. Could that be an opening line? Without the exclamation mark — that was something she'd learned in the Buckhurst writing class. Avoid them like the plague!

A few blank sheets of paper are lying on top of the muddle. She takes another sip of her peg, pulls back the chair and sits down.

Then she picks up her pen.

2

London 2009, an autumn afternoon. Bea is up in her study, right at the top of her tall new house. She moved in months ago, but boxes are everywhere, still, though the furniture found its place within days: the old oak chest in the dining room, the bureau and portraits in the first-floor sitting room. In the kitchen, the Rectory clock ticks steadily.

Fred and Nancy have Panther, up in their hall. They have his skin, and the ivory elephants, marching across the mantelpiece in the London flat they bought when he retired, and came home. He took everything out of store, keeping the photograph albums Will left him. The tapes of his stories were left to her.

'*Have I told you the one about* — '

'*Yes, Daddy.*'

'*Would be nice if somebody took an interest for once . . .*'

She's taking an interest now. She's opening boxes, looking at things she hasn't looked at for years, or has never looked at, just stuffed in the loft of the old house after her mother died, fifteen years ago. That's what you do when you're bringing up children, working, having a life. You think: one day. One day I'll go through it all.

It's all sky and tree-tops up here, though even on a Sunday afternoon you can hear sirens wail from the main road. She can hear them now; she can hear her son's rap music, throbbing from the room below. She leans back in her chair and looks out of the window, at pigeons blown about in the wind, and a plane moving slowly beneath the clouds. Going away? Coming home? Fred and Nancy used to be in one so often, leaving and returning every year. He always rang her when they got in.

'My darling! How are we?'

He still does it, it still makes them laugh.

It's just the two of them now: everyone else has gone. Their father. Their mother, who went on writing till the very last days of her life.

Hugo has gone, her first love, who flew back from New York for Will's funeral. '*Of course I'm coming. He was like a father to me.*' And poor lonely Agnes, who would have made the most wonderful mother — she left them each such a generous nest egg.

Fitz and Eleanor are gone: Eleanor first, and Fitz, for all her ailments, living on into her eighties.

Op-pop-pop-pop-poposite the ducks
Is the spot where I unbend . . .

She and Fred still sing it now and then.

Planes cross the sky, trees toss in the autumn wind. Steven's gone, too: the love of her life, dying — like Hugo, like so many of their generation — far too young.

Deep breath.

Now then, what have we here?

Boxes of letters: from her grandparents — the

Parent-Birds — to her mother. *Enclosing a birthday cheque . . .*

From her other, unremembered grandmother, to her father, out in India. *Darling Willie . . .* From Will to Flo: love letters before their marriage in India, love letters afterwards, whenever they were parted.

All I want is for you to come home . . . The envelope is smudgily postmarked Market Hampden, addressed to a hospital in Northampton.

Why was she really in there?

What else is in this box? Will's prayer book, brought back by his father from Palestine after the First World War, and used for so many years that the olive wood binding fell off. Flo had it rebound, wrote a little note inside: *For William, with love from Granny.*

Bea picks up her scissors, runs them through the thick tape on another big cardboard box. Inside: a heap of old exercise books. One, a tattered dusty pink, has a drawing of Britannia on the front, sitting there with her trident and shield and helmet, looking out over the hills. 'British Made', says the line beneath her. Inside, her mother has written in hasty pencil: *January 1950. We are living on a farm! Down in the depths of Devon!*

Beneath the diaries are manuscripts: heaps of them. And pages of notes, pinned rustily together, and what Flo used to call little scribblings of this and that. They go on — she looks at the last page of the last diary — to within three days of her death.

For a long time Bea sits there, surrounded by

all this. She's tired, and even now she has to be careful. Sometimes, still, she's just not there for a moment. And she closes her eyes for a little while, drifting off, as the autumn wind rattles the window catch. Then she opens the last box. All Will's dozens of tapes are in there, slotted into their Boots cases, each card index written up in Biro.

Ploughing with Bulls. Indian Wrestling. Artificial Fertilisers. Cutting & Irrigation. The Tiger of Tulsipore.

'Testing, testing . . . '

'Fred! Bea, my darling! Come and listen to this!'

The Blind Punkah Wallah. Hinduism. Animism. The Troop Ship Home.

Right at the bottom, a couple of framed pictures are wrapped up in yellowing newspaper. She takes them out, blows the dust off, coughs.

That photograph of Will in Indian Army uniform. He's in his thirties, looking at the camera with a cloud of light behind him — a period photograph, that's how they did it then — smiling the dearest smile. Perhaps he gave it to Flo on their wedding day. At the bottom, he'd written in fountain pen, *Always. Will*

The music downstairs is turned down, there's a shout.

'Mum?'

'Shan't be a tick!'

She unwraps the last framed picture. It's Will's wartime poem, the one that hung in the downstairs lav in Ryehurst. She saw it every day of her life, she knows it by heart.

Out of Burma, out of Burma,
By the long and dusty road . . .

She knows all the pen and ink drawings that surround it, though she'd forgotten the captions: Mule Transport in the Hills. Tribesmen Acting as Guides. Food Dropped by Aircraft. Rivers in Flood.

'Mum!'

'Coming!'

But she doesn't move. As the autumn sky grows dusky, she goes on sitting there, amongst everything that surrounds her. Look at it all. Just look at it.

What is she to do with all of this?

WHAT IS SHE TO DO WITH ALL OF THIS?

Indian Refugees from Burma

Out of Burma, out of Burma,
By the long and dusty road,
By the bullock, by the steamer
Thousands came and bore their load.

On they plodded, and behind them
Left their homes and all they knew,
Walking into India, China,
By the roads that led them through.

Way behind them, struggling armies
Fought and sweated in the sun.
Onward swept the Nippon banner,
Refugees were on the run.

Not so long and we will go back,
Aeroplanes will fill the sky.
We shall fight, and we'll go forward
And the Japs will turn and fly.

We shall go and watch the paddy
Growing bright green in the rain,
Green trees waving, love and laughter,
Children playing and no more pain.

W. S., the *Times of India, 1942*

Acknowledgements

Two fine editors helped to shape this novel. Charlotte Mendelson took the runaway first draft and set it back on track. Thereafter, Mary-Anne Harrington's insight, interventions and intelligence were invaluable. I thank them both greatly. Yvonne Holland was a sensitive and meticulous copy-editor for whose good work I am very grateful.

Thanks also to my agent, Laura Longrigg, who kept the faith, and who fired me up more than she knew. And to Peter Gorb, who served in the Indian Army as a young man, and who saved me from a fearful solecism — or, as Will Sutherland would have it, a ghastly bish. Affectionate thanks to my brother, who read two very different drafts, and liked them both.

Lastly, I thank my son, Jamie Mayer, ill throughout the long, long writing of this book, whose courage, strength, generosity and undimmed wit mean that its final dedication is, unequivocally, to him.